Praise for *The Se*

'An excellent and atmospheric hist

'An atmospheric reconstruction of Barcelona at one of the pivotal points in its history. A gothic thriller of great inventiveness'
BBC History Magazine

'An enjoyably over-the-top gothic thriller'   *Sunday Times*

'If you loved *The Shadow of The Wind*, pop this on your reading list. A gripping adventure, packed with action and atmosphere'
Good Housekeeping

'You've never seen Barcelona this way before – gothic, dangerous, romantic and diabolical. A breath-taking, genre-busting enigma for fans of *The Shadow of the Wind*'   *NetGalley*

'There is madness, selfishness, cruelty and corruption, concluding in a bizarre grand guignol of Lovecraftian horror. There is a weird, Gothic feel to the novel, a sensation that the characters are in ethereal and disturbing times. It is an enjoyable, racy read'
Historical Novel Society

'A cracking slice of Spanish gothic . . . The translation from Thomas Bunstead gives the prose a fin-de-siecle feel with a lyricism that ensures even the most violent of descriptions have an uncomfortable beauty to them. The characters are all fascinating, but it is turn-of-the-century Barcelona that is the star of the show. Measured yet exciting, brutal yet poetic, Llobregat has crafted a great novel'
SciFi Now

'A debut novel that has the power to become a phenomenon in the wake of *The Shadow of the Wind*'   *El Mundo*

'A masterful thriller: passionate, brutal, historically exact'
Hamburger Morgenpost

Jordi Llobregat began writing at the age of twelve after watching the film *The Man from Acapulco*. He currently combines writing with his work as head of a company that works on community development in cities. He is director of the noir fiction festival, Valencia Negra. *The Secret of Vesalius* is his first novel and has been published in nineteen countries worldwide. He lives in Valencia, Spain.

Thomas Bunstead's translations include work by Eduardo Halfon and Yuri Herrera, Aixa de la Cruz and Enrique Vila-Matas. A guest editor of a *Words without Borders* feature on Mexico (March 2015), Thomas has also published his own writing in the *Times Literary Supplement*, the *Paris Review* blog and *>kill author*.

THE SECRET OF VESALIUS

Jordi Llobregat

Translated from Spanish
by Thomas Bunstead

riverrun

First published in Spain in 2015 by Destino, Planeta
This English translation first published in Great Britain in 2017 by riverrun
This paperback edition first published in 2018 by

riverrun

An imprint of

Quercus Editions Limited
Carmelite House
50 Victoria Embankment
London EC4Y 0DZ

An Hachette UK company

A CIP catalogue record for this book is available
from the British Library

PB 978 1 78429 306 2
Ebook 978 1 78429 303 1

10 9 8 7 6 5 4 3 2 1

Typeset by CC Book Production
Printed and bound in Great Britain by Clays Ltd, St Ives plc

For you, Mother

Short and easy is the path of speculation, but it leads to no place; long and difficult is the way of experimenting, but it leads us to the truth.

Galen (129–217 AD)

Today he can discover his errors of yesterday and tomorrow he can obtain a new light on what he thinks himself sure of today.

Maimonides (Mose ben Maimon) (1137–1204 AD)

Man's ingenuity is his only way to eternal life.

Andreas Vesalius (1514–1564 AD)

ONE

1888
Barcelona: Port Vell, near the Lazaretto Dock

Scanning the murky reaches for a third time, the old man cursed between gritted teeth. The silence across the water was broken only by the sound of the waves slapping against the hull. Rain gusted down, soaking the poop and the tobacco crates stored below. At this hour, with the first hint of dawn in the sky, a sea mist had enveloped the old port, making vague, looming shapes of the boats at anchor and the dockyard huts, dropping a thick veil down over the shoreline. Manoeuvring the jetty pilings in such conditions was not to be taken lightly. He was an old hand though, and would have a few more runs at it still; that wasn't what worried him. Try as he might, he could not shift the feeling: something was afoot, something ill. That was the sensation like ballast gravel grinding in his stomach.

The wind picked up, turning the water choppy. The many creases around his eyes deepened as he swept his gaze back along the boat, taking in his sleeping son and the mast; the cotton sail, furled tight, was coming loose in one place. Adroitly he went and unfastened it, and, somewhat relieved to see the cloth bulge with wind, fastened the end to the bitt. Clenching his fists, his fingers in their wool gloves creaked like old ropes. The rain and cold had long penetrated the weave of his clothes, down to the bone. He sighed. Operating the boat was getting no easier; soon he would have to step down. He had the strong sense he would not live to see the end of the century, and the marvels of which men spoke. But then again, what matter a pack of clanking machines? What match could such contraptions ever be for a good man with two strong arms? He spat vehemently over the side and tacked the boat a quarter turn.

A little light began tinting the sky, revealing the city's foggy outlines. High above on the port side, the peak of Montjuïch reared up. The old man aimed for the unloading spot deep in the Lazaretto Dock, a place out of sight of the castle watch and clear, too, of the steam ships that began crossing at that hour.

The current dragged the boat towards a cluster of rocks. He was working the tiller to bring them back on course when something in the water caught his eye. It was less misty in the inner harbour; he could discern the white surf lapping the groynes, and there, a few metres away between floating scraps of wood and the dangling block-and-tackles, a bulky object had bobbed up. A wave washed over it, and when the swell receded the thing had gone again. The old man clicked his tongue and waited. It wouldn't be the first time a piece of cargo had fallen off the side of some rich merchant vessel – a stroke of luck for whoever happened to find it.

A minute passed, and then another, and, grudgingly, he began to accept that perhaps his mind had been playing tricks. But, readying to exit the current again, he heard a splashing sound. The object surfaced, a few feet closer now, listing this way and that in the water. A smile spread on the old man's face, his teeth a jumble of blackened stumps, and he swung the boat around: it was an oak chest the size of a wine barrel, with stamps along it that looked, to his eye, French. The binding ropes were intact, so the piece would still be watertight. The French were known for their porcelain, for spirits and fine cloth, any of which he could sell for a tidy sum. Gripping the tiller, he turned around to his son:

'Up with you now,' he said. 'Up and get the gaff.'

The youngster looked up uncomprehendingly, and his father gestured to the chest. He jumped up and hurried back to rummage among the nets and ropes, finally extracting a long pole with a metal hook at the end. As they drew closer, the father issuing instructions in a low voice, the boy reached out and snagged the chest. The old man, using a shorter hook, caught one of the ropes at the opposite end. Little by little they brought it closer, and then prepared to lift it in.

'That's it, easy . . . Jesus and Mary!'

Suddenly a hand – human – had grabbed the old man's arm. Dumbstruck, the old man stared at it; he was being pulled down towards the dark water. Before he could react, a wave struck the boat and, as quickly as it had come, the apparition was gone.

The boy grabbed the fishing lantern, pulling back the shutter: a shaft of light fell on a body gripping the side of the trunk, trying to stay above water. It turned its face towards the light: in place of eyes were two dark openings. A sort of grimace or snarl overtook its features, it seemed to be trying to speak, but, instead of words, a gurgling issued forth, followed by a low moan. It didn't look likely to withstand the sea's buffeting much longer.

The father hesitated for a moment, before barking at the son:

'Keep the chest steady.'

The boy stood stock-still. Ashen, he couldn't take his eyes off the creature. Another wave came, putting distance between boat and chest.

'Damn it, boy!'

'Father, are you . . . Should we?'

The chest began to go under again.

'Come on, heave!'

The son took up the gaff again and dragged the chest close, finally pinning it against the side. The old man steadied himself, before seizing the creature's outstretched arm – it was cold and slippery to the touch. Shutting his eyes and breathing deep, he hauled it aboard.

The creature rolled onto the deck, then lay still on its back. Rather than the tail of a fish, as the old man had expected, waist-down there was a pair of legs. It was naked, and instead of a pelt had skin of a brilliant, almost transparent white. Its stomach bore a terrible gash, black at the edges. The boy was reminded of the scaled fish you saw at market.

The old man moved closer, leaning cautiously down and prodding the form for any sign of life. Seeing further cuts all across the chest, a shiver ran through him. Pushing lightly, his hand sunk into the skin, which had all the solidity of butter. A sharp stench reached his nose, sending him stumbling back into

4

the tobacco crates. The boy went over to help him up, and the pair, huddling close together, eyed the battered figure as it lay completely still.

'What have we brought aboard, father?'

'As Christ is Lord, I do not know.'

A moment later, the body of the creature lit up: a momentary brilliance that revealed, beneath the skin, a structure that seemed to resemble the branches of a tree. A single pulse of light. In unison, father and son made the sign of the cross.

RETURN

Twenty-four days before the start of the World Fair

TWO

'That's all for today, gentlemen.'

The lecture theatre filled with the sound of benches being scraped back. Standing at the front, the young professor gathered his notes and placed them in his satchel, watching the students file out. Much as he tried to give off an air of gravitas, he couldn't help but smile; only a few months earlier he himself had been one of them, and now here he was, completing his second week of lectures on this side of the lectern.

He went over to a window. The sky was full of dark grey clouds but that could do little to alter his mood. His path to that lectern had been long and winding, and no one could say he didn't deserve his position. Looking out over the quad, he was about to let out a contented sigh, when a voice sprang up behind him:

'Professor Amat!'

A young student stood at the door.

'Yes?'

'Apologies, Professor. Sir Edward wishes to see you.'

'I'm on my way.'

Just listen to that. Professor. Professor and faculty member at Magdalen College, one of the most prestigious colleges in all of Oxford. He'd been brought in as cover for Professor Brown, who had an unfortunate case of gout, but that hardly detracted from the achievement. He was on his way; he'd have his own post in no time. When the opportunity had arisen, he'd grasped it with both hands. Now, gathering his things, he left the room in which he was to give lectures in Greek, for the whole of that trimester. As he made his way along the corridors, he felt students' eyes upon him. He remained an object of some curiosity.

Stepping outside, he gathered his gown about him. It had begun to rain and, though May was near at hand, an icy wind was swirling around the quad, scouring the cloisters. He walked quickly along the earthen path, a constant hubbub issuing from inside the lecture theatres; it was also the sharp end of the academic year. He passed the college chapel on his right, catching a few notes of the choir rehearsing, and came through the lychgate into an ivy-lined quad. Cutting along the gravel path that divided the flowerbed, he felt the rain on his brow and neck, but even a thorough drenching wouldn't stop this feeling of wanting to jump for joy.

The porter had been watching out for Amat and swung the door open as he drew close. Walter was a college institution. It was commonly held among students that he had occupied his post since Magdalen's inception – four hundred years in the past – and his stooped and wrinkled appearance did suggest something of that. He was also well known for his ability to get his hands on tobacco, spirits, and many a delicacy beside, and at not unreasonable prices. Such fare was of course prohibited within the college walls, which meant that Walter did a roaring trade.

'Mr Amat! Or should I say . . .' His half smile gave him away. '*Professor* Amat . . .'

Daniel inclined his head. For all that Walter considered him a 'damned foreigner' – as he'd dubbed him the first time they met – there was a mutual fondness between them.

'Well, Walter, how are we this morning?'

'Not so well as yourself, I dare say. It's cold, and when it's cold my bones ache.'

'An iodine solution would do you good. I know a man.'

Walter looked offended.

'Put myself in the hands of some sawbones? Why would I want to do that?'

Daniel smiled.

'I believe Sir Edward is expecting me.'

'Of course, of course, *Professor*. Don't let an old man hold you up, least of all an old man who's not much longer for this world.'

Daniel couldn't help but laugh.

'Thank you, Walter. Oh, one thing: later on, I might have need of one of those bottles you keep in your store . . .'

'I'll see what I can do,' Walter said, feigning a look of resignation. 'Can't make any promises, mind.' He turned and, muttering to himself, disappeared back into the lodge.

As Daniel climbed the stairs, he thought of all the great scholars to have trodden these same steps. Up on the first floor, at the end of a short passageway, the door to the dean's office was ajar. Daniel knocked nonetheless, and heard a voice bid him enter.

The dean's study was nothing if not spartan. Walnut shelves

11

lined the walls, dark rugs covered the floor as far as the desk, and a modest fire burned at the back on the left – a painting of the Battle of Bannockburn hung on the chimney breast. Daniel knew the place well. He had spent many hours in Sir Edward's study, some of them, by his reckoning, the happiest of his life. Sir Edward had been his first tutor when he started at the college, and their instant rapport had only deepened in the years that had followed.

'My dear Amat, whatever are you hanging about in the doorway for?'

Sir Edward Warren was past his fiftieth year, but the deep bags under his eyes and his lank, receding hair did little to detract from his kindly air. An eminent historian, he was also known in elite intellectual circles for his skills as an orator. Specializing in ancient languages – also Daniel's subject – he had assumed the post of college dean a decade earlier, following the previous incumbent's death.

'Good day?'

Daniel tried to order his thoughts; his mind was skipping from place to place. He felt euphoric, and at the same time very weary.

'Wonderful, Sir Edward. Just wonderful!'

'How pleasing. High hopes, my boy, high hopes.'

'Thank you, Sir. I'll try not to let you down.'

Dismissing this with a waft of his hand, Sir Edward settled back in his chair.

'How long now since you came to us? Six years, unless I'm mistaken?'

'Going on seven.'

'Seven years! How it passes.' He squinted. 'I still remember the day you walked through that door, fresh from Barcelona.'

At the mention of the word, Daniel's face darkened. Sir Edward, however, seemed not to notice.

'Yes! Soaked to the bone in that downpour, and with just that single suitcase to show for yourself. I could hardly understand you with that accent of yours, and your general appearance, my goodness!' He laughed. 'I was of a mind to call the constabulary, did you know that?'

Daniel shook his head.

'I have always wondered what brought you to these parts . . . And you, in turn, always so tightlipped on that very subject.'

'Oxford is world-renowned, Sir, as you know. I simply wished to study here.'

'Mm. Yes, of course.' Sir Edward straightened up. 'In any case, you're no longer that green lad. No, you've left him far, far behind. It's a man I see here before me, yes indeed, quite the candidate!'

'As I say, sir, my only hope is—'

'Yes, yes. Well, during this fortnight in Professor Brown's shoes, by all accounts, you've acquitted yourself in exemplary fashion. In fact, that's why I sent for you.' Sir Edward paused. 'Your capabilities are beyond all doubt. Yesterday was our monthly head of faculties meeting. Among other things, a proposal was agreed upon, unanimously in fact: we're offering you a post in the faculty of Ancient Languages. What do you say to that?'

13

A wave of emotion washed over Daniel. He couldn't believe it – so soon! Sir Edward's smile broadened at the younger man's stuttering response.

'Well? What do you say? Do you accept?'

'But of course, Sir! Of course. It's . . . fantastic! I can't begin to . . . I owe you everything.'

'Nonsense. You've earned it. You've shown first class dedication, first class. In all my years I've seen very few as well-fitted to the job.'

Sir Edward got up and went over to the drinks tray, pouring two generous glasses of brandy.

'And my daughter, eh?' he said. 'She'll be pleased no doubt? I'm delighted she accepted the proposal. I'm very much looking forward to welcoming you in to the family as my son-in-law. The dinner tonight, we're going to announce it then. Alexandra is all I have left. I'm sure you'll make her very happy.'

'I love her very much.'

Sir Edward nodded, passing Daniel one of the glasses and raising his own. He dropped his voice. 'Alexandra is, as her mother was, a lovely little thing. I feel I ought to warn you of something, however, lest you reproach me further down the line for having let you advance unprepared . . . Oh, she's beautiful, capable, knows how to run a household, it's just . . . That temper of hers! You never know when it will rear up.' He winked. 'Well, it'll be the Welsh in her I suppose. Dragon country and all that!'

They both laughed. Daniel had a deep fondness for his father-in-law to be. When Daniel had been most in need, Sir Edward had taken him in – no questions asked. His world had come crumbling down, and Sir Edward had been there to pick up the pieces, offering wisdom and fellowship. There was no way he could ever repay the man.

'To your health, Amat, and to the many grandchildren you're going to give me!'

They clinked glasses, and, out of respect, Daniel took a small sip. Then, placing the glass down on the table, he got to his feet.

'I need to see to a few matters before dinner tonight, Sir Edward. With your blessing . . .'

'Of course, of course, that was all. A little bird tells me some student colleagues of yours have organized a gathering? Fear not, my lips are sealed. Just don't be late for dinner – or Alexandra will have your guts.'

Laughing, Sir Edward saw Daniel to the door.

'Oh,' he said, raising a finger, 'I almost forgot.'

Going back over to the desk, he sifted through a pile of documents, finally alighting on a mustard-coloured envelope.

'A telegram came this morning.'

'For me?'

'Indeed, indeed. The mark says Barcelona.'

As Sir Edward handed it over, Daniel's nerves nearly gave him away. The old man didn't notice the trembling of his hand, and Daniel managed to stow the envelope without dropping it.

'I'll . . . read it later on,' he said. 'So many errands!'

'Yes, yes.'

Leaving the office and making his way downstairs, Daniel set off as fast as his quivering legs would carry him.

⋆

15

Back in his old student quarters, he collapsed into a chair. Finals, the professorship, the engagement to Alexandra; it had all happened so quickly that he hadn't had time to move out – his trunks were ready in a corner, but he had yet to pack any books or clothes. All of which, at that moment, could not have been further from his thoughts. The morning's jubilation had melted into nothing. The professorship, the wedding, it all seemed to belong to some other person's life. He looked over at the small envelope on his desk.

How? After all this time?

His hand went to the scars on his neck, an unconscious gesture that had, during these last seven years, developed into a tic. He ran his fingertips across the dead tissue, a constant reminder of the fire; those ridges and folds would never let him forget. He had to laugh: how could he have thought it would just be blotted out? A simple telegram was all it had taken: the spell was broken.

He got up from the chair and went and tore open the telegram. Inside was a pink sheet of paper. Unfolding it, fingers trembling, he scanned the filigreed lines, but couldn't take in what they were saying. He took a deep breath and started again.

Seven years, just like that.

He went over and braced himself against the window frame. Outside, rain continued to fall, darkening the college grounds. They had found him. He had known they might, sooner or later, but he hadn't imagined . . . Perhaps, he thought, he ought to be in pain, or feeling some kind of sorrow, but all he felt were searing sensations: sensations of rage, of guilt. He shut his eyes and rested his head against the glass, tried to stem

16

the anguish. Clenching his jaw, his whole body became tense. The scar throbbed. Crumpling the telegram into a ball, he threw it to the far end of the room. Only then did the tears come, intermingling with the raindrops that streaked the windowpane.

THREE

The snoring shook the small, dirty room. A sheet pinned to the window frame allowed daylight in at the edges. It was the usual Raval guesthouse – as good a place as any to pass out drunk. Cramped, stuffy, with drips in several places, occupants would usually rent for a season and move on. The current inhabitant had been staying for five months.

'Be damned!'

A figure stirred on the straw mattress. Glancing wildly around, the man appeared to be trying to remember where he was. Swinging his legs over the side and getting up, he stumbled back. Hands on head, he unleashed a series of curses in a gravelly voice.

'Bread!' he called. 'And some of that Alsace wine!'

Groaning, the man got down from the bed again. He tottered over to the desk and began swiping aside mounds of old newspapers and scribbled-on sheets. Finally, alighting on a large brass clock, he exclaimed triumphantly. Undoing the clasp and seeing that the hour hand was nearly at midday, his giddiness seemed suddenly to drain away.

'Midday? No . . .'

He began dashing around in his undershorts. Filling the basin and splashing cold water on his face, he cursed continuously. The ache at his temples would not abate; he plunged his head right in. This set him shivering, and he dried himself off with the bed sheet. Trousers, shirt, and boots quickly followed, and on his way out he took a gulp from the coffee cup on the side – immediately regretting it. The dark liquid, quite cold, tasted like a stagnant pond – it was the fourth time he'd used the same grounds, he remembered. Spluttering, snatching down his straw hat and checked jacket from the stand, he dashed from the room, fixing his bow tie as he hurried down the stairs.

'Señor Fleixa!'

A man with a large paunch stepped into his path. He glared at Fleixa under drooping eyelids. The man smelled strongly of garlic, which did little to help clear Fleixa's aching head.

'Señor Gonzalez! I was just thinking about you. How's your lovely wife?'

'Three months' rent you owe me, nearly four. The room's up.'

'Three months? How is that possible? Well, not to worry, my friend. I'm owed some pay from the reports I've been writing recently – we'll have this trifle solved in no time. As you know, Señor, being a well-known journalist entails certain social obligations, and I've had some unforeseen costs as a result.'

'I know all about your social obligations. You said the same last month.'

'There must have been a mix up. Your wife was kind enough to let me defer my latest payment.'

'Jacinta? When did the two of you speak?'

19

'Oh, yesterday, around midday, I think . . .'

'But she was at Mass at midday.'

'Oh, later on in that case. Don't pay me any mind. I can be the most forgetful person.'

A look of comprehension spread on the landlord's face. Perhaps, thought Fleixa, it hadn't been the best idea to bring Jacinta into it; better, perhaps, not to mention the agreement they'd come to after the previous day's amorous encounter. Gonzalez was known for his dull wits, but perhaps even he was beginning to intuit his wife's long-running infidelities. Fleixa didn't much feel like hanging around to find out either way, and made a dive for the gap that had opened up to the man's right.

'Wait just one second!'

Pretending not to hear, Fleixa carried on down the stairs.

'At the end of the month,' he called back up. 'You'll have your money, I promise!'

A stream of insults followed him out the door.

He hurried down the street, shouldering his jacket as he went. The overcrowding here in the Raval was extreme, and it stank of several kinds of rot; migrants from across Spain had been piling in for years now, drawn by the promise of factory work. But Fleixa liked it still; he relished the bustle of it all. The cobblestones resembled a small river in places, so ill equipped was the drainage system to deal with the heavy rain they'd seen of late. The earth in between had become a mud bath. Fleixa glanced from ground to sky as he made his way through the barrio.

'If it carries on raining like this, the port will be up here soon. So much for the start of summer!'

He passed a shopkeeper emptying slops into the street, and then a pair of colliers pulling their coal cart behind them and openly eyeing a group of women across the way. The journalist, as was his custom, tipped his hat to the ladies. They, sheltering in a doorway, didn't seem very suitably dressed for the weather. One of them stepped out to speak to Fleixa. An infant boy with a dark shock of hair clung to her neck.

'Dolors was looking for you last night, rapscallion.'

'Manuela, hello! Have you done something? You are looking especially lovely this morning.'

Straightening her hair, the woman smiled bashfully; she had perhaps three teeth in her mouth. Her ample breasts were barely concealed beneath her blouse, and the child bounced against them. She smelt of brandy, onions and firewood.

'You do know,' she said, 'when you get bored of her, you could always come and see me . . .'

Now it was Fleixa's turn to smile.

'Be a good girl, now, and tell Dolors I'll see her later on.'

She snorted, and with a twirl of her skirts went back over to the group.

Exiting the alleyway, Fleixa came out onto Las Ramblas, which teemed with people. Fruit and vegetable carts headed for La Boquería market vied with horses and traps. Along came the Catalonia Line tram, handbell ringing out. Match sellers, newspaper venders and florists cried their wares as the housekeepers hurried past, and well-to-do ladies and gentlemen strolled by. Fleixa dived through the mass of people, crossed to Calle del Pi and, after a few minutes' walk, arrived at the newspaper offices.

The *Barcelona Correo* had been established ten years earlier, and had gained a foothold as one of the main papers in the city. Sellers would call out the title each morning, along with that of the monarchist *Diari de Barcelona*, the Liberal Party's *La Vanguardia* and the *Noticiero Universal*, which was the newest, and made great claims of independence. Residents of the city were avid readers of the news, and the papers were their best way of keeping up to date. The *Correo*'s headquarters stretched across the four floors of an old gothic building whose stone façade gave an air of respectability that kept the owners happy. The porter greeted Fleixa in his typical respectful manner.

'You, Señor Fleixa, are late.'

'Serafín! The news keeps no fixed schedule, everybody knows that.'

'Tell it to Don Sanchís. I could hear him shouting your name from here.'

Don Pascual Sanchís was editor in chief at the *Correo*. Not a man known for his good temper, he was rumoured to have smiled once and once only: the day the *Correo* broke the story of Councillor Rusell's affair and the edition had gone into three runs. His office was always dense with cigar smoke – he was rarely seen without an enormous Montecristo lodged in his mouth – and he ruled with an iron fist. The *Correo* would not have been such a success otherwise.

Fleixa felt ill at ease as he went up the stairs; it was never good if Sanchís was after you. And the man's mood was hardly likely to improve when he found out that Fleixa hadn't yet closed his latest piece. But what could he do if a source failed to show? Three nights in a row he'd been to the meeting point at the Set

22

Portes tavern. The matter had become a little more complicated on the last of those occasions; Fleixa had drunk some wine – to pass the time – and let himself become involved in a game of cards. He had not won. Feeling quite certain that Luck could not desert him twice in the same night, he'd taken the tram over to the Hippodrome: another seventy-five pesetas down the drain. That was on top of the three hundred he already owed La Negra, a moneylender with a reputation for reclaiming her debts. She was just about the only one he could still borrow from, though it seemed her patience was wearing thin. And the *Correo* had stopped paying him advances – he would have to work for the rest of the year for nothing.

He was out of breath by the time he made it up to the editorial department. A couple of printer boys came past and he ignored their greetings, heading straight to his shared office. On his desk, on top of the stacks of dusty papers, was a pair of large shoes. The man to whom the feet belonged was sitting reading that morning's news.

'Good day,' said Fleixa, collapsing into his chair.

'My!' came a singsong voice from behind the paper. 'Señor Bernat Fleixa himself! To what do we owe the honour—'

'Leave it out, Alejandro.'

Alejandro Vives had been appointed Politics Editor four years earlier. Slim as a lighthouse and nearly as tall, he had small eyes and a very long nose – it was said that his nose would find out a story long before the man himself. He always seemed to be in a good mood, even around Fleixa – Alejandro was just about the only member of staff who hadn't given up on him.

'Rough night?' he said.

Fleixa weighed up the sarcasm in the question. Alejandro continued to read.

'Not the best,' said Fleixa. 'How is Sanchís today, by the way?'

'I believe he's been somewhat desirous of your company.'

'Fine, he can desire all he likes.'

Rummaging through his desk drawers for some tobacco, Fleixa glanced over at the paper Alejandro was reading – it was that day's *Correo*. Something caught his eye and he stopped. His eyes grew wide as he scanned the column in the bottom right-hand corner.

BODY FOUND IN PORT

A corpse, identity unknown, was found down by the Lazaretto Dock in the early hours of Sunday morning. A pair of fishermen brought the body in. The authorities are not treating the death as suspicious, pointing to a mishap in the area that had been reported in the early hours. With no criminal investigation taking place, the family will be able to bury their kin. It would seem that the individual was a doctor of some renown, but the family have opted not to divulge his name. The ceremony will take place at midday today at the Montjuïch Cemetery.

Felipe Llopis had the byline.

'What the hell happened to my piece?' Fleixa cried.

Fleixa left the office, crossing the department floor in the direction of the editor in chief. There were several barely concealed smirks as he passed – an article being pulled and replaced by another, that was bound to be common knowledge. Fleixa was fuming. Not bothering to knock, he thrust open the heavy glass door. On the far side of a table filled with galley proofs, teletypes and copies of rival papers, stood a man so broad he seemed to shrink the room around him. Seeing Fleixa, he squinted, knitting his brow.

'Why's my report been pulled?' Fleixa cried.

A voice came from behind him.

'The death of a hundred chickens, down at the Sans warehouses, is, after all, undoubtedly front page copy.'

A young, beaming man in an impeccable suit was leaning against the back wall. Felipe Llopis always combed his fair hair with oil, and his moustache and delicate goatee were immaculately sculpted. The female typists fawned over his elegant ways, and he had even managed to charm his way into the esteem of his colleagues. No one knew who his sources were, or the secret of his knack for always landing a story first. Which was why the *Correo* had poached him from *Campana* the previous year. In Fleixa's eyes, he was the perfect imbecile.

'Llopis! I thought something smelled in here!'

'Your natty jacket, no doubt.'

'What do you mean—'

'Enough!'

Sanchís thumped the table. His booming voice meant they now had the attention of the whole department.

'Felipe, we'll talk later. Shut the door behind you.'

There was even a certain grace to the way the young reporter stood up from the armchair. He winked on his way past Fleixa, who merely glared back, clenching his fists.

'Damn it, Pascual, letting him rob my column like that!'

'Sit down and be quiet!'

Fleixa sat down, before immediately disobeying the second part of the command.

'Why's that cobbler in my City Life column?'

'First of all, it's my column, not yours, as with the rest of this paper. And that cobbler happens to deliver news. You, meanwhile—'

'I'm close on that story I was telling you about, any day now. It's going to blow everything else out of the water.'

Sanchís shook his head, jowls flapping. Fleixa was put in mind of a British bulldog.

'How long have you and I known one other?'

Fleixa shrugged.

'You're not making this easy for me. You show up late, work when you feel like it, it's been weeks now and only fillers from you.' A pained expression entered his face. 'Years we've known each other, Bernat, and I've never seen you like this. Look at your clothes, and could your eyes get any redder? You stink. Back at the cards? How much do you owe?'

Fleixa didn't answer.

'I'm going to come clean with you: I'm thinking about giving you the push.' He pointed his cigar towards the department. 'Llopis wears fancy suits and he reckons himself quite the aristocrat, but he's out there day after day. He gets himself in the right places, and once he's there, damn if he doesn't root around. He brings me what I need: copy. Same as you not so long ago. This is a *news*paper, Bernat, we live or die by that. Look at the city. Barcelona's changing. The world's changing. Before we know it

26

the World Fair's going to be underway. *Times* are changing, and men like Llopis are right there at the coalface.'

Fleixa cleared his throat.

'I just need a bit more time.'

Again the flapping of Sanchís' jowls. He took a deep breath and massaged his neck. The smoke in the room had settled a little before he came to speak again.

'I know I'm going to regret this . . . A week I'm giving you, seven days, and that's it. Then I'll make a decision, and I won't go back on it. Clear?' He thrust the cigar in the direction of the door. 'Out now, and get yourself a wash, for God's sake.'

As Fleixa went out, he heard the man murmuring behind him.

'A newspaper, it's a newspaper I'm running, damn it.'

The sound of the typewriters and conversations in the department were back to their normal level now. Fleixa caught sight of Llopis at his desk, surrounded by a group of young hacks. Llopis nodded as he passed, and in reply Fleixa stuck his middle finger up and carried on his way. An alarm was going off in his head, and it had nothing to do with Llopis: he had that sense of forgetting something, some important detail or other, but couldn't pin it down. He puffed out his cheeks. The hangover wasn't helping.

'How did *that* go?' asked Alejandro as Fleixa came back in.

'Could have been worse,' he said.

His colleague, reclining in his chair, was still leafing through the paper. Then Fleixa remembered. He began foraging among his notes.

'Time?' Fleixa demanded. 'What's the time?'

'What? Pawned your watch again?'

'What's the time, damn it!'

'Nearly one o'clock, why—'

With that Fleixa dashed from the room, scattering papers in his wake.

FOUR

Montjuïch Cemetery enjoyed a beautiful view out across the sea, though not on this day: midday had just chimed on the bells at Poble Sec, but so deep was the gloom it could almost have been the middle of the night. The rain beat down, and flashes of lightning lit the marble mausoleums. Saints, angels and virgins, all of them weeping furiously, seemed to become animate when Daniel glanced their way. He pinched the bridge of his nose and shut his eyes. The journey from Oxford had been long and he was tired.

He shifted his weight, the gravel crunching beneath his feet like cockroaches. The Mass had been brief, the minimum of fuss: his father would doubtless have been pleased. Daniel had refused the invitation to speak. His memories were of an elegant man, always immaculately presented, and of the distant stranger he had become after the death of Daniel's mother. He had thrown himself into his medical work, which from then on had become the single governing influence in the life of the family. How well Daniel could still hear the man's dignified voice, commanding the children to be silent: the great man was trying to work. Silence, always silence, broken only by the occasional lecture, and that always on the same topic: how the children were to follow after him, honouring the name by becoming doctors too.

Something he had not done.

He looked over at another grave, that of his brother. His hand shot to the scars crisscrossing his nape. Pursing his lips, he focussed on the soothing sensation of the raindrops bathing his neck – though he also knew, very well, that even such a torrent could never wash away his constant sense of being ill-at-ease. He looked at the scattering of mourners. Four umbrellas, like dark toadstools, sheltered men in long black coats and top hats. Old colleagues of his father's. All wore the same indifferent expression; they had attended many such affairs.

Also attending was a municipal clerk, representing the local authority. His father had been nothing if not well-connected. Don Alfred Amat i Roures, eminent doctor and university professor: his burial was no small matter, though in such weather the functionary would doubtless make his excuses at the earliest opportunity.

Four or five students were hanging back to Daniel's right. They shifted about uncomfortably in the downpour, huddling close in their jackets; he imagined they'd be leaving soon enough as well. He thought he glimpsed a hipflask being passed between them.

No more than a dozen people, and that included the cemetery workers who just then began passing the ropes beneath the coffin. A life of sacrifice, dedicated solely to the advance of medicine, only to end your days under a mound of dirt tossed down by a few strangers. The men began lowering the coffin, which wobbled unceremoniously before coming to rest with a small splash at the bottom of the grave. Meanwhile the priest – over whose head an altar boy, himself drenched, held an umbrella – intoned from Ecclesiastes. The creaking scrape of the ropes as they were pulled from beneath the coffin drowned out the priest's concluding words. Daniel leaned down and tossed a handful of soil onto the varnished oak of the coffin. The impact seemed to echo throughout the cemetery; Daniel was slightly surprised not to see his father clamber out and tell him off for being so noisy. As the shovel loads of earth began filling in the grave, the mourners bid hurried farewells. A freezing sea wind had picked up, and the rain continued to come down; there were better places to pass such an afternoon than in the cemetery of Montjuïch.

His father's colleagues were the first to approach, offering their condolences. Guarded expressions, a few words on his father's qualities – a great doctor, a great man of science – and so on. Daniel barely registered the tributes. Nodding, he automatically held out his hand to shake, but avoided their eyes. The last of the professors, walking with a stick, came forward. He had no umbrella, and the water trickled through his sodden hat.

'Condolences. I'm very sorry f-f-for your loss.'

Daniel murmured a thank you, offered his hand, and looked past the man to the next in line. But the man didn't move on, instead clearing his throat and continuing in his whispered stutter:

'I-I'm Joan Gavet. I was, let's say, a f-friend of your f-father's.'

Daniel nodded unenthusiastically.

'I h-hope your return to Barcelona has brought you *some* pleasure, after all these years.'

'Not exactly. In fact, the moment I stepped off the train I was involved in an incident.'

'No! What m-manner of incident?'

'Oh, it was nothing,' said Daniel, regretting having brought it up. 'My luggage was stolen. I only brought a few clothes, one or two personal items, nothing that can't be replaced.'

'All the same, I-I'm awfully sorry.'

'Really, no matter. In any case, I don't plan on staying long.'

'Oh?' said Gavet, who seemed disappointed. 'A shame, I-I'd h-hoped we might have a chance to meet, talk a little. A pleasure to h-have met you, all the same.'

And with that, the singular doctor turned and made his way through the rain.

The rest of the mourners dispersed like ravens at a gunshot. Daniel readied to do the same, but then noticed a young man still standing at the graveside. He looked genuinely stricken, and for a moment Daniel's heart went out to the stranger: someone *had* cared about his father, after all. The youngster glanced up, his almond-shaped eyes momentarily meeting Daniel's – but the expression immediately changed, he seemed to regret having given something away, and immediately looked down, before gathering his coat about him and hurrying off along the path.

Daniel watched as the men shovelled in the rest of the earth. He took a deep breath of the sea air. After one last look at his father's final resting place, he placed his hat on his head and was making to leave when he caught a hint of jasmine on the air. Across the path, under a cypress tree, stood a figure dressed in black.

A graveyard illusion, Daniel wondered? He approached slowly, fearing that the figure would disappear. It was a woman wearing a veil; she lifted her head, watching as he approached; her eyes were just as green as he remembered. She held an umbrella in her gloved right hand, and her astrakhan coat close about her in the other. A few strands of jet-black hair had fallen loose from her fascinator, and these swayed in the wind. Daniel stopped a few paces from her, and they looked at one other, weighing the years. She was the first to speak.

'Señor Amat.'

Daniel inclined his head. 'Irene,' he said, barely containing the waver in his voice. 'Good of you to come.'

'It was the least I could do. I was fond of your father.'

Daniel looked in her eyes for the young girl he'd once known – her voice had changed more than her features, the Caribbean accent fading, the timbre deepening. She removed a lace handkerchief from her bag and dabbed at her eyes, lifting the veil to do so; he caught a glimpse of mulatto skin.

'What a long time it's been,' Daniel managed to say.

'Too long.'

'How have you—'

'Fine, fine. Good of you to ask.'

She glanced towards the cemetery entrance. A cloaked coachman stood waiting. A brief look of concern entered her features, and as she put away the handkerchief her hand seemed to tremble very slightly, but she composed herself just as quickly.

'I ought to go,' she said.

Daniel felt the urge to stop her, but what could he say? She waited – Daniel seemed about to speak – but when the words didn't come, she gathered herself and left. Then, on an impulse, he hurried after her, catching her at the elbow. He felt the warmth of her body. A host of memories collided in his mind; the cemetery faded to nothing . . . Seeing that she was glaring at him through the veil, his reverie ended.

'What do you think you're doing?' she said.

'I should . . .' he said. 'I should have written.'

'But you didn't. Maybe it was better that way.'

'I'd like to come and see you before I leave—'

'You can't. Not now.'

Removing his hand from her arm, she set off again. Daniel watched her go, passing beneath the dripping cypresses and out along the path, through the rain.

Alone once more, Daniel cast a final look at the spot his father lay buried, before turning and making his way towards the cemetery gates. Irene's incursion had affected him – what a fool he was! Why had it not occurred to him that she might come? Forgotten feelings stirred inside him. Why did it matter, after all this time? He'd made a new life for himself, he was betrothed, had a position at Oxford: his was an altogether enviable future. She was the past. A past that was in no danger of returning.

As Daniel came out onto the road, he was brought from his reverie by the sound of panting and wheezing.

'Señor Amat? *Damn* this rain.'

A short, moustachioed man was just behind him, hands braced against his legs as he tried to catch his breath. Wearing a checked jacket, a bow tie and a straw hat, his steamed-up glasses had slid to the end of his nose, revealing bulging eyes. Blinking the rain away, he smiled, which cocked his moustache jauntily. Daniel did not remember the man having been at the ceremony.

'Do we know each other?'

The man proffered a wet hand.

'Bernat Fleixa,' he said, before reaching into his jacket. 'My card.'

Daniel scanned it. His eyebrows shot up.

'Journalist?'

'That's right, Señor. With the *Correo*.'

Handing back the card, Daniel turned on his heel.

'I've got nothing to say.'

Fleixa hurried after him.

'Well, really,' he said, 'it's more a matter of what I've got to say to you. You're the spit of your father, did you know that? Far more youthful, that goes without saying . . .'

'Ah! You knew my father!' said Daniel. 'But of *course* you did.'

'Doctor Amat and I had certain dealings. In fact—'

'Listen, Señor Fleixa,' said Daniel, turning brusquely to face him. 'If you, in fact, *had* had any dealings with my father, you would know the low esteem in which he held journalists. He'd rail against your kind at any opportunity, and the slander that is your stock and trade. Even the weeklies were beyond the pale, by his reckoning. Never in a thousand years would he have two words to say to a man such as yourself.'

'Well, in fact, he did. As it goes, he sought *me* out, Señor.'

Now it was Daniel's turn to take deep breaths. He felt suddenly worn out. The journey, the ceremony, Irene . . . All he wanted now was to sleep, a good long sleep, and then to

35

board the return train, the one whose destination was his real life.

'Please, a minute of your time,' said Fleixa. 'That's all I ask. After that, you need only say the word and you'll never hear from me again.'

The man was a pest; Daniel quickened his pace.

'Wait!' came Fleixa's voice. 'You've got it all wrong. Your father and I arranged to meet, but he never showed. He was prevented . . .' Fleixa caught up with Daniel, and, glancing around, went on in a low voice. 'Señor Amat. I believe that your father was murdered.'

FIVE

The Europa, one of the many cafes lining the Plaza Real, had in recent years become quite fashionable. At this mid-afternoon hour, though, only a few tables were taken. A group of regulars, enveloped in cigarette smoke, were busily discussing the recently imposed grain duties.

Daniel and Fleixa took a table at the back, neither saying a word as the waiter poured their drinks. Once they were alone, Daniel spoke first.

'Could we begin, Señor Fleixa, with you telling me exactly why I ought to trust you?'

'Your father seemed to. Look—'

'No, you look. Let me be clear. The fact I'm even here talking to you is, to my mind, madness. It's impossible that anyone could have wished the death of my father, simply impossible. You've got five minutes to explain yourself, and then I leave. After that you're never to contact me again.'

'Sounds fair,' said Fleixa, throwing back the glass of absinthe and clearing his throat. 'All right. Three weeks ago, I received word from your father at the newspaper offices, urging me to come and meet him at the church in San Miquel de Port. Make haste, the message said.'

Daniel nodded; it *was* like his father to make an invitation sound like an order.

'Go on.'

'We met the following day. While we were talking, he was constantly looking around, kept stopping mid-sentence. He seemed in a tremendous hurry. He wasn't, how can I put it, particularly warm towards me, and I got the sense he liked the clandestine nature of our meeting little more. But discretion was clearly paramount, otherwise we'd have met at the newspaper or the university. Well, no sooner had we sat down than he handed me this mountain of papers.'

Fleixa took out a grey, leather-bound portfolio and placed it on the table.

'And this is?' said Daniel.

'My question precisely,' said the journalist, undoing the knot on the bundle. 'Your father told me about a study he'd been carrying out, looking into the hygiene in the city's poorest barrios. For a number of months he'd been gathering data, particularly from the Barceloneta area, and then analysing it. I don't know if you know that area of town? It's undergone huge changes in the past few years. Construction companies have been moving in, the Land and Sea Engineering Agency, and Catalan Gas too. It's cheek by jowl down there, with huge numbers of families coming in from across the country, all in search of work. The study, your father explained, aimed to establish a relationship between the miserable working and

38

living conditions and the illnesses these people suffer. These papers are his findings.'

Daniel made no attempt to hide his surprise: this didn't sound much like his father's line of work. He'd been personal physician to several of the most moneyed families in Barcelona, was very much connected with the city's upper classes – nor had he ever minded crowing about it. Shining a light on such murky matters would hardly have been to their liking.

'This doesn't sound like the sort of thing—'

'Quite,' said Fleixa. 'Hardly a task to win you many friends. Nonetheless your father had applied himself to it tirelessly, if the contents of these papers are anything to go by.' He paused to call for another drink. "What am I supposed to do with all this?' I said to him. I hardly think my employers would want to get on the wrong side of the richest men in the city – some of them including the *Correo*'s owners. But your father said this was the tip of the iceberg.

'When he began his investigations, he found, as he'd expected, numerous causes of death. Accidents in the work place were the main culprit, but also contaminated water, scabies, pneumonia, consumption, and . . . starvation. Death is a fact of life for these people, as your father learned. He became increasingly involved in the work. He began coming up with hygiene rules, and started pressuring the town council to deal with the water and sewage problems, treated some of the sick himself, even paying for medicines out of his own pocket. The upshot being that he gained the trust of the people in the area.' Fleixa downed the second absinthe. 'One afternoon, an old joiner confided in your father. He spoke in a hushed voice, your father said, about a malign presence that had taken hold of the Barceloneta. In the previous weeks, girls had started disappearing. Always around twilight, when they were on their way back from the workshops, or out on errands. Their bodies would show up four or five days after, always in a terrible state – they each seemed to have been bled, and some were missing limbs. The most terrifying thing, the joiner had said, were the enormous gashes each of them bore, which looked like bite marks, only with burnt edges.

'The joiner, according to your father, was genuinely frightened. He went on to talk about the search parties that had been set up in the area, since the authorities had done nothing. But their efforts had been in vain – the disappearances had continued unabated. Fathers had started keeping their daughters under lock and key, praying the demon wouldn't come for them in their beds. Your father, naturally enough, dismissed the stories as ill-educated superstition. He forgot about the whole thing until, a week later, they came to get him. Another body had been found, in the most astonishing state.'

Daniel leaned in closer.

'Astonishing in what way?'

'Your father was reluctant to go into detail. I pushed him – this would be important if I was going to cover the story. Your father agreed to tell me more – at a later date. But those further meetings, unfortunately, never came to pass.' Fleixa gestured to the waiter again. 'He did tell me that the last girl was a particularly young one. Almost a child. Your father, Señor Amat, could hardly control his rage as he told me about it. On his orders, the Guardia Civil took her to the morgue for an autopsy. Your father

40

thought that the report might lead to the capture of the monster responsible. But he was never able to carry it out.'

'No? Why not?'

'The girl's body disappeared that same night.'

'That's not possible.'

'Exactly what your father said. The room she was kept in had only one exit, and a guard was posted the entire night. The man made a statement saying he never once left his position, and no one had come in.'

'People lie. I assume the authorities have looked in to the matter.'

'Seems they were rather patronising when your father went to them, in fact. They somehow managed to cast doubt on the body ever having been brought to them. And your father's colleagues at the university don't seem to have been much help either.'

Daniel imagined his father's frustration, when once a single word from him would have been enough to make people jump. How things must have changed while he'd been away . . .

'Doctor Amat told me he suspected the police.'

'The police? But that's absurd.'

'Perhaps.' Fleixa shrugged. 'His investigations had made certain people very uncomfortable, and your father was convinced that they wanted a cover up. But that didn't stop him. He initiated a parallel study – the findings of which you have before you.'

Fleixa pushed a sheet of paper across the table that looked the same as the others. Daniel recognized the careful hand of his father. The paper rustled in his hand when he picked it up. Taking a breath, banishing the flood of memories, he began to read. On the left-hand side was a list of names, and to the right, a column of numbers.

'A . . . list?'

'One that took him a long time, and a great deal of work, to assemble. I don't imagine Barceloneta's terrified populace were the easiest people to extract information from. It was only because they held him in such high esteem that they complied at all.'

'But what is it?'

'On the basis of their testimonies, your father gathered a list of the names and ages of the missing girls, the dates their bodies were found, and their *conditions* when found.'

Daniel counted sixteen lines, before looking up at Fleixa incredulously.

'I know,' said Fleixa.

Daniel looked back down at the list. A girl named Gracia Sanjuán had been found with her legs mutilated; another named Adela Reig had had her eyeballs gouged out; another, Sara Fuster, was missing an arm. The first victim had been found in January, and the most recent three weeks before Daniel's return. The youngest was just fifteen years old. The sheet of paper suddenly felt heavy in Daniel's hand. He reached for his glass; his hand less than steady. He sipped the water as nausea gripped him.

'And these marks down this side?' he asked.

'Coordinates.'

'Coordinates?'

'Precisely where each of the bodies was found. Most of the girls showed up in the sewers, or floating in Port Vell itself.'

The pair fell silent. Daniel could see why the man thought his father's death suspicious. He hadn't touched a drink in seven years, but just then felt the need for some burning brandy inside him. He resisted though, downing the water instead. It tasted rusty to him, like blood.

Meanwhile the journalist settled back with a satisfied look on his face. His five minutes were up, and Daniel wasn't going anywhere.

'But your father and I agreed I wouldn't print a single word until he had more proof.'

'Proof?' said Daniel. 'What kind of proof?'

'Your father knew this list wouldn't cut it. He thought he might be able to find the person, or persons, responsible, and then, with my help, bring them in. I didn't hear from your father after that, until Monday past, when a hurried note came from him. He'd found what he needed and was ready to run me through it.'

'And what did he tell you?'

'Unfortunately, that was the meeting he didn't make. I went to the appointed place three nights in a row.'

Daniel didn't know what to think.

'It was an accident,' was all he managed to say. 'They told me his death was an accident.'

'Did they by any chance let you *see* your father's body?'

'No,' he admitted. 'They said the water had left him badly disfigured.'

'If your father was right and the authorities were trying to cover up these crimes, the same would surely go for his death . . .' Glancing over his shoulder, he lowered his voice. 'Señor Amat, this is a game involving far weightier interests than you might think. A large number of the dead were factory workers. If this were to go public, the worker unions that have recently been set up would have the perfect chance to make a name for themselves; they could even call a general strike. The city's been a powder keg of late. The workers are making demands for better conditions, and they're becoming better organized. The factory owners have the police and the Guardia Civil on their side, as well as pickets-for-hire to go in and break up protests. Word is they wouldn't be averse to hiring a few gunmen as well. Some kind of flare up seems inevitable. The governor, meanwhile, he's desperate to avoid anything of the sort, and he's been leaning on the town council, who in turn are up to their ears preparing for the World Fair. It's very much in the balance whether everything will be ready in time for the opening ceremony – a strike would certainly put paid to that – and then think about the consequences for Barcelona internationally. Do you see what we're talking about here?'

'Why are you telling me all this?' asked Daniel.

'I want the exclusive.'

'The exclusive?'

'That was the agreement I had with your father.' Fleixa leaned closer. 'I think you and I can help one another.'

'How's that?'

'You have access to his belongings. His findings must be somewhere.'

Daniel felt uncertain. The whole thing was . . . just so astonishing. How much of it was true, how much might be a trick of some kind? Could his father have invented some imaginary conspiracy? But why? And then he suddenly realized. How naïve he'd been – letting himself get carried along in the fantasy of it

44

all. He contained a bitter laugh. For a moment, he'd let himself be taken in by the story too – forgetting what his father was really like. Daniel nearly smacked the table in frustration.

'Well, Señor Fleixa, I'm sorry to disappoint you, but this is all a wind-up. My father was an unusual person. More than capable of dreaming up such nonsense, if it was somehow to his benefit. If you knew him as well as I did, you'd know. He's simply been using you.'

'What reason could your father possibly have for wanting to make this up?'

'Frankly,' he said, gathering his coat and hat, 'I neither know nor care.'

'Don't!' Fleixa got to his feet as well. 'I know it's an outlandish tale; I had difficulty believing it as well. But I've been able to verify your father's claims now.'

Daniel shouldered his coat.

'Meet me tomorrow night,' said Fleixa, 'and I can show you, for certain, the truth of it all.'

Daniel paused at the door. How he longed to leave, get away from this city of curses, and back to Oxford. His father was dead: it was time to put his past behind him. In England, his fiancée awaited him, his beloved Magdalen, a chance to teach. He sighed. The journalist seemed convinced. Perhaps he ought to give the man a chance – perhaps it would be definitive proof, in fact, of the story's flimsiness. Then he could go back to England with a clear conscience, knowing he'd done what he could. If not, he'd be constantly asking himself if there hadn't been at least a grain of truth in the whole thing.

'All right, all right,' he said. 'I'll put off my return.'

A smile spread on the journalist's face.

'Fantastic. You won't be sorry. Here.' They shook hands. 'I'll meet you tomorrow night at eleven, in front of the Fortuna statue at the port. Wear dark clothes, nothing too showy. Oh! And bring your father's briefcase, if you'd be so kind. Do you think you can?'

'I don't see why not. But what for?'

'You'll have to trust me on that one.'

SIX

With unerring steps, the masked figure made its way along the centre of the gangway between the shelves. The oil lamp it carried was the only source of light in that dark labyrinth, the flame catching in the glass receptacles that lined the shelves, briefly illuminating the grotesque shapes floating inside; like the ranks of some silent army, hundreds of vials and jars stood in meticulously neat rows.

The most recent specimen was the best so far. Progress, finally some progress . . .

He made his way through into a hexagonal room. All other sounds were drowned out by a constant buzzing whir, like a beehive. Here the temperature dropped, and the air grew damper still. Noting the familiar rushing of water several feet below the flagstones, he imagined, not for the first time, being submerged beneath that torrent. He came past a fenced-off well to the right; the surface was a glittering, cobalt circle whose reflection cast onto the ceiling. He stopped and held the lantern up to a metal pole that reached high into the dark above. He caressed the copper coating, which was warm even through his gloves; warm like a living being. The man emitted a guttural noise, resting his forehead against the pole for a moment and murmuring to himself.

Despondently, he moved away from the pole and over to the centre of the space. He placed the lantern down on a side table and turned up the flame. The light fell on a large block of marble in front of him. Hewn twenty years earlier as a single piece, it had slightly curved edges and was the length of an adult body; the slight roundness somewhat gave it the impression of a completely flat plate. Mounted on three pillars with dragonheads at the tops, the curved portions were in perfect harmony with the purity of the straight lines – the craftsman had poured a lifetime's skill into the work.

The man ran his hands over the smooth surface, fingering the channels along which the bodily fluids of his victims would run before pouring off through a metal aperture in the middle. The power of the stone pulsed at his fingertips – he thrilled at the force of that energy. Then he drew his hands suddenly back – as though from a shock. Staring intently at the marble, he moved away very slightly, and slowly began to undress.

First came the leather gloves; he moved unhurriedly, depositing one and then the other on a small table to the side. Orderliness was of the utmost importance. Every single thing he did was in an orderly fashion. Next came the jacket and the waistcoat, which with unhurried movements he folded and laid next to the gloves. Bow tie, shirt, trousers and undergarments followed, all placed in a neat pile.

Steam rose from his body in the chill underground air. As

he moved closer to the light again, marks on his torso became visible – they looked akin to the gnarls and whorls of tree bark.

He climbed onto the marble table and lay down. As his skin touched the gelid stone he felt the pores of his skin contract, and half-shut his eyes. His scars distended, the pain began to diminish. His breathing became more even. He listened to his heart as it slowed. And then, as so many times before, it all began.

First he began to feel the presence of all those who had lain there before him, the spirits of the bodies he'd taken from graves and that had yielded up their portion of eternal peace in the name of science. One after the next – each came to his mind in an unending sequence. The deathly force ran through him, the remnants of a lost vitality, soothing his pain. A moan escaped his lips. He stiffened as the next of the bodies, or their essences, cascaded through him. This was different to the previous part – a presence, verging on the physical, radiated so strongly that it overcame his senses. The young, pubescent girls, still alive when they touched the cold stone; their minds still working and their desperate hearts still pounding, until the very last moment when, like all the rest, their blood would flow into the centre and the marble would absorb every last drop of their warmth. A tide of arousal washed up inside him as, in agony, he orgasmed, crying out, before lying back again. He was still. Only then did the pain subside altogether, and only then was he able to turn his thoughts to her.

'Soon,' he said, recovering his breath. 'We'll be together again, so soon.'

The humming noise droned on.

THE NOTEBOOK

Eighteen days before the start of the World Fair

SEVEN

María Lluch looked no older than thirty. She wasn't what you could call young, nor was she as exotic as some of the overseas girls, but on the streets of the Raval her plentiful bosom and firm body meant she'd never had to try particularly hard to avoid going hungry. That, though, was before she'd begun losing weight so rapidly. Securing lodgings in the cold end-of-spring nights became another matter. Every shift had been a struggle to bring in the few pesetas that would have allowed her to carry on. A hard existence, but no harder than that of thousands of souls in Barcelona; María had borne it without complaint. What was the point in complaining?

That morning she was lying down, her eyes closed. She looked deeply relaxed, indifferent to anything that might disturb her repose. A shadow reared up in front of her. That of a man. A hint of compassion flickered across his face before he suddenly raised one hand in the air, light glinting off the blade. He plunged it into María's chest and, with great precision, drew it down to her abdomen, opening an enormous rend in the flesh. He plunged it in twice more, higher up the torso, drawing up and away from the original incision, leaving a tremendous 'Y' shape. Finally, María's breasts hung loose to either side.

María did not cry out. No one raised the alarm. On the contrary, all around there were murmurs of appreciation, until the man, weapon still in hand, cut through the hubbub in grave tones.

'Gentlemen,' he said, 'a little quiet if you please. As you will have noticed, the incisions ought to be made either in a capital 'T' or a 'Y' shape, depending on the specimen. That gives good access to the thoracic cavity. Saw, please.'

An assistant brought over the requested instrument, and hush fell on the lecture theatre. That morning's Anatomy class was being given by one of the most eminent surgeons in Catalonia, Doctor Manel Martorell. Dressed in a neat dark suit, with a leather apron over the top, he was imparting one of his magisterial lectures in the Dissection Hall of the old Royal College of Surgeons, the headquarters of the Medical Sciences Faculty.

The space was illuminated by a bright ceiling light. Oval-shaped and neoclassical in style, the century-old design was the handiwork of the architect Ventura Rodríguez. There were entrances in both wings, and four rows of long marble benches with crimson cushions – all seats taken at this particular moment. There were several wooden chairs at the front for professors who might wish to sit in. Final-year students were always in attendance, but such events were also open to the public, who would flock to see an autopsy.

As a rule, the bodies of females weren't used for study. The smell of carbolic acid drifted across the room, mixing with the smoke from the censers that hung beside the dissection table. But a sweet rotting scent was still in evidence, reminding those present of death's peculiar pungency. On the front bench, several of the students were whispering amongst themselves.

'See that?' said one. 'The old man actually kept his hand steady!'

Muffled laughter came from the group, at the centre of which sat a young man with dark eyes, his black hair slicked back and a sharp goatee on his chin in the style of the Romantics. He was leaning over the wooden bar in front, ignoring his friends' jokes.

'What do you say, Fenollosa?' said one. 'Coming for a few cups later on?'

He didn't deign to answer; his attention was on the incisions being made. The prostitute's pale skin seemed to blend in with the marble surface. Though there were channels for transporting the blood and the other bodily fluids, gobbets had solidified here and there in the sawdust on the floor, like a livid sort of wax.

'Very well, gentlemen. And who among you can tell me the cause of death?'

Everyone seemed to think the question was directed at someone else. Doctor Martorell did not look pleased.

'I must remind you, gentlemen, that it is *surgeons* you aspire to become. Nothing less.' He paused, looking pointedly around. '*Apparently* you wish to add your names to the illustrious roster of this university. Talent is required for that, a talent that I frankly doubt that any of you here present possess. Perhaps none of you. I do hope I will be proved wrong, however, at least with one or two.'

The dark-haired youth got to his feet, to a ripple of murmurs.

55

'If you'll allow me, Professor, I believe I may be able to provide an answer.' He spoke with undisguised arrogance. 'Simply by observing the stomach, so skilfully extracted by yourself, we can see that the folds in the mucous membrane are all flush now, undoubtedly due to the partially ulcerated mass also present in the stomach. The strong likelihood, therefore, with no pathological study to confirm the idea, is a malignant tumour. This, coupled with this woman's unhealthy style of living, led to her death.'

Martorell plunged his bloodstained hands into a basin his assistant had supplied.

'Very good, Señor Fenollosa. Your diagnosis is a textbook one, to the letter.'

A salvo of applause and cheering broke out in the young man's group, reverberating around the hall.

'Gentleman, please! A modicum of seriousness. We aren't at the bullfights now.' Gradually the room fell quiet again. 'A shame that the patient's death prevents her from confirming your postulation, Fenollosa . . .'

At that moment someone could be heard clearing his throat.

'Yes?' said Martorell.

A hand had been raised, two rows back: a smooth-faced young man with glasses slipping down his nose.

'Something to add there?'

'Yes, Sir,' said the young man in a small voice, already seeming to regret it.

'Very well, do not keep us in suspense. We'll all end up like the señorita here, at this rate.'

The young man blushed as laughter went around. Fenollosa

56

swivelled to eye him. Everybody knew that when he spoke, rejoinders weren't called for – except for this upstart, it seemed.

The young man got to his feet and again cleared his throat.

'Well?' said the professor, not accustomed to being made to wait.

'I was wondering, Señor, whether we might have ventured a diagnosis *without* any invasive procedure?'

'Go on . . .'

'The supraclavicular adenopathy on the left side is, I believe, clear for all to see. An inflammation that suggests intra-abdominal disease – scrofula, possibly, or a tumour in the neck or head. But if that were the case, further lymph nodes would be in evidence on the neck. No doubt she had been vomiting, and complaining of stomach pain and anaemia. By the looks of her body, she'd been shedding weight for perhaps several weeks.'

Doctor Martorell looked at the boy with renewed interest. His approach showed a practical knowledge all too scant among the students, for all that they were in their final years. With a poorly disguised smile he turned back to Fenollosa.

'It seems someone dares disagree with you, for once. Let us make the most of it. Which of you can tell me what would have been the best medical course of action with the young lady?'

Fenollosa could feel the eyes of the room upon him. The son of Doctor Fenollosa had to live up to the example of his brilliant, venerated forebear. Students knew of the link, as did the teaching staff, and indeed his father constantly reminded him about it, time and again. As if he needed reminding.

He got slowly to his feet, glaring at the insolent upstart. A few whispers went around.

'Go on, you show him.'

'Show him who's boss.'

Fenollosa allowed for a theatrical pause and, turning to the public, began to proclaim. 'In my view the most effective intervention would have been a partial gastrectomy to remove a small portion of the stomach, the part where the tumour was, and then to join the remainder to the duodenum.'

A nod from Martorell was enough to prompt rapturous applause in the group of friends.

'But, Sir . . .'

The gentle voice of the unknown youngster dampened the cheers.

'Yes?' said Martorell.

'My colleague is undoubtedly in the right. Even so, he is perhaps unaware that the technique he describes has been superseded. Doctor Billroth modified the procedure thirteen years ago now.'

'Indeed!' exclaimed Martorell. 'And would you care to run us through those modifications?'

'Of course. Billroth proposed that a suture be placed in the stomach at the level of the jejunum, as that will block off the duodenal knot, in turn allowing for larger resections. We should also bear in mind that in the last twelve months Kronlein has successfully carried out a total transverse-jejunum implant, termino-laterally, and antecolically, which improves the chances of recovery.'

'Very good, young man—'

'But none of that fully answers the question.'

'Ah? And what, in your view, would the correct answer be?'

Martorell seemed to be enjoying this. The student was completely untouched by nerves. The whole room was hanging on his words; some had even started taking notes.

'The best way to proceed would have been to not intervene, seeing as it was extremely unlikely that this woman's life could have been saved anyway. One look at her Virchow's Node and we'd have been able to see that metastasis had set in, the illness was quite advanced, and so our duty would have been to save the poor woman from an unnecessary and highly unpleasant operation. The best prescription would have been palliatives for her physical pain and something to soothe her soul.'

Martorell's admiration was clear to see.

'Brilliant, quite brilliant.' He swung round in the direction of Fenollosa. He was enjoying this. 'Anything you'd like to disagree with? Some clever comeback?'

Fenollosa bit his lip. His friends urged him to knock down the argument, but he knew there was no answer he could make. He gripped the wooden bar, his knuckles turning white.

'No, Señor. Nothing to add.'

A deflated murmur went around. Martorell turned back to the other student, who had taken his seat once more.

'Would you mind telling everyone your name, young man?'

As he stood up again he looked mawkish, all his self-possession seemingly gone.

'Yes, Sir. My name is . . . Pau, Pau Gilbert.'

'Very good, Señor Gilbert, my congratulations. Gentlemen,' he said, 'this is precisely what I mean when I say that things may be done well, or they may be done *very* well. You must not limit yourselves to the medical manuals. It is we who are marking out the frontiers of science in this day and age. Use your brains, gentlemen,' he said, turning his gaze back to Fenollosa. 'That is, if you still have any.'

The chamber filled with laughter once more, and the lecture came to a close.

All the talk as people filed out was of the exchange. Fenollosa, surrounded by his supporters in one corner, watched as Gilbert hurried out of the room, a bundle of books held against his chest.

Pau Gilbert cursed himself over and over as he hurried away, head down; he was determined to ward off any attempt to engage him in conversation. Stupid! Had he lost his mind? Risking everything, and for what? To air his huge intellect? To show off his knowledge, far superior to any of his imbecilic peers, superior, even, to anything one was likely to gain in this paltry faculty? He puffed out his cheeks, shaking his head. Then again humility wasn't something he was blessed with, and well he knew it – and what a brat that Fenollosa was, what a grasper! He couldn't help but be irritated by his petty contributions, and by his obsession with making sure everyone knew exactly who his father was. He'd pipe up, and his little friends would cheer as though it were Wagner in the Liceo. 'Stuck up children from moneyed homes – no reason for them not to take life as a joke.' He was nowhere near as comfortably off. He was there to qualify as a surgeon, and nothing else mattered, absolutely nothing. He wouldn't be stopped in that, but he mustn't make such childish errors again, or draw attention to himself. He picked up the pace, hoping to make himself scarce as quickly as possible.

*

With a brusque wave of the hand, Fenollosa cut into his colleagues' chattering.

'Anyone know anything about this Gilbert?'

'I heard he started halfway through the course,' said one of the taller young men. 'That he transferred from a foreign university.'

'Doesn't seem he has much in the way of a social life,' said another. 'Strange bug.'

'Apparently he's an ace when it comes to procedures.'

'He's just some upstart.'

'Right, an upstart who showed Professor Steady how to close up a wound.'

'Prof Steady wouldn't know how to close his wife's legs!'

The group burst into laughter – but not Fenollosa. He kept his eye on Gilbert right to the end of the corridor, until he disappeared from sight.

EIGHT

The fog rose up from the port, enveloping La Fortuna Dock, consuming the Paseo de Colón cobblestone by cobblestone and extending its grey tongue up and along the neighbouring streets. Daniel blew on his hands and rubbed them together. Stamping his feet against the carriage floor for warmth, he checked his watch for the third time. It had been five minutes since the driver had enquired whether they were to continue waiting. Daniel had begun to wonder if agreeing to the rendezvous hadn't been utter madness – but then he heard footsteps echoing along the street outside. Seconds later, from out of the shadows, Bernat Fleixa's wiry frame appeared.

'Good evening, Señor Amat.'

The journalist got into the carriage and sat alongside Daniel, weighing his appearance approvingly. Daniel wore a simple, knee-length grey wool jacket and dark trousers, a pair of walking boots completing the outfit. He had also, as requested, brought along his father's briefcase. Fleixa, for his part, was dressed in his usual outlandish manner. He called up to the driver with the

62

address, and the carriage sprang forward, the wheels crunching beneath. Neither man spoke. They left the Paseo and its magnificent buildings behind, and crossed the Plaza del Palacio, passing Estación de Francia before turning onto a strangely quiet street towards the sea. When they came onto a street called Calle Ginebra, the carriage stopped.

'What's happening?'

'I'm sorry, Señor, but this is as far as I go.'

Daniel began to object, but Fleixa put his hand on his arm.

'That's fine,' said the journalist. 'We'll get down.'

The pair began along the dark street, as the driver turned the horses around and headed back the way they'd come.

'Why didn't you let me speak?'

'No point. Carriages just won't go into Barceloneta at this hour. We'll need to walk a little way, but not too far, and doubtless the air will do neither of us any harm.'

Ahead of them, a rank of rectangular constructions reared up in a military-looking formation that led down to the sea. Damp salty air filled their lungs. This part of the city, unlike Las Ramblas, was poorly lit, only the occasional streetlamp casting a pool of yellow gaslight. The buildings were so tightly packed together, so cluttered and disorderly, that Daniel doubted whether the place would be any brighter in daylight. Mud from the uncobbled streets had washed up and covered the walkways, as though they were down at sea level already.

'So are you going to tell me where we're heading?' asked Daniel.

'We're meeting someone,' answered Fleixa, not breaking stride.

'Guessing games, wonderful. Who?'

'An acquaintance of your father's. Someone who was very important to his work. He runs this part of the city, albeit in a not entirely official capacity.'

'You've met him yourself?' said Daniel doubtfully.

'Not exactly. In fact, I don't know if he'll agree to see us. We have to hope your parentage will do the trick.'

'And if not?'

Just then, two men emerged from the murk and approached.

'I have a feeling we'll know fairly soon.'

The taller of the pair was dark in complexion and had a crooked nose. He appraised Daniel and Fleixa with an amused look in his eye. Daniel noticed he was dangling a dead rat by the tail, and gulped. His companion, shorter and thicker set, walked coolly around them. His vacant expression made Daniel wonder whether he suffered from some kind of mental retardation. The man, sensing them eyeing him, gave a rotten-toothed smile. He was dandling an iron bar in his left hand. They both smelled as though they had just climbed out of a drain and perhaps, Daniel reflected, that might not be so far from the truth.

'And you are?' asked the one with the rat.

'We're here to see Vidal,' said Fleixa evenly. 'He's expecting us.'

The man made an exaggerated show of considering the idea. He began shifting back and forth on his feet, the rat swinging in his hand.

'Vidal? I don't know any Vidal. How about you, Crip, know anyone by that name?'

The other man shook his head, gazing steadily at Daniel. His fingers opened and closed around the piece of metal.

64

'See, no one we know,' the tall man said, shrugging theatrically. 'Looks like you're stuck with us – right, Crip? Question is, who are *you*, and what is it,' he said, motioning around, 'that brings you here?'

Daniel half-expected the rat to fly from the man's hand. Then, rather than answering, the journalist took a step forward.

'I don't see why that's any of your business.'

'Oh?' said the man, thrusting his pockmarked face into Fleixa's. 'You're in our territory now, and that means we need payment . . . Wait, these clothes of yours – you police? You *smell* like police. What do you say, Crip?'

The other let out a guttural noise, baring his teeth. Daniel couldn't help but shrink back.

'My friend isn't that fond of police. He got hooked as a little boy, spent three nights in Amalia prison, and let's just say they gave him quite a warm welcome. He's never been quite the same—'

'You'd be better off not wasting our time,' Fleixa said. 'Vidal isn't a man to be kept waiting.' The man was a good head taller than him, but Fleixa didn't seem intimidated, as though he somehow knew they'd come through unscathed. Daniel wasn't so sure. He readied himself for a fight, one they were sure to come out of badly.

But then Fleixa whispered something in the man's ear, causing him to stand away, looking Daniel up and down. His eyes paused on the briefcase, and his scornful look vanished. With the hand that held the rat, he indicated behind him.

'Third on the right. Green curtain. Let them past, Crip.'

As he and Fleixa moved off, Daniel ventured a glance back

over his shoulder. The men had gone over to a spot behind a low wall, where a small bonfire burned. The taller one took a stick from the ground and skewered the rat with it. Daniel decided not to watch the next part.

'What did you say to him?' he whispered.

'I said that you're a doctor, and Vidal is expecting you.'

'I'm no doctor!'

'He doesn't know that.'

'And that was enough?'

'Doctors are a rare thing in these parts. Here people really are in need of attention, wouldn't you say? Anyway it worked.'

'That was why you said to bring my father's briefcase.'

'Anyone can tell it's a doctor's.'

'And if they'd looked inside and seen it was empty?'

Fleixa shrugged.

No sooner had they drawn level with the indicated house than several men stepped forward from a nearby doorway, surrounding the pair; fishermen, by the look of them. Daniel promptly felt a pair of leathery hands frisking him. Clearly enjoying his discomfort, the man in question stood up in front of him, almost nose to nose. The odour emanating from him was a mix of perspiration, fish and alcohol. With the searches concluded, the curtain-door was drawn back and the pair were told to enter.

'I'll do the talking,' said Fleixa.

They came into a low-ceilinged room with half a dozen small gas lamps burning. For furniture all it had was a table, an arm-chair and three decrepit chairs. A fire blazing in the hearth made the small space stiflingly warm.

A door opened and into the room came a very short man, barely five foot tall. He approached the visitors.

Manel Vidal seemed very much at ease in the intense warmth. He wore a beige, rather untidily tailored coat, fully buttoned. His jowls spilled over the top of a lilac neckerchief and a small cigar hung from a pair of very thin lips. He sucked in the smoke and as he exhaled puffed out his chubby cheeks like a child. His eyes were hidden behind a pair of blue-lensed spectacles.

'Take a seat, gentlemen.' He spoke in little more than a whisper.

One of his men brought the armchair over to him and Vidal hopped onto it. Daniel noticed that the armchair was higher off the ground than the other chairs, so Vidal's interlocutors would always be lower down than him. An old woman in a black shawl came in and placed a bottle of watered wine on the table, along with cups, two large loaves of bread and some rancid-looking cheese. She went back out again without a word. No one made any movement to serve them.

Clasping his tiny hands together, Vidal sat and waited.

'Señor Vidal, my name is—'

'—Bernat Fleixa, you're a reporter with the *Barcelona Correo*. Don't bother yourself, I know you. People have read your articles to me. Interesting, brilliant even in places. You are quite the stylist. A little prolix, doubtless, though that's forgivable seeing how keen you are to kindle debate. Really you ought to ease off on the adjectives, you overuse them and, to my mind, it can come across a little overwrought.'

Fleixa opened his mouth, unsure whether he had just been praised as never in his life, or if he ought to take offence.

'Well, I—'

'You friend, however . . .' Vidal interrupted again, puffing out smoke.

'My name is Daniel Amat.'

Vidal sat bolt upright in his seat. A note of caution entered his voice.

'Related to Doctor Amat, by any chance?'

'I'm his son.'

'He never mentioned any sons . . .'

Now it was Daniel's turn to stiffen. Had his father completely erased any memory of his existence? Was he so ashamed? Daniel shifted uncomfortably in his chair; that accursed fire! What was he doing here? Why hadn't he taken the first train back to Paris? He was surprised to hear himself begin excusing his father:

'I left the country a long time ago. My father and I weren't close during that time. I've just come back to Barcelona for the funeral.'

Vidal said nothing, smoke whisping upwards from his mouth.

'Fathers and son should never allow enmity to come between them. What happened?'

'It was all a long time ago.'

No one said anything. Even Fleixa glanced at his watch.

'There was . . . an accident. Many people died. My father held me responsible.'

Vidal clicked his tongue and tilted his head oddly.

'A heavy load you bear! Strange, isn't it, the ones we love the most tend to do us the most hurt? But we only ever get one father. You ought to consider yourself fortunate, Señor Amat. At least you were lucky enough to know him, you even got to hate him. My father, an uneducated fisherman, rejected me the moment he set eyes on me, and left my mother to rear me alone. I've never known anything more about him, but I do not blame him. You ought not to either.' He sat back in his chair. 'Losing a loved one *twice* is no usual thing; my condolences for this double loss. The doctor was a good man.'

Daniel nodded. He didn't know what to say.

'You speak to precisely the cause of our visit,' said Fleixa. 'We have reason to believe Doctor Amat's death was not an accident. And that you might be able to help us.'

Vidal puffed on his cigar before answering. 'Of course it wasn't an accident.'

Daniel steadied himself against the table.

'So . . .' said Fleixa.

'The doctor paid for his daring. The Black Hound took him.'

He abruptly spat on his hand and, holding the palm flat in front of his face, began whispering something in what sounded like a gypsy tongue. Behind Daniel and Fleixa, the men made low groaning sounds.

'The "Black Hound"?' the pair said.

'Not a name to go shouting around. All of Barceloneta knows of the beast, but fear keeps their lips sealed. It's an old curse around these parts, a condemned soul: half dog, half ghost. People say that Lucifer posted him at the gates of Hell. And once in every one hundred and eleven years his master lets him off the leash. On moonless nights he comes out of the ocean to quench his black soul. When he comes, it means death is sure; nothing stops the beast, his hunger is endless. He devours souls, his eyes are like coals, and his enormous fangs are fire itself.'

69

Daniel stood up in a fury, knocking over his chair: 'Are you trying to say my father was killed by a . . . a *demon dog*?'

He felt strong hands restraining him, and then he was being slammed against the table. Stunned, a few moments later he felt a knife at his neck. He tensed, expecting to feel the blade plunge in, but after a moment Vidal waved his hand and Daniel was released. The men stepped back. Fleixa, who was sweating profusely, had looked on aghast. Daniel sat back down and tried to catch his breath.

'Apologies, Señor Amat,' said Vidal with a half-smile. 'My men are rather . . . *anxious* about my safety. Excuse them.'

Touching a hand to his bruised shoulder, Daniel cleared his throat.

'No, Señor Vidal, it's me who should apologize. I forgot that I'm a guest under your roof.'

The dwarf acknowledged this with a tilt of the head.

'Please understand my unease,' Daniel went on. 'My father is dead, and I want to get to the bottom of it.'

The room fell quiet again, only the crackling of the flames to be heard. Vidal slowly lifted his hands to his face and removed the spectacles, revealing a pair of milky white pupils. The imposing racketeer, the pimp to whom all pimps in that part of the city answered – the man with the power to ignite or extinguish an uprising in Barceloneta should the feeling take him – was blind.

'The truth is a complex thing,' he said. 'You should be careful what you wish for.' Then, to his men: 'Bring him closer.'

Just then a boy of seven or eight appeared in the room, accompanied by a man holding him by the arm. His wool cape was far too large for his scrawny body, and a dirty shock of hair, doubtless lice-infested, came spilling out from under his cap. Daniel was surprised to see that, in spite of the rags the boy wore, he had on a pair of very good boots. The man knocked the boy's cap off his head. The boy leaned down and picked it up, defying his captor, though he did not put it back on his head. He glanced warily around the room. His eyebrows shot up when he saw Daniel, but he quickly resumed the same sullen expression.

'This is Guillem, and a clever little so-and-so he is,' said Vidal with a tut. 'Lives around the docks. He knows the sewers like the back of his hand – your father used him as his guide. Guillem is the last person to see your father alive.'

'You knew my father?' asked Daniel.

The boy glared back, pursing his lips. Vidal's man gave him a slap on the neck.

'Yes!' he said, as though his tongue had been given a yank.

Daniel smiled, attempting to make the boy feel more at ease.

'And you worked for him?'

The boy nodded. 'I said no to start with. Thought he wanted . . . the same as the others.'

'The others?'

'Other gentlemen like him. Good clothes, money in their pockets. Come by and give you a few pesetas to go in the coach with them, for a ride. Sometimes they give you a buttered roll.'

Daniel shuddered.

'But he wasn't like that. He just wanted me to show him the way. It was him who gave me these boots.'

'And where did you show him the way *to*?'

'He was interested in the tunnels, we went down three, four times.'

71

'And the last time you saw him? When was that?'

The boy counted on his dirty fingers.

'Eight days back. He seemed nervous, didn't talk much. We went down, same as the other times, 'cept this time he wanted to go further in. I told him there was no way, it was too dangerous where he wanted to go. You can't. No one does. But he wouldn't listen. And then he never came out.'

Daniel was about to ask another question, but with a flick of Vidal's head the boy was prodded and bustled from the room.

'Your father, Señor Amat, wanted to help us. You've seen how it is around here. He spent a lot of time helping the sick, in the last weeks he even brought another doctor along to assist him. Brought medicines as well, helped with the births of a few more souls unlucky enough to pitch up in this place. He became a friend to us, a good friend. When we told him of the curse, he wouldn't hear of it – until he saw the girl's body. Even after that he refused to accept the evidence, which is that the Black Hound takes what it's owed, whenever and however it wants. Your father was determined to find other explanations. We tried to stop him, but he carried on and on with his inquiries . . . and paid for it with his life. Possibly his soul as well.'

The final phrase hung on the air.

'You truly believe,' said Fleixa, 'that all these murders are the work of some kind of demon?'

Daniel caught the note of fear mixed in with Fleixa's incredulity. Vidal turned his vacant eyes in the direction of the journalist.

'It doesn't matter what I think, Señor Fleixa. The good Lord abandoned this barrio long ago, so it's little wonder that the beast walks among us – and sates itself whenever it likes. You only have to look around you: this is his dwelling place, there's no doubt.' Then, turning back to Daniel, he said, 'I was very fond of your father, lad. That's why I'll give you the same warning I gave him.' He paused, puffing out smoke. 'Do not seek after that which is beyond you. This is not a thing to be understood. Return to your life and forget this place: it is cursed.'

NINE

The moon seemed suspended between the clouds as they set off in silence along the empty street. After the suffocating heat inside, the brisk sea air struck their faces like shards of glass. They wrapped their coats about them and adjusted their hats against the chill.

All that, thought Daniel, and it boiled down to some absurd superstition. His father had clearly let himself be taken in by the fantastic tale; his senility did the rest. All good sense having deserted him, he'd embarked on a search for an imaginary assassin. He'd become so fixated that, as the police said, some accident had befallen him, or he'd simply spent so much time roaming those miserable reaches that the inevitable bad end had come. That was all there was to it. Now Daniel was free to return to England. He'd done what he could, and ought to feel satisfied . . . but he didn't. It felt like failure. Glancing at his companion, he saw that he wasn't the only one with his head hung low; Fleixa looked just as despondent.

They crossed Calle San Juan, making for the Plaza de la

Fuente and Paseo San Carlos, where a carriage could be hailed. As they passed the San Miguel Church, a clatter came from behind a pile of empty fishing crates.

'Who goes there?'

A shadow slid along the church wall and disappeared.

'It's that damned boy of Vidal's,' said Fleixa, clearly relieved. 'Probably after some money from us.'

Guillem materialized on the next corner, standing up behind some more crates. His large eyes were fixed on Daniel, who motioned for him to come closer, but the boy kept away, inspecting the pair with great caution.

'Are you not afraid,' said Daniel, 'to be abroad, all alone, at such an hour?'

'I'm not,' he said. 'I've got the doctor's magic to protect me.'

'What magic might that be?'

The boy frowned.

'Is it really true you're his son?'

'I am, I give you my word.'

Daniel held out a coin to the boy. Guillem leapt forward and snatched it from his hand, before retreating to his spot behind the crates.

'I'll show you if you like,' said the boy, and after a pause nodded in Fleixa's direction. 'And I don't mind if he comes.'

And without any further ado, he turned and headed back down the alley. Daniel shrugged and looked at Fleixa as if to say, *Why not?* They both fell in behind the boy. After a few minutes they emerged from the alleys and backstreets onto a wide promenade above the seawall, against which waves crashed. The boy had led them to the old port. Gas lamps lined the Paseo

Nacional, and beyond them were large merchant ships, packet boats and dozens of fishing vessels, all bobbing on the water in anticipation of dawn.

Guillem went straight across the deserted avenue and, coming to the inner wall, leaped straight over the top. Daniel and Fleixa, both startled, expected to hear the sound of the body plunging into the waters below. But when they followed, leaning over the edge they found a series of steps cut into the stone, leading down to the water's edge.

'You thinking of going down there?' said Fleixa.

'It doesn't look like we have much of a choice!'

The boy was already halfway down, shadows enclosing around him. The steps were shallow, irregular and covered in moss – no easy descent. The pair clambered over, the briny atmosphere intensifying; Daniel felt sure they were bound for a watery grave. When they reached the last step, they both stopped and looked around: Guillem was nowhere to be seen.

'Where's the little devil got to?' exclaimed Fleixa.

A whistle startled them. A little way along the wall was a tunnel entrance, the height of a man and invisible from above; a thin watercourse spilled out from inside. Guillem was sitting on the edge looking impatient. Seeing they'd spotted him, he got to his feet, shifted aside some pieces of timber and extracted a beaten tin lantern. He lit it, and the interior of the tunnel suddenly blazed into view. Someone had etched the word 'VIVITUR' into the brickwork.

'This is the magic?' asked Daniel.

'The doctor did it for me,' said Guillem solemnly.

'Are there other . . . magic words like this?'

'Yes.'

'Will you show us?'

The boy thought for a moment, pursing his lips, before nodding once more and heading down into the tunnel.

'A joke of some kind,' said Fleixa. 'Must be.'

'Stay here if you wish.'

Daniel began after the boy, whose shadow extended and flickered behind him in the lamplight. The men had to stoop. The tunnel forked and forked again, the constant murmur of water accompanying their progress. Every now and then a sizeable rat would rear up, screech and flee. The oil smoke billowing from the lantern offset the stench of sewage. Daniel quickly lost his bearings. Without their little guide they'd have no chance of finding their way out. Suppressing his disquiet, he dusted himself off, trying, without success, to shift the dampness sticking to his clothes. He heard Fleixa muttering to himself behind. When they came to another fork in the tunnel, the boy stopped and held the lantern up, illuminating a wall on which the word 'INGENIO' had been etched. As soon as the pair caught up, Guillem turned down the marked tunnel, and a few metres further on the sewer opened out into a chamber the height of several men. Fleixa stumbled in and puffed out his cheeks, Daniel also sighing with relief at being able to stand up straight, and smiling as the journalist let out a stream of invective.

'For the love of God! This place is disgusting. What are we even doing down here?'

'Following the marks my father made.'

'Damn it all, where's the sense?'

'It's some kind of message, I think. I still don't know what it means – that's why we ought to carry on to the end.' And then, gloomily, he said, 'Don't worry, there are only three words to go.'

'How do you know that?'

'Shh!' said Guillem. 'Not so loud. This is Picker territory now.'

'Oh, come on, boy!'

Guillem looked at the journalist like the imbecile he clearly thought him to be.

'What are "Pickers"?' asked Daniel.

'Tall tales,' said Fleixa. 'A speciality in this city, as you've surely noticed.'

But Daniel looked inquisitively at the boy all the same, and Fleixa grudgingly explained. 'They say that, a few decades back, certain people began scratching a living down here. Beggars, wanderers, criminals – the kind who would rather hide in the sewers than face the law. More and more are supposed to have joined the ranks, some say they set up their own community, appoint their own leaders, have their own laws. They spend their days scavenging – picking – anything of value. Hence the name. And people also say that they emerge at night looking for anyone foolish enough to come wandering around down here, and that if they get you, you'll never be seen again. They trade the bone marrow they extract from the bodies, supposedly. Personally,' said the journalist, 'I think it's an old wives's tale. Can you imagine anyone actually living down here?'

'I'm not making it up,' said Guillem, frowning.

'How have you come to know this place so well?' said Daniel.

'I was sleeping rough with my little brother. That was before. And one winter it snowed, everything froze and we had nothing to eat. So we came down here – and the Pickers took us in. They know their way around perfectly, they don't need any light to navigate, they're even better than the rats. These sewers run beneath the whole city. You can go from place to place without anyone knowing. Us children were the only ones allowed to go up to the street, we were sent to get food. Most of them don't go up for years, they go crazy. A certain amount of time passes and you can't take sunlight any more. When my brother caught fever and died, that was when I left.' He glanced up through the darkness. 'We need to hurry, it's going to rain.'

And with that he hopped off the boulder he'd been sitting on and headed along the passageway.

'What does he mean?' Fleixa asked Daniel.

The boy's answer echoed around the chamber.

'When it rains, the tunnels flood.'

The pair looked at each another in alarm.

'So we should go back then?'

But Guillem didn't answer. As he went on ahead with the lantern, the space fell into darkness.

'Doesn't look like we have much of a choice, Fleixa. He's got the lantern.'

They advanced in the wake of the boy. The tunnel sloped downwards for a hundred metres and then broke off to the right. Fleixa thought he could hear thunder, and kept on demanding to go back. But the boy forged ahead. As they came into yet another tunnel, they were surrounded by the sound of buzzing. Daniel put his hand against a wall and felt a light vibration. He wanted to ask where the sound was coming from, but it was too loud to speak over – a moment later they came into another chamber and the sound died away again.

After a few more minutes' walk, Guillem pulled up and again held the lantern up to reveal an inscription: *ERUNT*.

'The final one,' declared Daniel, peering at the wall.

'How do you know that?'

'Because they form a phrase: *Vivitur ingenio, caetera mortis erunt.*'

'Which means?'

'Man's ingenuity is his only way to eternal life.'

'I'll be hanged if I understand *anything*.'

Daniel, looking pensive, said nothing, but continued peering at the wall.

'What's beyond here?' he asked Guillem.

'More tunnels.'

He regarded the rough lines his father had carved into the brickwork. He tried to understand. The words were meant for him, but he couldn't fathom the meaning – what would his father have wanted to bring him here for? He wasn't a man to act aimlessly. Daniel ran his fingers over the surface – and then the brick moved, dislodging a small shower of sandstone.

'The light,' called Daniel, suddenly excited.

The mortar here was a different colour to the rest of the wall, and came away with a little scraping. Using a pencil Fleixa lent him, Daniel quickly excavated the joins, freeing the brick. Daniel snatched the light from the boy and held it up to the gap. Thinking he saw something at the back, he took off his jacket and rolled up his shirtsleeve, and thrust his hand inside. He didn't think he could get it all the way back – but by stretching to his absolute limit, he could feel something jagged against his fingertips. He managed to pull it out, and in the lamplight it was revealed to be a small packet.

'The doctor said you'd find it,' declared the boy.

They left far more rapidly than they had entered. Guillem spoke no more, but hurried along glancing upwards into the darkness. After what felt to Daniel like an eternity they finally made it back to the same outlet they'd entered by. Back atop the seawall once more, they took deep gulps of the fresh air; Fleixa for one had never been so glad to see an overcast Barcelona sky. A few drops of rain began to fall, soon becoming a downpour. They ran over to shelter in a doorway. Before they realized, Guillem had padded away and disappeared into the backstreets.

TEN

Several cups of hot coffee later, Daniel and Fleixa were still staring at the object before them on the table, which looked out of place on the polished marble top. Flat and rectangular like a cigarette holder, it was wrapped in a piece of mud-stained bandage. They were in a café in the environs of the university, and only after a good long while had the cold of the sewers begun to dissipate from their bones. Fleixa was drumming his fingers impatiently on the table, and Daniel looked up at him. Eventually Daniel took a breath, adjusted his spectacles, and went about unwrapping his father's final bequest.

It was no straightforward task. The damp of the sewers had caused the fabric of the old bandages to cake together into one stiff, coagulated block. A rancid odour rose as he began pulling it apart.

'Stinks!' murmured Fleixa, taking a sip of his brandy.

After several minutes' work, and having to put up with Fleixa's fidgeting, finally Daniel pulled clear the last layer. Lifting his hands away, he discovered a delicate silver jewel box. Daniel gulped. His fingers hovered at the clasp, before finally sliding it free. As he opened the top, a breath seemed to escape along with the trace of an antique perfume. A pirouetting figure in mother-of-pearl stood at the centre.

'Surely not!' Fleixa almost shouted. 'We risk life and limb down in those sewers, and all for nothing?'

Daniel paid him no mind. Surprise lit up his face, an unexpected memory – his eyes sparkled with emotion. He put his fingers to the ballerina and wound her round, three times, to the left. The music box tune twinkled in the air as the figure spun back around. Daniel beamed; Fleixa only raised his eyebrows.

The music and figurine came to a stop. Daniel again wound her around, but this time once to the right, and then twice back around to the left. Now, instead of music, a click was heard and a panel sprang open, revealing a hidden compartment.

'My mother loved this jewellery box,' said Daniel.

Carefully he slipped the panel out and placed it to one side. There was a small grey notebook in the velvet-lined interior, which he removed. Exchanging glances with the journalist, Daniel unfastened the leather strap and opened the book. The paper was of excellent quality and, aside from a few damp marks, in good condition. The pages themselves were filled with neat handwriting. And on the inside front cover, a name appeared: 'Doctor Frederic Homs'.

'Looks like a notebook to me,' said Fleixa, his disappointment obvious.

'I've seen similar ones before,' said Daniel. 'My father used them to make research notes, and often as diaries. What I don't know is why he's gone to such ends to stash the notebook of *another* doctor. Maybe the writing will tell us.'

They began to read.

Notes on the convalescence of my wife Luisa Homs

19 December 1885
2.a
Initial check up reveals the following symptoms: the patient is
not suffering from fever. Stools are plentiful if whitish in colour
and somewhat on the small side. Pulse has been taken every
two hours and on all counts patient seems weak.

Blood pressure results show clear hypertension resulting in
loss of liquids. Treatments have been applied.

'His own wife!' said Fleixa. 'And not at all well, from the sounds of things.'

'Cholera,' said Daniel.

Again Fleixa arched an eyebrow. Daniel, not lifting his eyes from the page, explained. 'As a child, every single morning my father would give us a test. Symptoms. If we wanted our breakfast we had to guess the illness the symptoms he described pertained to, and the best course of treatment. Get it wrong, and that day we'd be packed off to school on an empty stomach. Very effective teaching method, I can assure you.'

22 December 1885
6.b
For a portion of last year (until September) the patient resided

84

in Valencia with some members of her family. There was a
bad outbreak of cholera in the area between June and July.
It would appear that the efforts of one Doctor Jaime Ferrán
stemmed the spread of the disease. It was the first time that a
vaccine had been used to immunize humans against bacterial
illness: a great medical advance. Unfortunately some of our
colleagues in the profession have questioned the approach.
Regarding the current case, the bacillus injection was adminis-
tered too late.

The patient has been complaining of cramps and is increas-
ingly dehydrated. Apathy and loss of lucidity also in evidence.
Treatment to continue.

Note: seek advice of Doctor Ferrán.

The ensuing pages described the efforts of Frederic Homs to find a cure for his wife. Certain notes included the elaborate chemical equations upon which the doctor based his experiments. As they read on it was clear that the treatments had been ineffective and, try as Homs might, his perseverance went unrewarded. The writing became less formal as the pages went on, allowing a glimpse of the desperation caused in the writer by his all too evident impotence in the face of the disease.

10 January 1886
17.d
My dear Luisa, I must ask your forgiveness. Since your
admittance to hospital my pain and anguish have pitched
me into a most lamentable sort of chaos. The longest weeks of
my life. I only have to think of our being separated – I break

*down. I will not cease in my work to find a cure, I promise
you. Trust in me, my beloved.*

13 January 1886
22.a
*Good news, our most esteemed Amat has joined the fight! All
the rest have given up, offer nothing but condolences, avoid
having dealings with me, but our good friend applies himself
with the selfsame zeal as I. Hope!*

16 January 1886
35.e
*Dear, dear Luisa. I have come to the library to better apply
myself. I sometimes think my place is at your side, and I
ought to be there with you, rather than wasting all these many
hours in books and experiments. I know, though, that you
know I do it only for your own good. And I shall succeed,
whatever the cost. Be strong.*

The medical history had given way to affectionate letters. Homs
would dive into the deepest slough at every new problem, and
soar euphorically at any slight good result.

21 January 1886
60.b
*A great discovery today! If my overwrought mind does not
deceive me, I have found something beyond our wildest
dreams. I do not know whether to believe in what I have
found, nor do I wish to bestow upon you false hope.*

86

23 January 1886

64.b

*The more I go on in my research, the more convinced I am
that Vesalius's Liber Octavus is our only hope.*

29 January 1886

67.f

*A most terrible day, my dear. A falling out with our friend.
When I shared my findings, he became as enthused as I.
Not only did we seem to have alighted on a solution for you
but, if our predictions were correct, it was sure to go down
as the greatest scientific discovery of the close of this century.
But in the night we fell to bitter disputes. Amat does not
want to go on. Terrible things he said, speaking of God and
of the sacred order of things – the which he claimed we would
contravene. It's true, I see it now, I lost my head, I insulted
him most unacceptably. Our fellowship is perhaps destroyed.
Perhaps, but it's all one: I now see that this is a solitary quest,
mine alone, and that should the opportunity present itself I
must not hesitate to go down any path, be it even the Devil's
own.*

Daniel and Fleixa looked in the following pages for Homs's
great discovery, apparently the cause of the fallout with Doctor
Amat, but could not find it. There was no mention of the revelation, as though Homs had wanted to keep it a secret even from
himself. The notes from the following days, increasingly erratic,
concerned deadends and defeats in Homs's quest.

3 (4?) February 1886

Have not eaten a meal this day and do not remember the last time I slept. The date? Day and night begin to meld into one single thing. Deep cut upon smashing some distillation jars – forgot I had left a Bunsen lit. Problems with the delivery of corpses and delays in receiving the correct chemical compounds. But worst of all – these I believe to be far from coincidences: I know that Amat is trying to sabotage my attempts. Yes, my dear, your eyes do not deceive you: our most excellent friend has set himself against finding a cure. Such low acts – I am astounded! He has been in conversation with the board at the hospital, and has turned them all against me. The vice-chancellor has been to see me, concerned for my wellbeing, he claims. As if I was ignorant of his true intention – to spy on my findings and advances. They want to take over my work, but I won't allow it, I will overcome their worst intentions. I'll finish. Even if, as Amat says, God Himself is against my inquiries – I will finish with God as well if needs be.

a	b	c	d	e	f	g	h	i	l	m	n

o	p	q	r	s	t	v	x	y	z		

'And this table?' said Fleixa.

'Couldn't say,' said Daniel. 'Some chart of equivalences between the different experiments, doubtless.'

Several blank pages followed, and then Homs's final notes.

Date unknown
#?
I am exhausted, dear, and I am burning up. I have been suffering the occasional hallucination, I think I see you beside me and you look worried – you are worried at my regrettable state. It is not possible, I know, for you have been in a coma these past days, but it is a consolation all the same to have you beside me as I go about my experiments.

Date unknown
#?
I have been losing weight – a good deal, I suppose, given that my ribs are now protruding from my sides, and my hands look like talons . . . I know that my appearance, more akin to a beggar in the street than to a man of science, is a discomfort to my colleagues – I know and care not. The deuce with them! Forgive me, dear, but I feel my spirit on the rack – thus these words that enter my pen. It ails me that I cannot unravel the secret of my marvellous discovery. I know I am on the right track, I feel it. There, it is just there, I reach out for it. I have followed the steps as the book indicates, every instruction one after the other, and yet and yet! Something I must be doing wrong!

Date unknown

#?

Only a few hours sleep these past four days, perhaps I ought to rest a little – but I cannot stop. Not now, not when it is so close.

And there the diary ended.

'Is that it? Nothing more?'

Thumbing through the final pages, all of them blank, Daniel shook his head.

'What could your father have been keeping this for?'

'Truly, no idea.'

'Possibly,' Fleixa went on, 'it connected in some way with his own inquiries.'

Daniel closed the notebook with a sigh.

'So,' said Fleixa, his enthusiasm renewed, 'next is to locate Doctor Frederic Homs, see what we can learn from him. Wouldn't you say?'

'I'm sorry, Señor Fleixa, but I don't think I can go on with all this.'

'How's that?'

Daniel avoided the journalist's astonished look. He'd made up his mind, for good or for ill.

'My father's inquiries show that there is some relationship between him and the terrible fate of the young women in Barceloneta. That means his death was not an accident. I appreciate your help in establishing that. But all the same, tomorrow I will go directly to the police and place the matter in their hands.'

'Have you lost your mind? What makes you think they'll care

90

more about what you have to say than they did when your father went to them?'

'I understand your annoyance, I do. But this is a matter for the authorities. Trapping the culprit, bringing him to justice – this is beyond you and I alone.'

'But—'

'Forgive me,' said Daniel, getting to his feet and extending his hand, which Fleixa, though stunned, took. 'Our adventures end here, Señor Fleixa. This coming Thursday I will be on the Paris train, and from there shall return to England. Thank you again for everything.'

ELEVEN

Pau was hurrying to the hospital. The end of term exams were upon them, everyone was on edge. The professors had become more uncompromising, using any pretext to dole out extra work. With so many classes and such a heavy load of practical projects it was nigh on impossible to give time to anything else. Though none of that would be an acceptable excuse today, he knew.

He scurried along the passageway, not bothering to take in the portraits of distinguished alumni, and out onto the street. With a terse hello to a fellow student, he entered the hospital building. He crossed the orangery and went up the steps two at a time, ignoring the reproachful looks of two nuns coming down. He felt hopeful as he hurried along: the results must have been beginning to show by now. But how quickly hope gave way to worry! If it didn't turn out as planned, then what a bind he'd be in! As he approached the women's ward he turned down a corridor that led to a covered patio, before pausing in the passage and glancing around, checking he hadn't been followed. It was mid-afternoon, not a busy time in the hospital, and that made it easy to pass unnoticed – but he couldn't take any chances.

He scanned the section of the patio that was most shielded from prying eyes and, advancing down that side, lowered his face. Which was why he didn't see that indeed he was being watched – from a second floor window. Thinking himself in the clear, he stopped at a large door in the corner, took out a bunch of keys and opened it. He crossed the threshold and shut the door quietly behind him, resting his back against the wall inside and letting out a sigh. Coming in through another, short passageway, he arrived at a vestibule, where the familiar odour of antiseptic filled the air. Daylight broke in through a high window. The rusty remains of several mattresses had been leaned up against the wall, and alongside them were a dozen or so washing baskets, full of dirty bedclothes. At the back, where the room was dimmest, was a door, to the side of which a low table stood bearing a covered food tray and some clean linen. He carefully gathered both and, knocking softly, went in.

Three quarters of an hour later, Pau came back out. He dropped a bundle of dirty clothes into a basket and put the tray, now empty, back on the table. He retraced his steps, through the covered patio, back across the hospital gardens. Several patients were out for their evening strolls, trying to make the most of the last rays of sunlight. Arriving back at the university and climbing up the stairs, Pau allowed himself to smile. Half enthused, half relieved, he whispered to himself, 'It's working!'

TWELVE

'Your father's death was an unfortunate accident. There's nothing more to be said.'

Inspector Sánchez, content he'd clarified the matter, sprawled his large frame back in his desk chair. He spat a pea shell into the waste-paper basket by his feet. His chubby, infant-like hands gesticulated as he spoke, and when he paused, they dipped into a newspaper cone full of *altramuz* – salted peas. His upturned nose and tiny eyes seemed out of place on his large face. Receiving no immediate reply, he attempted a smile, but it was not an expression to which he was accustomed, and the result was a sort of strange grimace. Daniel ignored the policeman's condescending tone.

'These papers show a chain of events. At the very least they raise questions about the cause of death.'

'Well . . . That's quite a claim to make. May I?'

Daniel handed over the portfolio containing his father's documents, though he decided to hold back on Homs's diary. He still didn't know how it was that the whole fitted together.

'And you say that your father came by this information via his own private investigations?'

'Yes, as I've already explained.'

'Interesting . . . These notes are most interesting, but change nothing. The opposite, in fact: they rather confirm our suspicions.'

'In what way?'

'It could hardly be clearer,' said Sánchez. 'When this list of crimes was compiled, its author was in a clear state of perturbation. They are the ravings of an obsessive, neither more nor less. At the time of writing, your father was plainly on the verge of a nervous collapse.

'A few weeks before the, what shall we say, *fatal accident*, Señor Amat came to see me. Were you aware? And he himself placed these documents in front of me. Like you, he sought to evince something linking these deaths together, but without presenting a scrap of evidence. Some shadowy murderer, butchering citizens left and right . . . God help us – you couldn't make it up!'

'But—'

'Please do not be offended,' said Sánchez, raising his hands in a placating way. 'I suppose the fact that you and your father hadn't spoken for, what, six, seven years? Learning of his death, and by telegram too, that must have been quite the blow. I understand. When all is said and done, he was still your father.'

Though it was cold in the office, Daniel flushed. He tried to keep calm, reminding himself of what he had wanted to get out of this meeting. His presence clearly put the Inspector on edge, and he didn't know why. He just had the sense the man wanted him out. Manners urged him to follow the prompts and leave – but he was damned if he'd make it that easy.

'You're trying to tell me these dead bodies are all made up?'

'Oh no,' said Sánchez. 'They are doubtless far from made up.'

Daniel didn't expect that. Sánchez popped another salted pea into his mouth, and before he could speak again there was a knock at the door. An official came in with some papers for Sánchez to sign, which he did, ignoring Daniel's impatient looks. The official went away and Sánchez began again.

'In this city, Señor Amat, such cases are commonplace. Almost half a million inhabitants live here, so altercations and, unfortunately, the odd violent death, are by no means rare. You can cook up all the lists you like. As for the dead people your father has chosen to group together here, there's little doubt that their means of subsistence weren't exactly . . . *exemplary*. A beating from their pimp, a client who got a little too frisky, a catfight over some particularly profitable street corner . . . It's gossip and tittle-tattle that makes it into something else.'

Daniel tried not to think about the match seller girl, fifteen years old, on the list, or the grocer's daughter, twenty. Without his knowing it, his back had become tense, and the pain was pulsing through his neck scars.

'And the state their bodies were found in?' he said. 'What do you put that down to?'

'Señor Amat, the water and the vermin in those parts can leave a human body in a very unfortunate state. You ought to see what a few hungry rats can make of a large hunk of meat.'

His laugh resounded around the room. But Daniel wasn't

smiling, and Sánchez fell quiet, burying his hand in the *altramuz* once more.

'Barcelona has more than its fair share of murderers, prostitutes and anarchists. I've got quite enough in the way of tall tales to think about – like the rumours about the labourers planning to gang together in some kind of association, a "General Union of Workers" they're calling it – can you imagine? Not that I want to cause alarm: we keep the peace, we are the thin line between order and the potential for chaos, anarchy and larceny. We are the ones that keep the people safe. And we know how to do our job.'

'I'm not sure I see it like that,' said Daniel, finally letting his ire get the better of him. 'It seems to me that you have done nothing at all to shed light on the truth of this matter. You've moved swiftly only in quelling any noise about the deaths of these young women, citing, most flimsily I might add, their social conditions. As for my father's death, that you have declared it an accident rather than anything else – anything, say, closer to the truth – is merely to avoid complications for yourself.'

'Señor Amat!' Sánchez grimaced, pursing his fleshy lips. 'You'd do well to be more careful than to go throwing around such accusations. Where's your gratitude? It was only the influence of certain people close to us that prevented your father's name being dragged through the mud.'

Daniel could hardly believe his ears. What was the man trying to insinuate?

Sánchez hauled himself out of his chair, which creaked as if in relief, and went over to the door.

'I agreed to see you out of respect for your father. My time is far too precious to fritter away on nonsense. I won't, however, hold it against you; your loss has clearly affected you. As a show of good will, I'm going to hold onto these documents,' he snatched the portfolio from Daniel's hand. 'You have my word that we will be looking into things.'

He stopped to spit out another shell. He watched it fly through the air, with the attendant spray of saliva. The shell hit the edge of the waste-paper basket and bounced out. Annoyed, he turned to Daniel again.

'The thing I find myself asking, Señor Amat, is whether you haven't perhaps lost your bearings since coming to Barcelona? I believe the best thing for you now would be to return home.'

Leaving the station, Daniel took a carriage back to the halls of residence where he was staying. The World Fair meant that all hotels were completely booked, and the dean had refused to let him stay in a hostel, offering him his father's old rooms for the duration of his stay.

Reflecting on the exchange with Sánchez, he became lost in the rattle and jolt of the carriage. Could the whole thing really be a mad invention of his father's – fuelled by the superstitious tales he'd been told in Barceloneta? Could he really have taken his own life, as Sánchez seemed to be suggesting? Daniel couldn't bring himself to believe it. His father's pride would never have allowed it, not when he viewed it as the coward's way out. But years had passed, many years, and he had no way of knowing the extent to which things had changed. The more people spoke to him of his father now, the greater the sensation grew: he hadn't really known the man at all.

The carriage pulled up outside the university, on the Medical Faculty side. Daniel paid the driver and went in. He greeted the porter and made for his quarters, pleased by the prospect of a lie-down. He had not slept well during his time in Barcelona. For a number of days now the lack of sleep, allied with all the emotion, had been preventing him from thinking at all clearly. He would try to recover his strength and, the following day, come to some sort of a decision.

It was late and the corridors that led to the staff lodgings were empty. When he reached his own, as he went to take out his key, he stopped. The door was ajar; he was quite certain that he'd not left it so. He went in and had to stifle a cry: the place had been ransacked. The drawers, wardrobe and his suitcases had all been turned out, and his shirts and suits were in a mess on the floor, the mattress had even been torn open; the cotton insides hung out like the guts of a disembowelled corpse.

Looking over at the table, he saw that the jewellery box was gone. He searched everywhere for it but to no avail. Patting his inside pocket he was relieved to feel the notebook still there; he'd decided to take it to the interview with Sánchez only as an afterthought upon leaving. Fleixa was right: the contents of those pages must be important in some way, for all that they were ignorant of the reasons.

THIRTEEN

Fleixa was grateful for Dolors's body heat beneath the sheets. The stove had consumed the last of the coal a while earlier and the room was icy. Light from the streetlamp outside filtered in through the curtains – it was very much still the night, but he couldn't sleep. His mind was swirling with the Vidal encounter, the adventure down in the sewers, the notebook belonging to Doctor Homs. Over and over he asked himself: had Doctor Amat deceived him? Could it all be the product of an infirm mind? Something told him no. He'd wagered a great deal on that story – if it turned out not to be true, yet another blow to his journalistic name was in store. Which Llopis would doubtless seize upon to usurp his position at the paper.

He shut his eyes and returned to the question of the murders. Daniel Amat was clearly not what he claimed to be. The interview with Vidal had prompted several questions: what exactly had happened seven years earlier? Why had Daniel fled for England, never to speak to his father again? What was his secret? Open questions were meat and drink to him: instinct told him there was a story in them somewhere. He tutted in frustration as he remembered, in spite of his protestations, Daniel's decision to go to the police. There was an end to the whole thing. He could write something short about the crimes, maybe they could stretch to a column, but it would be nothing more than conjecture. He was going to need something bigger to explain the delays to the newspaper. One more problem to add to all the many others.

The Raval had been buzzing with talk for several days: Fleixa was a wanted man. He'd lost a fistful down the Can Tunis races and it had now been several weeks since his loan had expired. La Negra was not known for her leniency with clients who found themselves short of funds. On top of which, the landlord wanted the rent – apparently he had ceased being swayed by his wife. Fleixa had been left with no other option but to take refuge with Dolors who, roughly ejecting a client when Fleixa knocked at the door, agreed to take him in for a few nights. He turned over again and looked down at the woman lying beside him. Though well into her thirties, Dolors, when she slept, had the look of a young girl.

They'd met three years earlier. He'd just published his piece on the tram takings robbery, in which several people inside the Barcelona Tramways company, including the chief executive, had been implicated, as well as a town councillor. It had been quite the scandal, and his report became the talk of the town. A few weeks later, as he left the newspaper offices one night, he was assaulted by a group of masked thugs. He was down on the ground, being kicked and beaten, when Dolors came around the corner and raised the alarm – shouting and screaming until the

101

men took off. She took him back to her home semi-unconscious and with a large knife wound to the stomach. Fleixa shuddered to remember – he held his hands up to see if they were trembling. Dolors patched him up and stayed by his side until the following day, when he went into a fever. She made him drink cup after cup of a homemade herbal remedy, she changed his sheets, she put cold compresses on his brow until the fever abated; he needed tending to for a week. When he asked her why, what had been in it for her, she just shrugged and smiled. Since then they had seen one another with a certain amount of regularity, and sometimes, when she wasn't working, would spend the whole night in the same bed. As time went by it came to seem like the perfect arrangement. Dolors was what she was, and didn't want attachments. Just then there was a noise out in the street, and the prostitute's eyes came sleepily open. She yawned.

'Can't sleep?' she said.

'No,' said Fleixa. 'Thinking.'

She shifted under the sheets as Fleixa watched – in the half-light, he could make out her lips curving upwards into a smile, and her saffron-coloured hair splayed out over the covers. Fleixa was startled to feel her hand upon him. She rested her head on his shoulder.

'It isn't good to think too much. Leave it till tomorrow, come here. It's cold.'

He did as he was told.

FOURTEEN

Daniel woke early, having again slept badly. The meeting with Sánchez, his room being ransacked: he'd ended up with many more questions than answers. The police clearly had no intention of reopening his father's case, and there was no point reporting the theft of the jewellery box. Rousing himself and putting on his clothes, he decided to go and take it up with the dean.

Santa Creu Hospital occupied a distinguished gothic edifice. Built four centuries earlier as a single place for the city's various hospitals to inhabit, in the intervening period an array of new passageways and wards, and stairways joining them, had been added. Placing the Royal College of Surgeons next door had been an unmitigated success, seeing that it had allowed for the practical education, for over one hundred years, of Barcelona's future medical practitioners. The city had produced a significant number of distinguished medics as a direct result.

A hospital porter pointed Daniel to the patient gardens as

Doctor Suñé's most likely location and, thanking the man, Daniel made his way up a flight of steps and into the porticoed courtyard.

He found Doctor Luis Suñé i Molist crouching down before a young boy. The middle-aged man's hair was scraped back over a balding pate, while a gleaming moustache capped his broad smile. The young boy wore a grey dressing gown, marking him out as a patient. The doctor was speaking, one hand resting on the boy's shoulder. Daniel approached.

'Sister Inés will be with you,' Daniel heard him say. 'All you need now is to eat properly, take as much sun as you can, and your daily walks. You'll be home again in no time.'

Daniel took in the boy's ailment with some dismay: he was on crutches, missing one leg. The boy, tears in his eyes, smiled at the doctor and turned away, heading down a corridor with the sister at his side. Doctor Suñé watched him go, and then, sighing, stood up with some difficulty, straightening his arms against his knees. Only then did he notice Daniel.

'Señor Amat,' he said, momentary surprise giving way to a grave expression. 'I've been informed of the robbery. You must accept my apologies, I just cannot understand it. We've never seen anything of the kind. They told me they moved you into different quarters, is everything as you would wish it to be?'

'It's fine, thank you. In fact, I was wondering about taking advantage of your generous hospitality a few days longer. It would seem that my father left quite a number of issues unresolved.'

'But of course. Stay as long as you wish.'

'And might we speak?'

104

Suñé gave him an inquisitive look. He called over a sister and sent her ahead to prepare some rooms.

'I'm sadly short of free time,' he said to Daniel. 'But you're welcome to accompany me on my rounds.'

They began along the corridor. Suñé constantly had to stop to answer questions, or receive some briefing or other; deliberate and measured in all he did, he was decisive in giving out instructions and providing solutions to the range of questions posed.

'We'll be able to talk more easily in here,' he said as they came to a separate part of the hospital, away from the wards. 'Go ahead.'

'As you know,' Daniel began, 'my father and I had not seen each other for a long time. And now, returning to the city, I have learned certain things about the man that make it seem . . . how can I put it? As though I never knew him.'

'I held him in great esteem,' Suñé said. 'I studied under him. Everyone admired his enormous talents for doctoring and research. But after the awful events seven years ago, it's fair to say that your father was never the same.'

Daniel nodded for him to go on.

'Your father left the city not long after you yourself went away. Berlin, or Vienna, I believe, for a period of two years. He never said much about it. When he came back he seemed quite recovered, rejuvenated you might almost say. He began teaching again, picked up his research projects where he'd left off, even began seeing patients. Everything went well for a time, until he began looking into the hygiene question. To begin with it was a side project, a hobby almost, but it ended up occupying him entirely, body and soul – physically and mentally, he simply gave it everything. We tried to warn him – little good that did! It wore him out. And anyone who tried to help, he simply pushed away, most gruffly – you know how he could be.'

Daniel did. His father could be quite unpleasant when he tried.

'He seemed to be on the up again for a time, but then began acting peculiarly, going missing for several days at a time without notifying anyone, taking walks around the colleges at night, carrying out very delicate experiments in his own quarters. His interests turned increasingly outlandish, and I would go so far as to say that he lost touch with reality. People, colleagues and friends, began to turn their backs.

'He suffered a series of nervous episodes, and a time came when I had to prescribe laudanum if he was to have any chance of sleeping at night. But he was still racked by nightmares, and would frequently be heard calling out – your name, and that of your brother.'

Daniel nodded, head bowed.

'My brother died in the fire.'

'That I know,' said Suñé, taking a deep breath. 'Your father was tormented by the memory. He relived it over and over again. And then came the fantastical tales of a demon murderer, which led to him losing his mind; the only demon was inside him. Your father didn't die because of an "accumulation of unfortunate coincidences", no.' Here Suñé placed a hand on Daniel's shoulder. 'Forgive me, but it is my firm belief that your father took his own life.'

'It isn't possible. My father—'

'Was a brilliant doctor and a man of many virtues. What happened between the two of you is in the past. As far as everyone

106

else is concerned, his death was an accident. We'll honour him and remember him as he deserves to be remembered.'

Could it be true? His father losing his mind? But he'd left Homs's notebook – how to explain that, if his father was insane at the last? Or could it have been yet further *proof* of his madness?

The pair left the quiet anteroom and came through into another, busier section of the hospital. Doctors and their assistants conversed in the corridors, while pairs of nuns, in their immaculate white robes, hurried here and there. A group of students, with a professor at their head, passed Daniel and Suñé. Daniel recognized one: the youngster from among the group at his father's funeral who had gone over to the graveside.

'Do you know who that student is?' he asked the doctor.

'Which one?'

'The one at the back, with the folder under his arm.'

'Ah, that's Pau Gilbert. Brilliant young man, though not the most popular with his peers. He was the last acting assistant for your father.'

Daniel watched the youngster and the group as they made their way along the corridor, and when they passed from sight turned and followed Suñé into a long hall. The roof was supported by a dozen or so pointed arches, and between these a line of windows let in the sunlight. Fifty iron bedsteads stood along either wall, with an aisle down the centre for the doctors to move up and down. A few of the beds had white curtains drawn around them for privacy.

'This is the Santa Maria ward,' Suñé explained, 'the Tramuntana section. Men here, women in Sant Josep. Many a long hour your father spent in this place.'

All the beds were taken, and Daniel saw that a few pallets had even been set up on the floor. Suñé guessed his thoughts.

'We're oversubscribed, no getting round it. A delicate situation, though it was worse during the cholera outbreak three years ago. We're going to be moving to a new hospital quite soon, thank the Lord. Some land has become available over by Mount Pelada, I'm hoping that . . . ' He stopped and waved his hand. 'Oh look, Doctor Gavet. He's one of the best we have, I'll introduce you.'

Daniel recognized Gavet from the funeral as well – the man who'd offered his stuttering condolences at the end. He was sitting next to the bed of a patient with a bandaged head. The invalid was explaining something, and becoming quite agitated, and Gavet endeavoured to calm him. The light from the bedside lantern fell on the patient's face, and for a moment Daniel thought he recognized him, though he couldn't remember where from.

'It's excellent work that Doctor Gavet is doing here,' said Suñé. 'Dawn till well past dusk he's at it. Many are the patients who owe him their lives. The man he's speaking to is one of a number of labourers who were brought in last night after an accident at the World Fair site. His two workmates died this morning from their wounds.'

Daniel watched as Gavet consoled the injured man, who was writhing about. He called over a nurse, who dispensed a calmative. Looking up, Gavet saw the dean and, after exchanging a few more words with the patient, came over. He seemed incensed.

'Damn it all, Suñé, i-it's unbelievable. These men, they're

working the most *ridiculous* shifts. We can't let it go on. It's the *third accident* this week at the power station.'

'Try to be calm, there's little we can do apart from our jobs, you know that. Do you know Señor Amat?'

'We met at the cemetery . . .' Daniel began to say, but Gavet, with the slightest of nods, muttered a protest then turned and walked away.

'You'll excuse his zeal. He's a very dedicated man, and what's more, he's quite right. We've been seeing all sorts of injuries from the World Fair site. Hardly any of the companies put safety measures in place, to them that's all a waste of time. There are vast numbers of men working there, and a high accident count. Anyway, Señor Amat,' he said with a tired gesture, 'as you can see, I've got a lot on my plate. Work calls. I hope I've been of some help.'

'Yes, Señor, I appreciate your time. If you'll allow, I have one final question.'

'Go on?'

'What can you tell me about Doctor Frederic Homs?'

Suñé frowned.

'Why are you interested in Homs?'

'I found some books belonging to him among my father's things,' he lied. 'Seems they were friendly.'

'That's true, there was a great friendship between the two – for a number of years. Then certain . . . problems arose.' Daniel nodded inquisitively. 'Very well. Homs taught chemistry, and was a well-known anatomist. His dissection classes were very popular among the students. He ran the library for a year, and did a commendable job. It was when his wife fell ill that he began causing a stir. I don't know all the details, but it was at that point, too, that the relations between him and your father began to cool.'

'Do you know where I might be able to find him?'

'What are you planning exactly, Señor Amat?'

'After such a long time without contact with my father, I simply want to speak with someone who was close to him these past years.'

'Unfortunately, that's not very likely.'

'Why, may I ask?'

Suñé shot him an annoyed look.

'Look, this is no straightforward matter. When the gravity of his wife's situation became clear, Homs gave up teaching, along with all his other duties at the hospital. He spent weeks, day and night for weeks and weeks, trying to find a cure for her.'

'And what happened?'

'He did not succeed. The wife died.'

Daniel felt a stab of pity for Homs. The notebook was ample evidence of the man's dedication. His pain at her loss, the feelings of impotence, must have been quite terrible.

'And is Homs still on the staff?'

'He is not,' said Suñé, shaking his head. 'Homs was consumed by his struggle, a struggle he was never likely to win, when the reaper came for his wife. He didn't recover from the loss, he just couldn't get over it, and his wits deserted him. To the point when one night some doctors at the hospital – your father included – had to stop him carrying out an autopsy on a boy.'

'And why would that have been so extraordinary?'

110

'The boy was still alive.'

Daniel fell quiet.

'For the last year and a half, Doctor Homs has been a patient at the New Bethlem Mental Sanatorium.'

FIFTEEN

Carmeta hurried along as quickly as her legs would carry her. In the empty street, her footfall rang out like a nightwatchman's cane. How late it was! Thirteen years old, she was an apprentice seamstress at the home of the Pons family, a mansion on the Paseo de Gracia. She'd been ordered to complete a job at the last minute, a ball gown for Leonor, the eldest daughter of Doña Herminia. Normally this would be a job for Adela, Carmeta's senior, but she had been ill in bed for the past three days. The difficulty of the task combined with Carmeta's lack of expertise resulted in many extra hours of work, with a good few complications along the way. Fortunately, she had succeeded in completing the dress, and to her mistress's liking as well.

By the time she arrived at Plaza Catalonia it was already past nine o'clock. The last tram had come and gone, a storekeeper told her; she was going to have to walk home. She groaned at the long walk ahead; the warmth of the coal stove suddenly that bit further away. It wasn't the first time she'd made the journey by foot; some weeks she chose to save the twenty centimos and soak up the life of the streets instead. She loved the walk along Las Ramblas more than anything, the elegant ladies, the haughty gentleman riding in carriages to the Liceo or the Hotel Principal. And she'd never skip La Boquería market, with its thronging stalls and vibrant cafés. The smells, the colour, the sheer incessant movement of all those people – she loved to soak it in. Before taking work at the Pons household, she'd rarely left her native barrio, and Barcelona was a new and exciting world to her.

But not today. Night had fallen, rain looked likely, and a long walk was the last thing she felt like. All the shops and newspaper kiosks had dropped their shutters, only the occasional café still had its lights on. She gathered her shawl about her; truly, the night was cold. And she couldn't afford to let herself fall ill, not even for a single day. She had to be working. The five pesetas she brought home each week were a great help to her parents, each of whom spent long hours working the Sants looms.

Her steps led her past Casa Figueras, the pasta factory. The relief on the corner of the building was very pleasing to her eye. She understood little of what people were saying when 'modernism' was mentioned – her mistress spoke of it, saying that it was becoming fashionable in the city, provoking admiration and mockery in equal measure – such discussions went over Carmeta's head. All she knew was how much she would like to be able to carry herself like the country girl in the relief, what she'd give to look like that.

She crossed the street over to Las Ramblas de Sant Josep. Drops of rain began to fall, the prelude to a downpour. Skipping over the first puddles she came to, she dived into the backstreets of El Born. Nightwatchmen would light the lamps throughout the course of their patrols, and the yellowish gaslight come to pervade the streets. Carmeta learned to look after herself long ago, she'd had to, and her eyes and ears were peeled as she went along. Barcelona was a place of wonder, but it could also be cruel to any person who failed to stay alert – even more so now that the Black Hound was abroad. She smiled to herself in an attempt to shake off the fearful tale.

In kitchens and sculleries across the city, the curse was all they talked about. Versions abounded, some claiming that the Hound appeared on the darkest nights and took the form of an enormous, dark brown mastiff, others claiming it to be black as the night itself. The beast's eyes glowed like coals, and hellfire burned at the back of its maw, most agreed. There was one stable hand she knew who said its paws left impressions in the flagstones. People said it had claimed at least a dozen girls, and never failed to brutalize the bodies. Not that she believed any of it – nothing more than the fancies of stable boys trying to win the attention of the serving girls.

She came onto Paseo San Carlos, which was quite deserted, with the bullring a grey smudge off to the left. And then the heavens opened. The force of the rainfall took her aback, and she thought to shelter under an arcade, but the pull of a warm bowl of soup won out. She was tired, her soaking dress clung to her body, and she'd begun to shiver. If she stopped she'd surely end up catching cold. It wasn't far now either, and so she gathered the shawl about her as best she could and turned down an alley between two narrow buildings.

The proximity of the sea announced itself in the salty, misty

114

air. Now she couldn't see more than five feet ahead. Two men appeared pushing a handcart, came past Carmeta and disappeared again without noticing her. As she turned onto Calle Concordia the nearest streetlamp suddenly went out – there were always shortages of gas in this part of El Born, and the slightest cold or drop of rain was enough to keep the nightwatchmen from their duties. And then, all the other lamps in sight went out at once. She carried on regardless – gas cuts were as common around here as a scandal at the Liceo.

Then, bending down to tighten her laces, she heard footsteps behind her, which stopped almost as soon as she noticed them. Until then the only sound had been her own laboured breathing. But now she was sure she'd heard footsteps. She paused where she was and listened, but now could only make out the sound of the waves at the shore, and the faint whistling of the wind though the posterns. She began forward again, an unpleasant tickle now lodged in her stomach. In those dark, unfrequented streets, the stories suddenly didn't seem so fanciful any more. Going past a tavern with lowered shutters, she heard the steps once more – now accompanied by the sound of heavy breathing. Unmistakeably. She picked up her skirt and quickened her pace, trying to glance back at each corner she turned. An enormous mastiff pursuing her – her mind was suddenly invaded by the image of it. And then a howl rent the air, and Carmeta was off and running, along the alleys, across streets, until she came out in front of a grocer's – shut. Her breath came out in white puffs. She'd lost her shawl and her hair hung loose. She could hear no noises behind her now; she thought she must have given whatever had been following her the slip. But then a shadow leaped at her.

She fell to the floor, shielding herself with her arms and crying out for help. After a moment though, she realized she wasn't being attacked. She stopped screaming and opened her eyes. A pile of empty crates surrounded her, and she could see, up ahead, a cat fleeing along the alley.

She would have laughed, but it was too cold. Elvira and Àngels would have a real hoot when she told them back at work tomorrow – the Black Hound had taken a swipe at her! What a ninny she was. Getting to her feet, she went down the next street. This one was dark too, but it was also her home street, and she could make it to her door blind from here. Her mother would not be pleased about the lost shawl – but she'd find an excuse. Still smiling, she removed a long key from her bag. She sighed. She could smell the soup over the fire, and thought she heard the sound of two of her brothers fighting. Placing the key in the lock, looking down at the chink of candlelight on the front step, she wondered if Josep, her youngest brother, her very favourite, would still be awake.

It happened too quickly for her even to cry out. She was seized suddenly and lifted backwards with incredible force. She tried to grab hold of the door handle, but it was out of reach before she knew it. A blow to the head left her stunned, then she felt a sharp twinge, and a warm sensation that spread across her whole body. She slumped to the ground insensate. She could make out the window of her home, lit from within, and there behind the curtain, the silhouette of her mother. She seemed to be looking out onto the street; they were waiting for her. Help, she wanted to cry out for help, but her mouth would not come open. Her head swam. As her assailant began to drag her away, her heels caught in the mud. Her eyelids were heavy, but she was still able to make out her home as it grew smaller in the distance. Tears were running down her cheeks, though she could no longer feel them.

NEW BETHLEM
MENTAL SANATORIUM

Fifteen days before the start of the World Fair

SIXTEEN

Daniel left the Telegraph Station in the grand former residence of the Marquis of Cintadilla. It had been far from easy writing the note explaining his delayed return to Oxford. He had spent an hour trying to come up with an adequate excuse, and finally decided to avoid going into detail. Stepping out of the grand doorway, he put on his hat and crossed Plaza Urquinaona, making his way purposefully towards a rank of carriages, hailing one. He was driven along to the Ronda de San Pedro, the streets busy with all manner of vehicles, from covered landau carriages down to sedan chairs carried by pairs of men on foot. Barcelona was a never-ending swarm, constantly in motion as people headed for factories, markets or upmarket cafés, depending on their social standing. None of which could have been further from Daniel's thoughts, so focussed was he on the task in hand.

The carriage advanced along the Paseo de Gracia and, crossing the Tarragona train lines, came onto Calle Mallorca, where the buildings became more spaced out and new constructions began to intersperse with old family residences. They were at their destination within a few minutes, an elegant mansion with white walls and a slate roof. The growth of the city had meant that the moneyed citizens could begin to build their homes away from the centre, keeping any insalubriousness at arm's length. Certain aesthetic trends were clear to see among this burgeoning bourgeoisie, but for Irene's husband, this new-fangled modernism was clearly not destined to last, and he had instructed his architects to build him something quite different. Daniel rang the doorbell and was received by a young girl with bulging eyes and olive skin. She looked Daniel up and down.

'Buenas tardes,' she said – she had a considerable, and quite endearing, lisp. 'Can I help?'

'Buenas tardes,' said Daniel, removing his hat and handing over his card. 'Daniel Amat. I would like to see the Señora.'

Stepping inside, Daniel couldn't help but admire the opulence of the place. The hallway was larger and more elaborate than usual, even for a family of their standing. The curtains, drawn across the lofty windows, were woven with fabric imported from the colonies. Paintings covered the walls, and vases and classical-looking sculptures stood between the sumptuous Louis XVI furniture. One such piece would fetch as much as his yearly Oxford salary. It was Doctor Suñé that had given him the address, and who had also informed him of Irene's match with one of the city's leading industrialists. They had married seven years earlier. Time hadn't stood still for anyone; it was only natural that Irene had found a husband. Indeed, hadn't Daniel himself built a new life? Wasn't he, too, engaged? So why did it rankle? He was yet to complete a full circuit of the room when the servant girl reappeared.

'The Señora sends her apologies,' she said. 'She is currently indisposed. No visitors.'

Daniel liked that the girl didn't try to dress it up; her mistress wanted rid of him, that was all.

'Take her this,' he said handing over a small box. 'And tell her I do not mean to leave until I have had an audience.'

The servant, clearly flustered by his tone, took the box and withdrew. She came back after a short while and silently led him through to a homely reading room. When they came in, a wet nurse gathered up a baby girl and disappeared through a far door. Before he had time to think, his attention was diverted by the scene before him: reclining in a rocking chair, Irene had the case open in her lap, running her fingers over the cameo inside. She was gazing off towards the window, through which the setting sun broke, caressing her skin, as though she wished to escape with it. Daniel pretended to clear his throat, Irene turned to face him and the last ray of sun dipped away, taking with it that image, that moment. On this occasion she wore a close-fitting green dress with a high neck and long sleeves. A San Jorge cross hung from her necklace. The years had laid creases at the corner of her eyes and mouth – Daniel hadn't noticed at the cemetery. And how would he look to her, he wondered? As she got up from the chair, Daniel noticed some bruising on one of her wrists, over which she hastily pulled her sleeve.

'Astonishing, that you would be so bold as to come here.'

A glacial look accompanied her words. Daniel was little surprised. She despised him, and with good reason. But knowing that didn't make him feel less uncomfortable.

123

'I'm sorry, please believe that,' he said. 'I won't be long in the city and had to come.'

'You shouldn't have bothered.'

'I wanted to give it to you in person. I know how important it was for you.'

Irene gave a faint nod. Daniel's mind hurtled back to the moment when she gave him that agate bird as a gift. Seven years – and a lifetime – ago. 'It's for you,' she had said, smiling to stop the tremble in her lips. 'It's a tocororo. If you put them in a cage, they die from the pain . . . ' The last words either had spoken before the accident that was to separate them forever.

'Thank you,' said Irene. She shut the case, her previous coolness returning. 'And what is it you hope for in return? My forgiveness, by any chance?'

Daniel cleared his throat before answering.

'No, I don't believe that would be possible.'

'You left, you disappeared without a word,' she said, her voice growing louder. 'What did you expect?'

'I don't know. Nothing. I didn't think I'd see you again, in all honesty.'

'No word from you, nothing, in all those years.' Her knuckles whitened as she gripped the box.

'At the time, I thought it would be the best thing for you.'

'The best thing!' She let out a hoarse laugh.

They'd moved closer without knowing it. Daniel could smell the jasmine oil on her skin, and sensed the accelerated beating of her heart – or was it perhaps his own? Irene looked furious, and, though Daniel tried, he could not look away. Her beauty magnetized him. He tried to hold himself back, but moved a step closer and put out a hand; Irene shuddered at his touch, moving brusquely away and turning her back. Her face flushed.

'Why are you here?'

Daniel knew his answer was unlikely to ease the situation.

'I've got some questions about my father.'

Irene turned to face him, making no attempt to conceal her surprise. Daniel went on – though it might be the end of whatever was left between them, still he had to know.

'When I received your telegram with the death notice—'

'I sent no telegram. How could I have? I didn't know where you were.'

Daniel was confused. If not her, who could it have been? It had been signed 'Irene' – someone who knew their shared history had decided to masquerade as her. And how would that person have known of his whereabouts? And what could be their reason? *Why did they want him back in Barcelona?*

'What do you want to know about him?' Irene said.

'They said at the hospital that you saw a lot of him this last year.'

'I did. When he came back from his travels I felt it was my duty to visit him. Your father was always very kind to me. But what makes my visits of interest to you?'

Daniel made the decision to tell her. 'I'm looking into the circumstances surrounding his death. I don't believe it to have been an accident, I think he was murdered.'

Irene's hand shot to her mouth. But there was a moment in which – her eyes couldn't hide it – he saw that, in fact, the idea wasn't new to her.

125

'When you visited him,' Daniel went on, 'did anything my father say seem out of the ordinary?'

'Not especially. During the final weeks he did seem more preoccupied than usual. I put it down to his work. When he became immersed in one of his studies, you know how he could be, he'd go days without eating. Then we'd meet up – it wouldn't take long for him to return to his normal self. And yet . . .' She furrowed her brow. 'Five days before his disappearance there was something. When I arrived I found him lying on the floor in soaking wet clothes. I called for help and a young man appeared, he said he was your father's assistant.'

'The young man – quite fine featured?'

'Yes, that's him. Between the two of us we managed to get your father onto the bed. We made him comfortable, and after a few minutes he began to talking, in a delirious way; he seemed to be asleep, but he talked and talked, though it all seemed like ravings.'

'What kind of thing?'

'I could only make out the odd word. A search, something that God was against, a demon dog? He woke up after a few hours and asked for water. He seemed calmer, and tried to reassure me; he just said he'd been working too much. His assistant left us alone at one point, and he gripped me by the arm and pleaded with me to forget everything I'd heard. He fell into a deep sleep – after mumbling your name a number of times. I left him to rest. That was the last time I saw him alive.'

Daniel was trying to piece it all together when the door flew open, the impact shaking the walls, and a man came in. Irene stepped towards him, putting a solicitous hand on his arm.

126

'Good evening, my love. I believe you and Señor Amat know one another?'

'My very good friend, what a surprise to find you here!'

Daniel's astonishment was so great he barely registered the words. Bertomeu Adell, only son of a wealthy family from the county of Empordà, had changed a great deal in the previous seven years. His hairline had begun to recede, and he looked sallower than Daniel remembered. Nor had he always worn a moustache – though he still had that same air of self-satisfaction that Daniel knew from their days as friends. And the signs of his wealth were clear to see: his finely tailored jacket, the gold chain looping down from his waistcoat pocket, his gleaming Italian boots, and the ivory cane that he wielded like a rapier. He scanned the room inquisitorially. Adell was one of a group who would always attend the parties and galas when the Giné sisters came to Barcelona, and that was how he'd met Irene and Ángela; Daniel himself had introduced them. Adell had always desired the younger of the sisters, and eventually his courting had paid off.

Daniel offered his hand, but his old friend only placed his own on Irene's waist, yanking her near. Irene seemed to shrink upon contact.

'You look well,' said Adell.

'Thank you,' Daniel managed to say, with a slight nod. 'And it's lovely to see you, however I wouldn't wish to importune either of you further. I was just leaving.'

'So soon?' said Adell, letting Irene go, taking Daniel by the elbow. 'I think not. It's such a pleasure to have you in my home – such an *unexpected* pleasure.'

Daniel failed to think of an excuse, and allowed himself to be guided over to one of the easy chairs. Adell put down his cane and sat opposite him.

'Cognac, Irene. Two.'

'I'll get Juana,' she said, picking up a silver bell from a side table.

'No,' said Adell. '*You* serve us, I said.' Rolling his eyes, he turned back to Daniel. 'Are you married?'

Daniel shook his head.

'You're lucky. Women are a headache, make no mistake: their fickle moods, their caprices – you're constantly off balance. In truth they are little different from children: soft in mind, soft in spirit. And incapable of surviving without the protection of men. What would they do without us?'

Irene, avoiding Daniel's eye, went over to the drinks cabinet, and next there came the tinkling of glass; Daniel couldn't help but notice how her hand trembled.

'*Try* not to spill anything, darling.'

'Actually, could I have—'

'Ah yes, you're a whisky man, aren't you? Some of our best whisky, Irene, for our friend Daniel. That's what they drink over on the Isles, right? Doesn't matter to me, I've got several cases from a recently established distillery in Scotland, Glenfiddich, something like that. Little matter – just that people have been talking it up, and the name is unpronounceable – that's all I know! Might buy a few shares, haven't quite made my mind up.'

'I'm happy without a drink. I don't drink, in fact.'

Adell was dumbfounded. 'Teetotal?' he said, and burst out laughing, beating the arm of his chair – so hard, Daniel thought it might break. Eventually Adell's laughter subsided. He dabbed his eyes with a handkerchief and, sighing, took a sip from the glass Irene had brought over.

'That'll be all,' he said to her. 'Out.'

Irene left the room without a word. When she came past her husband, she shot Daniel a look, some sort of appeal, but one that Daniel did not understand.

'It's been a long time, has it not?'

'It has, yes.'

'And what line of work are you in now?'

'I'm a lecturer, I have a degree from Oxford University.'

'Well, not everyone in the world is destined to become a doctor.' He leaned back in his chair and swirled the cognac around his glass. 'I only studied it because Mother and Father forced me. To them a surgeon was a very reputable thing to be, and I didn't wish to let them down. I didn't warm to the subject at the start, but later on grew to love it . . . Ah!' he said, squinting. 'To hold the life of a fellow creature in your hands like that – to me it's something quite heady. Goodness knows how but I became the model student. That fly-by-nighter you surely remember, I left him far behind. I am a much changed person, my friend.'

'So you have a degree in medicine?'

'Oh, no. Not that I wouldn't have made a wonderful doctor. Unfortunately, when my father died, someone had to see to the running of the family business. I had to give up my studies in the final year.'

'I'm sorry.'

'Don't be, in the end it worked out rather well for me. Don't you think?' He gave Daniel a probing look. 'Tell me, and be honest, what brings you here?'

'To thank your wife for her kindness to my father.'

'Yes, but of course. She's got quite the soft spot for charitable works. She's so . . . *giving* with her time. Overly, to my mind. A woman's place is in the home, seeing that her husband and children have all they need.' He took another sip of the cognac. 'Such a terrible accident, your father's death. To drown in the port. My word. Not that I haven't heard the odd malicious rumour, I must say . . . How can I put it? It doesn't seem your father was having the best of times. Such a shame for him to feel that pull, that temptation to end it all.'

'What do you mean?' said Daniel, getting to his feet.

'Rumours, that's all, loose talk. You know how parochial it can be here.'

As his indignation rose, Daniel could feel the tension in his scars. How had this man managed to win Irene's hand? Daniel knew her as a woman with a fine mind, an independent spirit. She'd rejected many a suitor before Daniel and she were in love, and he could never have imagined her on the arm of someone like Adell. But how much, how very much, had changed in his absence, and how little he understood any of it. And in any case, he thought bitterly, who was he to judge?

Adell seemed amused. 'And how does the old city seem to you?'

'Different. Very different.'

'Nothing compared to the changes in England. They know how to get on. Here we keep going with this namby pamby government. Point-scoring seems just about the only thing they care

130

about, when what this country needs is strong leaders. Sagasta? That bleeding heart? What should we expect? You know about the disturbances, I'm sure, every other day it seems we've been having them. The workers, they've become idlers, idlers and vagabonds all. Now, these unions they're proposing? That's all we need. Ingrates, the lot of them. We put bread on their tables, roofs over their heads, and what do we get? Eh?'

Daniel doubted that his answer would be to Adell's liking, so he simply shrugged. On went the speech, growing progressively louder.

'Not that it's all gone to the dogs, thank God – there's us at least, the businessmen. We lay our capital on the line, not to mention our good names, just trying to keep this damned country going. This city would be nothing without us.'

'I suppose,' said Daniel, 'everyone plays a part in the progress of things.'

To this Adell said nothing, getting to his feet instead.

'You should see it with your own eyes, Daniel. I'd be honoured to show you around the site we're currently busy with, at the World Fair.'

'I'm not sure that will be—'

'Rot. I'm sure you'll be able to make time one of these days. You'd be surprised.'

'Well, I—'

'You'll come,' said Adell. 'Now, I'm very sorry, but I have a great many things to see to. I'm rather a busy man, you see.'

Daniel stood and shook the proffered hand, and, thus dismissed, turned and left the room, trying to give an appearance of calm – though he was feeling far from it. The servant girl was

131

there to show him to the front door, but Irene didn't appear. Coming through into the hallway, Daniel found another visitor waiting there.

'Doctor Gavet, what brings you here?'

Gavet seemed alarmed, on edge in some way, and responded with an inaudible murmur.

'Has something happened for them to have need of you?' asked Daniel.

'Oh, no. A routine visit. I-I'm the Adell f-family doctor. I must ask you to excuse me, I'm l-late arriving.'

Daniel stood aside to let him pass. Coming onto the street, it felt like a relief to be out in the evening air. He had thought that seeing Irene would improve his spirits. He'd thought he'd find answers, and in some way . . . what? What was he looking for? He didn't know. All he felt was that, once again, he was abandoning her, leaving her to fend for herself. He should not have come. He was about to hail a carriage when he heard footsteps behind him and, turning, found Irene's girl running along the pavement. Reaching him, panting, she handed over a folded sheet of paper. With a nod, she turned and went back towards the house. Daniel walked on a little before reading the short note.

If you still value me in any way, you'll forget about all of this and go back to England.

Daniel decided against taking a carriage; he needed to walk. Since returning to Barcelona everyone he'd come across seemed to want him to leave. And now Irene. But the more they wanted him gone, the more determined he felt to stay. This matter was far from being any clearer, the more he thought about it the more he felt certain that his father's death had been no accident. And he wasn't going to rest – he was surprised to hear himself saying it – until he found those responsible.

SEVENTEEN

Fleixa was in high spirits as he made his way to the office. He had spoken with Sanchís the day before and the editor had agreed, however grudgingly, to give him a few extra days. It seemed that Llopis had lost his way somewhat, his last piece had been a rehash of an earlier one, and he wasn't in Sanchís's good books any longer. Not that Fleixa's situation was really much better.

He and Amat had an appointment to visit the New Bethlem Sanatorium together the next morning. The younger man had decided to delay his return to England, at least for a few days, apparently having had a change of heart about looking into the death of his father. He reminded Fleixa of himself in younger days. He smiled – Dolors would laugh at that, let him know what a sentimental fool he was – and she'd be right. Then he remembered the encounter with Vidal, and his smile faded. The story of the accident intrigued him, as did the ensuing cut-off between son and father. A terrible thing, to lose a loved one in a fire, no question, but his instinct said there was more to it, there must be something else. Amat had swerved all questions expertly, but the journalist in Fleixa wasn't going to let it go that easily. His shift was hours from ending, and he meant to make the most of them.

Entering the *Correo* buildings, after a little of the usual sparring with Serafin, rather than going upstairs to editorial he took the spiral staircase down to the basement. The steps wound twice around a column and came out in a poorly ventilated corridor. He walked purposefully along the passage, away from the print rooms, and came to a dark red door. A small metal plaque said 'ARCHIVES', below which someone had written 'Do not disturb'.

The legendary *Correo* archives were the envy of many of the paper's competitors. The last fifty years of Barcelona in print was housed down there – all the newspapers, all the weeklies, all the journals. Articles that had never gone to press, too, internal memos and documentation pertaining to newspaper business. A specially fitted library with thousands of articles, the collection was considered nothing less than the Alexandrian Library of the city's recent past. It was also the place where new staff would be sent on their first day, to have their ears chewed by the chief archivist, Enric Curumillas. Fleixa knocked and entered, welcomed in by a blast of warm air. Even a mummy would have a hard time of it down here, he thought.

'Who's there?' came a voice.

'Me, Bernat Fleixa,' he replied.

'Come through to where the light is.'

Fleixa did so, making his way along an ill-lit gangway to a table on which an oil lamp burned. Bunkered behind stacks of files and cabinets, sat a man, short, thin and completely bald – the only hairs on his head being a goatee beard. His disgruntlement was obvious as he lifted his chin and peered over his reading glasses. He wore black silk sleeves to protect his shirt, and his hands, as veined as a river delta, hovered over a register. An unlit cigarette dangled from the thin purple line of his lips; he was a man who loved to smoke, but never did so inside the archive room.

'What the hell do *you* want? I'm busy.'

'Nice to see I'm still welcome, Curumillas.' He removed a small bundle from his jacket pocket and tossed it onto the table. 'A little tobacco for you, the good stuff.'

The old man grumbled but shot out an arm, pocketing the tobacco before grudgingly looking up again. The lantern created a shadow play behind Curumillas each time he moved.

'All right, what?'

'The fire at the Amat house, I need everything that was written about it at the time. It was seven years ago, so eighty-one, around May or June.'

'The twentieth of May.'

Fleixa's eyebrows shot up.

'Calm down,' said Curumillas. 'Someone else has been in recently asking for the same.'

'Really? Who was that?'

'You know as well as I the rules on archive confidentiality. A pinch of tobacco doesn't go that far.'

'Oh, but you'll never guess what, Curumillas? The other day, as chance would have it, I stopped by the Turkish Tavern . . .'

Now it was Curumillas's turn to show surprise, though he tried to hide it, shrugging and frowning. Fleixa carried on as if he hadn't noticed.

'Those opium dens – it's terrible really. All those people lying around on filthy little beds, the little braziers lined up next to each one, the haze enveloping everything. Wasn't it Ovid who said "Night came on, her peaceful brow bound with poppies, bringing dark dreams along in her train"?'

He paused for a few moments, savouring the archivist's livid expression.

'I'm sure the darkness in there, and all that smoke, must have been playing tricks, because you won't believe who I *thought* I saw in there, draped around one of those pipes . . .'

'There are words for the likes of you, Fleixa.'

'My mother said the same. However, if you wish for that story to remain untold, tell me, who was it?'

The old man swivelled round to face his desk.

'Let me see . . .'

He took a ledger from one of the drawers, opening it with the green bookmark and flicking back a few pages. Fleixa glanced down at the neat columns, organized by date, type of request, and name of petitioner. Curumillas ran an inkstained finger along the rows and columns, until he came to a name.

'Yes, here it is, it was a couple of days ago.'

The journalist craned his neck, but the old man spoke before he could make it out.

'Felipe Llopis.'

Fleixa grimaced, cursing Llopis: how did he manage to be constantly one step ahead?

'I remember the young man,' said Curumillas, making a face. 'Acting quite the big shot. Comes in here, starts *sneezing* all over my documents, complaining about the dust? Can you believe that?' He went on before Fleixa had a chance to comment. 'Then, like I was some wet-behind-the-ears newbie, he starts telling me I'd better find what he wanted "sooner rather than later". And that was it, off he went, not a word of thanks. All haughty, like he smelled shit or something.'

'And did he find them?'

'What's that?'

'The papers he was looking for, did he find them?'

'What do you take me for?'

Fleixa found himself smiling: you had to love Curumillas. A famous grouch he might be, and he might have some less than savoury pastimes, but he was the living, breathing chronicle of the last century of Barcelona life. That he had decided to bury himself alive in that drain was his affair. He was in his element amongst books and papers, as he himself put it. Fleixa almost felt bad spinning him a line.

'The thing is, Llopis and I are working together on a piece, we need these documents. He hasn't been here long, he doesn't know how things work – in fact, he even forgot to tell me he'd been down already. I'll pass on your complaint, and I'm sure he'll come and apologize. But since I'm here you might as well show me what you've managed to find. If you don't mind?'

Curumillas peered at him through smudged lenses. And, lifting himself out of his chair with a sigh, he picked up the lantern and gestured for Fleixa to follow him.

'This way.'

The old man, stooping, led Fleixa down a gangway past dozens of further rows of lacquered wooden shelving units, covered in a thick grimy film, each bearing an endboard with a complex table of letters and numbers, a code that only Curumillas knew how to decipher.

'Each aisle is organized according to years, months and days. All documentation is arranged by date in folders, and according to type – books, newspapers, magazines, periodicals – whatever they may be.'

He was proud of the enormous archive and the system governing it, and would always regale visitors, even longstanding staff at the *Correo* who had heard it all before.

They turned down one of the narrow aisles, shifting to single file. Though hunched, Curumillas moved swiftly, and Fleixa had to hurry to keep up.

'Here it is.'

Fleixa glanced around, trying to divine any distinguishing features to the spot. The old man, ignoring his bafflement, handed him the lantern as he dragged some steps nearer. He scaled them with difficulty, taking something down from the top shelf.

'Here.'

A cardboard binder dropped into Fleixa's arms. It weighed close to nothing.

'This is everything?'

'Twentieth May, 1881, fire at the Amat family mansion,' Curumillas said impatiently as he came back down the steps. 'That's the sum of the coverage: newspaper articles, reports by the Guardia Civil and the firemen, obituaries. Less information than usual, looks like it was probably swept under the carpet. You know how it goes, any suggestion of high jinks, someone's palms get greased, and nobody says much.' Curumillas took up the lantern. 'There's a table next to my office. You can have a look there.'

They retraced their steps, and Fleixa set himself up, lighting a small gas lamp on the table in question and laying out the contents of the binder. There were half a dozen folders, and he began with the first that came to hand. It contained a number of cuttings from the *Correo* itself.

ENORMOUS BLAZE AT AMAT MANSION

Calamity has written a new chapter in the history of our city. In the early hours of yesterday, an enormous blaze consumed the home of the Amat family. Two individuals are reported dead and several seriously injured.

Don Alec Amat Muria, son of the eminent Doctor Don Alfred Amat i Roures, and Señorita Ángela Giné Roser, who was visiting the family, both perished in the flames, doubtless asphyxiated by the huge amounts of smoke. Don Daniel Amat Muria – brother of Don Alec and fiancé of Señorita Ángela – suffered burns and the onset of asphyxiation, and was taken to the Santa Creu Hospital for treatment. At the time of writing his status is unknown, though hospital staff have informed us the situation is grave.

According to Don Romualdo Gualta, a clerk, who witnessed the blaze: 'It was like someone had opened a furnace door in the middle of the street.'

The conflagration continued until well into the morning, and the fire services, in spite of heroic and tireless efforts, were all but powerless to quell the flames.

140

To add to the sad news, we have learned that Señorita Ángela Giné and Daniel Amat were due to be married very shortly. All of Barcelona is saddened by this devastating event, above all as it has shattered the dreams of two young people in the prime of their lives. Condolences have been flooding in.

The style of writing was familiar to him, though he couldn't quite put his finger on who the writer might have been. He'd come back to that later. He laid the *Correo* cutting to one side and picked up another, bulkier folder, one that contained cuttings from several other papers.

The *Diario de Barcelona* led with Doctor Amat's position in Catalan society, lamenting his losses. *La Dinastía*, in keeping with its usual aggressive editorial line, took the opportunity to lambaste the government and demand better fire-prevention measures. The piece featured an illustration of a group of fire fighters tackling the enormous blaze, and in the foreground a figure, Doctor Amat presumably, embracing another, in all probability Daniel or the deceased son Alec. And lastly, the coverage of the *La Ilustración Española y Americana*, looking beyond the events, made reference to Doctor Amat's loss of his wife, a number of years earlier, also in an accident of some sort. There were several other pieces, but no new information. Putting the cuttings aside, Fleixa moved onto the next folder, the reports by the Guardia Civil and the fire services. Though he pored over them, they failed to shed light on the cause of the fire, simply pointing to the likelihood of an accident.

After an hour, he closed the last folder in disappointment.

He'd hoped to gain some sense of what it was that tormented Amat, but knew just as little as when he'd begun. Perhaps he was imagining things, and the young man was merely showing the strain of the tragic losses; not only a brother but a fiancée taken from him. But Fleixa, deciding to move on, still felt he'd been thwarted somehow. He began putting the documents back in order when something at the bottom of the binder caught his eye: a crumpled piece of paper. He took it out and smoothed it on the table. It was the notes taken by whichever journalist had covered the fire for the *Correo*. So nothing of interest, he thought as he scanned it. But then, reaching the end, he felt an ant nest erupt in his stomach: at the end of a list of possible causes, it said: 'premeditated???'. And it was at that point that Fleixa recognized the handwriting. Why the list? What had made the writer suspect foul play? Fleixa suddenly felt better. Something, he had something to go on. He tucked the sheet into his jacket pocket. Then, going over to a nearby shelf, he pulled down a folder and swapped the contents of the two; he was damned if he was going to make it easy for Llopis. Curumillas still hadn't come back by the time Fleixa passed his office, where he deposited the original folder. On his way out, though, he remembered something and turned back. The registry ledger was still where the archivist had placed it, and Fleixa opened it at the most recent entry, with his name, the date and the documents he'd requested listed at the top of a new page. His thought had been to erase it, but seeing that the pages weren't numbered, he simply tore out the entire page. Leaving everything as he'd found it, he turned and made his way towards the exit.

'Off then, Señor Fleixa?' Curumillas stepped out from behind one of the shelving units, his arms full of a stack of magazines.

'Yes, the documents didn't turn out to be very much help after all. I've left it all on your desk, ready to go back into the archives. Thanks for your help.'

'Fleixa.'

'Yes?' he said, one hand on the door handle.

The archivist gave him a couple of bony slaps on the arm, and began hobbling back to his desk. 'After you've given that Llopis fellow the runaround,' he said back over his shoulder, 'I want you to come back down here and tell me all about it.'

Fleixa let out a laugh, and pulled open the door. He could hear Curumillas singing softly to himself as the door swung shut.

EIGHTEEN

A group in white coats moved quietly along the corridors of Santa Creu hospital. It was customary to check on the patients early each morning. And in this, the final year of their studies, none of the students could skip the practical classes. Their knowledge still needed a good deal of honing if they were to qualify as surgeons.

'Really, young man,' said Doctor Segura to one of the group. 'Never, *never* would you prescribe calendula ointment for this kind of eczema. Perhaps you decided to sleep through that particular class?'

The student in question moaned, as though the previous night's dinner had suddenly repeated in his stomach. Several of the other students tittered.

'This poor woman's suffering is far from funny, gentlemen. If any of you had to go through what she is going through, you'd be on your knees, I can assure you.'

'She's just a serving girl.'

Pau looked at the boy who had made the comment. Medical

144

students, who tended to come from well-off families, often considered it beneath them to tend to the ailments of labourers, servants, or prostitutes from the Raval. Their ambitions were to set up in well-heeled clinics, to have aristocrats for clients. Whereas Pau saw things differently: his skills were a gift, an opportunity to serve others, whoever they happened to be. Death and illness were the great levellers. So his father had taught him, and hence his passion for his studies.

'Are any of you going to stop staring at your navels, and tell me what the correct treatment would have been?'

Pau stepped forward, paying no mind to the looks from the other students.

'Bearing in mind the patient's leukaemia, Señor, and the fact she also suffers frequent fevers, in my view she should be given Fowler's syrup of arsenic. There was a case, thirteen years ago, when a Doctor Heinrich Lissauer reported an excellent response.'

'Indeed, young man. Very good. And how, if you wouldn't mind enlightening your colleagues here, is this miraculous tonic prepared?'

Pau hesitated, not because he didn't know the answer but because it would mean drawing attention to himself again, just as he'd sworn not to. Finally though, faced with the professor's clear impatience, he had to answer. 'Take one drachm and eighteen grains of arsenic acid powder – well ground. Add the same quantity of pure potassium, which, though tartar salt also serves, I personally prefer. Place in a flask along with four hundred and fifty millilitres of distilled water. Mix and apply heat until the powders dissolve, take a new mixing container and pour in the liquid that remains. Then add water, taking care that the resultant amount, after the evaporation, remains four hundred and fifty millilitres. Cover the container and leave to rest for several days. And handle with care: though effective for certain treatments, it is toxic.'

'At least there's one of you who pays attention in my classes!'

Pau blushed, as Segura turned to the first student. 'You. You're to prepare the syrup, and then I want you personally to supervise this patient for the next week. And no mishaps. On with our rounds then, gentlemen.'

The students prepared to move off together, when Fenollosa stopped Segura.

'Sorry, Señor.'

Pau sighed, expecting some joke, either that or some long-winded irrelevant excuses, much like the others delivered by Fenollosa in recent weeks.

'Yes?'

'I speak for everyone here, Señor. Before we go on, we'd like to visit the other patient.'

'I don't understand. What other patient? All the patients are found on the wards, as well you know, which is precisely where our rounds will take us.'

'Not all, Señor.'

Fenollosa glanced at Pau, an amused look in his eye.

'Come on,' said Segura crossly. 'Enough of the games.'

'Rumour has it,' said Fenollosa, 'that there is a patient in a private wing of the hospital, and this patient is receiving treatment, but under lock and key. Is it some sort of experiment, perhaps? A particularly *recherché* illness? Or is it some distinguished personage, and discretion is therefore required? Questions abound,

146

as you can imagine. We'd like the chance to visit this patient, and to see if we can help with the diagnosis.'

A chorus of assent went around. Pau could feel his hands shaking. Professor Segura was perplexed.

'It isn't possible,' he said. 'I personally see to the admission register.'

Pau spoke up, trying to stay calm. 'Time's getting on, Señor. We ought to continue with the rounds.'

'Just a moment, Gilbert. If there's a patient in the hospital without my knowledge, it's something I need to clear up immediately. Please, Fenollosa, show us the way.'

The group set off, this time with Fenollosa at the head. Pau didn't know what to do. His colleagues' demeanour gave him the sense this was all pre-planned. He had no idea how he'd been found out, especially considering the lengths he'd gone to. He looked at the broad smile on Fenollosa's face as the other delivered an anecdote, to laughter from the others. For a moment he was overcome by feelings of rage, though his thoughts quickly turned to the matter in hand: how on earth was he going to avoid this thing that seemed to be crashing down on his head?

Having walked the exact same route Pau always took, they came into the storage areas. Once they had come through into a despatch space where the laundry was kept, Fenollosa stopped and turned to face the group.

'This is it,' he said, presenting the door with a flourish.

Pau tried physically to stop them from entering, but one of the students stepped out in front of him and two others grabbed hold of his arms. Doctor Segura, unaware of what was going on behind him, unlocked the door and went straight in.

The small room was well lit, thanks to a large window that gave onto the street, and which had been left ajar. Laboratory beakers stood here and there containing aromatic herbs, along with plant pots taken from the hospital gardens. The air was clean and fragrant. On the bed lay a girl, propped up against several pillows and trying to make herself invisible under the sheets. Her chestnut hair fell in messy clumps about her head. Her face was extremely pale and she looked out at her visitors like a cornered animal. Seeing how thin she was, the sweat bathing her brow, and the handkerchief covering her mouth, Segura backed away, pushing Fenollosa and the rest of the group back towards the door.

'Out! Everybody out, now!'

Out in the corridor, they nearly collided with one of the hospital nuns who was carrying a tray in her arms. Segura looked distraught as he shut the door, and when he saw the woman pushed towards her.

'You! Tell me what this child is doing in this room.'

'I . . . I don't know anything,' she said, shrinking back. 'I just come and leave clean sheets, food and water, twice a day.'

'Who told you to do that?'

'A doctor,' she shrugged. 'I don't know his name.'

Segura looked like he might explode. The sister glanced around, trying to understand what she'd done wrong, when suddenly her expression changed.

'Him,' she said. 'That young man gave me the order.'

Everyone turned to look at Pau, Segura gazing at him incredulously.

'Gilbert? You did this?'

148

There was no way for him to hide. He could see the delight on Fenollosa's face, and on those of his lackeys around him. They couldn't have planned it any better.

'Yes, Señor. I'm responsible.'

Segura's disgust was palpable. 'Do you think you could explain how a patient suffering *tuberculosis* comes to have been admitted, and then hidden away, in my hospital?'

A clamour erupted among the students. Pau felt his throat tighten. Fenollosa looked livid, that was some consolation at least. Pau had no idea how Fenollosa had learned of the patient, but in any case he clearly hadn't known what the illness was.

'You reprobate!' cried Fenollosa, fist raised. 'You've put us all at risk, you ought to be expelled!' A number of the others seconded the idea.

Pau held their looks, unruffled, before turning to face the doctor.

'She's called Elena.'

'I don't care what she's called, Señor Gilbert.' His own disappointment seemed to weigh more on him than the angry expressions of the other students. 'How long has she been here?'

'A week.'

'A week! Dear God! What were you thinking? Tuberculosis is not only high contagious, it's deadly – any child could tell you that. The whole hospital could have been infected!'

'She was left on the hospital steps in the early hours of Thursday morning, while I was on duty. She was coughing and feverish. What was I supposed to do, leave her in the street? I took all the necessary precautions. There's practically nobody in this section of the hospital. No one apart from me goes into

149

the room, I change the sheets myself, I feed her and administer all medicines.'

'And what treatment have you been giving her?'

The doctor's sudden interest signified a truce, a chance to explain himself. That, though, was only going to mean further problems. He cleared his throat.

'I administered a balm for the cough, and changed her diet. Resting in a clean room that's frequently aired, she's improved immeasurably.'

'That's it? You haven't bled her daily, no purgatives?'

'No, Sir, I haven't. There are doubts as to the efficacy of that approach.'

'You're trying to tell me you've managed to stop this illness with a bit of rest and some decent food?'

Pau tried to avoid Segura's glare, but he knew there was no way out of this.

'To begin with I . . . carried out a pleural cavity puncture, and injected nitrogen.' Segura looked alarmed, and Pau spoke more rapidly. 'Some studies by Toussaint have shown that tuberculosis lesions have responded well to a spontaneous pneumothorax. And Forlanini did the same with patients in a far worse state, with good results. A pulmonary collapse helps scarring.'

'God help me! You did this procedure with no surgical assistance whatsoever?'

Pau said nothing. Segura shook his head.

'Not only do you let into the hospital a person suffering the most dangerous illness known to man, you play fast and loose with dubious experimental procedures. These are grave and irresponsible acts, Señor Gilbert.'

'But the treatment has been working! Elena has stopped coughing, her mucus is clear now, and the fevers have abated. The dressings where I made the injection aren't infected, her breathing is better and she's regained her appetite.'

'Gilbert, you are one of the most brilliant students I've had, but your intellect is also your downfall. It might have worked this time, but rules are there for a reason. She'll be sent directly to the tuberculosis centre tomorrow.'

Segura turned and began walking away along the corridor, with Pau close behind.

'Please, Señor, not that. You'll be sending her to her death. All those contagious cases around her – it will make her far worse. She's getting better, she just needs a few more days in isolation.'

'You think it would be better to put the whole of this hospital at risk?'

'I know I haven't acted correctly, but surely she needn't be punished. I beg of you. She isn't a risk any more.'

But Segura only shook his head, starting back along the corridor with the other students behind. They all gave Pau a wide berth – as if he too were a health hazard.

A number of hours later, Pau left the hospital. Books and study notes in his arms, he walked quickly. He'd been lucky: after an emergency meeting of the heads of faculty, they'd decided to punish him with a 100 peseta fine and a doubling of his hours at the hospital. Any further infraction, and, he was told in no uncertain terms, he'd be expelled. Though he didn't know how he was going to pay the fine, it still felt like a relief; the most pressing thing remained the young girl. If she ended her days in the tuberculosis centre, it would be his fault. None of this would have happened if he'd kept his vanity in check and not given Fenollosa reason to want to attack him. Elena had needed his help and he knew he'd done the right thing; he heard his father saying so. The treatment, in spite of Segura's misgivings, was having the desired effect. There was no way he could abandon her now. He'd go to Segura the following day and try to change his mind. He'd take charge of her care, day and night if needs be.

So deep in thought was he that he failed to notice the man coming around the corner towards him; they crashed into each other, and Pau's books and papers went everywhere. The man cried out for him to be more careful, and Pau turned to apologize, but he disappeared into the crowd. Seeing the deplorable state of the pavement, he only prayed none of the books were ruined. That would be all he needed.

'You ought to watch where you're going.'

Pau looked up to find Fenollosa and his acolytes around him.

'Think you're *so* clever,' Fenollosa whispered, leaning down to pick up one of the books. 'But you're wrong.'

Fenollosa stood, let the book fall to the floor and then stepped on it. Beaming, with a tilt of the head, he pushed past Pau, followed by the others. Pau heard their laughter all the way down the street. Containing his exasperation, he bent down and gathered the book; the covers were hanging off. How would he explain that to the librarian? As he examined the pages, he noticed a piece of paper poking out – at first, cursing, he thought that a page had come loose from the spine, but on closer inspection found that it was a flyer for the upcoming International

Congress of Spiritualists. And then, turning it over, Pau had to stifle a cry; scrawled in charcoal on the back were the words:

I know your true identity. I'll be waiting for you tomorrow, at sundown, across from the Dominican convent.

He reread the note, and a chill ran through him. He glanced left and right. Suddenly there was menace in the crowded pavement. The anxiety that most days he was able to keep under control rose up, coursing through him like a torrent. He hurried to gather the rest of the books and dashed off in the direction of his rooms, controlling his trembling body as best he could.

NINETEEN

There was more to Daniel Amat than met the eye: Fleixa kept hearing Vidal's words, over and over, and to add to them now there was the note in the archives. Though only a glimmer of something, that something was doubtless significant. The young man's part in the fire – it didn't quite fit. And it was Fleixa's intention to find out why.

He picked up the pace. Night had fallen, and yellow light from the streetlamps reflected here and there on the rain-slick pavements. He adjusted his hat and jacket. At least, thank goodness, it wasn't raining.

Just then a burst of pain erupted in his face.

He toppled to the ground, crashing into some baskets mounded with horse dung, which spilled out across the pavement. He was dragged to his feet and knocked down again. He fell back against a shop front, the impact sending a wave along the metal shutters.

An enormous man had stepped out from a darkened doorway; he looked hewn from rock and was almost as broad as the street itself. He was wearing a vest in spite of the cold, and the bulging muscles beneath looked liable to burst. He wore a cloth cap, beneath which a pair of oriental eyes sparkled in amusement.

If it was a mugging, he didn't plan to put up a fight. If something else, he just hoped they didn't beat him too badly.

'Fleixa, Fleixa, Fleixa.'

He knew that falsetto voice. Further down the street, an unusually tall female figure now appeared. It approached Fleixa with feline steps, wrapped in furs over a long maroon dress. A cigarette dangled from between La Negra's crimson lips and her hair was a dyed-blonde bob; the gangster could have passed for a *grande dame* in any high society salon – if it weren't for her fearsome reputation, and what in fact hung between her legs.

'Ah, Armando,' Fleixa managed to say.

He heard a cluck, and the thug behind him grabbed Fleixa by the testicles and squeezed. Fleixa let out a yelp.

'Dear child, you *know* not to call me that.'

'Of course, yes,' he said, gasping. 'Forgive me. What . . . what brings you here?'

'You, sugar. You're what brings me here.'

La Negra laid a delicate, fake-nailed hand on her henchman's shoulder.

'That'll do, Little Pedro. We wouldn't want our beloved reporter to be hurt, not before time. Certainly not before he's paid his debts. You see,' she said, turning to Fleixa, 'Pedro used to be in the Wonder Brothers' Circus. Bending metal bars, that was his speciality. A featherweight like you wouldn't last more than a couple of seconds – better for you if you don't make a fuss.'

Fleixa nodded. Even if he tried, he wouldn't be able to move.

The smile on La Negra's face was anything but reassuring, but at least Little Pedro had loosened his grip a little – enough for him to breathe again.

'I'm not happy, sweet boy, not even slightly. Seems you've become a little forgetful of late.'

'I'm going to get your money, I swear. A little more time is all I ask.'

A high-pitched laugh echoed down the street.

'You're funny, you know that? *More* time?'

'My luck's about to change. I'm closing in on this scoop, and it's going to mean some serious money for me.'

La Negra leaned in and prodded a long fingernail into Fleixa's cheek.

'Look, Fleixa, I've always liked you. I don't know why but those sad, sad eyes of yours – they get me every time.' She sighed. 'But in my line of work, respect is everything. People ask me for money, and I lend it to them, that part's simple. But if I don't get my money back, well that's a bit more complicated. People talk, you know what I mean? Then that talk spreads, quicker than you can believe, and before you know it, I'm looking for another line of work. That's something I just can't allow, even for someone with your good looks. I'm sorry, but you've got a lot to learn about respect.'

Fleixa felt a fist to the face, and while he was still reeling, a knee in his stomach made him drop to the floor, gasping for breath.

'You're a pair,' he spat. 'Probably been giving each other backrubs all night long.'

He covered his head as the blows rained down. He took a

kick to the jaw that threw his head back violently, smacking him into the shop front once more. His mouth filled with blood. Just before he blacked out he heard La Negra's silky voice whispering in his ear.

'Tell that whore of yours to lend you the money. No more delays. We'll be seeing you again, sweet thing, whether you want to pay or not.'

TWENTY

Daniel and Fleixa took an early train out to Sarriá, nearly four miles to the north of the city. The journalist had a bandage around his head and a nasty black eye, and when Daniel asked what had happened he became evasive, so Daniel changed the subject, recounting his conversation with the dean instead. They talked about ideas they'd each had about Homs's notebook, without coming to any conclusions. It was clear that Daniel's father had secreted it in the hope that someone would find it, they just didn't know why. They hoped Homs would be willing to shed some light on the matter. Maybe he'd even be able to elucidate a link between the notebook and the spate of killings.

The conversation petered out and Fleixa fell asleep. As his companion snored loudly in his seat, Daniel looked out the window. They came through Provenza station, which stood at the city limit, and as they left Barcelona behind, the tall chimney stacks of factories passed by in quick succession. Built on what had previously been agricultural land, they were a clear sign of the rapid changes the city was undergoing. He saw groups of factory workers traipsing in for their shifts – men in their traditional knotted shirts and espadrilles, women in grey wool dresses and hair tied up in scarves. Grave faces, few words being spoken. Most bore a bundle that would contain salted sardines and beans, a meagre perk in hard, twelve-hour shifts. Everything he could remember from his childhood was changing, and so quickly.

They got off at Sant Gervasi and, rather than wait for the sanatorium coach, took a private carriage. A short ride brought them to the estate entrance.

The sanatorium, built twenty years earlier, was positioned some way up the southern slope of Mount Tibidabo. On a clear day the views stretched across all of Barcelona and way out over the Mediterranean.

Arriving, they paid the driver and made their way along a winding earthen path that cut through an orchard on its way to the main building.

'You know, Amat,' said Fleixa, who was trying to keep the mud off his boots, 'you still haven't told me why you changed your mind about looking into all of this.'

Daniel thought for a moment.

'I just feel more and more certain that my father's death can't have been an accident. Too many people seem to want to get rid of me, it makes me want to get to the bottom of it. He'd never forgive me if I didn't at least try. Culpability, guilt, it's an area I have some knowledge of.' Then, before Fleixa could follow up, Daniel hurried ahead. 'Come on, let's get a move on.'

They made their way through the grounds, which occupied a large portion of the sanatorium's five hectares. There was an area with vegetable patches and another, larger space, planted with lemon and apple trees; the central vantage of the sanatorium buildings meant patients could be kept under a constant watch without the place seeming like a prison.

'Think they'll agree to let us see him?' asked Fleixa.

'The director was a good friend of my parents.'

'In that case I'll be sure to mind my mouth, don't you worry.'

'Now I am worried.'

Fleixa began to protest, but then saw Amat's smile and laughed – which caused a stab of pain in his jaw, and he let out a groan.

They rang the bell and a nun came to the door. She seemed alarmed at the sight of Fleixa after his beating, and Daniel spoke in reassuring tones.

'Good afternoon, Sister. We're here to see the director.'

Letting them in, she left them in a charming courtyard that backed onto a small chapel. After a few minutes they heard a thundering voice.

'Better have a damn good reason for taking me away from my work.'

Over by a half-open door stood a man in a white coat, arms folded. Though into his middle years, Antoni Giné had a robust physique – his head looked as though it had been chiselled from marble before being set upon a pair of broad shoulders. He looked between the two visitors, evaluating and, Fleixa felt, classifying them on the spot. He had a head of thick, curly hair and proud, mutton chop sideburns.

'Thank you for seeing us, Señor Giné,' said Daniel.

The doctor's face turned livid the moment he saw Daniel, and, taking a couple of steps closer, he looked ready to attack him. Daniel stood his ground as Fleixa looked between the two – and then he realized: this was the father of Irene and Ángela Giné.

'When the nurse said your name,' he spluttered, 'I thought she must have been mistaken. I thought you were dead, Señor, and perhaps that would have been best. You have ten seconds to turn around and go back where you came from, otherwise I shall have my staff eject you.'

'Please, Señor Giné – trust me, I wouldn't have come without a very good reason. I need your help. It's to do with my father's death.'

Doubt entered the doctor's face. He eventually made up his mind, and when he came to speak, seemed suddenly to have aged. 'Your father's death was an unhappy blow. The bond between us was great and, out of respect for him, I'll hear you out.'

Daniel puffed out his cheeks – he realized he'd been holding his breath. Before they'd arrived, he hadn't been sure that Giné would let him say anything at all.

'His death wasn't an accident.'

Giné gave them a suspicious look, as though appraising a patient.

'I understand your doubts,' said Daniel. 'But we have proof that he was murdered.'

'Murdered? Good God. And what help can I be?'

'It would seem,' said Fleixa, 'that one of your nutjobs, before they went round the bend—'

Giné frowned. 'What did you say?'

'What my colleague *means*,' said Daniel, 'is that one of your

161

patients might be able to help us clarify the circumstances surrounding my father's death. We'd like to speak with him.'

'Many of the individuals here are extremely unwell, and they can't see visitors. Who was it you hoped to speak to?'

'A Doctor Homs.'

'That won't be possible.'

'It's absolutely essential that we see him, Doctor Giné.'

Giné took a deep breath.

'You misunderstand. It won't be possible because Doctor Homs left the sanatorium nine months ago.'

Daniel and Fleixa looked at one another uncertainly.

'Come to my office. We can talk there.'

He turned and went back through the door, with Daniel and Fleixa behind.

'Why this name?' Fleixa asked, to break the silence as they made their way into the interior. Giné looked at him quizzically.

'New Bethlem,' said Fleixa.

'Oh, yes, the name of the sanatorium. It's in honour of Bethlem Hospital in London. An allusion, that's all.'

'And do you have many patients?'

'Señor—'

'Fleixa.'

'Señor Fleixa, are you interested at all in psychopathology?'

'Which is?'

'It's the study of mental illness,' said Daniel.

Giné glanced at Daniel. 'I see you haven't forgotten everything your father taught you.' Daniel didn't answer, and Giné went on, his tone less severe. 'We're pioneers in this country. We've been looking into these illnesses for over thirty years,' he said proudly. 'We even published our own scientific journal until just three years ago.'

'But how do you study a "mental illness"?' asked Fleixa.

'Well, what you might think of as a "nutjob" is in fact just someone with an illness. In the last few decades, for people to begin to accept this, there's had to be considerable change in the general attitude. Unfortunately, there's still a lot of ignorance for us to contend with.'

Seeming to forget their presence, Giné began to hold forth as though at a university lectern.

'Galen summarized the work that had been done before his time on madness, strongly arguing for a doctrine based on the humours. According to that, if a person was melancholic, it was down to the humour generated in the kidneys, dementia was due to a lack of animal spirits, imbecility the falling away of animal spirits, and mania these same being in a state of perversion. In truth, these ideas were at odds with the knowledge Galen had of anatomy and of the physiology of the nervous system. Fortunately, after him other thinkers stepped forward, bringing more pragmatic views to the table – ones that would lead on to the study of the brain.'

Fleixa stifled a yawn – drawing a glare from Daniel. Giné went on unperturbed.

'In spite of everything, it's taken a long time for people with this kind of illness to be treated as they deserve – that is, as needful of medical attention. In this regard, New Bethlem has achieved considerable prestige. We've instated a regimen of freedom and expansiveness that is compatible with each individual's psycho-pathology, we have established methods for keeping them under observation around the clock, in scrupulously hygienic conditions and, above all, we put in place curative methods that match the ailments of each individual.'

The corridor they were coming down forked, leading them into a different wing, lined with doors to left and right. The moment they crossed the threshold, they were confronted with a chorus of shouting and wailing. Daniel and Fleixa looked at one another in alarm but Giné walked straight ahead, not breaking stride.

Fleixa paused by one of the metal doors and peered in through a small window. In the centre of the room, lying down on a metal cot, a bald man was thrashing around and howling. He wore a pair of fingerless gloves with padded wrists that were clamped to a leather belt around his waist, which in turn was attached to the wall.

Noticing that Fleixa had stopped, Giné came back to where he stood.

'Though all his mental faculties have departed him, this man remains agitated. As a way of abating his aggressive urges, we use this ingenious contraption for most of the day. He may not use his hands to harm himself, and his chest is not constrained as it would be if we used a straightjacket.'

'But . . . the poor man.'

'But imagine the alternatives.'

With that, Giné turned and continued the way he'd been going, and Daniel and Fleixa again fell in behind.

'We currently have around a hundred patients. The east wing is occupied by the men, the west by the women. And these we divide into three categories: those who are placid, those who are agitated, and those, like the man you have just seen, who require restraint. We have some extremely well-off patients here – on top of the one hundred and eighty pesetas fee, for an extra seventy pesetas they may have a personal nurse assigned. There are our second and third tier services also, naturally more economical.'

Finally they arrived at Giné's office, a cheerful space with large windows overlooking the grounds. It had barely changed since the last time Daniel was there – the same white display cabinets against the walls and, at the back, the same medical manuals, the stethoscope and collection of human skulls of all different sizes. Degrees and diplomas hung on the walls, and the desk, piled high with books, folders and all manner of documents, was clearly that of a busy man.

As he looked around Daniel also noticed a sepia portrait on the table. He suppressed a shudder. Though the subjects were younger in the picture, he'd have recognized them anywhere: Ángela and Irene standing behind their seated father. Their smiles suggested a great hope for wonderful years to come. A familiar image. And, seeing the date beside the portraitist's signature, Daniel turned pale; it was from the week before the fire.

Giné pointed to the chairs in front of the desk, inviting the pair to sit. When he saw what Daniel was looking at, he looked crestfallen.

'Truly, Amat. I didn't think I'd be seeing you again.'

'There isn't a great deal I can say to that, Doctor.' He hesitated. 'I went to see your daughter.'

Giné nodded bitterly.

'It was a heavy blow for her, losing her sister and you at the same time.' Seeing Daniel still at a loss for words, he went on. 'Of course, I knew about your relationship. When you disappeared, Irene had no choice but to accept Bertomeu Adell's hand in marriage. The poor girl.'

Giné watched Daniel for a moment, a look of incredulity spreading on the doctor's face.

'You didn't know?'

Daniel gave a look to show, indeed, he did not. Giné leaned back in his chair and turned his gaze towards the window.

'We've hardly talked since . . . what happened. And it's not for me to explain everything to you. If you want to know, you'll have to ask her.'

Daniel had many questions, but Giné clearly wasn't going to say any more, so he forced himself back to the reason for their visit. 'My father took it upon himself to investigate a spate of killings in Barceloneta, and that was what got him killed. He made sure I got a certain notebook, the original owner of which was Doctor Homs. I'm convinced there's some link, which was why we wanted to get hold of Homs.'

'I see,' said Giné, rubbing his beard. 'You'll understand, of course, that the reasons for Doctor Homs being admitted are confidential. I can, however, divulge that he had been getting better – which was why everyone was so surprised at the way things turned out. Now, though, I can see that what happened wasn't entirely illogical – it had to do with the death of your father.' Giné shut his eyes before continuing his tale. 'Homs's disorder had been provoked by the death of his wife. Even if we weren't banking on a full and complete recovery, we had managed to stabilize him. All his hopes for life had been dashed, and when that happens, a cure is nigh on impossible. We were actually close to giving up, but then things began to change; Homs struck up a friendship with another of the patients, another man of medicine, apparently. Homs seemed greatly revitalized in the ensuing months and we glimpsed the possibility, for the first time, of him getting better. With the surprising progress he was making, we even let the two of them set up a small laboratory. It had become quite an interesting case for us, we were excited.'

'But something went wrong, yes?' said Fleixa.

'It did,' sighed Giné. 'We found one of the night staff unconscious on the floor one morning, he'd taken a blow to the head. After we'd gone round to check all the patients were in their respective rooms, we found Homs's companion in the laboratory – dead. Not only dead but disfigured, virtually unrecognizable: terrible lacerations to his face and hands, undoubtedly sustained in self-defence. He had his identity card though; that and the clothes were the only way we knew for certain it was him.'

'Why,' Daniel and Fleixa said almost in unison, 'would Homs do something like that?'

'Nobody knows. The human mind harbours many a secret.' His voice grew quiet, and Daniel sensed that the events in question had affected him profoundly. 'It was nine months ago, and the motives are still a mystery to us. As I'm sure you understand, it was something of a low point for the institution.'

'But clearly not your fault,' said Daniel.

A dejected smile showed that Giné appreciated the comment.

'So Homs was only making a show of getting better?' said Fleixa.

'Seems so. He fooled us all. Even your father, Daniel. The very day before the awful event, he came to see him. He visited quite often. I remember his words that day about Homs's exemplary progress, and how he congratulated us for it. We were all taken in.' He shook his head sadly. 'We notified the authorities, but they were more concerned at the time with the uprising in La Maquinista than a mental patient escaping. Which means that Doctor Homs is still out there, and he truly is a danger. His is a kind of moral insanity. It wouldn't be any surprise if he were to kill again.'

He didn't need to go on. The first corpse had appeared in Barceloneta not long after Homs's escape. Everything pointed to Doctor Homs as the likely target of Daniel's father's pursuit.

'There's something else. A detail that makes Homs's actions all the more inexplicable . . .'

'Go on,' said Daniel.

'In the weeks running up to his escape, Homs complained of a severe pain in his ribs. We found a kidney tumour in one of his regular check-ups. The illness was very advanced. He couldn't have had more than a year to live.'

Before he could go on, a nun burst in.

'Doctor,' she said, 'we need you urgently. Ferrer has had another episode.'

'I'm coming,' he said, standing up. 'I'm sorry to have to leave like this, Amat. I hope you find Homs – and the proof you need. Now, you'll have to excuse me. I'll get an orderly to show you out.'

In the doorway, he turned to Daniel.

'It was not easy to accept my daughter's death. I blamed you for a long time. But it was an accident, that's all, a terrible accident. I still ask myself what Ángela was up to that night.'

He searched Daniel's eyes. 'You're still young, too young to bear that guilt. You must talk to Irene.'

And with that, he hurried after the nurse, leaving them alone in the office. Fleixa jumped up, rounded the desk and began rifling through the drawers.

'What do you think you're doing?' said Daniel.

'That quack can't fool me. We need more information. Come on, lend a hand.'

'Have you lost your mind?'

'Funny question to be asking, here!' he said, smiling, pulling out more papers. 'Now, do you, or do you not, want to solve your father's case? You take the filing cabinet,' he said, gesturing behind him.

Daniel hesitated, but finally went over to the cabinet with its three drawers. He tried the top one, which wouldn't open at first, so he yanked on it as hard as he could – with a loud snap the drawer came clean out, and a dozen or so patients' files scattered across the carpet.

The pair looked towards the door, where they expected the entire hospital staff to come pouring in. But, despite the noise, no one appeared.

'Quick,' said Fleixa, 'help me.'

They hurried to put the papers back. As his hand fell on a dossier, Daniel suddenly stopped; he thought his eyes must be deceiving him. He read and reread the name of the patient in question: Bertomeu Adell.

All haste forgotten, he slowly opened it and looked inside.

Adell had been admitted, it said, a year earlier, experiencing agitation and aggressive urges. According to the slim report, the family had decided to bring him in after he had nearly killed a servant for serving his breakfast in a way he found displeasing. His father's money and influence had prevented word from spreading, and meant he avoided prison – but the family had to agree to him being committed. The father had died a month later, and, in spite of Giné's protestations (the note was enclosed), Bertomeu was released.

'What's this?' said Fleixa.

'Nothing.'

'Well, while you've been amusing yourself, I've found what we need.' He held up a triumphant handful of papers. 'Come on, hurry. They're sure to be here any second.'

Daniel put Adell's notes back in the drawer and, with Fleixa's help, lifted and slid it back into place. Checking to see the place appeared just as they'd found it, they went out into the corridor. An elderly nurse was there as they came out, making them both jump.

'I've been asked to show you out. This way, if you please.'

Trying not to make their relief too obvious, the pair followed her back through the sanatorium to the main entrance. As they came outside, Daniel turned to the woman before she swung the door shut.

'Would you tell the director,' he said, 'how much we appreciate his help. And that . . . I'm going to do what I can. He'll know what I mean.'

The nurse nodded and bid them farewell. They made their way through the gardens and hailed the first carriage they saw, back to Sant Gervasi.

TWENTY-ONE

Once installed in the train compartment, the pair could relax. They had been lucky, arriving just in time for the first evening train to Barcelona. Buying tickets from the inspector, they found an empty compartment and drew the blinds so that no one could see in.

Safe from prying eyes, Fleixa took out the report.

'It's even more insane than I thought,' said Daniel.

Fleixa, concentrating on the thick sheath of papers, said nothing. The pages were organized according to date and, placing the initial administrative forms to one side, he came to the part about Homs being admitted and the treatments he was given.

```
Frederic Homs
45 years old
Profession: doctor
Widower; childless
    Suffering mental disturbances for three weeks
    to date (according to companions). Initially
```

noted as displaying incoherence and delirium, with debilitating fits. Hallucinations, visual and aural: frequent. Trouble recognizing friends and family. Recurring insomnia. Decision made to intervene immediately, to avert onset of full dementia.

Examination led to prescription of hot bath in the morning, with cold water poured over the head at the same time, then urtications. In the afternoons, two sessions of Scotch shower (hot and cold water in alternation), and electro-therapy. Fowler's syrup also to be administered to help eczema. And, to begin with, to bring down nervous tension, two measures of chloral hydrate a day.

With the initial treatments established, the pages went on to an exhaustive series of follow-up notes:

One month and two days into the patient's stay. No perceivable improvements. More intensive treatments recommended, including application of moxibustion to patient's nape to draw out insane humours. (Paper must be dry, match must be cotton or burlap.) To complement this, and given the patient's hallucinations, continued letter-writing and refusal to acknowledge her death, jimson weed with opium.

172

Homs's progress was outlined in the successive documents, a series of brief notes.

Two weeks into the patient's treatment, slight changes observed, nothing of any substance. Discharge from moxibustion points still considerable, symptoms not reducing. Further moxibustion led to sever redness of the canker. Electrotherapy has been increased.

So continued the treatment for several weeks, the notes showing periods of improvement and periods of deterioration. Homs seemed generally to be getting better, but not sufficiently. The view seemed to be that a complete recovery was beyond the powers of the sanatorium.

It was at that point that the friendship with the other patient began, a turning point in Homs's stay at the sanatorium, according to the notes. There was a considerable change over the coming months, to the point that his release was recommended. Finally, Giné had included a short note dated two days before the murder of Homs's friend.

Alfons Martí, male, 26 years of age, clear post-traumatic symptoms, admitted 15 February, year 1884, patient of Doctor Don Alfred Amat i Roures. After his isolation period, showed himself a most excellent companion to Doctor Homs. Important to observe closely the interaction between these two due to marked therapeutic impact.

'My father?' said Daniel, rereading the final note. 'The man Homs killed had been a patient of my father's?'

'Quite the coincidence, no?'

Daniel reflected for a moment, before nodding in agreement. 'My father would often have patients whose physical complaints were merely a mask for mental issues. In fact, he always insisted on an understanding of "psyche" to get to the root of a problem. His view was that a large number of illnesses were the result of some imbalance in the mind. Some branded him a heretic, but Giné, as a friend, shared his views. Which was why my father wouldn't have hesitated in referring patients.' His face darkened. 'It's a horrible coincidence. My father's determination makes sense now. Homs kills this man, this Alfons Martí, and my father felt doubly responsible: friend of the killer, doctor to the victim. Detaining Homs became a personal matter for him.'

Neither of them spoke again during the rest of the journey, each becoming immersed in his own thoughts. Night was falling as the train pulled into Plaza Catalonia again.

TWENTY-TWO

Pau came through the iron gate on Calle del Carmen. He was dead tired – he couldn't remember the last time he'd had a decent sleep. His eyes ached and the low level buzz inside his skull had become constant; he'd been working longer shifts than ever in his life.

Added to the hospital work, part of his punishment for taking in the girl, there were classes and private study time. At least Elena hadn't been ejected – that was some consolation. The tuberculosis had been found no longer contagious and she had been allowed to stay on until she made a full recovery. Doctor Segura had admitted the effectiveness of Pau's methods, though without reducing the punishment. Pau was relieved at how it had turned out, but he now had other things on his mind.

He took the note from his pocket and, for the hundredth time, reread it – and for the hundredth time, couldn't avoid the violent shudder. His secret had been discovered. He'd been as careful as he could, but all for nothing. Who could it be?

How had they worked it out? There was only one way to find out. Pocketing the note once more, he set off to the appointed meeting place.

At first he didn't recognize the man, he was in such a bad state. Waiting in the shadows of Calle Elisabets, across from the Los Ángeles Convent, he had aged far beyond his forty years. He stood glancing from side to side and stamping his feet to keep warm. His attire, which looked well made, was shabby and soiled, and his jacket hung off him. As Pau came closer he saw how red and sunken the man's eyes were, and how emaciated his features. He sniffed the air like a rat on alert.

'Good afternoon, Señor Gilbert,' he said with an ungainly bow and a semblance of a smile. 'That's the name you go by now, I believe?'

'Albert,' said Pau.

The man feigned offence.

'After all this time, that's the only thing you can think of to say? "Albert"? Not even a *how are you, nice to see you, what have you been up to these past years – these hellish years?*'

Pau said nothing. He shot a look along the street, checking to see if anyone from the university might be able to see them, anyone who might wonder what he was doing in the company of such an individual.

'Easy,' said the man. 'No one comes down here after sunset, even the nuns from the convent are inside warming their toes. But we can always go somewhere else if you prefer.'

Though Pau made it clear he didn't mind, the man began moving away. Pau followed after, and the man suddenly turned and pulled him close as they came to a doorway – he gave off an overpowering odour of wine and stale sweat.

'Unlike you, I've thought a great deal about you. And I can see things have gone well for you, ever so well.' He looked Pau up and down. 'Yes indeed, quite the gentleman you look.'

'What do you want with me?'

'No messing about, eh? Very well, Señor Gilbert, it is my belief that your father would have been far from happy with the way you have been behaving.'

Pau shoved the man back. 'Don't you dare,' he said, his voice wavering. 'Don't you *dare* speak my father's name.'

An unpleasant sneer spread on the man's face. Scratching his stubbly cheek, he spat on the ground. 'Oh, poor boy. Your father died, yes? Accident with the carriage – the roads *are* in such a state these days.'

Pau was clenching his jaw – he tasted blood in his mouth. 'Just tell me what you've brought me here to say.'

'Really, Señor Gilbert, I come here all nice and polite, but you, you act with the same lack of regard as your father.'

'He was far too good with you.'

'I didn't deserve the way I was treated!'

'She was practically a child, you villain.'

'A tart is what she was! She enticed me in, and then off she went shouting it from the rooftops.'

'You raped her and left her with child. Then she died in childbirth, and the baby too – how can you live with yourself?'

With a roll of the eyes, the man put a finger to his lips. 'Honestly, you'd be better off minding your manners.'

'Come on: whatever you want to say, out with it.'

The contempt Pau felt for the man was almost overwhelming.

Many years earlier, Albert had been employed as a servant at the house. To begin with he'd carried out his duties like any other servant, but then he'd become infatuated with a young maidservant named Francisca. His pursuit was common knowledge, as was the lack of encouragement from Francisca, who was then found one evening out by the coalbunker, battered and bruised, and with her clothes torn. The young girl, in her terrorized state, had refused to report him, which was the only reason Albert had avoided prison. Pau's father, however, had taken action, dismissing Albert and doing all he could to stop him from finding employment elsewhere. They found out that Francisca was pregnant soon after.

'You ought to be asking yourself how I found you,' chuckled Albert. 'I know you want to know, so I'll tell you: last week I happened to be walking down this very street. It was pouring with rain and I took shelter in an alleyway, just across from the hospital. I was trying to wring out my clothes when a student came out of the building and came by. He was in a hurry. He didn't so much as look at me, but I looked at him, oh yes. He seemed familiar, very. But how could it be, I said to myself, that I knew a young gentleman such as he? So I came back, a few times, I came back and looked again. I had to get to the bottom of it. Then one night, just as I was about to give up, it suddenly came to me – like a thunderbolt. At first I thought the drink must have been playing tricks on me. How you've changed! And imagine my delight when I confirmed it *was* you, for all that you had a neat haircut and nice new clothes.

You always go about alone, and you don't leave the hospital until after nightfall – very clever. Easier to avoid being noticed that way, yes?'

Pau didn't answer.

'As you can imagine, I thanked the Lord for this stroke of luck. I've not been having the best of times. It'll pass, but I need a little money. Isn't that what friends are for? You help me and I help you. I don't care about what you're up to, or who you're trying to fool with this masquerade, but the thing is with me, you see, I have such a hard time not talking, if you see what I mean? So, you help me out of the fix I'm in, and in exchange I won't go around sharing our little secret.'

Pau took a deep breath.

'How much are we talking about, exactly?'

'Oh, nothing you wouldn't give to an old friend.'

'How much?'

'A hundred and fifty pesetas.'

Pau stifled a cry. It was more than the cost of matriculating at the faculty.

'I haven't got that much.'

With a groan, Albert shoved Pau up against the doorway, following it up with a punch to the stomach that winded him. Then, yanking on his lapels, he bundled him to the floor, kneeling down on him hard.

'If you thought you were going to get away because of who you are, you're wrong. I'll have my money. You owe it to me after the way your father treated me, for all the hardship I've endured since that day. Hear me? If you don't want everyone to hear about your little game, you've got until the end of the week to get me that money. But,' he said, his face brightening, 'we can always sort it out another way, if you prefer.'

Pau tried to struggle clear, but Albert was too strong. Spittle was running down the side of his mouth, he stank of brandy, and Pau could feel a hand sliding down to his crotch. Pau managed to get a hand free, and crashed his elbow into his assailant's face, sending him stumbling back.

Albert hit him square in the face, and there was a crunch as Pau's head hit the wall. He felt unsteady, and toppled to the floor. A sinister smile spread on Albert's face as he dabbed at his bleeding lip.

'I'm going to enjoy this.'

He raised his fist to strike again, but just then the clattering of horses' hooves filled the street. Albert shot a look to his right and, cursing, leaned in close.

'Thursday at eight, at San Justo. Don't even think about trying to make me wait.'

Pau barely registered the words, or the sound of Albert's footsteps as he hurried away. There was a sudden movement next to him, voices, shouting. He was being lifted to his feet by a pair of strong arms.

'All right? Are you hurt?'

Everything was blurry. He recognized that voice though. Gradually, as his vision returned, his saviour's face came into focus – a face he knew.

A fire kept the room pleasantly warm, but Pau continued to feel the chill of the street in his bones, and the cup of coffee he'd been given was doing little to stop his shivers either. To his left

180

sat Daniel Amat. The thoughtful, bespectacled gaze of those sparkling grey eyes of his: so similar to his father. Trying to stem his bewilderment, Pau cleared his throat.

'You were lucky,' said Amat.

Pau nodded and took a sip of the dark coffee.

The man Amat had been travelling with put some documents he was reading to one side.

'Scandalous,' said the man. 'Robbing people right outside the hospital doors. Lightning quick too he was, otherwise no way could he have outrun me.'

Fleixa's words drew a wry smile from Daniel. So they assumed that Albert had been trying to rob him – Pau was relieved to hear that. He could use that.

Ignoring his companion's amusement, Fleixa got up and came over to Pau, offering his hand.

'I'm Bernat Fleixa. Maybe you've heard of me, I write for the *Correo*.'

Pau took the proffered hand, shaking his head. And though he tried to look apologetic, Fleixa's disappointment was clear.

'Sorry,' said Pau. 'I haven't heard of you.'

Fleixa feigned indifference, bracing his arms against the desktop. Daniel, evidently finding the exchange quite funny, turned to Pau with a gleam of curiosity in his eye.

'So what happened, exactly?'

'I was leaving the hospital, and that man came out of the shadows and tried to rob me. I was worn out, I'd just come off a very long shift, and I didn't have any energy – otherwise I'd have run away. He caught me off guard, that's all.'

'And did he manage it?'

181

'Manage what?'

'If he took any valuables, you ought to go to the police.'

'Oh, no, he didn't,' said Pau awkwardly.

No one said anything for a few moments. Pau used the lull to get up and place his cup on a side table. His head was spinning and he still felt weak, but the sooner he could get away, the fewer questions he'd have to answer.

'I greatly appreciate your help, gentlemen, I'm in your debt. I'm feeling much improved, so I ought to be getting back. It's very late and I have work again tomorrow at the hospital.'

With that, he nodded to them both and saw himself out. As the door shut behind him, Fleixa turned a quizzical look Daniel's way.

'Strange specimen, didn't you think?'

Albert Malavell stood in a doorway across from the halls of residence, sheltering from the gusts of rain. He looked up at all the illuminated windows. He didn't know which room it was, but that little mattered. It was enough to imagine the place. His hand caressed the dagger in his pocket, and he ran his tongue back and forth over the split in his lip.

TWENTY-THREE

The landau carriage sped towards the port, leaving the bustle of Las Ramblas behind. At the bottom of the road the horses had to circumnavigate some roadworks, at the centre of which a monument to Christopher Columbus was under construction.

The voice of the driver carried back to Daniel in the open-top seats.

'I'd bet a year's pay that monstrosity topples over before they get the column up.'

Daniel didn't bother to answer, looking admiringly instead at the complex iron structure, brainchild of the architect Juan Torras. The scaffold, over sixty metres in height, was the tallest construction Barcelona had ever seen. The four slender columns, made of angle iron, were traversed by three viewing platforms, forming a perfect square. Numerous iron braces had been driven into the ground to resist the buffeting of the wind. The column rose up in the centre, crowned by the seven-metre figure of the distinguished mariner, who had numerous extra support ropes attached to his person – as though he were Lemuel Gulliver on his famous travels.

The monument, intended to celebrate the World Fair, had been under construction for no less than seven years, and there had been a great deal of talk about the ingenious methods used to hoist the enormous ferrous castings. Rumours presaging a disaster were so rife that the Mayor himself had visited the architect's studios for assurance that the works would not come crashing down on the heads of passing citizens. Torras's answer had been to stand directly beneath the crane the day the statue, weighing all of six tonnes, had been raised. The naysayers had been proved wrong, and the architect's stock soared like the price of cereal.

Leaving the works behind, the landau entered the Paseo that had recently been recobbled and named after Columbus. To the left stood the Hotel Internacional, another building job thrown up for the Fair in record time.

Here by the waterfront, Daniel observed the tumult of activity, sailing boats, merchant vessels and fishing ships vying for moorings, the packet boats disgorging passengers and goods, and, on one side, fishermen unloading the morning's catch where the buyers milled around checking the wares.

The air was briny for a distance, soon to be replaced by the smell of soot from the Estación de Francia. With its gabled roofs and high, arched windows, the place was busy with travellers, porters carrying suitcases and bundles, carriages calling out for fares at the exit and waggon drivers hurrying to unload merchandise for the train to Madrid.

On the landau went, joining a path that led between the train tracks and the Parque de la Ciudadela, eventually coming to Calle Villena, which passed through a side gate into the precinct.

The guards at the entrance, recognizing the carriage, waved in greeting to the driver. They came along a grove of orange trees, at the end of which stood some huts containing piles of wood and brick crates. The driver, not bothering to get down from the cab, pointed the way between two scaffolded constructions.

'Pink bricks,' he said. 'You can't miss the place.'

Making his way along the faintly marked path, Daniel took deep breaths, enjoying the walk in spite of the morning chill. The air between the sea and the park was clear of the factory smoke that clogged most of the city. For a few moments the apprehension that had been gripping him subsided.

He came out from the shadows of the buildings and crossed to the other side, before stopping and suppressing a gasp. Stretched out before him was the site of the World Fair.

He recognized the different buildings thanks to a wall poster he'd seen the day before lampooning the works. To his left, the Palace of Industry and Commerce stood like a gigantic fan. Its seventy thousand square feet were due to house the latest technologies: a homage to the ingenuity of mankind. Across from the palace, the ruins of the old citadel had been turned over to lush gardens, complete with a waterfall and numerous copses of trees. On either side of the grove, what was to be the Conference Hall stood alongside the Martorell Museum; the opening ceremony was planned to take place here, with attendees including the Queen Regent, the King, and all manner of dignitaries from across Catalonia and country-wide. Beyond these, Daniel could make out the elegant Palace of Fine Arts, work of the architect August Font, and after that the Spanish Colonies Pavilion. A little further off, peeking out above the trees, the Amargòs glasshouse could just be seen, and the crenelated tops of the ostentatious Lluís Domènech café-restaurant. Enric Sagnier's León XIII Pavilion, slated to hold the papal exhibitions, was supposed to be opposite, but had been discarded after the works fell irretrievably behind schedule. After the gardens came a wide avenue – wide enough for six horse-and-carriages to come down it abreast – lined by hugely disparate pavilions, such as that put on by the Marquis de Campo, the American Soda Water Pavilion and the Philippines Tobacco Pavilion. At the end of the avenue stood the imposing Arco de Triunfo, which was to be the main entranceway.

'Who ever thought Serrano's madcap idea would ever actually come to pass?' said a voice behind him. 'Right?'

Bertomeu Adell approached, a box of snuff in one hand. After taking a couple of sniffs and massaging the bridge of his nose, a satisfied expression settled on his face.

'Everyone's been smoking these damned cigarettes these past, what, ten years? But for me, nothing can touch a good bit of snuff. The only downside,' he said, clicking his tongue, 'is it's becoming such a battle to get your hands on anything halfway decent.'

He came and stood beside Daniel, turning and taking in the view, the buildings and gardens, as though they were his own possessions.

'I'm pleased you decided to come, Amat.'

They set off, crossing the gardens, passing the Conference Hall on one side and coming through another pavilion, until they came out in front of a light red-brick construction.

Though smaller than the other edifices, it stood somehow

186

defiantly before the Barcelona sky. Its four-storey façade combined glazed ceramics and light red openwork, broken up by arched windows. A slender hexagonal chimney stack stood at the centre of the building, a thick white coil of smoke pouring forth.

Daniel wondered to himself what the function of the place might be.

'In honour of our long years of friendship,' said Adell, stopping in front of the principal doorway, 'I'm going to bring you into a confidence, dear friend. I've risked a good amount of my inheritance on this project. If anything were to fail to go to plan it would be quite the setback. But you, Amat,' pointing at him, 'you're going to make sure that doesn't happen.'

'What are you talking about?'

Smiling enigmatically, Adell went ahead into the building.

There was a large reception area just inside, with linoleum flooring and wooden panels halfway up the walls. The decorations, a series of motifs from nature, were nearly complete, and the air smelt strongly of fresh paint.

Without a word to any of the workers, Adell advanced, leading the way to a glazed double door. Daniel followed him through, and was about to ask for an explanation, when a sensation of vertigo hit him, and he took a step back.

The reaction seemed to please Adell, who smiled. He leaned out over the iron balcony they'd stepped onto, which stood twenty metres above the ground. A deafening hum filled the air.

Recovering from the surprise, Daniel took in the extraordinary sight below. The enormous space, not dissimilar to a cathedral, was divided up into two nave-like bays that ran in parallel, with pillars rising up at a number of points. The floor was covered with dozens of cables, as though a metallic squid were trying to wrap the place in its tentacles. In the nearest bay, on a stage, Daniel counted six steam engines. They reminded him of iron elephants resting against the walls. Just below the stage a gang of men, stripped to the waist and sweating, worked in unison to feed three furnaces. Flames licked at the open hatches, as if hungry for the shovelfuls of coal. The heat was palpable even from that height.

Five contraptions stood in the next bay – Daniel didn't know what they were. Far larger than the steam engines, they took up the majority of the overall space. Men moved across raised gangways between the contraptions, and were taking notes and measurements. Daniel realized the hum was coming from them.

'You have before you Barcelona's first electric power plant,' announced Adell. 'Those machines are continuous current dynamos supplied to us by the English firm Shuckert & Co. They put out almost three thousand kilowatts of power. We're going to be lighting up Las Ramblas, the Columbus Paseo, the Plaza Sant Jaume, as well as the whole of the Fair. And that's only for starters: we've got a few dozen investors at the moment, but soon enough more will be flocking in.'

Daniel was impressed. The building and the facilities wouldn't have come cheap, and the effort required for such a project was truly titanic. He suspected, however, that Adell hadn't brought him here just to show off. What did he want? What did he mean about Daniel guaranteeing the project's success?

A worker burst through the door behind them, nodding to Daniel before addressing Adell.

'I'm sorry, Señor, we need to talk.'

With a sigh, Adell nodded impatiently. 'This is Señor Casavella, he runs the plant for me. And he always has some problem or other, urgently in need of my attention. If you'll excuse me?'

The pair moved off a little way, but not far enough that Daniel didn't pick up snatches of their conversation between the sound of the generators. Casavella was clearly extremely concerned about something.

'. . . three times this week . . .'

'. . . deal with it . . .'

'Yes, Señor, I know, Señor, but Tuesday . . . reached capacity . . . pressure . . . No, we can't do that . . . I don't know, Señor . . . ups and downs . . .'

'Don't be ridiculous . . .'

'. . . explosion.'

Then a klaxon rang out to announce a shift change, drowning out the conversation entirely. Daniel watched as Adell drew it to a close with an angry swipe of the hand. Casavella desisted, nodding several times to whatever Adell said next, before taking his leave. Coming back past Daniel, he touched his cap deferentially.

Adell, bracing his arms against the iron handrail, seemed to have forgotten that Daniel was there. After a minute he appeared to come back to himself.

'My dear friend,' he said. 'It's come to my attention that you've been making certain inquiries.'

Daniel said nothing. Adell came closer.

'And I'd like for them to stop,' he said in a soft voice.

'What's that?'

'If it's a question of money, we can come to an arrangement.'

'I'm not sure I understand.'

Adell sighed impatiently.

'Let's see . . . Did you know? Water is fundamental for the steam furnaces, and that's why we installed a complex system running beneath the surface of this building that connects with the casks you see next to the furnaces. Any excess water is returned to the sewers. And some of the dead bodies in which you have been showing such a keen interest were found at the outflow points of *our* drainage system. This is, of course, just a coincidence, and a trifling one at that, but now that you and your friend the journalist have begun digging around, it's starting to draw attention – to me. Now do you understand?'

That, thought Daniel, would explain why no one had seen any of the bodies being thrown in the water. And Adell's concern wasn't surprising – he could be directly implicated in the deaths, however absurd that might be, but also, if they became public knowledge it would simply generate a scandal, a dent to his reputation. The investors wouldn't be happy, and the future of an electrified Barcelona could even be thrown into doubt.

'I think I see what you're getting at,' he said.

A smile of complicity spread on Adell's face, only to vanish as soon as Daniel spoke again.

'People might even hold you responsible for the crimes.'

'Oh, please, Amat, don't be ridiculous. I remember you as a person with some brains. To start with, what crimes? Accidents, very unfortunate ones, but accidents all the same. Furthermore, none of it has anything to do with me, but what I do see is that any publicity would not be good. You do know the World Fair opens in two weeks? Things are rather delicate at this present moment, we're just putting the finishing touches to the most important part of the system. There are certain misalignments in the pressure flows, and endless other issues, you can't begin to imagine—'

'Did you know of my father's investigations while he was carrying them out?'

'Of course.' He shrugged. 'Your father and I discussed it – though he refused to listen to good sense on the matter. Whereas – given how far back you and I go – I'm sure we can come to some agreement. The electricity grid is scheduled to spread across the entire city, enormous amounts of money will be pouring into it. Do you see? Electricity is the future. We can't stand in the way of progress, Amat.'

'A number of those dead bodies belonged to girls, hardly more than children.'

Adell waved a hand, as though shooing a mosquito.

'And why should that be my concern? They're with God now. Their deaths were an end to suffering, that's all. Really, if it weren't for the damned press, the likes of your friend Bernat Fleixa, to me it would be no different to a few dead dogs. But bad publicity, now that is serious, it could easily endanger my life's great project – and that I cannot allow.'

'And why should I do what you say?'

'I understand, my friend, I really do,' said Adell calmly. 'Your father died in a most unfortunate accident, and then some unscrupulous individuals begin mixing him up with some frankly laughable stuff about crimes, plots, fantastical machinations. You ask yourself whether they might not be in the right. You've been away for such a long time, how are you supposed to know what to think? I might have done the same. But the thing is, it's all a lie. Nothing you've been told is true. You're confused, and that means you can't see how badly you've tumbled into a hare-brained quest, or that no good will come of it.'

Daniel went to say something, but Adell silenced him with a gesture.

'It makes me sad seeing you like this. I feel, I suppose, obliged to help you – because we're such old friends, and because of Irene, too.'

'She has nothing to do with this.'

'I'm very well aware of your feelings for her in the past.' At this, Adell's face darkened. 'And yet it must have been a difficult decision for you, leaving like that. Sometimes you get winners and losers, isn't that right? And actually that leaves me in your debt.' He took an envelope from his pocket. 'There's a first class ticket in here for your return to England, and a small amount of spending money. Think of it as compensation.'

'I'm not interested. I—'

'Oh, I don't expect you to accept right away. The offer stands for three days. I hope you will decide, in that time, to accept – and put this whole sorry matter behind you. And if not . . .' Adell paused, all traces of gentleness vanishing. 'I'll find other ways of making you do so – *old friend*.'

And, as if they had come to an agreement, a coachman appeared next to them.

'One more thing,' said Adell. 'If you decide to see Irene again, you'll regret it.'

'Is that a threat – another one?'

'Of course, but not in the sense that you think. In this case, Amat, it isn't me you ought to be worried about.'

'So what are you trying to say?' Daniel was having difficulty controlling his rage.

'If I should hear about another meeting taking place behind my back, I'll take action, taking full advantage of my rights as her husband. It will cost my wife a great deal to disobey me again. I don't know if you follow me.' And he stressed each of the following words, one by one. 'Irene is mine now. And I'll use her as I see fit. Am I right in thinking you won't forget what I'm saying? Ironic, wouldn't you say, the situation we've got ourselves into? After all, the wellbeing of my wife, and the wellbeing of my very household, has come to depend on you.'

And with that, Adell turned and walked off along the gangway, as though Daniel had ceased to exist.

TWENTY-FOUR

The boy picked up a stone from the ground. Examining it, he decided it would do: not too heavy and not too light. Testing its sharp edge, he smiled to himself and placed it in his pocket along with the other five.

Lying on his front on the ground, he shot looks left and right, before springing to his feet and dashing over to a pile of sleepers next to a mound of dirt. His chosen hiding place. He came to a thicket, dived and rolled along the ground, raising a puff of sand. He'd scraped his knees, which were bare, but no matter – wounds he could show off later on.

Seemingly, he'd gone unnoticed. He carefully lifted his head above the wall and scanned the area. The position was perfect: he could see everything.

To his left, behind a boxcar, Xavi Sento had secreted himself. The boy could see Xavi's peaked cap and those eyes of his, large as lanterns in his small head. A little further off, next to a coalbunker, 'The Kid' Chato was making a racket as he tried to get his fat behind into position. The boy had to stop himself calling out a reproach. He looked to his left where, though he couldn't see him, he knew 'Fat Lip' Sesé was hiding. Everyone was in position, everyone knew the plan, and it was all going smoothly. No wonder – after all, the plan was his.

It had all begun three days earlier, when they were challenged by some boys from the village of Sants. They'd agreed to settle it on neutral ground, and the tracks next to the station at Villanueva had been chosen – just by the harbour entrance where coal was unloaded. There was plenty of ammunition to use, and endless places to hide. The guard would be tucked up in his cabin at that hour, and everybody knew that nothing would draw him out once he'd settled in for the night.

His thoughts were interrupted by a whistling sound – a stone sailing through the air – followed by a loud clang as it hit the boxcar next to which Chato had just hunkered down. He sighed. His overweight friend was highly effective in hand-to-hand situations, but when it came to guerrilla tactics he was about as subtle as a battalion. At least Chato had revealed the positions of a couple of their adversaries. He gestured at the others to hold fire.

Straining to hear, he managed to make out the crunching of stones a few metres away. Shadows moved between the boxcars. They were close, extremely close – they'd nearly come all the way to the sewerage outflow point – and that was where the trap would be sprung.

He got up again and set off running as though pursued by Cuban rebels. Sesé jumped up as he went past, and the two sprinted across the tracks. A few stones hit the ground nearby but missed them, and some shouts and taunts confirmed the enemy were in pursuit. They were nearly at the outflow, and could hear the sound of the waves below. Nen, Fran and Vélez were down there with whole piles of ammunition. Chato and Sento would come up from behind in a pincer movement, and victory would be theirs.

Reaching the embankment, he slipped and slid down the stony slope, ending up in the water, where his feet came into contact with something soft. Looking back to the top of the slope in anticipation of his pursuers, the noise of splashing over to one side drew his attention. He turned to look, confounded by the commotion Sesé was making.

Down on his knees in the water, his eyes wild and his body quaking, Sesé pointed at the boy's feet.

The boy looked down.

At first he couldn't make it out, but then a wave turned the body over again.

A girl, half submerged between his feet. Stripped of clothes, the body was so white as to look see-through. Her eyes were shut, as if in sleep – but from the stench, it clearly wasn't that. A trip he'd once been on with his father, to the butchers in Sants, flashed into his thoughts.

Another swell twisted the girl's head around unnaturally, and, between blackened muscles, he was able to see the bones of the neck. The flesh was gone, as if torn away by an enormous bite.

The boy felt something warm running down his inner thigh, and after a moment began to scream.

TWENTY-FIVE

The morgue was in the cellars of the Guardia Civil barracks. You entered through a doorway situated on a concealed alleyway – safe from prying eyes. But all along the edge of the building, at floor height, gratings released a telltale mix of disinfectant and an odour like rotten fruit.

Fleixa came down the alleyway and rapped on the door. The man at the entrance was an elderly former Guardia Civil. The journalist slipped him a few coins and he agreed to make himself scarce for as long as was necessary. Fleixa signalled behind him, and Daniel and Pau Gilbert stepped out from the shadows. The trio entered, and no sooner had they set foot on the stone steps leading to the cellars than the faint odours they'd smelled outside became overpoweringly strong.

Descending last, as Daniel watched the young Gilbert carefully picking his way down the steps, he ran through the previous few hours since Fleixa had brought the news of this latest death.

It was a golden opportunity to see for themselves the state of one of the bodies, and perhaps glean some insight about where to take their inquiries. Not that the matter was entirely straight-forward. They needed someone with sufficient medical expertise to examine the body, and there was only one person either of them knew: his father's old assistant, Pau Gilbert.

When they went to ask the young man for his help, he flatly refused. He seemed affronted. Insist though they might, he main-tained his position – that was, until Fleixa reminded him of the debt he owed after they'd come to his aid outside the hospital. Finally he came round, if reluctantly.

In the carriage that had brought them, the young man kept his thoughts to himself, refusing to be drawn into any kind of conversation. And now, as they made their way down the steps, he gave the clear impression of regretting his decision.

The morgue was situated in a long stone vault. Three gas lamps hung down from a cable running from one end of the ceiling to the other, allowing for the lamps to be retracted if they were in the way. As the trio came in, only one of the lamps was lit, leaving most of the space in darkness. Six stout wooden tables, with screens separating them, lined the wall, and four of them were occupied.

'The old man said ours should be back there,' said Fleixa, gesturing to the far end.

They approached the farthest table. There was a body covered with a length of sackcloth; something told them it was the one.

Clearing his throat, Fleixa leaned against the wall – at a prudent distance. The smell of decomposing flesh had impregnated the very walls. His guts lurching, he regretted having eaten supper before he came.

Pulling on a flax rope, Pau brought the lamp nearer and

opened the valve so that the circle of light widened, illuminating the three of them.

'Are you sure we can do this?'

'Just make sure you don't touch it,' said Daniel. 'We mustn't leave any marks. Just give us your opinion.'

Fleixa showed his agreement with a vague wave of the hand.

Removing his jacket, Pau took down a leather apron from a nearby rack. Identifying the causes of death without an internal examination was no simple task. Displaying a confidence he didn't feel, he opened an adjacent cupboard and took out a couple of metal trays, placing onto them a scalpel, a pair of scissors, a number of different forceps, an autopsy knife and a small bone saw. Though he wasn't going to open the body, he wanted to be prepared. He looked up at the two men.

'Ready?'

They nodded. Pau took a deep breath and removed the cloth.

They each had to stifle a cry. Fleixa crossed himself, muttering a series of curses, as Daniel took a step back, face ashen. Pau was the first to recover.

'The stitches on the chest suggest an autopsy's already taken place. Didn't you say we were the first to see the body?'

'The guard assured me no one had touched it,' said Fleixa, looking anywhere but at the body. 'It's exactly as it was found.'

Daniel couldn't tear his eyes away, thinking: had his father's death been so gruesome? 'Señor Gilbert, we don't have answers, only questions. I'm sorry to have dragged you into this. If you would like to drop out now, we'll understand.'

'Give me a minute,' said Pau, swallowing hard. 'I've never seen a body in this kind of state.'

'Don't feel under any obligation, if you don't think—'

'I said I'd do it.'

But still Pau cursed himself. What was he doing there? He had quite enough to worry about without adding an illegal autopsy to the list. He shouldn't have let himself be swayed by the journalist's reminder of his debt. At that moment, though, he'd thought there might be a chance they'd talk to the dean, which would endanger something far more important, and so he'd gone along with it. Now he wondered if he hadn't made a serious blunder.

Resigned, he turned his attention to the dead body again. He felt both excited and unsure. You could tell at a glance that this young girl had been through an atrocious ordeal. Mastering his feelings – as his father had shown him to do – he put his fears to one side. The individual that had previously occupied that body was no longer there, it had given way to an anatomical riddle, a mystery to be solved – nothing more. He pulled the cloth away fully now, uncovering the body down to its feet.

Fleixa continued to say nothing and avoided looking at what was on the table. He had been warned about 'extraordinary conditions', but he hadn't expected anything like this. The stench of this particular specimen was worse than anything in the rest of the room. It was all he could do to avoid vomiting. He felt incredulous when he saw the way the youngster looked at the body, how fascinated he clearly was.

'If you'd be so kind,' said Daniel in a low voice, 'as to tell us what you're thinking as you carry out your examination.'

Pau nodded, and began. 'Female, fourteen to sixteen years old. A metre sixty, approximately, and around forty-five kilos. Unclothed. Hair colour, difficult to determine: the entire body has been shaved, including head and pubis. No *livor mortis* to be seen – on the contrary, save along the edges of the wounds, which show black, the skin is profoundly white. It's as though she's been bled.'

'Same as my father said Homs's other victims were.'

Pau looked up. There were other such bodies? Homs? Who was Homs? All questions he'd have to ask – when the time came. 'Did they say it was found in water?'

'They did.'

'Yesterday, in the afternoon-evening?'

Another nod.

'The body is cold to the touch; in a body that's been underwater, *rigor mortis* usually sets in after two to four days, and then loosens. I'd say she's been dead for over a week: the lack of bloating suggests that she wasn't in the water for all that long. This is all highly unusual, but even more so is the consistency of the flesh, which is almost jelly-like. And look at the extremities. The bones and cartilage show an impossible degree of calcium deficiency.'

Daniel nodded for him to go on. Fleixa, recovered from the initial shock, was taking notes.

'We can see two open wounds – here, on the inner right thigh, and here, at the nape – and the edges of each are carbonized. The skin over the trapezius, and the medius and anterior scalenus muscles, has been peeled back. The clavicle looks to have been broken in at least three different places, the wound suggestive of an animal bite. And from the amount of flesh removed, by an enormous creature, I'd suggest.'

He moved to the far end to examine the feet.

'Again, serious burn marks on the toes, so serious that some of the phalanx bones themselves look carbonized . . . And look, how strange! All these Lichtenberg Figures!'

'Lichten-what?' said Fleixa.

'Lichtenberg Figures, or electrical treeing – these veiny formations you see on the legs and arms. They mean capillaries have burst beneath the skin.'

Pau looked closely at the cut that had been stitched together on the abdomen, before moving on to examine the head. It struck him that the cheeks were very swollen, and he quickly checked the eyes. He brought the lantern closer and increased the flame, took up the scissors and, before either of the others could stop him, made an incision on one of the eyelids.

'What do you think you're doing?'

'Wait – I think you'll want to see this.'

Taking up the pincers, he removed a suture that ran along the edge of the girl's eye. Then he rested one hand against her forehead, parted the eyelids, and sunk the instrument into the socket. Soft sucking noises accompanied his movements. When he pulled the pincers away, they brought with them a lump of bloodstained fat.

'They took out her eyes,' said Pau, smiling with satisfaction.

Fleixa hurried over to a grate in the floor and, bending double, was violently sick.

'It could even be,' Pau said, ignoring the journalist, 'that she was conscious at the moment of extraction. See here, at the corner of the eye? There's an incision, virtually invisible. You'd need a scalpel for that. The girl might have moved.'

'You're sure?'

'Not completely. But what I can say is that the work done here was magnificent.'

'Magnificent?' said Fleixa, wiping his mouth with a handkerchief. 'How can you call this carnage magnificent?'

'Look at this suture.' He pointed to the faint line on the other eyelid. 'If someone hadn't known where to look, they'd never have found it. The eyeballs were extracted, and they had to cauterize the sockets to stop all the blood from draining out. All of which takes tremendous skill, and a good deal of experience too. The work of a surgeon, I'd say, and not any old surgeon either.' Placing the pincers back on the tray, he crossed his arms. 'That should do, I think. Now would you mind explaining what this is all about?'

But before either man could answer, the guard burst in, face distorted.

'Quick! The Inspector himself is coming, and some others with him. You need to get out of here.'

Daniel helped Pau cover the body and put the instruments away as Fleixa turned off the light. They rushed over to the door. When they reached the foot of the stairs they heard voices, and a light shone down from above. They couldn't get out that way.

They hurried back along the corridor, which curved to the left and, after several metres, came to an abrupt end at an oak doorway. Fleixa tried, but it was locked. The voices could now be clearly heard.

Pau pointed to a large barrel leaning against the wall, and silently they positioned themselves behind it; their only hope was to shelter in its shadow.

The light from the men's lanterns broke up the shadows as

they made their way down the stairs and advanced towards the trio. Looking down, Daniel noticed with dismay that the tips of his shoes were in full light.

Inspector Sánchez appeared, flanked by three officers. If he happened to turn his head at this moment, they'd be seen. But the group just carried on down the passageway and proceeded into the morgue, leaving the trio in darkness once more.

Coming out from the hiding place they fled up the stairs and out. The guard shut the door behind them. After the foulness of the morgue, the cold, clear night air was a relief.

In the carriage on the way back to the university, Daniel turned to Pau.

'You're right,' he said. 'We owe you an explanation.'

Fleixa rolled his eyes, shaking his head, but Daniel went on regardless.

'I ought to warn you, though, that if we let you in on the whole story, you'll be just as implicated as us.'

'You don't say – more implicated than I am after tonight?'

TWENTY-SIX

'Not exactly the easiest thing to believe.'

At that hour of the night, Café Zurich was full, but Fleixa had managed to get a table. They were enveloped by cigar smoke and the hubbub of conversation; it seemed a good place for confidences.

Fleixa lounged in his seat, absentmindedly opening and closing his pocket watch, while Daniel ran Pau through the events of the past few days, including an explanation of Doctor Homs's notebook, which lay open in front of them. The young student looked alternately between the notebook and the faces of the two men.

'So you think this Doctor Homs is responsible for more murders like tonight's?'

'Indeed.'

'But why isn't this bigger news?'

'Fear is a wonderful silencer. And, apart from the families of these girls, no one really cares about their deaths.'

'The perfect victims,' added Fleixa, who'd now begun swinging his watch back and forth in front of his eyes.

The journalist wasn't at all keen on bringing Pau in. Instinct told him there was something amiss about the boy – and his instinct was never wrong. The delicate manners, the soft voice, the reserve – it had gone the instant he had the girl's dead body in front of him. He'd become enraptured at one point; he'd clearly enjoyed the task. And there was no way that could be normal. It made Fleixa retch, for goodness' sake, just thinking of the smell. No, the boy surely couldn't be trusted, though there was little he could do now: Amat had decided to involve him, and Fleixa's advice hadn't entered into it. But he still intended to keep a close eye on the youngster.

'You corroborated it,' said Daniel, unaware of Fleixa's train of thought. 'It would need a first-class doctor to sew the eyelids like that. And that's what Homs is.'

'And what could be his motive? Why commit such awful crimes?'

'That we don't know for sure,' Daniel conceded. 'On the basis of the journal and what we've found out about his departure from the sanatorium, we're guessing that Homs is trying to find a cure for his wife. He refuses to accept that she's dead.'

'And what has any of this got to do with your father's death?'

'They were friends. It seems my father helped with Homs's initial investigations, and then when it became clear that Homs was losing his mind, assisted in apprehending him and having him committed. The first bodies were found in the months after Homs's escape. My father thought he recognized it as his old colleague's handiwork, and sought to verify his suspicion: that Homs had turned murderer. My father felt responsible, and tried to catch him, but died before he could.'

'And why don't you take this to the authorities?'

'They've been trying to cover the whole thing up,' said Fleixa, putting away his watch and downing his third brandy. 'They think if word of the murders gets out it might prompt some kind of uprising in the city.'

'You're a journalist, you could go public.'

'I wish I could have by now. I need more than we've got though. We're very thin on actual evidence.'

'But something would still be done about it.'

'You don't understand. I'm not looking to write just a column. I want to get the front page with this.'

Pau sat upright, his incredulity clear to see. 'Your . . . *career* means more to you than stopping more deaths? That's obscene.'

'Obscene, is it now? Just you listen—'

'That's enough,' said Daniel. 'There's a new body now. It gives us a chance to prove these deaths aren't all just accidents.'

'Actually, it doesn't . . .' said Fleixa dejectedly. They both looked at him. 'Before we left the guard told me that Sánchez and his men had come for the girl's body. They hadn't arrived just by chance. She'll be deep in some common grave by now.'

'So we've got nothing.'

A silence fell between them.

'*Damn* . . .'

'All might not be completely lost,' said Daniel.

'How's that?'

'All right . . . Remember my rooms were ransacked? I've been thinking about it. The view at the university is that it was some student prank, but that makes no sense. I'm convinced whoever went through my things knew what they were up to. And Homs,

207

after all his years teaching at the university, would know the place like the back of his hand.'

'Homs? But why risk exposing himself like that?'

'Exactly! That's the question, what was he after? It was clearly risky, so he must have been looking for something important. And I think I know what it was.' He tapped the open pages of the notebook. 'He wanted his book back.'

'Why would an old notebook be so important?'

'I don't know.' Daniel's smiled vanished. 'I've been going over and over these pages for days now, and I have to admit I've come up with absolutely nothing. Maybe it's hidden in some way, or maybe it's something that would only be noticeable to Homs – in which case, we're never going to work it out.'

'May I?'

Pau took the book and turned back to the first page. Eventually, after reading for a few minutes, the other two looking on expectantly, he shook his head. 'I'm sorry, nothing's jumping out at me.' He went to pass the book back, but then stopped. 'Wait.'

Flicking back, he found what he was looking for. 'This is strange,' he said. 'Homs is a medical man, and one of some standing. Odd for him to make such a schoolboy error.'

'Go on,' said Daniel.

'It says in the notes on January twenty-third: "Vesalius's *Liber Octavus* is the only hope."'

'And that's strange because?'

'This *Liber Octavus*, or "Book Eight": there's no such thing.'

'Vesalius?' said Fleixa, slightly slurring now. 'Who's that?'

'Any first year student could tell you,' said Pau. 'Andreas

208

Vesalius was an eminent sixteenth-century anatomist, famous for challenging Galen's precepts. A big thing at the time, given that he'd been *the* point of reference for all medical practice since antiquity.'

'You don't say?' said Fleixa.

Ignoring the journalist's disdain, Pau went on. 'Galen based his anatomical studies on animal dissections, which generated a great many misguided ideas. Vesalius who, like any other medical person of that time, started out respecting Galen, opted to focus directly on human anatomy.'

'Which means?'

'There was a period in Paris when he carried out hundreds of dissections on the bodies of men, women and children. At that time it was no easy thing to even obtain bodies to do such work. His dealings with grave robbers are pretty infamous.' Daniel and Fleixa frowned. 'In exchange for a few coins, they'd dig up graves and bring him the bodies. Later, when he returned to Italy, he was allowed to study the bodies of dead criminals.'

'Sounds like a hoot,' said Fleixa, taking another drink.

Pau snorted.

'Don't mind him,' said Daniel. 'Carry on, if you don't mind. Maybe it will tell us why Homs mentions it.'

'All right,' said Pau, pausing for a moment. 'His undeniable genius, which some people saw as conceitedness—'

He heard an 'ahem' – the journalist was grinning behind his glass. Pau's face flushed, but he tried to ignore him.

'As I was saying, he was confident enough to begin criticizing other doctors of the time. He accused them of overlooking ana-tomical studies. In his view, science was an impossibility as

209

long as the truth about human nature continued to be sought in Scripture rather than in cold, hard facts. Anything that went against God's word in those days was of course discounted, but also considered the devil's work – it had to be guarded against, there was censure. All that being the case, Vesalius pointed out that Galen's work had been built up as a kind of Bible in the sciences, and went on to break with all the established ideas, blazing a new path for the study of human anatomy. The shockwaves were felt right through the medical establishment. When he published, though his ideas won some people over, by and large he was rejected by doctors throughout Europe. The man he'd studied under, Jacobo Silvio, came out against his proposals. He made so many enemies in Italy he was forced to give up his professorship in Padua and had to emigrate to Spain, where he became a member of Carlos V's court, as a king's physician.'

'Why do you know so much about him?'

'He's a hugely important figure in modern medicine, and anatomy, which he's primarily associated with, happens to be one of my specialisms. I gave a talk on his work last year, and a few weeks ago, when I started working for Doctor Amat, he got me to gather everything I could on Vesalius. To me it seemed slightly pointless, but of course I did as I was asked.'

'That's it!' exclaimed Daniel, suddenly enthused. 'My father wanted you to work for him because he knew about your Vesalius expertise. His inquiries must have led him in this direction. It can't be anything else, and it confirms that this note *is* significant.'

210

'Sorry,' said Fleixa, 'but how can a non-existent book by some writer who died three hundred years ago be significant?'

'It isn't a book as you understand the word,' said Pau. 'The "books" are the different sections in Vesalius's culminating work.'

'Well in that case,' Fleixa said, laughing, 'everything makes perfect sense.'

'Do you *want* to know or not?'

'Please,' said Daniel. 'Please carry on.'

Pau took a deep breath. 'At the age of just twenty-eight, Vesalius published his most important work, *De Humani Corporis Fabrica*, or "On the Fabric of the Human Body". It's considered to have given birth to modern anatomy, and it's divided into seven "books", each one dealing with a different part of the body. But the thing is, Vesalius wrote seven books, not eight.'

'A typo, perhaps?' said Fleixa.

'Could be—'

'On the contrary!' exclaimed Daniel. 'Don't you see? Homs wanted to get his notebook back because of the very fact it talks about this Book Eight.'

'Maybe I wasn't clear,' said Pau. 'Vesalius never wrote any *Liber Octavus*. For once I agree with Señor Fleixa, it's a slip most likely, probably down to the state Homs was in at the time.'

'Mind explaining,' said Fleixa, 'what "for once" is supposed to mean?'

'I disagree,' said Daniel, his blood still up. 'While he was trying to find a cure for his wife, Homs consulted Vesalius's manuscript and, somehow, learned of a chapter nobody knows about. *This* is the great discovery he talks about, the one he told my father about.'

'It also says,' said Pau, 'that your father refused to help any more because it was against God's teachings. Vesalius was hounded by the Church, and most of the medical professionals at the time went against his ideas. It could be that he made some colossal discovery but, knowing he'd be called a heretic, he was forced to keep it quiet, and decided to hide his findings away.'

'Right – and then Homs is the one to discover it, three hundred years later! But his wife *still* dies, and he loses his mind. My father hid the notebook, and with it the only possible way this secret chapter could be found.'

'All right,' said Pau, 'but supposing this Book Eight is real, what can it have to do with the deaths of all these girls?'

'That I can't answer. What I am sure about is that if we find it, it will lead us to Homs.'

'Where do we start?' said Fleixa.

'The most obvious thing is to get our hands on a copy of the Vesalius.'

'It's one of the main books doctors use in general practice, has been for a number of years now,' said Pau. 'Most libraries should stock it.'

'Wonderful,' said Daniel. 'And you, as a student, have access to a library. Do you want to carry on helping us?'

Pau considered for a moment. Daniel's enthusiasm was infectious. He knew he'd regret it, but then again, taking an old medical text out at the library could hardly land him in that much trouble.

'I can get to the library after my classes tomorrow.'

Daniel's face flushed with gratitude. 'If you agree, we'll meet at my rooms tomorrow evening, at around eight? We have to track down this Book Eight. Something tells me it's the only way we're going to prevent further bloodshed.'

TRUE OR FALSE

Twelve days before the start of the World Fair

TWENTY-SEVEN

Bertomeu Adell got down from his carriage at the Plaza de Sant Jaume. He cuffed aside a group of young beggars that immediately swarmed forward. Straightening his hat and taking his cane in his left hand, he couldn't hide his satisfied grin.

The Town Hall, which also housed the Council of One Hundred, stood across from the Provincial Offices: a group of buildings that had for two thousand years been the centre of social and political power in the city. Four Ionic columns broke up the façade of the Town Hall, above which, surmounting the portico, a pediment was set bearing the city's crest.

It was close to midday and the plaza was busy with foremen and ushers, gentlemen with secretaries hurrying after them. Also milling around were shoeshine boys, sweeps, beggars, servants of all kinds, and clerks on a multitude of errands. Adell ploughed on through the sea of bodies, and was received at the grand entrance of the Town Hall by two Guardia Civil.

He'd been invited for a meeting – a call he'd been waiting

a long time for – too long, he thought, swinging his cane for a moment like a wand of office. But he felt calm: his moment had come, finally he was to be recognized. His focus had only ever been on growing more wealthy – who's wasn't? – but the point was that his ventures had, as an aside, played a great part in the forward progress of the city.

He wanted to be one of Barcelona's leading men. What he really wanted was Deputy Cortes's place – for an Adell i Busquets, nothing less would do. His father, and his grandfather and great-grandfather before, had been eminent figures, and had all been made deputies. Their names were still spoken with respect, and now it was his turn. No more being called 'Steamy' when he wasn't there to reprimand the speaker – that reference to his family's past dealings with steam engines. From now on they'd have him along on any large projects, and invitations would come flooding in for the most select events and gatherings.

The thought of his wife came to mind, dampening his good spirits. Damn that woman, she'd never be content. Instead of behaving as befitted her station, she chose to constantly provoke him. Didn't know her place, never had. From the very moment they were betrothed she'd shown a rebellious streak. The worst thing was all the *opinions* – what made her think she was entitled to those? She read books, hardly a decent pastime for a lady. Less arrogant, more grateful, that was what she needed to be – hadn't it been his generosity that had saved her from a most shameful situation? To top it off, she'd become quite taciturn during these past weeks – coinciding with the return of a certain Daniel Amat – and her infantile shows of independence seemed a daily occurrence. She'd even sent him away when he came to visit her in bed – twice! She needed to learn her place – soon enough, he thought, soon enough.

An orderly stood waiting for him inside. He followed the man up the marble staircase, trying to defer the thoughts of his wife. Today was his day, *the* day, and no one, not even Irene, would put a blight on that. The sound of his cane striking the floor echoed back off the vaulted ceilings high above. They came through several rooms that were full of comings and goings, agitated ushers, busy functionaries; the place simply effervesced with industry.

The Mayor's office was far larger than he'd imagined. The six large gothic windows encircling the space, with their shutters open, afforded an excellent view over the plaza. A light haze of cigarette smoke hung upon the air. Several men stood at one end of an oval table that was covered in documents and plans. They ceased their conversation when the orderly approached.

Francesc Rius i Taulet, a man of about sixty, was in his fourth term as City Mayor. He wore one of the 'hulihee' beards, and with some pride – long mutton chops that hung down as far as the lapels of his suit, and joined together in a moustache; only his chin remained bare. Very overweight, he was rumoured to suffer from ill health, though his energies had been crucial in bringing the World Fair to fruition, and indeed in the transformation of Barcelona as a city.

Standing next to the Mayor was Elies Rogent, a famous architect and the only person present that Adell knew personally. Rogent had been the technical director for the World Fair, which meant they'd had dealings concerning the construction of the power plant. Their agendas were quite opposed: Adell recalled a recent argument over the quality of certain building materials, an argument that had stuck in his craw over the course of a few days.

A little further off, by some leather divans, stood the lawyer and great proponent of the regional tax schemes, Manuel Durán i Bas. He was chatting with Claudio López Bru, the Marquis of Comillas, a generous benefactor to the city – a generosity that rather ran against Adell's idea of a person of his status.

So four of the so-called Committee of the Eight were missing – the men who had underwritten the World Fair. This annoyed Adell; he'd hoped to be received by the committee in full. It would only be fitting, given the importance of the moment. But he quickly put it aside; this was, after all, just a first meeting. All due ceremony would come in time.

The Mayor beckoned him in, indicating where he was to sit. To one side stood a table with an array of spirits, coffee and pastries. Once each of the men had taken their seats, Francesc Rius came directly to the point.

'I suppose you know why we've invited you?'

Adell had toyed with the idea of showing reluctance, so that they would have to plead with him to accept: draw out the pleasure. He paused, relishing the idea, before answering in a haughty voice – the kind such men used. 'But of course, gentlemen.'

Clasping the arms of his chair, he leaned back. Soon it would be the Committee of the Nine.

A taut silence fell. Now, he thought, now the homages and

eulogies would come. He heard a couple of the others cough, and Rogent let out a disdainful snort. There went *his* invitation to the sumptuous party Adell was planning in order to announce his appointment – Rogent's *and* his frigid wife's.

The Mayor leaned forward, a grave look upon his face.

'Let's see . . . It seems you might have the wrong end of the stick.'

Adell blinked; this wasn't it, this wasn't it at all. Glancing around, he now saw how circumspect everyone looked, how far from relaxed. Also, no drink or cigar had been offered to him. He cleared his throat, on edge; he suddenly felt flushed. 'I'm sorry, I'm not sure . . .'

'We're simply here, Señor,' spat the architect, 'to get a proper handle on exactly *how* incompetent you are.'

Adell felt his face turn red: what was that supposed to mean?

'Please, Elies,' said the Mayor. 'No need for spite.'

'My thoughts exactly,' said Adell. 'Now listen, what's all this about?'

'Obviously,' said Manuel Durán, 'we're referring to the repeated power cuts these last few months. There are endless complaints about the cuts along Columbus Paseo, and in the grounds of the Fair. It's barely a fortnight until the opening ceremony, and I hardly need tell you what a disaster it would be, with the eyes of the world upon us, for the lights to decide not to work during the acts.'

'What precisely were you waiting for, before you came to inform us?' said Claudio López. The Marquis looked offended by the very sight of Adell.

Adell was dumbstruck. This? They'd brought him here for

221

this? The blasted cuts? His tongue felt like a piece of cardboard that had been glued down.

'Gentlemen,' he said. 'A few technical adjustments are all that's needed, it isn't—'

'Our current discussions,' said the Mayor, stony-faced, 'are about whether you are capable of resolving the issue. I'm a hair's breadth from rescinding your contract with the council.'

Adell almost fell out of his seat. Costs had spiralled, the backing of the investors was crucial. But the biggest problem was the sums of their money he'd had to make use of for his own asset management company – he'd had a run of rather bad luck there. The sugar markets, with Cuba in such a mess, had become quite unstable, and he'd sunk the lot into a couple of ill-fated operations. His whole inheritance wouldn't be enough to cancel out the money he now owed. The power plant was his last chance to get back on an even footing. And if this contract was cancelled, there was no way his use of these funds could fail to come out in the wash. He'd be ruined.

'Gentlemen, there's really no need to be so hasty.' He'd broken out in a cold sweat. 'You have my word, my absolute word of honour: these problems will have been dealt with in a week at the most.'

His words had a chilly reception.

'Señor Adell, you have three days to get the plant at full and reliable capacity. If not, the contract will be null, and you can be sure you won't be working in this town again.'

'Three days?'

'Not a minute more. Be warned, you don't want to make me regret having placed faith in you.'

Adell nodded and tried to smile, without much success. The meeting seemed to be at an end, and he went to get up, but the Mayor stopped him. 'One more thing.'

'A rather delicate one,' said the Marquis.

'All right,' said Adell. *What now?*

'Difficult as it seems to believe,' said Manuel Durán, 'we've been informed that bodies have been appearing in the plant's drainage network. Dead bodies.'

Adell had to hold his breath to stop from cursing the man.

'Perhaps you'd care to explain?' said the Mayor.

The four men peered at him quizzically. He didn't know how much they knew. Only a little, was his guess, and so, though he shouldn't lie, perhaps the whole truth wasn't entirely necessary either. He tried to calm himself and answer with a show of the utmost assurance.

'Your information is correct, gentlemen. Over rather a long period of time we've found the bodies of a number of unfortunate souls in the water. Personally, I'm not sure I see the problem.'

'Don't see the problem? Dear Lord! Why were the authorities not notified?'

'I didn't judge it necessary.'

'Wait, how many bodies are we talking about here?'

'A dozen. Perhaps more.'

'Jesus and the saints!'

'It has also been suggested to me,' said Durán, 'that the state in which these bodies were found is somewhat peculiar?'

'It cannot be the smoothest of rides through the sewers,' said Adell, 'and then there are the rats, and the fish, the dock water itself . . .'

223

'Awful!'

'There are rumours in Barceloneta,' said the lawyer, who seemed the best informed, 'of some sort of curse having provoked these deaths. Workers at the Land and Sea Engineering Agency have been flat out refusing to work night shifts, and that goes for the Nou Vulcà and Escuder factories too.'

To this further grave comments were added, and Adell considered his position. Inspector Sánchez had clearly decided to blab, in spite of the large sums he'd been paid not to. He'd need reminding where his loyalties lay . . . Dear Christ! As if he didn't have enough problems getting the plant operational. When the first body had been found he'd made a call: no one would care. That had been an error, he could see it now. He'd need to show more care.

'Nasty rumours, gentlemen, that's all. The victims have, to a one, been ladies of ill repute, and their deaths the result of a dissipated way of living. Under your watch, Señor Mayor, the city has of course become a much safer place, but not everyone acts within the law, or with the proper respect for the order of things. I hold my hands up: I have tried to keep these . . . *findings* from you, but only in an attempt to avoid burdening you, and indeed to be sure I am applying all my energies to the power plant.'

'Did it not cross your mind what would happen if the press got wind of this?' asked Rogent.

How that man vexed him – that tone of his! Of course it had crossed Adell's mind – he thought of little else.

'There are certain newspapers who would wish to defame the Fair,' said the architect. 'A story of this magnitude would unleash panic across the city.'

224

'And all this, mere days before the Queen is due for the cutting of the ribbon. The court might even decide to cancel.'

'Lord!'

'But not just that – exhibitors and visitors are expected from across the globe. What are they going to think?'

'That we cannot even keep our own citizens safe. It doesn't bear thinking about. They'll all cancel.'

'Especially with the World Fair taking place in Paris just next year, they'll simply skip Barcelona.'

'Gentlemen . . .' Adell tried to calm them, but to no avail.

'These "findings" are to be curtailed,' declared the lawyer. 'Absolute discretion is of the utmost importance.'

'Adell,' said Ruis, stabbing a finger in his direction. 'It is *your* responsibility to see that not a word of this makes it into print. You are to make yourself available to the police for interview, and let us know, immediately, of any news. I hope that's clear enough for you. Your position, not to mention your fortune, are on the line. If the World Fair in Barcelona should fail due to your incompetence, be assured, you will pay the price.'

As he left the Town Hall, Adell was as grey as the skies above. He got into the carriage and collapsed back onto the leather seats.

This had all started with the inopportune inquiries of that blasted doctor. Everything had begun to go awry at that very moment. The old man's death seemed to have solved it, but then, just at the most delicate moment, Daniel Amat had decided to make an appearance. Seven years away, and there he was again. And then he got that damned hack onside and picked up where his father had left off. Coincidences? Not likely.

He'd been too soft. A stop had to be put to all this. He couldn't allow for more mistakes, and less for any of this to jeopardize his real project, the one he'd been carrying out in secret. The sheer weight of his discovery – no one could even imagine it, least of all those fools on the Committee. When he went public with *that*, they'd all be kissing his feet. The whole city would kneel before his genius, they'd all come begging for the tiniest ounce of his glory. Daniel Amat had decided to get in the way, but not for long. He'd pay for today's humiliation, and soon.

TWENTY-EIGHT

Pau sighed and pushed *Observationes anatomicae* by Falloppio to one side. This wasn't turning out as expected: he'd been through the library's entire Anatomy section; not a single copy of the Vesalius was to be found.

The original library, once a plain room in the old College of Surgeons, had expanded considerably over the years, and nowadays occupied its own building next to the university. Its sturdy oak bookshelves led outwards from the ample central reading rooms in concentric rings, like a colossal, eight-sided theatre. At the third ring you came to a spiral staircase leading to a mezzanine floor. The domed roof, daylight filtering up from the windows below, rose to an apse that bore the city crest.

Pau loved this sensation: having the span of medical history at his fingertips. Unlike other students, he didn't find the silence in the library oppressive – quite the opposite. He took pleasure in the strong smells of wood, paper and stone. He felt at home here, perhaps because he had no other place to call by that name. And the library had a further advantage: Fenollosa and his friends made only rare visits, and when they did it was easy to avoid them.

He heard the bells of Santa María del Pi in the distance. It was getting late, the tables previously occupied by students were empty, the light from outside was waning and the lamps now barely lit the aisles. He had to get a move on if he was to keep his appointment with Amat and Fleixa.

He hated the idea of coming away empty-handed. He imagined the journalist's mocking expression. Not a single copy? He'd have to consult Señor Ferrán; it would mean his search wouldn't go unnoticed, but there wasn't any other way.

Gathering up his things, he headed for the librarian's office.

As he approached the end of the passageway he heard hushed, urgent voices. As he drew closer, the conversation seemed to turn more heated. Two men were arguing in the Chemistry section – the adjacent aisle. Pau advanced with caution. He didn't wish to interrupt a private dispute. And then, to his surprise, he recognized one of the voices.

'But, Father! I'm not a child any more.'

'That remains to be seen. I come for a visit, and the joke everyone seems to be cracking is about my son, my own son, and how some other student walked all over him in a public debate.'

'It was just a silly Anatomy class.'

'Don't you dare talk about the teachings of medicine like that.'

The younger man said nothing.

'Four generations of surgeons in the family, four. Each and every one of us *adding* to the good name. I graduated with distinction, and you, what do you do? You're a Fenollosa, for goodness' sake!'

'Please, Father, you're going too far.'

'Too far? Do you think I haven't heard about the dives you've been spending your nights in? Or that you've been showing up half-lit to class? Is this any way for a gentleman to behave?'

'Chip off the old block! Your whoring is legendary in the department.'

This was followed by a resounding slap. It wasn't terribly hard, but Pau saw, between the books, his classmate's face turn a different sort of scarlet. He looked like he might return the blow, but held back. The father, ignoring his son's incensed looks, straightened his jacket and shirtsleeves, gathered his gloves and cane, and turned to leave.

'I'm suspending your allowance for the time being. Finals are in two weeks. You're to apply yourself.'

The sound of his footsteps died away. Fenollosa dropped the books he was carrying and slammed his hand into the shelving beside him. His eyes glistened with tears.

The best thing Pau could think to do was to go back and wait for Fenollosa to leave. But as he turned, he bumped into a trolley, knocking a number of books to the floor with a loud clatter.

'Who's there?'

Pau tried to slip away, but it was too late.

'Gilbert! What the. . . ?'

He didn't know what to say.

'Make a habit of eavesdropping on private conversations?'

'No! It isn't what it seems.'

Fenollosa strode furiously along to the end of the aisle and advanced on the backpedalling Pau.

'Always in my way, stupid know-it-all . . . *Meddler*.'

He shoved Pau who, shorter and less heavily built, fell backwards, hitting the bookshelf behind him. His glasses were knocked to the ground. Fenollosa fell upon him, literally spitting his words into Pau's face.

'You got away with the episode of that street girl, but you're hiding something else, I just know it. I plan to find out what it is, and when I do they'll throw you out faster than you can say—'

'Gentlemen!'

Señor Ferrán appeared at the far end of the aisle. The chief librarian approached and, seeing the books spread across the floor, his look of incredulity gave way to genuine fury.

'What do you think you're up to?'

With some reluctance Fenollosa got to his feet. Pau rescued his glasses and tried to make himself presentable.

'Educated young men, and you roll about like ruffians!' He paused, daring them to correct him. His gaze came to rest on Fenollosa. 'You, out of here.'

Fenollosa stepped forward, and seemed about to make some rejoinder.

'Didn't you hear?' said Ferrán.

Glowering, Fenollosa gathered his belongings and turned to leave. He shot Pau a hateful glance as he came by and, a few seconds later, there came the thunderous sound of the door slamming. Ferrán grimaced, and as the reverberations settled, his face softened.

'Are you all right, Señor Gilbert? I wouldn't want my most faithful visitor to perish!'

'Thank you, Señor, I'm fine.'

'It looked to me as though you were assaulted. Want me to accompany you and we can file a complaint?'

'Oh, no, I don't think so. I appreciate it though. My colleague was a little . . . upset after a discussion we'd been having. About a pharmaceutical procedure. All a big mix up. Nothing, really.'

The man seemed unconvinced.

'I really ought to go and tell the dean, but I'll respect your decision.'

'I would appreciate that, Señor.'

'Perhaps,' said Ferrán jovially, 'a few *boxing* lessons in this new English sport everyone is talking about, eh?'

'Good advice, thank you.' Pau then remembered why he'd been coming this way to begin with. 'Oh, Señor Ferrán, I was actually on my way to look for you.'

'Oh?' His eyes gleamed in amusement. 'I ought to warn you, I haven't the first notion about this new pugilistic import, only a small pamphlet that's just come in from Madrid. You could take it out if you like.'

'It isn't that. There's a book I can't find.'

'Ah, now there's a matter with which I can perhaps assist. Come into my office and we'll have a look at the records.'

The office, a snug, scrupulously tidy space, stood in one corner of the labyrinthine library. The librarian moved a column of books to one side and put some documents in order, before settling into an armchair near the warmth of the fireplace.

'So, which book is it you're after?'

'*De Humani Corporis Fabrica*, by Andreas Vesalius.'

Ferrán's eyes lit up. 'What a masterwork. And normally we

231

have quite a few different copies, but in the refurbishment five months ago, several were lost, and in the most unfortunate manner.'

Sighing, he got up and went over to a chest with an array of different compartments, each with a golden knob. His hand skimmed across them like a pianist's, before alighting on one. Satisfied, he removed the drawer fully and placed it on the table. He took off the lid and revealed a row of index cards inside. The librarian, peering over the tops of his glasses, ran finger and thumb down the side. Pau waited expectantly. From the look on the old man's face, the news wasn't good.

'Seems you're too late. The last copies were taken out by a professor and a couple of students.' His eyebrows shot up. 'And how strange! The last one was taken out by the very individual you seemed to be on such good terms with just now.'

'Fenollosa?'

'Precisely. He borrowed it this very morning.'

The exact same day he'd come looking for Vesalius's manuscript. Coincidence, or was there something in it? There was no way for him to know, but the outcome was the same in any case: no book. His disappointment must have been clear, because when he looked up the librarian was smiling playfully.

'There might be an alternative.'

'It's that book I need, Señor Ferrán. Another one on anatomy won't do.'

The old man shook his head.

'I don't mean that. What I mean is there's a good chance these aren't the only copies there are.' He half-shut his eyes, casting his mind back. 'In the oldest part of the library, on the second

232

floor, there's a forgotten room. I call it "the attic". And it has a rather singular collection of books inside.'

'And I thought I knew my way around the library.'

'Not so strange really: no one knows about it.'

'And why is that?'

'A few years ago a professor who was still active at the university was made librarian. This was a departure from tradition, as usually only retired professors are appointed librarian.'

'You used to teach?'

'Of course – but my career, which was rather middling I might add, is by the by. As I was saying, this man put together an area for his own personal use, and created quite the stockpile of books – with no particular rhyme or reason to the collection.'

'What did he want such an area for?'

'The man was a rather fine researcher by all accounts, with a great future ahead of him. But not long after coming into the post, his wife fell ill.'

Pau felt a twinge of excitement. The librarian seemed not to notice.

'And from that moment on, the poor man dedicated every waking minute to trying to find a cure for her. Some say he even built a secret laboratory – I doubt it personally, but anyway. What's certain, though, is that his research led him to accumulate more and more books, including some from certain rather controversial disciplines. And the attic was where he placed them.'

'When you say "controversial"—'

'Oh, esoterics, the occult sciences, that kind of thing. Poppycock, most of it.' He clucked to show his disdain. 'A waste of time if you ask me. But then again, who knows how any person might react in that kind of situation. I remember seeing him in there for several days in a row at one point, never leaving the library. And all for nothing. The wife died, and he became unhinged. And then when the refurbishment happened, the attic was completely forgotten about in the plans.'

Glancing down at the flickering flames, the old man shook his head.

'A sad tale, most sad. As I remember, when it came to medical treatises, his main interest was Anatomy. Which is why –' he looked up at Pau – 'I thought you might find what you were after in there.'

'You don't happen to remember the name of the man, do you?'

Pau could hardly control his excitement. The old librarian shut his eyes for a few moments, and when he reopened them said, 'Homs it was. Doctor Frederic Homs.'

TWENTY-NINE

'Like I say, it's the devil's house.'

The driver followed these words with a crack of his whip, and the horse broke into a trot, leaving Plaza Antonio López behind. The Tilbury carriage came onto the Paseo de Isabel II. The man spoke with a broad, southern Catalan accent.

'It's been abandoned for seven years, from what I hear. Between you and me, I reckon it's more like twenty or thirty – at least twenty or thirty. Unspeakable things go on there, no word of a lie. It's cursed, Señor, the house is cursed.'

Daniel, seated beneath the hood of the two-wheel carriage, though aware of the man's chatter, was more concerned with keeping control of his nerves. The driver, thinking he'd impressed his passenger, went on.

'The whole family dead in a fire, how about it? Not a soul surviving. And that meant no one to inherit the place, so the council put it up for auction, but no one with half a brain wants to buy that sort of place. They'll have to knock it down, I tell you. About all it's good for.'

Daniel sighed. It hadn't been any easy decision to make. He'd been avoiding this moment since he set foot in Barcelona but this afternoon, with some time before meeting Fleixa and the young Gilbert, felt he couldn't put it off any longer.

The driver turned the carriage into a different street, and Daniel coughed to clear his throat. 'Driver, you'd be better going along Santa María.'

The man nodded and pulled on the reins, again cracking the whip over the horse's head. Daniel wanted to go the way he and his brother always used to go. The streets, so familiar to him, brought memories of his past life flooding back. They came along the Paseo del Born, quiet at that hour, and almost as far as Calle Montcada, before turning down a side street. The clamour of the city suddenly dropped away; the horse's hooves striking the cobblestones became the only sound. The driver finally took Daniel's silence as a cue to hold his tongue.

They cut along various alleys and backstreets before coming out in front of a high perimeter wall. This they skirted – in bygone days lime-washed and pointed with tiles, it was now mottled and cracked, leprous looking. The mortar had come away entirely in places, and the bricks stood bare. Finally the Tilbury came out onto a pleasant little tree-lined plaza.

'This is fine.'

'Sure, Señor?'

Daniel couldn't help but notice the concern in the man's voice. He handed him some coins.

'Don't worry. And don't go anywhere, I'll be back shortly.'

Getting down from the carriage, he set his hat on his head and started towards the house. It was one of the few mansions in the Ribera barrio. His father had always resisted moving to a better area – a waste of money, he always said.

His hands shook as he approached the imposing wrought-iron gate. He braced himself against the bars, which swung away a little with a creak. The lock was broken, replaced by someone with a robust chain. But that meant only the minimum of effort would allow access: you simply had to pull the two portions of the gate apart and slip through the gap.

Daniel glanced around. The street was deserted and on the corner the driver, cloak gathered about him, was rolling a cigarette next to the Tilbury. Stooping, Daniel ducked under the chain and shimmied through.

Stopping once more, he had to hold back an oath.

The place was completely overgrown after the years of abandonment. The gardens, once so elegant, were a chaotic jumble of greens and ochre. He was standing at the beginning of a flagstone path thick with weeds. Advancing a few steps, something scurried off through a nearby clump of long grass.

A few metres further on he came to an enormous linden tree. Daniel remembered how often he used to climb it. Now it stood like a decrepit old man, its leaves withered and the trunk faded. Unpruned, one of its trunks had grown too thick and snapped under its own weight. Beyond the linden stood the small, man-made oval lake. In summer he and his brother Alec would dip their toes – to be reprimanded immediately by the governess. In those days the water had been so clean and clear that the carp had appeared suspended in air, but now the bed lay empty, dust covering the cement zigzags at the bottom. Grass and weeds grew up between the crevices.

It was his first time back since the fire. When, weeks afterward, he'd left the hospital, following the argument with his father, he'd taken the first train to Calais, and from there sailed directly for England. He'd have carried on in that direction and never stopped if it weren't for Sir Edward. A little over seven years ago, that had been. He took in the heartrending transformation of the gardens that his mother had tended so lovingly, and that his father had maintained in her memory, and realized that, in fact, seeing the house could have been far worse. He sighed, resigned; no turning back now.

As he moved deeper into the grounds, the hum of the city dropped away entirely. Finally the only sound was the crunching of his shoes along the gravel. The breeze died down, and leaves and branches hung still as stone.

He came past the summerhouse, half collapsed. Alec, who had a great talent for acting, used to put on a show there at the end of every summer, lighting up the whole family with his witty impressions; their father would even come out of his office and take part in the merriment. Daniel would always take a supporting role, acting as stagehand or cast member. He shut his eyes to dispel the memories. And when he opened them, there the house was, as if it had been waiting for him.

His first impression was of an enormous ship marooned in a sea of dry grass. It had in times past been considered a splendid edifice. All three storeys still stood, and the spacious terrace on the first floor also remained intact. The Neo-Mudéjar turret extended skywards like an old lighthouse. Most of the glazed tiles had fallen from the façade, and those still in place looked tarnished and dull. The majority of the window shutters were broken and hanging off.

Daniel started up the steps to the front door. Putting to one side the agitation that gripped him, he made it up to the shady doorway. Remarkably, the family crest was still there on the doorframe and as his eye fell on the motto he remembered all the times his father would remind them of it: *Vivitur ingenio, caetera mortis erunt.*

A burst of frightened wings received him when he entered the spacious hallway. The late afternoon light filtered down through the holes in the roof, lighting up dust motes raised by his entry.

The devastation was even greater than he'd expected. A large number of the rafters had collapsed and the stairway, which the city's great and good had climbed in times gone by, was now piled with rubble. The wallpaper with its elegant designs had been vaporized. A grey shroud covered everything. Rain had entered through the gaps in the roof, presumably turning the grime on the floors to sludge, as the tiles were now covered in crusty marks where it had dried.

His heart seemed to contract as he moved deeper into the house. The effects of the fire were everywhere. The roofs and columns, which had once borne an expensive lacquer, now looked like the bones of a charred skeleton. The sateen drapes were rags stirring in the wind. Some of the ceiling lamps, though twisted by the flames, still hung down from the roof. Any pieces of furniture that had not been incinerated had fallen apart and subsided – in the very same spots they had once so splendidly stood. In spite of all the time that had passed, Daniel thought he still smelled burning.

He proceeded from room to room, wan light entering through the tattered shutters. His steps led him to the kitchens, which contained little more than the ashy remains of a table, a couple of chairs and some unrecognizable utensils. He stopped beside a door that was now a blackened plank. The entrance to his father's laboratory.

He hesitated before entering. A flight of stone steps inside the door led down into darkness. A surge of fear impelled him to leave, to get away from this place, go back to the security of forgetting: but the need to see it with his own eyes was stronger still. His memories of the night itself were blurry – the nightmares, far sharper, had eclipsed them. He'd never found out what had really happened. So now he was here. The time had come to find out: was he truly a murderer?

Kneeling down, he took out a pair of candles and some matches. After a couple of clumsy attempts he managed to light one of the wicks. The flame cast a circle of light around him. He took a deep breath and headed towards the dark doorway.

The wooden railing had disappeared, so he felt his way along the wall – the warmth of the stone made him shudder. He came down one flight and then another, conscious that to his left there was a ten-metre drop. The smell of the candle wax mingled with a stench from deep inside the building.

After a few more steps he then stopped, thinking he heard a muffled murmur. Surely not. His mind must be playing tricks. He heard something else and then, all of a sudden, a gust of air rose and extinguished the flame.

It was as dark as a well bottom. Losing contact with the wall, he flailed about in the air to try to locate it. It took all his

240

effort to master his panic; he managed to turn around. He could vaguely make out a light at the top of the stairs – he seemed to have descended further than he'd imagined. He inched his foot up and forward for the next step but missed it and stumbled, falling into the dark.

He cried out, expecting a long drop, and was surprised when, almost straight away, he felt first his knee strike something, and then the rest of his body slamming against a wall. He lay there winded. He'd managed to fall onto a lower part of the winding staircase.

Fear forced him to his feet; he massaged his injured leg. Being sure to keep one hand to the wall, he began hobbling back up the steps in the direction of the light.

When he came back through the door at the top he was completely ashen. He was having difficulty breathing, and his knee throbbed. Deeply shaken, he looked around, and it seemed to him that the house had come to life, and was closing in, shrinking, to stop him from getting away.

He scrambled back the way he'd come, feeling frenzied, stumbling and falling down a number of times. Somehow he managed to locate the hallway, came out onto the front porch and lurched down the steps, but when he reached the bottom his knee gave way and he fell face first onto the flagstone path. He turned onto his back and, with some relief, took a lungful of the cool garden air. The view of the sky seemed quite wonderful to him.

And then he felt himself retch, and just managed to turn onto his side as his stomach voided itself.

Once he was finished vomiting, he lifted himself, trembling, to his feet. His vision filled with tears. His father had been quite right never to return. Unbuttoning his collar, he felt his heart rate gradually decrease and his breathing become easier. He put his hand to his nape and ran his fingers over the scarred stretch of skin: the indelible reminder that, yes, he was a murderer.

Back inside the carriage once more, Daniel breathed a sigh of relief.

'Go,' he said.

The driver had been startled at his passenger's shabby state, but seeing the man's expression decided to keep his thoughts to himself. He stubbed his cigarette on the heel of his boot and stowed it in his tabard pocket. With a crack of the whip, the Tilbury was underway once more.

Daniel glanced behind them. Clouds were gathering above his old home, which was half hidden in shadow. As they moved off it seemed to melt into the air, like a figment of someone's imagination.

THIRTY

The roofbeams in the attic were low and sloping, and it smelled as though an animal had been left to rot in there. It seemed quite a leap to imagine Homs electing to work on the cure for his wife's illness here.

Pau lit the old lantern on the table. Discoloured sheets covered the furniture. Removing them, he found an empty bookcase, an old model skeleton that was missing a number of pieces, three travel trunks, large and well made, with labels stating that they'd once contained the doctor's laboratory instruments, a few dozen folders and some yellowing cardboard boxes containing a vast quantity of books.

At the sight of all those volumes, his resolve wavered. How long would all this take? In the unlikely case that Vesalius's manuscript was even among them, he'd need days to unearth it. Perhaps better to wait for one of the copies to be returned to the library, or even to go directly to one of the students who'd borrowed it.

For a moment that seemed a far more sensible route – but

then he imagined Fleixa's condescending smile. He picked up the nearest crate and placed it on the table, brought over a chair, and settled in for a long shift.

Two hours and seven boxes of books later, Pau collapsed back into the chair. Moments earlier he'd been glorifying in his good luck – he'd found Doctor Homs's personal library! What a sight Amat's and Fleixa's faces would be when they heard! And now he was beginning to see just what Ferrán had meant when he called the collection a farrago.

He'd gone through so many books he'd lost count, and the more he saw, the more bewildered he felt at the possibility of any unifying principle. Each box contained a mix of reputable scientific tracts and obviously fraudulent and superstitious displays of ignorance. Expensive editions of Aristotle's *Libris naturales*, Carl von Rokitansky's *Handbuch der Pathologischen Anatomie*, and *Leçons de pathologie expérimentale* by Claude Bernard mingled with pamphlets on esotericism, spiritualism and alchemy. It was strange in every way, and quite unbecoming of someone as erudite as Homs. Worst of all, there was no sight of the Vesalius.

He dragged over the next box. Rummaging around inside, he pulled out a volume with dark flaps: *The Book of Spirits: on the immortality of the soul, the nature of spirits and their relations with men, moral laws, the past and the future, and the prospects of humankind* by Allan Kardec.

This was a waste of time. Instead of revising for his exams . . . He shook his head and without thinking flung the book at the remaining boxes. He then watched on dumbly as they toppled over, raising dust and spilling dozens of texts to the ground.

There goes another hour, he thought, while I clean up this mess. Holding back a curse at his own stupidity, he decided, once he'd put the books back, to call it a day. He'd have to just bear the journalist's provocations – better than wasting more time.

He began gathering the fallen books from beside the bookcase – and stopped. Amazement spread on his face: a crack had opened in the wall.

Just what I need, he thought.

He brought the lantern closer. Even more trouble. He prodded the chink – how on earth could a few falling books have caused that kind of damage? And as he looked more closely, suddenly an idea came to him. He found one of the furniture cloths and wiped away the dust and cobwebs. There was a very fine vertical line through the shelf there and along the wall behind, as though someone had made an incision with an extremely sharp blade.

Tremulous with excitement, he placed both hands against the unit and pushed. When nothing happened, he tried again, throwing his whole weight into it: there came a cracking sound, and the shelves receded an inch. He shoved again and a hidden door swung open.

His hands shaking, Pau picked up the lantern again and went in. He could hear the sound of his own breath. Going further in, he wrinkled up his nose at the smell. The space was small and unelaborate, with a crude lab desk against one wall, a wardrobe, a bench and, on the other side, a rickety old bed and an iron stove. He'd found Homs's secret laboratory.

After the disputes with Doctor Amat and the questions at the university over his emotional state, Homs must have created this space in order to continue with his research uninterrupted. He would have been able to disappear, and to come and go as he pleased, without anyone knowing.

Pau ran a finger along the desktop, fascinated. The wood was mottled with stains from past experiments. Homs would have spent countless nights in that space, trying to find some way of saving his wife. It felt almost tangible to Pau, the sense of the desperate struggle that had driven him out of his mind. All the doctor's pain and obsession seemed to hover on the air. Pau shivered.

Something caught his eye as the light ran across the nearest wall. He lifted the lantern above his head and almost fell back with surprise. A single phrase, repeated over and over, covered the walls from floor to ceiling. Pau read it aloud: '*Vivitur ingenio, caetera mortis erunt.*' He ran his hand over the letters, written in charcoal. Certain stretches were close to illegible. What did it all mean? Was it linked in some way to the murders? Or just the product of an unhinged mind? Placing the lantern down on the lab desk, Pau took a pad from his bag and copied down the phrase. He would come back to it later.

Remembering why he was there to begin with, he went over to the cabinet, the only possible hiding place of the books. The doors were glass-fronted but too thick with dust to see through. Checking his excitement, he lifted the catch and pulled open one of the doors. The top shelf bore a number of medical manuals and some essays on cholera. One caught his eye: *De Dignotione ex Insomnis Libellis* – 'On the Diagnosis of Dreams'. A well-known work by Galen of Pergamon. Why would Homs have such a book? He picked it up and began leafing through, when his eye came to rest on another volume, apparently carelessly placed on the shelf below.

It was the only one with no words on the spine – it could even have been a notebook. His hands shaking, he took it from the wardrobe, placed it on the lab desk, and opened it.

The pages were crisp, slightly brittle to the touch. The lantern light fell on fantastical images of dismembered bodies, organs and skeletons, interspersed with bulky paragraphs in Latin and Greek. The crude beauty of the object fascinated him. Turning back to the title page, his eyes fell upon the Latin words: *De Humani Corporis Fabrica*.

Just then, he heard a floorboard creak loudly outside.

THIRTY-ONE

Irene rested her head against the window of the covered carriage, drinking in the cold air that blew over her chest and brought some colour to her cheeks. The smell of the rain and the flowers along La Rambla filled her senses. It felt like weeks since she'd been able to breathe.

She'd chosen a pearl-coloured evening dress and a velvet mantle for the occasion. The corset was restrictive, but remained preferable to the bustle that was still in fashion among some ladies.

She tried not to let her preoccupation show, so as not to worry Encarnita. Her husband had been in a fury of late, and that made her horribly fearful; these past years, Adell had been diligent in inculcating such feelings. She'd taken considerable precautions, and knew she could trust her maidservant, though she was quite aware that her husband would still end up finding out if she was seen with anyone in public. But she felt she had no choice.

Seeing Daniel at the funeral, and then his visit, had affected her more than she would like to have recognized. It had taken an enormous effort and sacrifice to resign herself to her marriage, to show docility and indifference – in the hope of protecting what was most important to her. And just as she'd reached the point where she felt the marriage was a lesser, and necessary evil, all the lies and half-truths upon which she'd built a life had come crumbling down – the moment she'd set eyes on Daniel.

He had changed, he was no longer the young, intelligent, if showy, man any more, the one whose conversation she so used to enjoy. Gone was the boy who would once look away when she laughed, along with the dreamer who'd had hopes for changing the world. He had a more contented aspect now, tempered by the years. But behind his eyes she could see dejection too – as though he no longer expected anything of anyone. Did he still suffer over what had happened? Did he, like here, harbour feelings of guilt? He had abandoned her, and she'd hated him for a long time. But the years had softened her rage, turning it to sadness, and her dreams had dissolved along with the memories.

Halfway along Las Ramblas de Sant Josep, the sumptuous landau turned up a small alleyway, and the buildings appeared to close in behind it.

Fleixa made his way across the newsroom and to the desk of Alejandro Vives, who at that moment was stretching back in his chair with his neck cradled in his hands. He cast a satisfied look across a couple of typed pages in front of him.

'My dear Fleixa, this here is the best article written since Sarah Bernhardt played Adrienne Lecouvrer at the Lírico.'

'I'm delighted for you. I was wondering if you had a moment?'

'Of course, what is it?'

'This,' said Fleixa, placing a newspaper down on the desk. It was an archive copy from the day after the fire at the Amat mansion. Vives frowned, his good spirits dashed.

'I remember this piece; I wrote it. A tragedy. You hadn't joined the paper by then, I don't think.'

'I also found these notes of yours, where you raise doubts about how the fire started.'

Vives rocked the chair forward and took up his notes.

'Did I?'

'Yes,' said Fleixa. He exaggerated, 'In your view it was pre-meditated.'

Vives looked at him gravely.

'It was a long time ago, I don't remember very well.'

'I'd appreciate it if you tried to.'

Vives looked annoyed. His previous ebullience gone, Fleixa was surprised to see he looked uncomfortable.

'Why are you so interested? Surely it's the definition of old news. Isn't present day Barcelona giving you enough to be getting on with?'

Fleixa gave him an impatient look.

'All right, all right,' Vives said, raising his hands. 'But what I'm about to tell you, you have to promise, it doesn't leave this room.'

'Naturally,' said Fleixa, settling himself on his colleague's desk. Sadness entered Vives's features, which intrigued Fleixa all the more.

'It was late, very late, and I was still in the office sorting out some problems with the next day's run. Then, as I was getting ready to leave, word of a mansion fire in Born came in – Martínez had sent his boy.'

250

Fleixa nodded. Martínez was a Guardia Civil paid by the paper – off the books – to send word of anything newsworthy. People suspected he was in the employ of several different papers, but after ten years of that no one minded overly.

'Go on.'

'When I got there, I remember being shocked by the sheer size of the fire; the flames illuminated the whole of the plaza in front, you approached and it was like broad daylight. People were shouting and screaming in the smoke, and the bells of the ambulances and the fire engines were ringing. Some Guardia lads were trying to clear a crowd that had gathered to watch, and the fire crew were trying to stop the fire from spreading to the adjacent properties, though the hoses weren't working properly – the steam pumps had got blocked.' Vives's gaze grew distant. 'I spoke to the officer. They'd given up trying to save the house. There was nothing they could do. He'd never seen anything like it, I remember him saying: it was like the whole place had been doused in pitch . . .' Vives's voice trailed off.

'Then?' Fleixa said.

'I went over to a group of servants standing on the pavement. A couple had wounds, but were in such a state they seemed not to notice. It could have been nothing, but I thought: the fear on their faces wasn't down to any fire. I tried to get a quote, but the only thing I managed to get out of them was that the fire hadn't started in the kitchen like the fire marshal had told me. Then I noticed a stable boy talking in a low voice with a maid. Apparently, when they got the young Señor Daniel out he'd been screaming, over and over, saying he'd killed everyone. I began asking questions, but the head butler showed up and they quickly buttoned their lips. I was shooed away.'

'If they were right, you know that Daniel Amat would have been confessing to the murder of his fiancée and his own brother?'

'I'm only telling you what I heard.'

'But that wasn't the end of it, am I right?'

Vives bit his lip.

'No, it wasn't. It really shook me up. It didn't seem open and shut to me, I couldn't stop thinking about what the servants had said. I began looking into the Amat and the Giné families. I asked everywhere, spoke to anyone I could find connected with either family, even bribed a few of the servants – all to try and work out what had happened that night.

'I managed to learn that, at the end of the eighties, Daniel Amat and his brother, Alec, a couple of kids from a good family, had one day been to a gala at the Liceo. In the interval, they happened to meet the Giné sisters and their father. Doctor Amat and Doctor Giné had been friends in their youth. Don Antoni Giné had established a practice in Cuba twenty years earlier, but certain problems had brought him back to Spain. He set up the New Bethlem Sanatorium, which had been a success, and he'd bought a magnificent estate in Collserola with the intention of settling in Barcelona for good. That meeting, however, wasn't in fact a coincidence: the two older men had orchestrated it.'

'Is this relevant?'

'Wait, Bernat. Don't make me lose my thread . . . So, the Giné girls, a very attractive pair by all accounts, had an insatiable desire to explore the city, which they'd only read about. Their elegance and their excellent education were widely spoken of.

252

Beyond that, the two girls couldn't have been more different. And largely, it turns out, that was because they weren't in fact sisters.' A smile briefly appeared on Vives's face. 'Irene, as you'll have guessed, was adopted. During the '78 uprisings in Cuba, Don Antoni, who was serving as a regimental doctor in a cavalry corps, came across her as a child, lying next to her mother's corpse after some skirmish in a village near Sancti Spíritus. It had been razed by the rebels. Being mestizo, she'd been abandoned by the villagers, and the Giné family, who only had the infant Ángela, took her in.

'Neither of the girls had been out of Cuba before, they didn't know anyone in Barcelona, so it was quite normal that Daniel and Alec should accompany them to functions and introduce them in their social circles. All the kind of things you'd expect: balls, the theatre, drives along the Ensanche. The girls caused quite a stir. The snowy-white beauty of one, the exotic good looks of the other: they couldn't help but stand out. They became a regular feature in the society pages.

'As for the two doctors, they couldn't have been more pleased with the way these friendships blossomed, to the point that, after some months, they agreed for their respective sons and daughters to marry. The only thing was, they neglected to find out if the youngsters were in agreement.'

'All very interesting, but what does it have to do with the fire?'

'Ángela was very attractive,' Vives continued, ignoring his colleague, 'and full of life. Daniel Amat was fond of her, but she didn't have his heart. She, however, felt a childish sort of love for him. At any other moment he might have been flattered, but the thing was that Daniel, in turn, had fallen for Irene – and in this case it was reciprocated. And to make it more complicated still, there was even gossip that the brother, Alec, had taken a fancy for Ángela, though I never found very much support for the idea. I don't know if you follow me.'

Fleixa did. He nodded.

'Irene wasn't entitled to any of the Giné inheritance. Don Antoni saw her as a daughter, treated her with great fondness, but that was as far as it went. Doña Francisca, the adoptive mother, also wouldn't have allowed anything more. Ángela was due to inherit. But Daniel didn't care about any of that, and he and Irene decided to reveal their feelings to the families, going against the fathers' agreement and asking for permission to marry. And if they weren't given it, Daniel was prepared to drop his studies, leave the family home and go away with her.'

'But something stopped him.'

'Disaster struck. I imagine you'll remember it – the repercussions were considerable. The Ginés were attacked on their way back from a charity event: their coachman fought back, shots were fired. Don Antoni took a slight injury to his arm, while Doña Francisca was gravely injured. Doctor Amat himself attended the Señora, but there was little to be done. On her death bed, she asked to speak to Ángela and Daniel and, with various witnesses, made them swear to carry out her final wish, which was for them to marry, have children, continue the family line. Ángela, in floods of tears, said they accepted. Her mother died a few hours later.

'And it was on the very same night that the tragedy unfolded.

'Irene broke it off with Daniel, feeling unable to oppose her half-sister's promise to her adoptive mother. Several witnesses

254

place Daniel in a number of taverns throughout the city that night, and two of the houseboys saw him come in very late. He'd been drinking, and rather than making his way to bed went down to the cellars, where his father kept a laboratory. The houseboys also said that Alec and Ángela had arrived in the house not long before, surely in search of Daniel.

'Though she was unable to verify the time, a maid who was snuffing the candles in the kitchen said that she heard a heated discussion from down in the cellar. She was alarmed, and considered waking the doctor, but when the arguments stopped she decided against interfering. Minutes later, the house was in flames.' Vives paused to light a cigarette. 'That's everything I found. The rest you already know. Sanchís made me leave it alone, case closed. People might hold it against me, but I have a family to feed. Daniel Amat disappeared soon after leaving the hospital. Following the burial, people stopped talking about Alec Amat and Ángela Giné. Until, that is, you come and decide to start poking around.'

'Do you believe Daniel Amat started the fire?'

Vives shrugged.

'Thanks, Alejandro. This has been a great help.'

'Great. Now do me a favour and don't breathe a word to anyone.'

Fleixa left the offices and, deep in thought, set off in the direction of the college, where he was due to meet Amat and the student. He ran through Vives's story. Suddenly Amat's tormented character made sense: forced to marry a woman he did not love and to forget, at the same time, the love of his life, only for it to come to the fire at the mansion, one he doubtless held himself responsible for. But what was the truth of it? What had happened down in that cellar? If someone had meant to start the fire, as Vives had insinuated, then why? A great many unanswered questions, but only one of them felt to him truly unsettling: was Daniel Amat a murderer?

He failed to notice the black carriage coming down the narrow street, until it screeched to a halt beside him. He was about to curse the coachman for the fright, but the coachman spoke first.

'Fleixa? Bernat Fleixa?'

'Maybe,' he said, wondering if La Negra could possibly be in possession of such a luxurious carriage.

The door opened and a young maid got out.

'Quick,' she said, 'get in.'

Fleixa did so, in spite of his misgivings. He looked up to find a lady of a dark, exotic beauty inside, and high society attire. Her brown skin melted into the unlit interior of the carriage, and her eyes sparkled in amusement to see the man in such a fluster. She was holding a closed fan. As the journalist appraised her, she pursed her lips ironically, sweeping aside a dark lock of hair from her forehead and giving him an intense stare. Fleixa coughed nervously, before remembering he ought to have removed his hat, which, feeling very clumsy, he then proceeded to do.

'I'm late for a meeting,' he said, and again felt ridiculous.

'Good afternoon, Señor Fleixa. Don't worry, the last thing I would wish is to waste your time.' Her soft voice had a slight Cuban accent. 'I don't believe we've had the pleasure. My name is Irene Adell.'

'Adell? Adell the industrialist – you're his wife?'

'Indeed.'

Not to mention you're also Daniel Amat's forbidden love, he thought, the woman he abandoned after causing your sister's death.

Irene half-opened the curtains with her long fingers and glanced out at the street.

'It's all right,' said Fleixa, seeing her worried look. 'No one need hear about this meeting, least of all from me. I'm capable of a little discretion. Though, to be frank, I have a sense you probably know what line of work I'm in, so you'll also know why discretion isn't exactly my speciality.'

The woman appeared to weigh his words. Fleixa hoped he hadn't put an end to the interview. He was extremely curious to speak to her.

'I quite understand,' she said finally. 'I trust that, once we've spoken, you *will* be discreet.'

Fleixa found himself nodding.

'I wanted to ask for your help with something.'

'If it's within my powers.'

'I want you to convince Daniel Amat to desist.'

Fleixa straightened up in surprise.

'I'm sorry, but you seem to be ahead of me: how do you know that Señor Amat and I know one another?'

'He came to see us on a personal matter, and your name came up when he was speaking with my husband.'

Fleixa came a little closer, suddenly even more interested.

'The inquiries you're both undertaking,' she said, 'will obviously entail certain risks.'

'I can hardly believe it!' The journalist laughed. 'Bertomeu Adell sending his wife to scare off the pesky journalist.'

A troubled look entered Irene's face.

'Apologies,' said Fleixa. 'Perhaps it isn't that.'

'I'm worried for Señor Amat,' she said. 'For his wellbeing. He's . . . an old friend. I don't want to see him put in an awkward position.'

'I share your concern, but why wouldn't you just go to Amat yourself?'

'I tried, but I fear I haven't convinced him.'

'I see. Still, I doubt that I—'

'Don't underestimate the effect you might have. Daniel speaks extremely highly of you. Your inquiries aren't my concern – that Daniel should be tangled up in them is. The bottom line is, I am willing to pay.'

She took an envelope from a small gilt purse and placed it in his hand. Fleixa opened it carefully, worried he might spoil the aroma that emanated from it. He almost whistled: it was enough to pay off La Negra and leave him with a good deal left over. Before he could change his mind, he slotted the envelope into his inside pocket.

'That's half,' said Irene. 'Half now, half, the same amount again, when you've done as you promise.'

'A most generous offer, Señora, and I'll do everything in my power,' he lied. 'I can't, however, guarantee that I'll be able to dissuade Amat.' Irene gave a questioning look. 'I'll do what I can, but I don't want to mislead you. Whatever I might say, the young man is intent on finding out the truth about his father's death.'

'I understand,' murmured Irene.

Fleixa was surprised that he felt regret – at not being able to offer the woman anything more. He wanted to say something to console her, but before he did, she lifted her head defiantly.

'There's something else I can offer you,' she said, 'an extra incentive.'

The journalist gestured for her to carry on; what apart from money?

'You'll know that my husband is involved in putting on the World Fair.' She waited for Fleixa to nod before continuing. 'So you will also know that he is in charge of construction at the power plant that's planned to supply electricity to the whole of the complex as well as the streets around La Ciudadela.'

'Yes, I know something of it.'

'Good. Well, Bertomeu is defrauding the investors.'

Fleixa started.

'That's quite an accusation, Señora. You're sure?'

'I'm in possession of certain documents that prove the syphoning of funds into other concerns of Bertomeu's, and others that show how those sums have been lost on a number of ill-advised ventures. Documents that will be yours if you do this thing for me.'

Fleixa tried not to show how excited he was: *this* was a scoop. Front page news, and then some. He couldn't help but admire the woman's daring: she surely wouldn't come away unscathed should her husband fall from grace. Was Amat's safety so important to her?

'You're aware of what it would mean if you were to inform on your husband like this?'

'I am. If Daniel Amat gives up his inquiries and goes back to

England, you'll have all the evidence you need, as well as the rest of the money.'

Irene tapped on the window with her fan, and the door opened. The maid stepped to one side as the journalist got down. Turning, he found Irene's eyes upon him – eyes, he thought, that one could very happily get lost in for a long time.

'I beg of you,' she said. 'Do this thing for me.'

Tilting his head, Fleixa touched the brim of his hat. The coachman geed the horses and the carriage pulled away, soon to be lost in the trees and shadows up ahead. Fleixa took a breath of the aroma that rose from inside his jacket – jasmine – and felt, with his whole heart, a moment of envy for Amat.

THIRTY-TWO

Placing the Vesalius and the Galen manuscripts in his bag, Pau came out of Homs's laboratory. Holding the lantern before him, he crossed the attic and peered out along the passageway. He was surprised to find all the lamps were out in the library, the only light the bluish brilliance of the moon through the windows. He checked his watch. He hadn't realized how late it had grown.

'Señor Ferrán?'

He would have expected the old librarian to come and fetch him at closing time. And now why wasn't he answering? Pau was certain he'd heard footsteps.

He peered into the shadows. The stillness, which at other times he so enjoyed, was now most unsettling. He found himself wishing the old man would appear from one of the aisles, annoyed at Pau's lateness.

Suddenly the thought came to him: what if the noise wasn't Ferrán, but someone else? He recalled Fenollosa's hateful look as they parted. He only needed to get Pau on his own to settle the score. This wasn't the most accessible part of the library, but the light from Pau's own lantern gave away his position.

He returned to the attic and placed the lantern on the table, closing the secret door and laying the sheet back over the furniture and boxes. The last thing he wanted was for Fenollosa to find out he'd been here, or what he'd found, particularly given they'd both been after the same book. Fastening the bag, he slipped out and crept back along the aisle.

Now the dark was to his advantage. He knew his way around the library far better than Fenollosa. If he thought he could get one over on him in here, he was wrong, very wrong.

He moved along to the adjacent aisle and hid behind the pharmacology shelves. Quietly removing a number of books for a peephole, and with the lantern still where he'd left it, he gave himself a good view.

Minutes passed and not a sound. Outside, clouds drifted in front of the moon, plunging the library into darkness again. The light from the lantern flickered inside the attic; the oil had nearly run out.

Hunched up in the cold library, Pau felt suddenly ridiculous. He remembered Ferrán once telling him how loud the old wood could be, shelves and floorboards warping and contracting in heat or cold. Most likely he'd imagined the footsteps.

He resolved to quit his hiding place. But, beginning to gather himself, he saw a shadow cross the lanternlight and enter the attic. Taken aback, he stood stock-still, before realizing now was the time to make his getaway. Fenollosa would see immediately that the place was empty.

Coming to the end of the second ring of shelves, he arrived

at the gallery railing. He could vaguely make out the maze of the library below. Feeling his way along the railing he came to one of the spiral staircases and descended – as quickly as he could, all stealth forgotten. He dived into the ground-floor aisles and, passing through several rooms, came finally to the central passageway. Realizing he'd been holding his breath, he let out a heavy sigh. The librarian's office was just there.

He went in without knocking – strange, he thought, for the lights to be out in there as well. The fire was still lit and as he entered he discerned a seated figure in the half-light: Ferrán was in his armchair, a book open in his lap. Pau said his name, and receiving no answer assumed the man had fallen asleep. He'd have to wake him.

Coming closer, he stifled a cry.

The old librarian's eyes were very much open, and a dark blot spread across the front of his shirt. The pages on which his hands rested were speckled with blood. A thin line of red ran around his neck; the incision had all but decapitated him.

A noise outside brought Pau from his stupor. He glanced at Ferrán once more and quickly left.

Scanning the dark, silent reaches of the library, his vulnerability was all too clear to him. The killer and the mysterious visitor up in the attic had to be one and the same, and there was every chance he was out there, waiting for Pau to venture forth.

He could barely check his panic as, hugging the bag to him, he dashed away from the light of the office and into the relative safety of the shadows.

★

The question kept repeating as he made his way along the aisles: who could it be? Not Fenollosa. He was capable of many things, but not murdering Ferrán in cold blood, surely? Who, then? And above all, *why*?

Leaving the biology rooms he came through into one of the wings of the library. He knew how easy it was to get lost in this section. He carried on for a few metres and then stopped, rested back against one of the shelf ends and slid down until his backside hit the floor. The manuscripts weren't light.

It seemed he'd got away. The killer, whoever it was, hadn't followed him. Only, Pau was now nowhere near the exit. He couldn't go back along the central aisle, that was too risky. He'd have to go the long way around to return to the foyer. He'd catch his breath and then do precisely that.

Then he sensed a presence in the adjacent aisle. Surely in his fear he was hearing things – but then, there it was again: footsteps. A shadow slipped over him and past. He tried to stay completely silent, hugging his legs and gritting his teeth. His heart was pounding so hard he thought the noise of it might give him away.

A few seconds later, the shadow disappeared, just as silently as it had come. Pau let out a sigh, feeling his shoulders drop.

Suddenly there was an explosion of books beside him; a gloved hand had burst through and was trying to grab him by the arm. Pau cried out and fell to one side. The hand withdrew. Through the gap in the books, Pau could just pick out a hooded figure in the darkness. It stood there, drawing measured breaths, the moon lighting up the blade in its hand.

'Who . . . Who are you?'

He received no answer. Struggling up, Pau strapped the bag on his back and fled without a backward glance. The killer started in pursuit, pacing along in the adjacent aisle, following with what felt to Pau like predatory patience.

Then he recalled that the stack separating them gave way a few metres up ahead; the two aisles would join in the ensuing room. If he didn't get there first, the killer would have him. He sped up – as did the killer.

They arrived into the space at the very same instant. Pau feinted to go right, but then suddenly stopped and threw himself at his pursuer.

The killer took the bulk of the impact as Pau slammed him back into a wrought-iron pillar. They fell to the floor in a heap. Pau, the first to get up, didn't wait for the killer to recover; he set off running, but straight away felt a tug on his trouser leg, and a spasm of pain in his arm, and stumbled. He just managed to keep his feet, and escaped down the nearest aisle.

As he advanced into the darkness, a cry of frustration from the killer echoed behind him. He shuddered.

He was running now without any thought of direction. He turned left and right, and changed course so many times he soon became lost. He thought he glimpsed hooded figures at the end of every aisle. His fear spurred him on until his legs would carry him no further. Once he had stopped, aside from the pounding in his temples, the library was completely still.

He checked the wound. Fortunately it was only skin deep and didn't restrict his movements. He fastened a handkerchief around it as he considered his next move. A few deep breaths:

he couldn't give up now. His only chance was to head straight for the foyer.

He traversed a number of aisles and came out into an open space surrounded by pillars and some glass-fronted display cabinets. The great dome stretched high above him, and he could half make out the dozens of partitioned tables and chairs. He'd arrived in the library's central reading room.

At a creak somewhere over to his left he dived beneath a nearby table. He clasped the bag to him and tried to be completely quiet, holding his breath as he mouthed a silent prayer. Outside, the clouds again covered the moon, dropping a dark mantle over everything.

Then, there was the killer once more. He stepped into the space, padding silently along as though the marble floors had been carpeted just for him, then halted. He appeared to sniff the air, and then came forward between the desks, before stopping mere centimetres from Pau's hiding place. Pau trembled at the sound of the killer's gloved hand running across the polished surface just above his head.

Then, as suddenly as he'd entered, the killer turned and left.

Pau gave it several minutes before coming out. His whole body was shaking now. He was struggling to stay steady on his feet, but forced himself on.

Leaving the reading room, he advanced with great caution along deathly quiet aisles. Each time there was a gap, just before he reached it, he'd pause and listen. But the killer seemed to have gone away, and he was nearly at the exit now. He was going to make it.

At that moment, all around him, the library grew suddenly bright.

As he came to the next corner, a wave of heat struck him. The Human Physiology section was in flames. The fire was devouring curtains and creeping forward along the tables and shelves. As it consumed the books a cloud of sparks and incandescent ash began drifting down. Soon the whole library would be ablaze.

Fury gripped him: the killer had started the fire to draw him out. It would spread, and soon become uncontrollable. If he didn't do something quickly, this place he loved would be reduced to ash. He had to get out, had to fetch help. And for that, he'd have to pass through the fire. Covering nose and mouth with a handkerchief, he advanced upon a gap in the flames.

He managed to make it to the foyer, eyes streaming from the smoke and heat. Stumbling blindly forwards until he found the door, his hands were still trembling as he groped around for the handle – he felt a wave of relief as his hand alighted on it. But though he turned it, nothing happened. In desperation, he turned it and pulled with all his might, but the door would not budge.

And then he felt a presence behind him. He turned to see the killer emerge from the flames, positioning himself between Pau and the library rooms – cutting off any possibility of escape. He calmly scanned the rest of the room, and then his eyes came to rest on Pau once more. He held out a hand.

His request floated on the air, as the fire crackled on. Pau knew straightaway what it was he wanted. But he also had a sense that even if he were to hand over the book, it wouldn't guarantee him his life.

'No.'

The figure moved forward so quickly Pau barely saw it. He received a blow to the face that unbalanced him, and then another to the ribs that sent him tumbling into a table. The flash of pain in his ribcage nearly caused him to drop the bag.

The killer grabbed him by the throat and pinned him back against the table. Pau was unable to move. The glove gave off the smell of blood. Pau tried to resist, but found himself completely drained of energy. The silver blade came sailing through the air towards his chest. He brought the bag up to protect himself, and the blade plunged into the leather, tearing it and causing the Vesalius manuscript to fall out. With a triumphant grunt, the killer let go of his victim and grabbed the book.

Pau tried to get away, but after a few steps his vision went blurry and he dropped to his knees, on the verge of passing out.

Having placed the volume inside his cloak, the killer turned his attention to Pau again. His shoulders shook as a sound issued from beneath his hood, like the rasping screech of some kind of bird. He took a step closer. This was it.

Suddenly, the door rocked on its hinges. Two further blows followed, and with a loud crack, the lock seemed to be about to break. Shouting could be heard outside, and bells had begun to chime.

The killer looked at the door and then at Pau. He hesitated, then seemed to smile. Bowing with an elegant flourish, he turned on his heel and was gone.

In the same moment, the door flew open and in burst Daniel and Fleixa, followed by the head porter and several students.

'Gilbert!' cried Daniel. Then, seeing the fire, he took a step back, his face distorted. 'Dear God!'

'Let's go!' said Fleixa, as the pair dragged Pau to his feet.

The porter was directing the students to bring water and raise the alarm.

'Homs,' whispered Pau. His throat was stinging.

'What's that?'

'Homs was here, in the library! He started the fire. He's just fled. And he's got the manuscript!'

THIRTY-THREE

As Daniel and Fleixa came out onto the street, they saw a two-horse landau driving away down Las Ramblas. They broke into a run but it was already far away.

'Damn! Could that have been Homs? Do you think?'

Daniel's answer was drowned out by a clap of thunder. Rain was falling heavily, and firemen's bells could be heard clanging in the distance. Making to go back inside the university, they heard shouting and the sound of hooves on the cobbles.

A cabriolet emerged from the sheets of rain. The driver, standing in the seat up in front of the hooded cab, slammed on the brakes, bringing the vehicle to a halt in front of the pair. It was Pau. Reins in hand, his face flushed, he called down to them.

'Get in!'

'What do you think you're doing?' objected Daniel.

'Just get in!'

Further down the street, a group of men appeared armed with riding whips. They rushed forward menacingly.

'You stole it?'

'Borrowed!'

'Have you lost your mind?' said Fleixa.

'Stay here if you'd rather, and you can explain to them.'

The journalist glanced at the approaching mob and, with a curse, got up. Daniel hid his smile as he took the seat next to Pau.

'Hold on tight. I'm not stopping if either of you fall out.'

Whirling the whip in the air, he cracked it above the horse, which set off again and was soon at a canter. The delicate cab was tossed from side to side and seemed in danger of flying clear of the chassis.

They saw the landau come past the Church of Bethlehem and turn onto La Rambla de los Capuchinos in the direction of the port. They reached the same turning within seconds.

Las Ramblas, bright beneath the newly installed electric lamps, were all but deserted, and the few people they did pass were sheltering from the downpour under café awnings. As the carriage flew by, a few cries of protest rang out. The lights and the trees passed by in a blur. Fleixa gulped – at this speed, any impact would be mortal.

'How did you know where to find me?' shouted Pau, driving the horse on.

'You didn't show, so we thought you'd still be in the library. Then we got there, saw the smoke.'

'Look!' cried Fleixa.

Up ahead, outside the Teatro Principal, a group of workmen were driving a team of mules to clear a caravan standing directly across Las Ramblas; a wheel had come off and numerous sand-bags lay in heaps. Homs would have to stop. A jolt of excitement ran through the trio. They had him.

Some of the men, noticing the approaching carriages, came forward waving their arms.

Rather than slowing the landau, Homs appeared to drive the horses even harder; at the sight of the enormous vehicle, the men abandoned the mules and scattered. With no one to keep it standing, the caravan toppled, spilling the rest of its contents across the cobbles.

Pau pulled on the reins. They watched Homs's suicidal dash in fascination: he surely couldn't survive this.

But just at the last second, the landau changed course, veering away and cutting through the thin gap between caravan and theatre.

One of the landau doors flew open and, along with one of the vehicle's lamps, bashed into the wall and were dragged screeching along it. The wheels scraped, sending up a shower of sparks. It looked briefly as though the landau would get stuck, but it had enough speed to bump aside the prone caravan and, with a violent jolt to the cabin, it passed through and continued on its crazed passage.

'We've lost him,' said Fleixa, half relieved.

But Pau's response was to urge on the horse, getting it up to a gallop again.

'Surely not?!'

The journalist's protest gave way to a cry of terror as Pau heaved sideways on the reins, sending the horse towards the gap. They avoided one of the piles of sandbags, and narrowly missed a banana tree, but all three passengers were thrown in the air as the wheels mounted the pavement. Loud grating noises came from the springs in the suspension and the wheel axis whipped about like a lizard's tail – but the thing held together. They shot on up Las Ramblas.

'Madness, madness . . .' said the journalist over and over, pinned against the back of the cabin, which was half hanging off now. A branch from the tree had become caught in the canvas roof, and the shreds fluttered about.

Daniel, gripping a handle, watched the younger man with incredulity.

'Where did you learn to drive like this?'

'Who told you I'd learned to drive?'

They heard Fleixa whimper behind them. Pau ignored him, geeing the horse once more with a whip of the reins. Homs's carriage forged on along the parallel street; a gap had opened, but they were gaining on him.

By the time they arrived onto La Rambla de Santa Monica the two vehicles were mere metres apart, with only the tree-lined central pavement separating them. The cabriolet horse was galloping as fast as it could, its hooves intermittently slipping in the incipient mud. But still Pau urged it to go faster, with Daniel's cries of encouragement in his ear.

Suddenly a public urinal appeared straight ahead of them. Pau heaved on the reins, and they narrowly avoided being thrown out. A gap had again opened up between them and the landau.

'He's getting away!' shouted Fleixa.

'I know, I know.'

'Catch him up!'

'What do you think I'm trying to do?'

273

Daniel was about to intervene, but words suddenly failed him. The other two also fell silent.

Trees and houses receded as they left Las Ramblas behind. They were about to join onto the Columbus Paseo when a giant reared up directly in front of them. Daniel recognized the immense monument surrounded in scaffold. They were headed straight for it.

Then Homs's landau was veering towards them. The two cabs crashed together with a grinding of wood and metal. Locked together, they flew down the last stretch of the Paseo. It wasn't an even contest: Homs's forced them towards the scaffolding, they in the lighter vehicle were powerless to resist.

Just as it seemed both were about to pile into the monument, Homs's landau broke away. By a matter of centimetres it avoided the nearest of the monument's braces, before disappearing into the shadows of the shipyards.

The cabriolet careened ahead. Daniel and Fleixa tried to apply the brake lever, and there was a juddering at the wheels. They slowed a little but then, with a crack that shook the whole carriage, the brakes snapped and came flying off.

Just as it was about to strike the first iron post, the horse suddenly swerved away. Daniel wanted to cry out in relief. And then the wheel axis reached breaking point, and as it split in two flung them into the enormous iron structure.

The impact with the scaffolding was formidable: the right wheel flew up into the air, throwing the cabriolet to one side as its momentum carried it forward. Fleixa was thrown to one side, and though Daniel tried to grab him, he ended up hitting his own head and collapsing unconscious into the cab. Pau seized hold of the railing, trying in vain to steer.

They ploughed on, severing some of the ropes and cords that held down the couplings. Splinters flew from the shattered wheel. A metallic groaning issued from the scaffold. The cabriolet, a wreck of wood, metal and canvas, but until this point somehow still attached to the maddened horse, now split off, and the cab flipped over and went sliding on, raising water and mud as it went. It came crashing towards the seawall, with such momentum that it flipped over it. For a brief moment it seemed to float upon the air, before falling into the dark expanse of the port. The cold of the water brought Daniel to. The remnants of the cabriolet sank beside him. He could make out Fleixa in the dark – he was treading water and waving his arms. A little way to his left, Pau floated motionless. He swam over as quickly as he could. The youngster had a nasty cut to the forehead. Daniel got hold of him and dragged him over to some stone steps.

'Help me, Fleixa.'

Together they extracted Pau from the water and lay him down beneath a streetlamp. Pau, his face very pale, looked even younger without his glasses. He was unconscious and didn't appear to be breathing. Daniel decided to remove his wet clothes, and began tearing open his shirt, but as the first buttons came off, Daniel suddenly stopped. Next to him, Fleixa let out a curse and took a couple of backward steps.

Gilbert's torso was bound in strips of cloth. Beneath, there was the outline of a female body, breasts.

The shock paralyzed them both for a moment, before Daniel

stood up, resolved. There would be time for explanations later on.

'Quick,' he ordered the journalist. 'Get the legs.'

He removed the jacket and shoved it under Gilbert's shoulders, tilting the head back. Kneeling down, he took her wrists and crossed them over the base of the ribs. He took a breath, and brought his weight down on her thoracic wall, before lifting her arms straight up in the air.

The whistles of the nightwatchmen began to fill the air, and the lights in the nearby houses began coming on. It wouldn't be long before they had quite the audience.

Several times Daniel repeated the procedure, but without any reaction from Gilbert.

'Damn it, come back!'

Daniel brought his fist down in frustration, causing Gilbert to jerk forwards and begin gasping for air. Daniel and Fleixa supported her as she coughed and vomited a large amount of seawater. Sighs of relief went around. They carefully lifted her up and laid the jacket across her shoulders, forgetting it was as wet as the rest of her clothes.

'You all right?'

Pau nodded between shivers.

'Wonderful. Now I think you've got some explaining to do.'

THIRTY-FOUR

Pau, wrapped in a woollen blanket, shivered uncontrollably. Head bowed, her wet hair fell forward over her face. A steaming cup of coffee was clasped between her hands.

A circumspect Daniel watched the flickering firelight as Fleixa hobbled back and forth across the room muttering to himself, pocket watch in hand.

'Will you please just sit down?'

Fleixa grumbled, but did as he was asked, taking a chair and placing it at a prudent distance from the girl, seemingly worried he might catch something from her.

They'd come back to the university. To their great surprise, they'd escaped the attentions of the nightwatchmen and the Guardia Civil. More incredibly, they'd come away from the crash with little more than bumps and bruises, and Fleixa's limp was only a sprained ankle. He'd be better in a few days.

Daniel regarded Pau – though he wasn't even sure if that was her name. How stupid he'd been, he thought. Pau had always seemed somehow unusual, with that slight frame, the delicate manner, never meeting your eye. Though he'd suspected there might be something being hidden, *this* had never entered his mind.

'You owe us an explanation.'

Pau looked up and let out a sigh.

'It's complicated.'

'Oh really?'

'Come on, Fleixa, more pressure is hardly what's needed.'

'It's a long story.'

'We've got time. Start at the beginning.'

After a pause, Pau began to speak. 'I was born to a well-off family. My mother died in childbirth and I had no siblings. My father was never interested in taking another wife, and so I was an only child. He was a doctor, a good one, and we lived relatively comfortably. When I was about to turn fourteen, he was invited to take up a post at the University of Glasgow, which he at first said no to, on my account. I did all I could to make him change his mind; I was young but I still understood what a wonderful opportunity it was for my father.'

'Glasgow is one of the most prestigious universities in the world,' said Daniel. 'You father must be quite the doctor.'

'Yes, he was,' Pau said proudly. 'We finally made the move, settling in a place called Beith, an hour outside Glasgow. He gave classes in the mornings and had a small clinic at home where he saw patients in the afternoon, mostly free of charge.'

'What has this got to do with *this*?' exclaimed Fleixa.

'Let her tell it,' said Daniel. 'Do us the favour of staying in your seat and not interrupting.'

Pau nodded a thank you before going on. 'One night as I

was preparing for bed, my father came in to see me. I don't think I'd ever seen him look so concerned. He'd been called to an emergency, but the man who usually helped him was ill. I'd helped him on occasion, minor cures and the like, and so I dressed again and went out with him.'

She moved her body a little closer to the fire.

'There had been an accident in Lochwinnoch, a town about half an hour from us. Some boilers had burst and a number of people were killed, others badly wounded. As you can imagine, the scene we found there was unlike anything I was accustomed to.

'The place they'd set up as a waiting room was overflowing with the wounded. The awful smell has never left me. We went into the consulting room, and inside, on the operating table, lay a boy, roughly the same age as me. He looked terrified. There was a large patch of blood on the sheet that covered him. My father said a few soothing words to the boy and took the cloth away; his clothes were singed and in rags, and most of his torso looked like it had been flayed, or like he'd been boiled. One of his legs bent back oddly. The pain must have been unbearable. I remember my father looking to see if I was going to be able to do this. I immediately washed my hands in hot water, just as he'd shown me, and hurried to get his implements ready for him.

'The boy was just one of the injured. We worked into the early hours, I lost track of time completely. That boy died, in spite of my father's efforts, but we did save a good many others. And that was how it all began; I discovered my vocation. Becoming a doctor was all I wanted to do with my life.'

'So your father trained you?'

'Exactly. I had to badger him, but he started allowing me to go with him to see patients – I suppose he hoped I'd be put off. But instead I showed him that I was really serious about it, and he allowed me to carry on.'

'But as a woman, you shouldn't have even been there helping him.'

'We found ways. I've always been slight, so it wasn't hard to hide my . . . feminine characteristics. I cut my hair and started wearing trousers and shirts. I only spoke when I had to, and then would put on a deeper voice, and used the kind of vocabulary you'd expect of a doctor. We started telling people that I had gone back to Barcelona to marry and that my twin brother had come to assist my father. The servants at the house knew but told no one.'

Pau peered into the cup.

'We spent three years like that, the happiest years of my life.' Her eyes sparkled at the memory. 'I found I had an innate talent for all things medical, and more than anything just a passion that meant I could devour books, and wanted to be working with my father all the hours God sent. Instead of learning to sew and play piano, I was there applying ointments and mending people's wounds. My father was not a young man then, and began to find the constant travelling to Glasgow, and the clinical work, very taxing. I gradually began to take over from him; some patients I began seeing without him. People started to know me, and it became quite normal for them to address me as "Doctor". My father was proud.'

Pau's lips began to tremble, and neither of the others said anything as she stopped to reflect.

'One night word came from a place called Saltcoats, a village quite nearby. The farmer's wife had gone into labour. There had been storms in the area for the previous couple of days, the rain was still coming down, the roads were just awful. And my father, as if it had been high summer outside, prepared his bag and got into the cart with the man who'd brought the message. That time he didn't let me come along; I'd been ill the past few days and still had a touch of fever. No need for us both to get drenched, he said to me. He kissed me before he left. And on their way back from the birth, the driver lost control of the cart and it came off the track. As they fell, one of the wheels flew off and struck my father, killing him.'

Pau sipped mechanically at the coffee, which was stone cold by now; she didn't notice.

'I couldn't live in Scotland with my father dead. I went to London and enrolled at the Florence Nightingale School for Nurses, part of St Thomas' Hospital. But I knew straightaway it wasn't for me.' A determined look entered her face. 'A surgeon was what I wanted to be. I'd already spent several years engaged in the kinds of tasks a young doctor would give anything to be working on. My father had only seen the future doctor in me, whereas, in the eyes of society, I was nothing but a woman, and therefore no good.'

Hard not to see the injustice, thought Daniel.

'I spent several weeks considering my options. There was little pressure financially: my father had left his affairs in good order, and I had an income from that. My view was, if I wanted to be a doctor, I shouldn't let anything stop me. If I had to become a man, so be it – hadn't I been a man already, for a number of

281

years? But it couldn't be in England. I resolved to come back to Barcelona in my new guise: no one knew me here, I'd train as a surgeon here. I managed to raise some fake, very expensive certificates from the University of Edinburgh, took the first train to Portsmouth, and then came directly here off the boat to present my qualifications. And was allowed to start in the Faculty of Medical Science as a final year student.'

'And what's your real name?' asked Daniel.

'Pau Gilbert – there wasn't any need to change it.'

'And has this got anything to do with that man attacking you in the alley?'

'Yes,' she conceded. 'He was a servant at the house for a short time. He saw me and recognized me. He threatened to reveal my true identity, unless I hand over a large sum of money.'

'The cur! What do you plan to do? Perhaps we could help.'

'It's my affair.'

Her determination impressed Daniel. She clearly didn't want to carry on along that line, so he decided to change the subject.

'But it is true that you worked for my father?'

'Yes, and he was very good to me. I was careless one day, and he worked out my secret. I was amazed: instead of going straight to the Faculty Board, because he saw that my medical skills outweighed the limitations of my sex, he agreed to keep my secret – if I would help him in his quest. I think that, in his way, Señor Amat, your father felt as unjustly treated as I did.'

Once more Daniel was hearing talk of his father in terms he barely recognized. The man he'd known, Don Alfred Amat i Roures, would have thought Pau's imposture scandalous, but not only had he shown understanding, he'd agreed to help maintain the subterfuge. Daniel felt a pang of regret over his ignorance of his father's true character – seemingly so different from the one he remembered. Perhaps reconciliation wouldn't have been impossible after all.

'All right,' said Fleixa. 'What now?'

Daniel turned to the journalist.

'What do you suggest?'

'It's a pretty odd situation.'

'For my part, it doesn't bother me if Pau's a man or a woman. You?'

'Well . . .'

'Today's been rather full in my view,' said Daniel, cutting him off. 'Rest is what we need. After all that's happened this evening, I say we ought not to be seen together tomorrow. Wednesday afternoon we'll make a start trying to get the book back.'

'All three of us?' asked Fleixa, incredulous.

'Of course. Providing Gilbert agrees.'

'But Amat! We can't . . . we can't . . . She's a woman!'

'A woman who happens to have risked her life trying to get that manuscript back, and whose medical knowledge seems pretty unsurpassed. If my father thought she'd do, who are we to argue?'

Fleixa grumbled, but said no more.

'So you won't tell anyone?' Pau asked.

'You have my word, your secret is safe with Señor Fleixa and me. Right?'

The journalist shifted uncomfortably in his seat, but nodded to show he was with them. Daniel smiled and turned back to Pau.

283

'We need your knowledge but we also need your bravery. What do you say, will you agree to help us?'

'I'm just as keen as you to try and catch this murderer.'

'Excellent!' Daniel exclaimed. 'We need to get organized. First there's something else to deal with though. You can't stay at the university, Pau.'

'Why not?'

'Homs knows your face now, and where to look for you. He might come after you again.'

'I don't have anywhere else,' she protested. 'And I don't want to drop my studies either. It's Finals soon.'

'Your life is in danger. And it won't be for long.'

'But where can I go?'

Fleixa raised his hand and, for the first time that evening, smiled. 'I think I have just the place.'

THE BLACK HOUND

Eleven days before the start of the World Fair

THIRTY-FIVE

Walking arm-in-arm with Fleixa, Dolors was beaming. The journalist had asked her out for *chocolate con churros* at La Mallorquina, directly across from the Liceo. He never usually spent money on her and so, invited to stroll at his side in the pale morning sunlight, she felt nothing less than a queen.

The looks she attracted from passersby couldn't have mattered less to her, or that Fleixa seemed more pensive than usual. She'd put on her best dress, a present from a client years ago. The cold of the day left her indifferent too, and her plunging neckline drew the eyes of many a gentleman – and the scowls of many ladies. Dolors loved to promenade like this, playing the upper-class lady, and, holding Fleixa close, for a moment allowed herself to feel that this life of hers hadn't been filled with such bad luck.

Fleixa's thoughts, meanwhile, were on the increasingly complicated case. Less than twenty-four hours ago they'd been chasing Homs along these very streets. The pain in his leg and the stinging cuts on his arm were reminders of just how close they'd been to catching him.

And what about Gilbert? Gilbert the girl! Who could have foreseen that? From the start he, *she*, hadn't seemed right to Fleixa: now at least he knew why. Daniel had insisted they go along with her masquerade, and for the moment there was nothing Fleixa could do but comply.

And then there was Sanchís, on at him to publish – it didn't matter what, just publish, his editor had said – yelled, to be accurate. Llopis was keeping track of all Fleixa's moves – he'd been sniffing around down in Barceloneta a couple of days before. The boy had a good nose, Fleixa couldn't deny it. He was still a fool though.

And then, lastly, Irene Adell. The money was hugely welcome, and if he blew sharp practice on the part of a lead industrialist, the defrauding of World Fair investors no less, it would make for astonishing copy, but convincing Amat to give up his quest was hardly going to be straightforward. Irene Adell clearly wasn't concerned about the spate of murders, she simply wanted Amat out of the city. Perhaps, Fleixa thought, he could carry on under his own steam with Amat gone. The whole of the front page would be his, guaranteed, not to mention him becoming the most famous journalist in Barcelona – perhaps in all of Spain.

Just then, he jumped. Dolors's shameless hand was going where it shouldn't.

'Behave,' he said, but she gave a disarming wink. And her quick caress had had its effect. 'How about we head back to your rooms?'

She unlinked arms, creasing her lips like a cross child.

'Not yet, Bernat. Let us walk *a little*.'

She turned away and advanced along Las Ramblas ahead of him, sashaying provocatively. Fleixa couldn't help but smile at her unabashedness – everyone was watching now. He burst out laughing as she bowed exaggeratedly to a scandalized couple, who, hurrying away, tried to pretend they hadn't noticed. Still chuckling, Fleixa took her by the arm again.

'Want someone to call the Guardia?'

'I can't help it if I have impeccable manners,' she said. 'Anyway, I could hardly have ignored them; that gentleman and I are already quite well acquainted.'

Fleixa frowned; he never liked hearing about her other clients. To change the subject, he brought up the reason he'd asked her out. 'I have a favour to ask, Dolors.'

'Of course!' she exclaimed, letting go of his hand. 'Now I see.'

'See what?'

'There had to be a reason you were being so nice.'

Her disappointment hurt Fleixa. And, he was surprised to find, he was actually reluctant to break up the nice time they were having. But it had to be done. With a deep breath, he went on. 'I need you to put someone up for two or three days.'

'In my rooms? What do you think this is, the Internacional?'

'She's in a bad spot. Somebody's after her, she needs to lay low for a little while.'

Dolors stopped next to a flower seller, showing exaggerated interest in a bunch of daisies. '*She?*'

'It isn't what you think.'

'And I shouldn't mind anyway, right?' she said, not looking at him.

Fleixa cast a look to the heavens. 'She's a young girl. She's in danger. The person responsible for the crimes I've been looking into knows where to find her. She needs help, Dolors.'

She considered the request. 'If she's somehow important in putting an end to the curse, I'll do what I have to. Some of the Black Hound's victims were friends of mine.'

'There is no curse, and there is no devil dog – I've told you. That's all servant gossip.'

'If you say so. The girl can use Manuela's room, she's gone home to see her parents for a few days. I'll try and spruce the place up a little.'

'Thank you, sweetheart.'

'Save it – this is going to cost you.'

'That's all right, though I'm going to need to defer payment.'

Dolors paused with her hand on a gardenia petal, and turned to the journalist.

'How much do you owe now?'

'A little.'

'How much.'

'Five hundred, give or take.'

'Five *hundred* pesetas!' she cried.

People stared. Fleixa linked his arm in hers again and pulled her along, much to the flower seller's annoyance, who'd thought he had a sure sale.

'Quiet! Do you want all of Barcelona to find out?'

'I don't have that kind of money, Bernat.'

'I'm not asking you for money, dear. I'm on top of it.'

'Who have you borrowed it from?'

'La Negra.'

'La Negra? *That's* why I've been seeing so much of you. This is serious – you ought to be hiding properly, or getting out of the city.'

'I can't leave now. Anyway, take it easy. I know what I'm doing.'

Dolors gave him an incredulous look, and was about to reply when a nearby commotion drew their attention.

They were up at Plaza Catalonia by now. Over the road, a couple of newspaper vendors seemed to be being mobbed. Fleixa wanted to carry on, but Dolors tugged on his arm

'All those people!'

'Enough rubbernecking, let's head back.'

'Come on, spoilsport.'

She broke away and went over to the crowd, making liberal use of her elbows, apologizing and smiling in turn as she waded forward. Fleixa received some insults as he tried to keep up, and he pulled his hat down low to try and hide his face; he didn't want anyone to recognize him today.

People's anger seemed to rise the closer they came to the vendors, and there was fear in the air too. He caught a few strands of the conversation: something about the authorities doing nothing. He couldn't help but worry that it was the previous night's incident they were talking about.

Then he saw the young cripple boy selling the *Correo de Barcelona*. The cart he was leaning against was all but empty of papers. They were going like hotcakes – Sanchís would be thrilled.

But then he heard the headline, and his heart skipped. Leaving caution aside, he dived directly through the bodies, ignoring the queue that had formed.

'Give me that paper.'

'I'm sorry, this gentleman is just taking the last one.'

A very overweight man with a top hat and cane was standing in front of the boy, and gave Fleixa a look of clear disdain. The coins were ready in his hand.

Fleixa snatched the paper from the boy and handed over the five centimos. The man's voluble protests fell on deaf ears as Fleixa strode away, a surprised Dolors in tow.

They found an empty bench on the Plaza and sat down. Fleixa almost tore the pages as he flicked through to find the piece. As he read, each new paragraph felt like a blow to the gut.

TERRIBLE EPISODE IN LA BARCELONETA: AUTHORITIES DO NOTHING

The most awful sequence of events has taken place in our beloved city, with no one acting to put a stop to it. Several bodies have been found in the vicinity of the World Fair site in recent months, each exhibiting signs of extraordinarily violent deaths. The authorities have tried to keep a lid on things, but to no avail. The city is abuzz with rumours.

The murders would appear to be linked. Each of the bodies is said to have been subjected to some sort of animal attack – an animal with the most enormous jaws. There is talk of the presence of a demon-animal that people are calling 'The Black Hound'.

Your correspondent caught up with his Excellency the Mayor at an event held at the Palacio de la Virreina: though initially reluctant to comment, Señor Ruis did urge calm, as well as caution. He played down suggestions that the killer could be on some twisted moral quest (a number of the victims have plied their trade in the less virtuous realms of our city), pointing to the fact that one of the victims was a man, and gave similarly short shrift to the idea of a philanthropic executioner wishing to draw attention, at all costs, to the plight of these unfortunate souls. A bloodthirsty maniac, was the Mayor's view, one, he assured us, whom the Guardia Civil would shortly catch: once the individual becomes aware of the efforts being made to locate him, he would surely turn upon himself the same weapon he has used against his victims. No reward was offered, with the Mayor citing those occasions when the promise of a reward has led to the death of innocents, who are then offered up as criminals. The Mayor expressed confidence in his deputies. Asked for his thoughts on the curse of the Black Hound, Señor Ruis rejected the idea as an old wives's tale, and exhorted all Barcelonans to trust in the authorities.

Down in La Barceloneta, however, the fear is palpable. Taverns and shops are suffering as people opt to stay indoors, and women will no longer venture out after dark. And numerous witnesses have spoken of an enormous canine seen roaming the streets . . .

Who might the mysterious killer be? How has he evaded his pursuers all this time? Is it, as so many believe, really the Black Hound? Is some diabolical entity abroad on our very own Ramblas?

The byline went to one Felipe Llopis.

Shutting his eyes, Fleixa balled up his fists and squeezed until they hurt. And then, without bidding Dolors farewell, he rose and headed back down Las Ramblas. At the first bin he came to, he screwed up the *Correo* and flung it inside.

THIRTY-SIX

Papers flew as a heavy fist slammed down onto the desk. Bertomeu Adell cursed. The gall! He glanced back down at the article that, by now, all of Barcelona would be talking about.

The *Correo* had broken the story, even going into particulars about the dead bodies, and then the other papers' second editions had run with it. All the headlines were similar in tone: *World Fair Murder Spree: Black Hound to Blame?*; *Authorities Fail to Act as Murder Spree Goes on*; *Curse Throws World Fair into Doubt*.

The city was in uproar. In the cafés they talked of nothing else. Apparently special editions had had been ordered after the ordinary print runs had sold out. Some of the pieces even mentioned him by name. The Mayor had sent several messages demanding an explanation. It wouldn't be long before he'd have to go and show his face at the Town Hall again.

He struck the table once more. *How?* And who was this Llopis, who seemed to know so much?

The work at the plant continued unabated, though the gory details were also being shared around there like a flask of brandy.

The cries of the owner inside his office had not gone unnoticed, nor what sounded like the smashing of glass. No one dared say anything.

'Casavella!'

The foreman came out from behind one of the steam engines, sweating from the work, and made his way to the office at the end of the bay. Through the frosted glass, Adell saw the figure stop and hesitate, and roared out, 'Get *in* here!'

Entering, Casavella couldn't hide his astonishment at the state of the office; it was as though the storms that had been lashing the city this past week had stopped by. The refreshment table was in pieces next to the stove, papers were strewn across the floor, a buckled lamp lay beside a packet of loose tobacco that had been shredded, the leaves mixed in with coffee and spilt milk.

Adell, sitting at his desk with a dozen or so newspapers before him, was so flushed it reminded Casavella of the boilers he was in charge of. The veins in his neck stood up and he was breathing heavily. As Casavella came in he instinctively took a step back.

'Where are you going?' said Adell, looking up. 'Get in here and shut the damned door.'

The foreman gulped, and did as he was told, and took up position in a corner, awaiting instructions. Adell was clearly making a great effort not to fly off the handle – though he still more or less spat his words.

'I'm going home. Have them bring my carriage around.'

Casavella's eyes grew wide as he noticed his employer's blood-soaked sleeve. He thought he should see if a doctor was wanted, but when Adell saw what he was looking at, his face turned angrier still.

'What?'

'Nothing, Señor.'

'Get someone to come and tidy this lot up. I want it ship-shape when I return. Understood?'

'Yes, Señor.'

'Well, so why are you standing there gawping? Stupid or something?'

'No, Señor. Sorry, Señor.'

Casavella went out, followed by Adell with one of the papers in hand. He marched along the central gangway between the generators, with all the workers studiously avoiding eye contact.

The landau was outside waiting for him. Before he got in he ran his hand over a number of deep scratches on the door. They'd been waxed, but that had done little to hide them. A silver lamp in the shape of a horse hung loose. Once Adell had taken up his seat, he said to the coachman, 'Ramón, change this door, would you? First chance you get.'

The reply reached him through the roof hatch. 'Of course, Señor.'

'Good – I don't want to have to tell you again. Now, home.'

They were back within a few minutes, the landau stopping in the mansion's inner courtyard. Getting down, Adell ignored the butler who stepped forward to greet him and proceeded directly to the library.

A man awaited him there, pacing nervously back and forth in front of the street windows. Adell, instead of greeting him, went over to the drinks cabinet and served himself a large measure of cognac. Drinking half in one go, he moved over to an armchair and sat. He pointed his guest to another chair and the man, complying by also taking a seat, began to speak.

'I got your message, Señor Adell, and as you can see I've come, but I think you should know I consider it not very prudent for us to meet in your home like this. One of the servants might recognize me, and who knows who they might tell. Better we were discreet,' said Inspector Sánchez, reaching into his pocket for a newspaper cone.

'Don't you dare start stuffing your face in my house.'

The policeman, shocked by Adell's tone, did not reply. Sniffing, he replaced the salted peas.

Adell interlaced his fingers as if at prayer, bringing them pensively to his lips. His countenance radiated rage.

'You've seen the papers?'

'I . . . have.'

'I wouldn't have thought it.'

He threw the copy of the *Correo* at him and Sánchez, speechless, gathered the sheets to him.

'Well?' spat Adell. 'Haven't I paid you enough to avoid this kind of thing?'

Sánchez shook his head as he cast an eye over the article. 'It's gossip, nothing more. This reporter doesn't have anything concrete, I'm convinced. He's written a piece based on street talk – he hasn't actually seen any of the bodies himself. We made the last one disappear the second it was found. No one laid eyes on it but us,' he lied. He knew *someone* had been to the morgue, but didn't see any reason why Adell needed to know that.

'Can you get your tiny mind around the ramifications?'

297

'I believe so. The Mayor sent me a message last night, and he seemed bent on putting a stop to the murders as well. I've tried to keep it as quiet as I can, but I don't know how much longer I can do that.'

'I do not have time for this . . . How does this hack know so much about the *states* the bodies were found in?'

'He could have tapped one of my men – I can't be responsible for every single person on the force. Though if it was, rest assured I'll find out who, and they will be punished. The man at the *Correo* is just going on rumours, Señor Adell, I'm certain of that. There's been talk of this Black Hound in Barceloneta for quite some time now. Girls are disappearing, people are scared. There's nothing I can do about that.'

The industrialist leaned closer to Sánchez who, though he was a good head taller, still felt intimidated.

'But there should be.' Adell sighed deeply, before sitting back again. Taking another gulp of his cognac, he went on. 'Daniel Amat's still in town, he's got some hack helping him, as well as a medical student now. They're starting to poke around in things that don't concern them, truly. Didn't I tell you to warn him away?'

'I told him in no uncertain terms that nothing would come of his inquiries. I told him it wasn't a good idea.'

'Well, tell him again – spell it out!'

Sánchez shrugged. Adell had to stop himself from screaming.

'In case you haven't noticed, Inspector, I won't be the only one to suffer should these inquiries go on. With my contacts, I'll be able to send you to the farthest reaches of Santiago de Cuba to ply your trade. Are we clear?'

Now Sánchez was worried – though the thought also occurred to him about whether Adell had really paid enough for all this.

'Of course, Señor. Leave it to me. I have some ideas.'

'You don't want to let me down, Sánchez. Truly, you do not want to let me down.'

Reaching out and picking up a small bell, Adell called in a servant to show Sánchez the door.

Once he was alone, Adell tried to calm himself. He took some slow, deep breaths, the way they'd shown him at the sanatorium. In this state, he knew he was capable of doing something he'd regret. He needed to calm down, and to think. Think, that was the thing, *think*.

Then he heard the boards creaking above him.

He jumped out of his chair, came dashing through the hallway and ran upstairs. Reaching the top, he saw the door to his office swinging shut.

'Little slut,' he said to himself. 'She won't get away with it this time.'

He threw the door open and entered. Irene, jolted by the loud bang, fell to the floor. Her dress and petticoats fell open and Adell drank in the sight of her long ebony legs. A rush of desire filled him as he took in her Creole curves; his eye came to rest on her bust, which rose and fell with her agitation, accentuating what lay beneath. She could see what he was thinking, and with a disdainful look got to her feet. Ashamed, should he be, thought Adell? His excitement turned to fury.

'What do you think you're doing? Didn't I forbid you from coming in here?'

'The girl left a hair tie.'

'She's like you, spoiled. I'm going to have to pay closer attention to her upbringing.' He smiled, knowing the reaction his words would produce. 'A little boarding school discipline will do her good.'

'No! You wouldn't dare!' Irene rushed at him, but Adell knocked her aside.

'Ungrateful half-caste bitch. I'd be better served by a whore down in the Raval.'

He slapped her, knocking her back into the desk. Adell went and made sure the door was locked. He walked slowly towards her, removing his belt deliberately. Irene's eyes dilated in terror but she didn't cry out; her body started to shake violently.

'Is there anything you want for?' Adell whispered. 'Haven't I given you far more than any other person would in the same situation? And this is how you repay me, disrespecting me under my own roof. Not any more. You *will* learn, even if you have to learn the hard way.'

Bringing the belt down, Adell felt his excitement grow. He raised it again, and delightful sensations coursed through him. He'd feel much better after this – much, much better.

THIRTY-SEVEN

Much as Fleixa would have enjoyed cracking Llopis's head open, he managed to control himself as he passed him in the newsroom. Llopis thought he'd won the battle, but he'd show him: winning the war was a different matter. He knocked on the office door and a voice bid him enter. The heat from the stove, along with the perennial fug, hit him like entering a sauna.

'Praise be, if it isn't Bernat Fleixa.'

'Good morning, Sanchís,' he said, shutting the door and taking a seat before he was offered one.

The veteran editor gave him a look over his glasses. 'My God, the day is a good few hours old and you do not yet smell of horse shit. How can that be?'

'New man.'

'Of course!' Sanchís put aside the paper he was reading. He crossed his arms, gave a sceptical squint. 'What is it then?'

'I've read the piece you let Llopis publish.'

'And?'

'You know I was after that same story.'

301

'I know what you've *told* me . . .'

'It's *my* story.' He paused, trying to stop his feelings from running away with him. 'He's a scribbler, a penny-a-liner, he hasn't got a clue. I want you to let me run with the story from now on.'

Sanchís arched an eyebrow.

'You do, do you? You're telling me how to run the paper?'

Fleixa knew he was on shaky ground, but couldn't help himself. 'How could you publish something like that? The Black Hound? Some imp going around killing people? Since when has the *Correo* run pap like that?'

Sanchís's face turned a shade of scarlet. Because he knows I'm right, thought Fleixa.

'That edition sold out in two hours. All the other papers took the same line, after we broke the story. My printers downstairs are working over, *over*time. People die in this city every day, but what people love to read about is a mystery – they're like flies to shit for the gory details.'

Fleixa couldn't contain himself. 'Christ in heaven, Sanchís! There's a whole lot more to it than the gossip Llopis has dished up for you.'

'More? Really. So where's this bombshell you've been promising? Tell me! Where? News, Fleixa, news. I said it before, in the streets they want news, and the juicier the better.' Then, in a lower voice, he added, 'You can't say I didn't warn you.'

'What's that?'

Sanchís came around the table and opened the door. 'Llopis, in here.'

The younger writer seemed to be expecting the call. He took

his time walking to the office, and came and stood before the two men. Sanchís prodded Fleixa in the chest.

'Until I have something from you I can actually put in print, this discussion is over. And until such time, I'm also promoting Llopis to head of current affairs. Whatever he says, goes.'

'Are you being serious?'

'And plain, I hope: do as I say, show me there still exists a journalist in that thick head of yours, or you're going to have to find yourself a new employer.'

Llopis's smile seemed on the cusp of touching both ears – Fleixa could almost feel the man's ego inflating – it was like the enormous globe they'd installed outside the Liceo for the inauguration. Fleixa thrust his face into Sanchis's, and, before he could stop himself, the words were out of his mouth.

'To hell with you.'

He turned and left, ignoring the shouts behind him and, as he crossed the newsroom, trying to stop the trembling of his extremities. He was aware that everyone was looking, though his vision was clouded. He didn't know how it had come to this. What was worse, he had no idea what to do next.

THIRTY-EIGHT

Pau paused on the landing. Her trunk was so heavy she'd struggled to get it up the narrow staircase. Taking the note the journalist had written, she checked the address once more. She couldn't imagine why the landlord had looked so amused, nor why he had winked, when she asked for Dolors.

She hoped it was the right course of action. Abandoning her rooms in college hadn't been her preferred option, but Amat had been very insistent, and Fleixa seemed to think it was a good idea as well. She was surprised at how much they seemed to care about her safety and, truth be told, after what had happened in the library, she'd also been worrying about the possibility of another encounter with Homs.

She sighed. Rather than getting better, things seemed to be getting worse. If she didn't want her identity revealed, she was going to have to pay Malavell the very next day, though she didn't know how she was supposed to raise that sort of sum when she only just had enough to cover her costs on the course. She couldn't let that happen, and she didn't want to bring Daniel or Fleixa into it; yet she still had no idea what she was going to do.

She brought the iron doorknocker down twice and waited.

The door opened, and a buxom woman appeared. She wore a black wig over her red hair, and a loosely tied dressing gown that revealed rather more than Pau would have wished to see. She had a segment of mandarin between her teeth, and her hands were covered in the juice.

'Here's a good-looking lad,' she said. 'You're a bit early, but I'll let you off this time. Come in.'

And, before Pau could speak, she disappeared inside. Pau stood in the doorway for a moment, before again hearing the invitation to enter. Unsure, she picked up the trunk and made her way along a narrow passageway that opened into a bedroom, where the woman waited.

The bed occupied almost the entire room, with a large throw and an array of coloured cushions strewn across it. Across from the bed stood a simple dressing table, bearing an array of bottles, brushes and hairpins. A full-length mirror, covered in stains, hung above it. A chair mounded with dresses completed the furniture. The air smelled strongly of citrus.

'Why don't you put your trunk down over there? Just arrived after a long trip? No, let me guess . . .' Her face lit up. 'You're leaving the city for good, and you thought you'd have one last hurrah. Here, I'll go and slip into something more comfortable. Be right with you.'

She vanished into the next room, and Pau heard running water and the woman singing a song. She was back after a couple of minutes, in a short cotton camisole. The fabric clung to her wet body. With a deliberate slowness, she leaned back against the doorframe. A fragrance of roses wafted forward. Pau was having trouble speaking.

Then the woman was on her, in a whirl of flesh and perfume. As Pau took steps backwards, her legs struck the bed and she fell onto it. The springs creaked as she hit the mattress. She tried to get up, but before she knew it the prostitute was straddling her, a playful expression on her face. She removed Pau's glasses and caressed her face. Then, sitting back up, she dropped one of the straps of her slip and brought Pau's hand up to her breast.

'No! Please!'

'Shy are we? There's a remedy for that. Leave it to Dolors.'

She began undoing Pau's shirt buttons and, try though Pau might, the woman's weight had her pinned to the bed.

'You've mistaken me for someone else!'

'Someone else?' said Dolors, breaking her caresses. 'What do you mean?'

'Or I've got the wrong place.'

'Who sent you here, sweetie?'

'Señor Fleixa?'

Dolors's expression changed to one of perplexity, then amusement. She began to laugh. She moved from Pau's lap and got down from the bed. Her single bare breast shook as she stood laughing, before she hooked the strap back over her shoulder.

Pau shot off the bed. she'd kill the journalist – this was some trick on his part. He'd be dying with laughter at that very moment, no doubt.

306

'You're the girl who needed helping?' said Dolors, looking her up and down. 'But you look like a young lord.'

Gathering glasses and jacket, Pau began dragging the trunk towards the door.

'There's been a mix up, Señora, a horrible mix up. Now, if you'll excuse me.'

Dolors came and stood between her and the door.

'I don't think so, dear,' she said, motioning for Pau to drop her belongings. Then, clearing the dresses from the chair, she motioned for her to sit.

'Shall we have a little something to warm us up? I think it'd do us both good.'

Not waiting for a reply, she brought a pair of cups out of the dresser drawer. She went through into the back again, returning with a cardigan over her shoulders and a porcelain teapot in hand, the stalk of some chamomile poking out from under the lid. She poured the tea on an improvised table.

'No sugar, but I have got this,' she said, bringing a small bottle out from another drawer and topping up each of the cups liberally. 'I'd never have said you were a girl. I thought it was my lucky day, such a sweet-faced boy at my door! Sure you're not one of those inverts?'

'No, no.'

The contents of Pau's cup did smell inviting – and were hot. She took a sip and the warmth of the grape liquor lit up her insides. She suddenly began to cough.

'Go easy on that,' said Dolors.

Pau nodded, attempting a polite smile. She had to admit, after that first hit, the alcohol did feel comforting.

'And so you're a . . .'

'A whore, yes. Don't worry, I'm a long way past feeling any shame at my calling. I was baptized María de los Dolores Algarrada Lucena, but most people find Dolors works just fine.'

She smiled to see the girl's timid looks. What a lamb! She made herself comfortable on the bed, took out a cigarette case and lit one, the aroma of tobacco and mint accompanying her exhalation.

'So you're the girl who needed to hole up for a few days. Sorry about before, but Fleixa didn't say you'd be showing up in disguise. What's your name?'

'Pau Gilbert.'

'Pleased to meet you then. Looks like we're going to be spending some time together.'

Pau was about to try and find a way of excusing herself, but then thought better. There was nowhere else for her, with the college out of bounds, and besides, the woman seemed friendly enough.

'I wouldn't be in the way?'

'Not at all. I could do with the company.'

'Will we sleep in the same bed?'

This set Dolors off again, and Pau, far from feeling she was being laughed at, found her amusement contagious. Dolors was nice.

'No, dear, no! There's a small room next to this one. One of the other girls usually has it, but she's gone home for a few days. Everything else we'll share. The rooms are basic, as you can see.

Basilio, the landlord, doesn't know about you, so you'll need to try and avoid him if you're coming and going.'

'That's fine, Señora. Your kindness is greatly appreciated.'

The girl's formality also seemed to amuse Dolors.

'Look, I can judge a character, I have to be able to in my line of work, and for all that you're a strange little fish dressed as a boy, you're a love. I'll survive having you here.'

Pau felt comforted. It was also nice to not have to hide – it had been a long, long time since she'd been addressed as a woman.

'What's in the trunk anyway? Looks like you're moving abroad.'

'A couple of changes of clothes, some books.'

'Books?'

'Medical books. I . . . I'm a student.'

'Well! Women becoming doctors – that's news to me. So,' she moved in closer, 'you know a bit about ointments, that sort of thing?'

'A little, yes.'

'Maybe you can help me.'

'I'll certainly try.'

'Some scabs appeared a few days ago, somewhere . . . slightly delicate. And Lord do they itch! Very red, and itch like anything.'

'I could do an examination, if you agree, and see if I can suggest something.'

'That would be wonderful!' Stubbing the cigarette in her cup, Dolors got up from the bed, to a chorus of squeaking springs.

'Come on, I'll show you where you'll be sleeping.' She stopped halfway along the passage. 'Oh, and I love a natter, nothing better, so if I start sticking my nose where it's not welcome, just

309

tell me to stop, all right? Speaking of which – you *sure* you're not one of those inverts? Why go around dressed as a man otherwise? Had me fooled, that's for sure. Come on, spill the beans. If we're going to be friends, you might as well.'

'It's quite a long story.'

'That's no bother, dear. I've got more free time than a politician.'

THIRTY-NINE

Fleixa pushed his plate to one side. That way only lay a swift trip to the lavatory – the stink coming from the stew pot made that clear. He opted for the brandy instead, taking up the bottle and serving himself another glass. He'd already had several, but it could be anisette from the grubbiest Raval distillery and it would still be better than that food. Anyway, he'd had worse.

The air in the tavern, hidden in the depths of the Raval, was a pungent mixture of smoking tobacco, boiled cabbage and rancid sweat. It was also stiflingly warm, though the customers, apart from one or two engaged in hushed conversation, by and large sat as far from one another as they could and there were only one or two gas lamps, burning low.

All morning he'd kept clear of any café or club frequented by journalists. Everyone would know, and he didn't feel like enduring the jokes. He still couldn't entirely believe he'd lost his job – he, one of the best in all of Barcelona, without a paper to work for. He'd entertained going back to grovel, but had a sense that it was too late even for that. Llopis had won, and that was all. He buried his head in his hands. At least, he thought, things couldn't get any worse.

'You don't seem your usual happy self, sweet boy.'

Looking up, Fleixa found two figures standing either side of him. La Negra smiled, though her eyes betrayed her true sentiment. He was about to say something when, at a gesture from the moneylender, the enormous henchman lifted Fleixa up by the scruff of the neck and began dragging him out.

No one seemed particularly concerned as Fleixa was transported across the tavern and out into the kitchens. At the back, a door gave onto a dingy alleyway that served as both warehouse and dumping area for the premises.

The change in temperature sent Fleixa into a coughing fit. He made to try and run away, but a shove from the henchman sent him flying into some crates containing a nearby hostel's dirty linen. His bad ankle gave way and he toppled onto a mound of bedsheets and pillowcases.

Then he was being lifted to his feet, and was propped against the wall. The alcohol stopped him from feeling overly concerned. Everything would be just fine.

'Negra,' he said, slurring slightly. 'This isn't necessary, you know? I've got your money. Here, in my jacket . . .'

He stopped when he heard La Negra's muted response.

'Sorry, this is beyond me now.'

She moved to one side and a larger figure stepped forward. Recognizing the man, Fleixa gave a small bow: he knew this was something far worse, without yet having a clue as to what that something was.

'La Negra's got a real sentimental streak, but at least she knows what's good for her, eh?'

Inspector Sánchez emerged into the light wearing a smug expression. He reached into his pocket and popped a salted pea into his mouth. Chewing briefly, he spat the shell into the dirty rivulet at their feet, which bore it, bobbing, past Fleixa.

'It just so happens the lovely lady owes me a favour, and a big favour at that. I've called it in, and now her debt is owed to me, do you see?'

'Not exactly . . . As you must have just heard me say, I've got the money. The debt's done.'

'Problem is, interest rates have just gone up.'

'I really don't know what you're talking about. I've had a little to drink, you might be able to tell.'

'Yes, well I'll do my best to make the situation clear. First, here's what I know: because, as you'll see, Señor journalist, I know a lot. I know, for instance, that along with that meddler Daniel Amat you have been looking into the rumours about the Black Hound, and I know that you've got a young student in on it now, and I even happen to know that you've just lost your job. Damn if I don't know a lot!' Sánchez spat out another pea shell.

'What do you want?' Fleixa said.

'Just an exchange.'

'That's all?'

'I need you to do something for me, Journalist.'

'You want me to put Amat off as well?'

'Oh, far from it. I want you to help him along, in fact. Do as I say, and by and by you and I will sit down to a nice glass of wine, like old friends. We'll have a nice chat, and you'll tell me everything you know, absolutely everything. And in exchange, we'll have another think about those interest rates. And, naturally, it will all be our little secret.'

'You want inside information, is that it?'

'You're really going to turn your nose up? We both know you haven't in the past.'

'And if I refuse?'

Sánchez gestured to the henchman, who stepped in and grabbed Fleixa's right arm. The journalist didn't bother to resist.

The Inspector came forward too, an apologetic look in his face. He took out a metal object – a cigar cutter, Fleixa saw. Sánchez took hold of Fleixa's middle finger, and delight entered his features as he inserted it into the small guillotine and lightly squeezed the shutter. Blood dribbled down, and, at the sharp pain, Fleixa's drunkenness suddenly dissipated. He immediately broke out in a sweat.

'Agree to help me, and the debt's written off, but if you don't –' Sánchez paused to place another pea in his mouth – 'you won't be doing any more scribbling, and that's for sure. I'll take each and every one of your fingers, and after that I'll take that whore of yours, and do with her as I please.'

Behind them, La Negra rolled her eyes disapprovingly, but didn't move to intervene.

'All right, all right, I get it!'

'You know what?' said Sánchez, who'd pulled the contraption away and was brushing it up and down along Fleixa's fingers. 'It's funny, but I'm not sure you do.'

Then, as if it were happening to someone else, Fleixa watched as Sánchez slotted the cutter over his little finger, and pressed

314

it completely shut. Pain coursed up his arm, and then with a snap the blades broke through the bone. The finger dropped to the ground and rolled into the stream, which carried it away. Blood spurted out, soaking Fleixa's sleeve, and his legs gave way: he crumpled like a marionette. His pocket watch fell from his waistcoat and into the filth of the alley floor.

'I have a feeling you'll remember our agreement now,' said Sánchez, wiping his hands on a cloth. 'Look at it this way: I've done you a favour! You can pass yourself off as one of these cripples, back from Cuba, people will take pity on you. You might even beg a better salary than you got working at that rag.'

Turning, Sánchez's boot struck the watch.

'What have we here?'

He picked it up before Fleixa could do anything. And having wiped it clean, opening the cover, he let out a cry.

'You keep a picture of your whore?' He laughed, showing it to the others. La Negra didn't seem amused.

Swinging the chain, Sánchez leaned in close to Fleixa. 'Maybe you'd like to let me have it, as a sign of our new association?'

Fleixa tried to protest, but then he felt his stomach heave and a wave of nausea ran through him. He was violently sick.

'Really!' Sánchez stepped away to keep his boots clean. 'Were you raised in a barn?' Turning away, he addressed La Negra, who was standing with her arms crossed, not looking impressed. 'That's done then. Take care of him, would you, we don't want him bleeding to death.'

Fleixa stayed hugging himself on the floor, and watched vacantly as La Negra's man wrapped his hand in a cloth. The Inspector clucked, and lobbed the watch into his lap.

'So you can see what a good heart I've got.'

Sánchez turned and walked away down the alley. He paused at the end, placed another pea in his mouth, and disappeared out onto the street.

Clasping the watch to his chest, Fleixa shut his eyes. He hoped unconsciousness would come quickly.

FORTY

Daniel felt the sea breeze on his face. Grey clouds were moving in. Seagulls wheeled in the air, their cries heralding the arrival of another storm.

He'd gone walking, and this was where his footsteps had led him: the Poniente pier, one of his favourite places as a child. He used to come in search of solace following the death of his mother; a pall had come down, then, on the family home. From that bench on the promenade, he used to watch the big steam ships leaving at nightfall, destined for ports unknown – far away in the Americas, elsewhere in Europe – and imagine fantastic adventures for himself, far from this life of unrelenting sorrow. The sun would dip beyond the horizon, and Alec would come and bring him back to the house.

He leaned back against the bench. Three small boys were fishing with a line and hook, and the clumsiness of one was making the other two laugh. Couples were making the most of the pause in the rain as they strolled arm in arm along the seafront, while a group of sailors called out to a pair of young girls, making sure they knew just how lovely they looked, as the girls, all giggles and blushes, hurried past.

Placing his hat next to him on the bench, Daniel took a creased envelope from his overcoat pocket. An express courier had arrived with it that afternoon. And though he'd read it twice already, he removed the pastel sheet and looked it over once more.

His fiancée Alexandra had written to say her father couldn't continue excusing his absence to the rest of the faculty – not without jeopardizing his own reputation as dean. Some of the others wanted to give his post to a certain Hillager, the son of Lord Hillager. She wrote of Sir Edward's dejection: he couldn't fathom why Daniel, whom he considered his own son, would want to throw it all away.

Alexandra couldn't understand his prolonged stay in Barcelona. Though she signed off with words of affection, Daniel also knew she must be prey to doubts. And, true to character, at the end of the missive Alexandra urged him to make a decision: if he returned immediately, all could be resolved, but if not, she would consider their engagement to be at an end.

He folded the letter and looked out across the sea, fixing his sight on the point where water and sky met.

He could take the train to Paris that very night, connect onwards to Calais, followed by the boat to England. There was nothing stopping him from gathering his belongings and doing precisely that. Nobody would blame him. To stay on meant to risk losing everything he cared about: his professorship at Oxford, the confidence and friendship of his tutor, not to mention Alexandra's love.

Considering it, he also had the sure sense that nothing he

318

could do would stop his guilt. Alexandra was right. His father was dead and there was nothing he could do about it. He'd even put his life in danger, and the lives of others. This wasn't his responsibility. Everyone wanted him to leave, so why not listen?

A name entered his thoughts.

He should never have gone to see her. He was betrothed to a quite wonderful young lady, and Irene had a husband. Their lives had taken separate paths, the feelings they'd shared seven years before had been consigned to a pile of ash – ash and ghosts. He ought to return to England and carry on with his life. Bury his past as deep as he could, in a place where none of it could return to hurt him.

The only thing was . . .

He got up from the bench and went over to the pier wall. Below, the waves crashed against the rocks, as though they were somehow privy to his thoughts. He looked at the letter in his hand. Tears came to his eyes. Sighing deeply, he slotted the letter back into his jacket pocket.

. . . he couldn't.

FORTY-ONE

The hooded figure was struggling to breathe. He felt suffocated by the feelings of anger that, like a thick and heavy sap, flowed in his veins, and made his head pound. And how his head pounded: it was like the second hand of a gargantuan clock, on and on and on. *The gall!*

His anger seemed to intoxicate him: he had to grab hold of furniture to steady himself. He crossed the room without looking at the pole, which continued its silent vibrations. Feeling harassed by the constant buzzing drone, he passed the vitrine-lined shelves and the blazing stove, beyond which a long oak table stood, covered in the laboratory equipment.

He stepped forward and with a great swipe of his arm knocked distilling jars, separating flasks, burettes and sample cases to the floor. Glass scattered everywhere. The chemical solutions, loosed from their containers, began trickling through the shards towards the drain.

He dumped the manuscript bearing the words *De Humani*

Corporis Fabrica onto the clear expanse of the table. The firelight played on the leather flaps: the lettering appeared to quiver.

He tore open the manuscript, his stomach lurching as he thought about his mistake . . . He turned the pages manically. Long blocks of text in Latin were interspersed with original etchings of body parts. The illustrations, occasionally occupying entire pages, showed dismembered bodies in disconcerting detail, dissected limbs, human skeletons in unlikely postures. Many were the collectors, in the furthest reaches of the continent, who would pay vast sums for the manuscript, but that couldn't have mattered less to him: there was something he needed to find, he *had* to find, and as the pages went on he felt more and more desperate at his failure to do so. He checked in the margins, he checked in the line breaks, he pored over every single filigree and line in the drawings. Reaching the end, he slammed the book shut, the impact resounding against the vaulted arches above. He buried his head in his hands for a moment before letting out a sob, which soon gave way to wails. He picked up the costly volume and hurled it from him, as hard as he could. With what sounded like a crunching of bones, it dashed against the inside of the stove, the precious illustrations writhing as they came into contact with the flames.

Pushing the hood back from his face, he tried to calm himself. His hair covered his sweaty face, and there was a dried thread of spittle at the corner of his mouth. Lifting his hand to wipe it away, he noticed a stab of pain in his arm, and then that his whole sleeve was soaked in blood.

He remembered sustaining the cut on fleeing the library – on the window he'd escaped through. During the chase he'd made a tourniquet of a handkerchief, but that had ceased to have any effect.

He got up and took a small suitcase from a double-doored wardrobe. Settling himself on a stool, he rolled the dripping sleeve up as far as his elbow; there was a very deep cut on his forearm, and it was bleeding freely. He noted with interest how close he'd come to severing the cephalic vein – he could see right through to the cubital extensor. He felt a gust of dizziness. Serious blood loss wasn't something to play around with. It was a wonder he hadn't passed out yet.

From the case he took a glass bottle, gauze, steel needles and some silk thread soaked in carbolic acid. He laid them out carefully on a silver tray to the other side of him. Uncorking the bottle, he emptied its contents over the wound. The iodine tincture bubbled, and a stinging sensation, almost like singing, flashed along the limb. He managed to keep his hand in place until all the liquid was gone. A small puddle of disinfectant and blood clots began to gather at his feet. He waited a moment, cleaned the cut out and, seeing the necessary blood spring from it again, prepared the suture.

The pain was his penance: he deserved to suffer. She had trusted in him, he'd let her down. He'd been so close to victory, and it had slipped away – because of *his* stupidity, it had slipped away. He placed the piece of wood between his teeth.

The semicircular needle wouldn't just slide in – he had to shut his eyes and thrust it into his flesh. Another flash of pain. He thought about how he'd been fooled – how that young man had stolen what, by rights, was his alone. With one end of the thread in his mouth, he pulled on the needle, drawing shut the

322

wound. He let out the breath he'd been holding. It was his fault. He had let doubt enter his mind, he had hesitated, and that was what had led to the moment of weakness. Not a mistake he'd be making again.

He plunged the needle in once more. His brow shone with sweat, and his jaw trembled with the effort. He'd find that young man again, and this time there would be no hesitation. He wouldn't let her down again.

Pulling on the suture, he bit down hard on the wood to prevent himself from crying out.

LIBER OCTAVUS

Ten days before the start of the World Fair

FORTY-TWO

Sleep would not come for Fleixa. After La Negra's man had carried his semi-conscious body to Dolors's door, all he could remember were the prostitute's alarmed cries, which, though he tried to stop her, then gave way to insults. But La Negra didn't react to the tirade and, before leaving, even advised Dolors to disinfect the wound.

The woman called Pau in to help, who did so without complaint. After bathing the wound in water and iodine she gave him some stitches, placed clean bandages on, and recommended laudanum to help him sleep. Then she left the two of them alone, and Dolors got him into bed and brought some warm broth, which he was unable to finish. He dropped down into a restless sleep.

Some way after midnight he woke and found Dolors curled up on the other side of the bed, on top of the bedspread, having left all the sheets to him. He sat up and felt immediately dizzy, then draped the sheet over her before laying his head back down on the pillow.

He brought his bandaged hand up in front of his face. It wasn't so different to how it would look if Sánchez had already taken all his fingers; Fleixa shuddered at the prospect. Money had suddenly become the least of his worries – he had little desire for his hand to be turned into a fingerless stump. He tasted bile in his mouth for a moment. It wasn't that he felt particularly good about the prospect of betraying Amat, but what choice did he have? He hadn't been given very many options. There would be a few days' grace, but then the Inspector would be back, and he'd want information. It wasn't to his liking, but he'd do what the policeman asked. And when it was all over, get out of the city, go away. Irene Adell's advance amounted to a small fortune. He could live off it comfortably for a time, anywhere.

At his side, Dolors turned over in her sleep, the sheets falling away to reveal her shoulder and the top of one of her breasts. Avoiding putting weight through his bad hand, Fleixa covered her again. She murmured in her sleep, and came closer to him; the warmth of her was a lovely sensation. How did she manage to smell so good? He carefully moved some of her curls from her face; when she was like this, relaxed, not made up, she went back to being that young girl from a village in Valle de Arán, recently arrived in Barcelona in search of a better life. He loved all her wrinkles and freckles. Even in sleep she had a mischievous look, which made him smile. She was always surprising him: she always expected good things of life. And whatever came, she managed to make it seem for the best.

No commitment, no ties. Most men would love that kind of arrangement. But recently, when he'd been away from her, knowing she might be with someone else had begun to rankle.

They'd been seeing more of each other these past weeks, and he knew it wasn't really just because of his creditors. He'd even caught himself missing her once or twice, when he spent a night back in his hostel.

Dolors stirred and opened her eyes.

'You're awake?' she said.

'Shh,' he whispered.

'What is it? Your hand hurting? Is it bleeding again?'

'No.' He smiled at her concern. 'I was just thinking.'

'At this hour of the night? Mad as a goat, you are.'

'Doubtless. In fact, I've been thinking about . . .'

'Me too.'

'Take it easy with me, I'm very weak.'

'You look just fine to me.'

After, Dolors lay back down beside the journalist with a sigh. Neither of them spoke as they lay enjoying the heat from each other's naked body. Fleixa took the opportunity to recover his breath. He was feeling worse than he was letting on, but didn't want to worry Dolors. Once he felt somewhat recovered, he plucked up the courage to say what had been going round and round in his head.

'What do you think about going away for a while?'

'Away? Away where?'

'I don't know, just away from Barcelona. For a while. The two of us.'

'You sure you're feeling all right?'

'I'm fine.'

The journalist gazed up at the ceiling as Dolors lay close again and began stroking his chest.

'You really are the strangest creature, Bernat.'

He leaned close to her and took a deep breath of her hair, then tipped her chin towards him and searched in her eyes for an answer. Dolors gave a perplexed smile. Fleixa was surprised by what he was feeling: it was all so simple, he thought. And for her? There was only one way to find out.

'Will you marry me?'

Dolors shot out of the bed, not bothering to cover her nakedness. She opened and shut her mouth a number of times, gawping at the journalist, as he, avoiding her eye, continued speaking.

'I've had a bit of good luck. I've come into an absolute pile of money. I could take care of you, of both of us. We could go on a trip, you've always said you wanted to see Madrid. I say let's do it – we could even go to Rome or Paris, it doesn't matter. Right now, in the morning. You and me. Only, of course, if you want to.'

He ran out of breath. He turned to look at Dolors again, who stood saying nothing. He couldn't tell if it was delight on her face, or a look of horror. She stood stock-still, her eyes shining. Then her lips slowly parted, becoming a smile, and she put her hand to her mouth. She's laughing, she's going to laugh at me, he thought, feeling suddenly embarrassed. He felt full of doubt, and then panic. Marriage? What was he thinking? She must have thought he'd lost his mind. For God's sake, he paid her for all these favours. What an imbecile he was.

Then there was a knock at the door. Pau stuck her head around the door, covering her eyes with her hand.

'Sorry. I need to use the bathroom.'

FORTY-THREE

It was bad enough hiding out in a brothel without having to be confronted by the sight of a naked Bernat Fleixa. Pau's face continued to burn as she came out onto the chilly street. Walking very briskly, she tried to dispel her feelings of embarrassment. The journalist didn't seem particularly pleased either, above all after Dolors's amused response. Ignoring her entreaties, he had jumped out of bed, dressed, and left as well, slamming the door behind him.

Pau had been told not to go out, but there was a meeting she couldn't miss.

It had been no easy thing, gathering the money. She'd managed to pawn an old microscope of her father's – it had made her weep to do it, but she had no choice. The money she needed to complete her studies had run low and she had nearly nothing to make it to the end of the month. And now all these extra complications, on top of her already precarious situation.

She reached Calle Hercules, passed the Town Hall and made for the Church of San Justo, where Malavell had set the meeting.

At least it was a long way from the hospital – the lower the likelihood of anyone seeing them together, the better.

She paused in the entranceway, allowing her eyes to adjust to the darkness inside the church. She made her way along one of the aisles, careful to avoid the large puddles – the roof leaked in many places. Her footsteps resounded along the flagstones. There were only a few candles, pinpricks of light in the large nave, and the ceiling and the transepts stood in total darkness. A cold wind seemed to spring from the walls themselves, making the church far from welcoming. Little wonder the place was empty.

Pau came as far as the transept, finding nobody. She looked in the chapels. No sign of Malavell. She turned on her heel, about to give up, when her old servant stepped out from behind a pillar.

'Good day to you, Señor Gilbert,' he said, his eyes sparkling. 'I hope I didn't make you jump. It's a pleasure to see you again. Shall we sit? We wouldn't want some parishioner to come in and wonder what we're up to.'

Pau nodded: the less conspicuous they were, the happier she was. Anyone might come in, later to recognize her at the hospital.

They went and sat in one of the pews in the San Félix chapel. Pau kept her distance, staying as aloof as she could. And before any preamble could begin, she took out a leather pochette and pushed it to him along the pew. He did nothing to hide his excitement, reaching out his bony fingers and grabbing it.

'Not, of course, that I don't trust you,' he said, opening the pochette and checking inside, 'but you just never know these days.'

He smiled a brown-toothed smile. Now Pau wanted to get something clear.

'So you've got your money. I never want to see your face again, and especially not anywhere near the hospital or the college.'

'But of course, Señorita. I'm a man of my word.'

At that, Pau got up to leave, but the man reached out a ragged arm and grabbed her, before shoving her against one of the stone pillars. Before she could respond, he brought his weight up against her. He had a knife.

'No need to run off *quite* so quickly though.'

'Let me go!'

'If you think this money is enough to cover what your father did to me, you've got another think coming. There's something we didn't finish the other day.'

'Have you lost your mind? We're in a church!'

'Know what? I know the priest here, and he happens to have a bit of a weakness for the old claret. I made a small donation, and he's gone for a drink. There's no one to bother us. It's just me and you, my dear.'

'No!'

They wrestled for a moment, but Pau simply didn't have Malavell's strength. He got on top of her and brought the blade to her throat; feeling its edge, she stopped dead. The man tightened his grip around her, an overpowering smell of old sweat washing over her.

'I'm going to get paid in full,' he whispered lecherously, laying a hand on her upper chest and beginning to fondle her.

Pau writhed in desperation, and felt a nick from the blade, but that wasn't going to stop her. In fury and fright she beat and kicked, forcing Malavell off, and then managed to catch him between the legs. A look of surprise crossed his face before he crumpled to the floor, the knife skittering away. Pau leapt to her feet and raced out of the church, leaving her old servant moaning and crying where he lay.

In spite of the ache in a tender area, as Albert Malavell made his way down the street he felt wonderful. The purse in his pocket was a lovely sort of weight: his plan had come off. He could have a new coat now if he liked, and a decent meal, though the first thing he planned to do was get a bottle of brandy to celebrate – followed, perhaps, by a trip to his favourite cathouse. The money would last a while.

Perhaps, he thought, he could even have demanded more – that girl had been born with a silver spoon in her mouth. Daughter to a quack, for goodness' sake, surely she'd been left a decent income.

Considering the idea, he pulled up in surprise: why hadn't he seen it before? No need for this to be the end – why not simply make this the first of several payments? Leave it a few days, let her feel she was in the clear, and then, when she least expected it, go and make fresh demands. He'd make a pretty packet that way. Anyway, she owed him for that little scene in the church – no way she wasn't going to pay.

He resumed walking, an extra spring in his step, when he heard footsteps behind him. He reached for the dagger.

'Easy, easy, my good man. I'm not going to divest you of any of those hard-earned coins.'

The upper-class voice belonged to a young man with dark hair, very stylishly turned out. He kept a handkerchief to mouth and nose as he surveyed Malavell haughtily.

'What a stink. You're in need of a bath, Señor.'

'And who asked you?'

'I am sorry, I don't usually fraternize with people of your kind.'

'What? Who are you?'

'Oh, a friend.'

Malavell looked him up and down.

'It's pretty clear, Señor, that friends is something we are not.'

Still smiling, the young man nodded.

'Yes, you're probably right. But there is something we have in common.'

'Oh?' said an impatient Malavell, running his fingers over the knife hilt. 'What's that then?'

'A certain interest in the person you've just been dealing with,' he pointed his cane back in the direction Pau had fled. 'I, like you, am an admirer, and really quite interested in this individual's wellbeing. Could I possibly buy you a drink – or perhaps two? I have a proposal to make.'

The young man held up a small bag of coins, and shook it. Removing his hand from the knife, Malavell smiled wolfishly; Fenollosa turned away, and he fell in behind. What a night this was turning out to be.

FOURTY-FOUR

'Gentlemen. The p-p-potential for the use of electricity in medical p-p-procedures, is really quite something.'

Professor Gavet hobbled back and forth across the small, wooden stage, supporting himself with a cane. He looked up over his glasses every now and then to check the students were still there in the lecture theatre. In spite of his stutter, the source of great fun, he was often invited to lecture, and, curiously, the defect grew less severe any time he entered a classroom.

Pau had arrived early. Sitting on the back row, she tried to make herself as inconspicuous as she could. Fenollosa's group was, as ever, bunched together in the front row, though Fenollosa himself was nowhere to be seen. That felt something of a relief. They hadn't seen each other since the library confrontation. Better that way.

She was still shaken by the encounter with Malavell and didn't want anyone to notice. After several days' absence, and against the wishes of Amat and Fleixa, she'd decided to go back to class.

Though it didn't seem the day would be of any great benefit, given how much trouble she was having concentrating.

Amat and Fleixa had stayed true to their word and not told anyone her secret. The commotion surrounding the death of Ferrán was no longer even a topic of conversation at the university. The corpse had been found in cinders, so no one had picked up on the old man's wounds – no one had been looking. The official line was that it had all been an unfortunate accident. No one seemed to have wondered what she was doing in the library at that hour, no one had asked her any questions. And yet she felt responsible: Ferrán's death weighed heavily upon her.

She found herself anxious for the end of the class, when she'd be seeing Amat and Fleixa again. After installing herself in Dolors's rooms, she'd begun examining the Galen manuscript she'd also taken from the attic, and what she'd found had astounded her.

A willowy student in Fenollosa's group raised a hand. This stopped Gavet's flow, and drew Pau's attention.

'Yes, Señor Martí. Something you'd like to ask?'

'As far as I understand, Señor, at the start of the century they did experiments to see if corpses could be brought back to life. Is that one of the possibilities you see in the future?'

Murmurs went around the lecture theatre. Gavet chuckled, without breaking stride.

'As usual, my dear Martí, a touch of h-h-humour in your contribution.' His eyes sparkled with amusement. 'Unlike other times, h-h-however, where a joke is all you attempt, here you h-happen to have alighted on a point of interest.'

He put the cane to one side and rested his hand on the table.

'Luigi Galvani, a name you ought to know, gentlemen, though I have my doubts about your capacities to retain such i-information . . . at the end of the last century, h-he discovered, quite by accident as it turns out, something he h-himself went on to call *bio-electrogenesis*, which gave birth to a whole new scientific theory. Perhaps, Señor Marti, you might be able to tell us the name of that theory?'

Seeing the student shake his head in embarrassment, Gavet smiled indulgently.

'Let me see i-if I can assist. Galvanism, it's called, after the man who came up with it. It states that the brains of all animals produce electricity, and that electricity transfers along the nerves, accumulates in the muscles and, at a given moment, is sent onwards and produces the movements of the muscles. Galvani set out the f-fundamentals of cardiac stimulation in his tract *De viribus electricitatis in motu musculari c-commentarius*. The theory h-held until a good way into this century. His own nephew, Giovani Aldini, carried out numerous studies in the h-hope of curing paralyzed patients, and even tried reanimating dead bodies.'

'So, Señor Gavet,' said another of the group, winking at his companions, 'it's your belief that, in certain circumstances, electricity could be used to bring someone back to life?'

A few laughs went around the lecture theatre.

'Your comments, gentlemen, make so little sense to me. I'm surprised, I-I thought you were too old to believe in such tales.'

The student looked abashed.

'Aldini's experiments were a resounding failure. The only noteworthy result of his public presentations, i-in which he gave shocks to the bodies of executed prisoners, were for a few audience members to pass out. Which couldn't be further from the therapeutic uses of electricity, our true subject h-here – and something deeply worthy of study.' He straightened up. 'We have evidence of its use in Egypt, Greece, and even China. The Roman doctor Scribonius Largus writes in his *Compositiones Medicamentorum* of using electric rays – the fish – to treat gouty arthritis. Then there was the Greek doctor, Dioscorides, who proposed the use of electricity for anal prolapse, and Avicenna even talked about its utility in treating migraines and epilepsy. There are dozens of examples I could give.'

'But what is your opinion?' said the student. 'Do you think we will be able to resuscitate people one day?'

'My dear boy, I wouldn't wish to try and set out the limits of medical science. Anything's possible, I suppose, but I can assure you that it would be no easy thing to bring even a spider back to life in a laboratory.'

More laughter loosened the atmosphere, and Gavet went on with a smile on his face.

'Eighteen years ago, a Doctor Steiner anaesthetized a patient with chloroform, and managed to bring h-him round. That's the closest anyone's come to resuscitation.' He paused, glancing at the clock. 'Interesting though this is, gentlemen, I think that's enough for today. F-for our next class, revise Ramón Araya's *Electroanesthesia*. Good afternoon, I'll see you the day after tomorrow.'

The lecture theatre emptied out in a hubbub of comments and discussion. Pau was on her way out too when she heard Gavet call out to her.

'Señor Gilbert, h-have you got a moment?'

Once everyone had gone, he looked up from some documents and signalled for her to come nearer.

'You haven't been in class this week, and I've been told you're not sleeping in your room at college.' He looked at her over his glasses. 'As one of your teachers this semester it's my duty to be concerned. I hope these oversights don't mean that anything's wrong.'

'No, Professor.'

'F-finals are upon us, which makes this sort of behaviour even less appropriate. I don't know if you understand me.' Gavet looked genuinely concerned. 'I need something to tell the Board, you've already been a subject of much discussion, and some of my colleagues are looking quite unfavourably on your tendency to ignore rules. If I'm going to speak up for you, I-I need to know I'm doing the right thing.'

Pau felt thankful for this kind show of interest. Out of all the lecturers, Gavet had always been the most attentive, always ready to help the students. She didn't like the idea of lying to him, and tried to think of something not too far from the truth.

'I believe you know about the tasks I was helping Doctor Amat with?'

Gavet nodded.

'I know students aren't supposed to practice until they've qualified, but since Doctor Amat's death I've carried on his work in La Barceloneta.'

'I-I see. Obviously it's against the rules, but the cause is an altogether worthy one, which excuses you – but that doesn't explain why you've been staying away.'

340

'Sometimes the work has gone on late, and I've had to spend the night.'

'What? Isn't it dangerous down there? All kinds of lowlife and ruffians, no?'

'Not at all, Señor. I've been lodging with a prostitute ...' Pau knew immediately she'd made a mistake. Gavet looked stupefied. 'Oh, it isn't what you think, Dolors is a lovely woman.'

'Dear Lord!'

'It's strictly a business transaction.'

Gavet looked like he was struggling for air, and his stutter grew suddenly more pronounced.

'Señor Gilbert, spare me! I-I-I will come up with something to tell the Board, but you must h-h-have a hundred per cent attendance record from now on. Understood? And above all, you must cease relations with that, with that *person*!'

Pau nodded numerous times. It wasn't hard to imagine what Gavet was thinking. But how, without divulging everything, could she explain? A murderer being after her, the Vesalius manuscript – he wouldn't believe a word.

Thanking him, she turned and left, before she could create any more problems for herself.

FORTY-FIVE

The rain poured down, soaking the streets. As the sun set and the light faded, a wind blew off Montjuïch, scouring the city. The streets seemed quieter than usual, and those that had ventured out were sheltering at wine merchants and taverns.

Dolors, on the other hand, felt only warmth in her crimson cheeks. She walked along briskly in her best polka dot dress and a shawl. She couldn't stop herself from smiling, just as she didn't seem to be able to master her thoughts, quick and slippery as eels. Fleixa's proposal went round and round in her thoughts.

Had he really meant it? Of course he had, she knew that. Never had she seen him so embarrassed. Before she could even answer he'd begun apologizing. Then the girl had come in and found them naked, which hadn't helped matters: she hadn't been able to stop herself from laughing, while Fleixa, thinking he was being ridiculed, had stormed off – which had made her laugh all the more. And by the time she realized what she'd done, he was long gone.

To be somebody's wife. She could not bring herself to believe it. Other men had sworn affection, promised to make an honest woman of her, but she'd always refused, knowing their enthusiasm wouldn't last, they'd only change their minds, and then the problems would start. And it wasn't any different with the journalist – or was it? She was far from certain.

He'd always provoked a special affection in her – so short, and always so sickly, and at the same time so full of himself. And he could be downright unbearable at times. But he always treated her with respect, to all appearances as though she were an honourable woman. And his proposition had unleashed an earthquake inside her – was this love? She didn't know. Perhaps life was reaching out a hand to her. Perhaps she'd be able to leave her miserable existence behind, as she promised herself she would, day after day. She trembled at the thought.

A couple of sailors came past, eyeing her openly. The younger of the two said something that made the other one laugh. Doubtless they'd just come into port, probably on one of the steamships that crossed every two months between here and Puerto Rico or Havana. They would have had their wages, and that money would currently be burning a hole in their pockets: an easy job – double the pay, half the effort! And yet she didn't stop for them.

She turned onto Presó Vella, or Old Prison Street, though it was also called Calle Amalia, after Queen Amalia. She saw a youngish girl come out from a nearby doorway, gathering her hair under a felt hat. The loose-fitting dress she wore barely covered her, and she hurried to wrap a red wool shawl about her body. A young man, himself probably no more than sixteen, appeared from the same doorway – from his shirt and espadrilles he looked like a factory apprentice. Glancing at Dolors, his face turned scarlet, and he turned and hurried away without a word.

'Any time, good looking,' said the girl, placing money in a purse between her breasts and nodding at Dolors. Her name, though probably not her real one, was Mercedes; it wasn't uncommon for them to give themselves a new name; many wished to leave their past selves behind. This one didn't look like she'd make it into her twenties. She had pretty, almond-shaped eyes, but they were lifeless, and though she dyed her hair the original chestnut colour had half grown out. Down here in the Raval, nothing was more fleeting than beauty.

'God, it's cold,' she said. 'Last thing you feel like is dropping your knickers, especially if the poor bastard can hardly pay.'

Dolors nodded. You often had to accept the bare minimum – that was when you'd take them into a doorway or down an alley, rather than back to the room. And if you were lucky and the place was sufficiently dark, you could just use your thighs. You'd be done with most of them in under a minute, what with the nerves they tended to suffer, and the alcohol they'd usually imbibed.

Mercedes finished sorting out her dress, and looked up at Dolors. 'You look different.'

'Different?'

'Yes, not as miserable as usual!'

Dolors didn't know what to say.

'I bet,' said Mercedes, pouting a little, 'you've been off with that lord, the one whose coachman's been around asking after you.'

'Asking after me?'

344

'Come on, girl, that won't work with me. Give me the juice. I'd say, by the way that driver dressed, and the way he spoke, his boss must have at least been the Maquinista owner. Rolling in it! And they seemed *really* keen on finding you.'

'Honestly, I don't know who it is.'

'If you say so.' Mercedes seemed annoyed. 'You don't have to tell me, I suppose. Anyway, I feel like a bit of hot food, what do you say?'

'Think I'm going to head off.'

'Back home? Already? I don't know what it is, but I swear something's up with you.'

Dolors watched as the young prostitute turned and headed in the direction of the tavern. Though it had only been a reflex, she really didn't feel like working tonight. Maybe she was coming down with something. Or maybe it was Fleixa's proposal, damn him: she couldn't stop thinking about it. She sighed. They were going to have to talk.

FORTY-SIX

'Couldn't we have found somewhere slightly quieter?'

Daniel and Pau both looked at Fleixa in annoyance. Their table had an excellent view of the stage, where a group of singers and guitarists sang, clapped and stamped their feet against the boards. The air of the *café cantante* was thick with noise and smoke. Not that it seemed to matter to the clientele, who were more concerned about where the roulette ball would land, or what card the croupier was about to turn over.

'You said somewhere discreet,' said Fleixa, himself focussing on the dancing girls. 'Where's better for not being noticed than the Café del Puerto?'

'What happened to your hand?' said Daniel.

'Oh, me being clumsy, nothing to worry about.'

Daniel couldn't help but notice the tremor in the journalist's voice though, undercutting the show of indifference. He'd been acting strangely since they arrived. Though cordial, he'd look away the moment any eye contact was made, especially with Pau, who had fallen silent, and seemed to be blushing. This accident must have had something to do with it, he thought. He was about to ask again when a waiter arrived through the crush.

'What will you have?' Fleixa said, waving his glass of brandy at them.

They both shook their heads.

'Killjoys! You don't want to make people suspicious, do you?' he said, giving an exaggerated wink.

They agreed to take some wine, and once they'd been served, Pau began filling them in on everything that had happened before they'd found her in the library. She told them of the difficulties she'd had finding a copy of the Vesalius manuscript, the hours she'd spent looking, and of the secret laboratory, with the phrase written over and over on the walls.

'Isn't that the same one your father wrote in the sewers,' said Fleixa, 'to tell us which way to go?'

'Yes,' Daniel said. *'Man's ingenuity is his only way to eternal life.'*

'Why would Homs be writing it so obsessively like that? And then your father using it too – it can't be coincidence.'

'I agree, but goodness knows what the link is. Maybe this mysterious *Liber Octavus* would give us some pointers. Anyway, what were you saying, Pau?'

She told them about finding Ferrán dead in his office, how she tried to get away through the labyrinthine library, and the encounter with her pursuer.

'Everyone at university thinks the fire was an accident. No one has the first clue.'

'And meanwhile we've made absolutely no progress.'

'We still need a copy of the Vesalius, since Homs took the one you found.'

But now Pau smiled.

'I've got something to show you,' she said, taking a canvas bundle from her bag. Carefully she placed it down on the table, unfolding the fabric to reveal a large book with dark leather covers.

'This is the other book I found in Homs's laboratory – it was next to the Vesalius. *De Dignotione ex Insomnis Libellis* – it's by Galen, and it's about diagnosing dreams.'

The other two looked mystified. Pau opened the book, and both men were taken aback at what they saw inside.

The print on the first page seemed to spring to life under the café lights. It was a highly detailed representation of a forensic presentation in a crowded lecture theatre. A scroll was depicted, with a mannered inscription: *Andreae Vesalii Bruxellensis, scholae medicorum Patauinae professoris, de Humani corporis fabrica Libri septem.*

Just then, the clamour in the café died down for a moment.

'And?' Fleixa said.

'It's Homs showing he has not only wit, but a sense of humour. No one would suspect Vesalius's most representative work to be hidden inside the covers of a book by Galen, his intellectual enemy, as it were.'

'So . . . Homs *hasn't* got the manuscript?'

'It seems there were two,' said Pau, tears of emotion in her eyes.

'Now I really am in the dark.'

'Here's what I think: when Homs found out they were going to have him committed, he decided to hide this manuscript, using the covers from a different book. Then he puts another copy of

Fabrica next to it as a decoy, and finally puts a huge number of other books in the vicinity to further throw people off.'

'But why go to all that trouble?'

'There were people who wanted in on his discoveries, so he tried to create a subterfuge.'

'But why this particular copy? You've told us it's a famous book, there must be hundreds of copies around, right?'

'My thoughts exactly. And there can only be one answer: *this* manuscript isn't a copy, it's an original. These pages are more than three hundred years old, in other words.'

The other two looked at it with renewed respect.

'But then . . . You're also saying that Homs fell for his own trick by taking the other book!'

'I just think that was bad luck. The two are very similar in shape and size, and when he took it from me in the fire, it wasn't exactly easy to see with all that smoke. And when you two showed up, he ran off as fast as he could – no time to check if he had the right book.'

'Sounds like a lot of hard work for some old book,' Fleixa sighed, pawing the book. 'Look, it's even got typos – this page isn't numbered right.'

Pau quickly retrieved the book from him, delicately placing it back on the table.

'This "old book", Señor Fleixa, is considered one of the most influential scientific tracts of all time. And, you seemed to have forgotten, I was nearly killed getting my hands on it. Don't you dare—'

'It's all right,' said Daniel. 'He didn't mean anything by it.'

The journalist responded with a mocking tilt of the head.

'Please,' said Daniel. 'We need to form some idea of why it's so important to Homs.'

'Fine,' said Pau, still glowering. 'The bad news is I've found no difference between this one and other copies I've seen in the past. And nothing about the *Liber Octavus* either.'

'Let the two of us have a look, maybe we'll find something.'

'Of course,' Pau said, pushing the manuscript towards them. 'Firstly, you ought to know that one of the most striking things about the book are its illustrations. There are more than eighty, and sixteen of those occupy full pages. They're the work of several different artists, though the first and most well known was Johannes Stephanus de Calcar, a pupil of Titian's. Vesalius himself also did a number of them.'

'What's so important about having pictures?'

'Vesalius argued passionately that anatomy and the fine arts shouldn't be separate, so he wanted to appeal as much to artists as to doctors. Their quality remains unsurpassed, and they have been copied many times. At the same time, they're a wonderful source of information, because of how much symbolism they contain. Look at the cover – that's Vesalius himself.' A man stood at the centre of the image: his forehead was high, his nose broad, and he had a full head of hair and an equally thick beard. The look in his eye, gazing directly out at them, seemed like a challenge to the reader, an invitation to come and discover his secrets. 'The scene represents the early days of dissections. At that time, because bodies would quickly rot, they'd start with the viscera, as you see –' Pau pointed – 'here, with this divider he's using to keep the cadaver open. In fact, the whole thing is a provocation. Vesalius was against the tradition of talking about dissection *ex cathedra*: here we see him relegating the barbers to a position beneath the table, while he prepares to dissect the body himself.'

'Barbers?' said Fleixa, trying not to laugh.

'Barbers were the original surgeons,' said Pau. 'They had to deal with dead bodies, which medical professionals at that time saw as being beneath them. Vesalius was among the first to break with that norm, and that was how he gained such good knowledge of the human body. With *Fabrica* he sought to demonstrate Galen's mistakes, such as the notion that the large blood vessels originated in the liver. So this illustration is his way of saying, the only accurate knowledge about human beings resides in human beings themselves.'

The page as she turned it seemed to creak, as if in complaint at all the years that had passed since it had been read.

'Vellum,' Pau said, 'which means it's definitely an original. I mentioned before that it was divided into the seven parts, or *Liber*. So the *Liber Primus* concerns bones and joints. The *Secundus* looks at musculature – that's where the most famous illustrations are. The *Tertius* looks at the heart and the blood vessels, the *Cuartus* the nervous system, the *Quintus* is about the abdominal organs, the *Sextus* the organs in the thorax, and the *Septimus* contains a description of the brain. In its day it was revolutionary. Modern anatomy starts here.'

The illustration they had before them now was of a smiling skeleton with the muscles peeled away; Fleixa couldn't help himself.

'It's disgusting!'

'It's one of the illustrations' great strong points. Vesalius went

351

for quite theatrical postures, very effective for description. This copy is different to others I've seen, it seems more . . . How can I put it? More alive.' She gave an admiring sigh. 'The symbols you see next to the muscles, tendons and bones correspond with a table on the following page, where you get an explanation of nomenclature and anatomical function.'

The oil lamps in the café did seem to add life to the illustrations. The figures writhed, silently shrieking in pain, as if they truly had been flayed. Fleixa shuddered – at the images, or at the fact he was going to have to report all of this to Sánchez later on – he didn't know.

'There's something inside the front page . . .' Daniel began to say, and brought the lantern on their table nearer. Then, holding the book up to the light, the shadow of some text became apparent, and as the other two looked expectantly on, he unstuck a thin piece of paper: on the lower part of the flyleaf there was a minuscule body of text.

'It looks like a dedication.'

'That's very unusual,' Pau said. 'Seeing as people tended to make the dedication as prominent as possible. Makes no sense to hide it away.'

The trio leaned in close. A quarter of the page was taken up by some intricate calligraphy, followed by Vesalius's elegant signature.

'It's in Latin.'

'You're right, Amat. Vesalius used the languages of medicine in those days: Vulgate Latin, Greek, Arabic and Hebrew.'

Daniel read aloud, translating. 'It's a personal dedication to King Felipe II, wishing him health and prosperity, and saying he hereby offers him the most treasured parts of his learning and wisdom. April 1565, it says next to the signature.'

'That isn't possible,' Pau said.

'What do you mean?'

'The only editions of *Fabrica* came out in 1542 and 1555. Vesalius gave Carlos V a copy of the first edition, nowadays that's kept at the University of Lovaine. But this is from ten years later; Vesalius was already dead by that time!'

'Maybe it's a mistake.'

'Maybe, but . . .' Pau fell silent for a moment, before looking up, her eyes glistening. 'Do you realize what this means? This might be a third edition, this ink might be from Vesalius's own pen – at a time when everyone *thought* him dead. An edition, in other words, of which there's absolutely no mention in any of the records. If I'm right, this is a one-off. You could probably name your price.'

'How much are we talking?' said Fleixa, looking at the stage as the guitarists and singers began another song. 'Forty, fifty pesetas?'

'Possibly slightly more. What about hundreds of thousands of pesetas?'

Fleixa spat out his brandy, and nearly fell off his seat.

'How's that?' Daniel said.

'More, probably.' Pau's fingers trembled as she ran them across the pages reverentially. 'There is no other anatomical compendium in the world quite like it. Millions, it could be worth.'

'A few old bits of paper and ink!'

Pau scowled at Fleixa once more. Not bothering to intervene

353

this time, Daniel took the book and scrutinized the pages close up. What was hidden in them, what was it that had led to so many deaths?

The song came to an end, and the artists left the stage for a break. Fleixa took the opportunity to belch and offer a toast to the illustrious anatomist.

'I've gathered a few facts about Vesalius,' said Pau, only addressing Daniel now. 'I wondered if I ran through them, whether it might help us decide our next step.'

'Good thinking,' said Daniel. 'Anything you think's relevant?'

'Well, in my view it's the latter part of his life that we ought to focus on.' She brought out a notebook. 'At the end of his time in Spain he stopped practising medicine, apart from waiting on the King, and dedicated himself to research. Some people in the medical profession hated that he had the King's favour, not to mention resenting his brazen attacks on Galen. And so when he started spending less time at court, that's when the malicious gossip began.'

'What kind of things?'

'Vesalius seemed to be carrying on with his autopsies, something which in those days, and especially in Spain, was frowned upon by the church, and even by some medical practitioners. So people started saying he was practising necromancy.'

'Fascinating!' said Fleixa, yawning. 'How is any of this supposed to help us?'

Ignoring the journalist, Pau went on. 'In 1564, a religious tribunal that was part of the Inquisition sentenced Vesalius to death, but King Felipe commuted it into a pilgrimage to Jerusalem instead. It isn't exactly clear what he was charged with, but the more reliable sources point to the possibility that he did an autopsy on a nobleman and, when he opened his chest, witnesses claimed that the heart was still beating. Which, if it were true, would be an unusual error for Vesalius to make, considering how many people he'd treated in his long career, not to mention the hundreds of dead bodies he'd used for study purposes.'

'And so what happened next?'

'He did his penance with the journey to the Holy Lands. Then, on his way back, though he was offered a Venetian ship by the crown, he boarded a decrepit boat used by pilgrims, and it sank off the Greek island of Zante. Vesalius is reported to have survived the shipwreck itself but, already quite old by that point, and having suffered injuries, he's said to have fallen ill and died. Other sources, though, say he lived on for another twelve years, spending the final part of his life in Greece.'

'Hard nut to crack, our Andreas!' said Fleixa.

'Perhaps, out of the reach of his enemies, it left him free to work on this third edition,' said Daniel. 'Perhaps that could have been when he wrote the *Liber Octavus*.'

'It is possible,' said Pau.

'Right, right, but how are we supposed to *find* this *Liber Octopus*, or whatever it is? Thinking of a little trip to Greece?'

'There must be some reason Homs was so intent on having *this copy*,' mused Daniel. 'Maybe it contains a clue as to how to find it.'

Pau shook her head dejectedly. She'd already been all the way through the book, and there was no sign of anything to do with the mysterious eighth section.

Just then pandemonium broke out over at one of the gambling

tables. Accusations of cheating, raised voices, and a full-blown fight erupted. The whole café was drawn into the chaos. The initial unrest was like touch paper, and within moments insults and fists began to fly all around.

'Let's get out of here,' said Daniel.

As they were standing up to leave a waiter, who had been trying to calm the combatants, was shoved into Fleixa, who in turn fell into the table, knocking over bottles and glasses – some of which were half full. Pau tried to save the manuscript from getting soaked, but couldn't move quickly enough: half of the last illustration they'd been looking at was covered in wine. And, before their eyes, in the middle of the crimson blotch, three of the symbols on the illustration began to glisten like tiny stars. In a sudden excitement Daniel grabbed a glass of red wine from a nearby table, and poured it onto the book as well – much to Pau's dismay.

'What do you think you're doing?' she cried.

'*Look*,' he said.

And they all stared in wonder as a constellation of glimmering circles appeared across the picture.

FORTY-SEVEN

Dolors's mind felt like a steam engine on full boil. She had decided to go and show herself at Fleixa's offices. If he wasn't there, the journalist had talked to her about a colleague he trusted, Vives was the name; he'd surely know where he might be. She needed to clear up this misunderstanding once and for all.

Turning the corner, she pulled up at the sight of a lavish landau coming along the street towards her. Not the kind of vehicle one would usually see in the Raval. Dolors couldn't help but be impressed by its expanses of dark, shining wood, its silver fittings. The horses had to be the most handsome she'd ever laid eyes upon.

To her surprise, it came alongside her and stopped. The driver, in a fine wool coat, inclined his head, and she caught a waft of something – a smell that brought to mind a visit she'd once made to the Santa Creu Hospital when one of the girls had been ill.

'Come closer, woman.' His voice cracked like the whip in his hand. Her first response was to send him on his way but, out of habit, she approached.

'Your name Dolors?'

At this she took a step back, eyeing the man.

'Maybe, maybe not.'

'Right. Well, I've just been talking to a friend of yours who said I'd find you down here. I had to buy her a drink before she'd tell me anything.'

Dolors shrugged. Mercedes and her mouth.

'Nothing to be afraid of, I mean no harm.' The man sounded gentler now. 'Been trying to find you for days.'

'Me? But why?'

'Another gentleman spoke to my master about you. He's asked me to find you and bring you to see him.'

Dolors didn't answer straightaway. This was the client Mercedes had mentioned. No one would go to such trouble for a prostitute – maybe one in El Paralelo, where all the new cabarets and theatres were, but not a Raval scrub like her. It was unheard of.

'I'm knocking off for the day.' She turned to leave. 'Tell your master it will have to be some other time.'

'Wait,' said the man, taking a purse out and, as she turned back again, lobbing it down to her. Dolors swore as she caught it – feeling how heavy it was. She tipped out a good number of duros, the solid silver piece that was worth five pesetas. She was rapt by the gleaming coins; even when the man spoke again, she could hardly tear her eyes away.

'Plenty more where that came from, if you accept. He's a very rich man, and generous with it.'

This was already a fortune to her, more than she'd earn in a year. And the man would pay her even more? She eyed the landau uncertainly. How much would one of those set you back? It was very beautiful, even with those scratches along the side. The owner must be unimaginably rich.

'Who is your master?'

'A very important gentleman, one requiring the utmost discretion, naturally.'

Seeing her indecision, the man went on. 'He has his fancies, is all – and he knows what it costs to have them satisfied. Are you really going to turn down this sort of opportunity?'

She looked at the duros again. She could do this job and never have to sell her body again. And it would be a little ridiculous for her to turn moralist now. Luck was smiling on her for once, why spurn it? She could start a new life with this money. Fleixa wouldn't have to know how she got it.

'All right,' she said.

'Wonderful!' said the man, hopping down and opening the coach door for her. 'There is one thing though . . .'

'What now?'

'Well,' he said, looking serious. 'As I say, he's quite particular, and one thing I know is that he can't stand polka dot dresses.'

'You can't be serious?'

'We could go past your home, you could change quickly. Really, anything but polka dots will be fine.'

'You're telling me to how to dress? Your master's mad.'

'He's an out and out gentleman, I assure you, but he is quite specific about certain things. It won't take five minutes to change – worth it, considering the money, wouldn't you say?'

Dolors felt like saying no, but those heavy duros quickly stifled any objections. What did it matter – she'd only have to take her clothes off anyway. The coachman, rubbing his gloved hands together, was clearly anxious for her answer.

'Fine, we'll do what he wants – but it's going to cost more.'

'Clever girl. He'll shower you with coins, don't you worry.' Smiling, he held out his hand to help her up. 'It's your lucky day.'

Dolors whistled when she saw the carriage interior. The door closed shut behind her. She told the driver the way, and the carriage set off. Drawing the blind on the small window, she dandled the purse distractedly in her hands. She tried to calm herself, saying this would be the last time. Life was going to change. Afterwards, she'd go and find Fleixa, and her answer would be yes.

FORTY-EIGHT

Ordering more wine, the trio moved to a table in a corner. The hubbub of the café, all the voices and music, fell into the background as their excitement grew.

They did the same with the next illustration, pouring a little wine onto it, and the same with the next. And again, small circles appeared around the symbols identifying the different parts of the body: small, glittering circles.

'Vesalius knew what he was about,' said Pau admiringly. 'He's used soda paste. The acid in the wine reacts with that, and the symbol in question, invisible before, gets this shimmery halo around it. It's so incredibly simple.'

'Right,' said Fleixa, 'but what does it mean? Presumably he's picking out certain symbols and not others for a reason?'

'A message?' said Daniel.

'Just add them together, and that's it?'

'It can't be that easy,' said Pau. 'They must be organized in some way.'

They turned their attention to the last illustration they'd poured the wine onto. It was of a dissection in its advanced stages. The skeleton looked off towards a landscape in the distance, turning its back on the reader – giving the reader a view of the deep layers of the musculature. Small, twinkling circles surrounded it, picking out symbols Vesalius had chosen to highlight three hundred years earlier.

'Maybe we need to hold it up next to another copy,' suggested Fleixa.

'Good idea, but too complicated,' said Daniel. 'I feel like the solution must be here, in this manuscript. Maybe there could be a link between this one and the rest of—'

'You're right!' exclaimed Pau, turning the book around to show them. 'The images and text don't make sense without each other, that's the whole way the book works. I was telling you, the symbols all correspond with the explanatory table on the subsequent page.'

'And the text comes in a particular order,' said Daniel. 'Of course! So let's copy out the symbols he marked, in the order they come in the tables. Can't hurt to try.'

They set to it, Daniel and Fleixa turning the pages and calling out the symbols in question to Pau, who transcribed them in her notebook. It turned out that sixteen of the seventeen full page illustrations contained the marks, but none of the smaller illustrations. After an hour Pau pushed the notebook towards them with a look of disappointment. They'd filled several pages, but not with anything that made any sense.

Ł>z7oLюгZoZ░ω░7ʌƐωZƷ+ǫaω‡◊7o6
>L6Łυf░f+rzL░7r░░░LƐz76░ю>L░Ł
zƐ7Z>+6◊+rz+░7Ɛω∞ωρo░76f◊7◊ɡL
76◊Ɛ+ZaюZ7∞fLz+<çǫLΔo+Zfρ7ƺ░∞+ǫ7<L
P7Zzω7Δof+6za░76LZƐ+░LZ7ª6ωǫƐ7г
Ɛ+Z░Ļ6ƺ7ʌf∞f◊7◊ . . .

'I don't understand it,' she said. 'I was sure you were onto something, Amat.'

All three felt gripped by uncertainty.

'This Vesalius is taking us for a ride!' exclaimed Fleixa.

But then, apropos of nothing, Daniel began to laugh.

'Of course! Why didn't I think of it before?'

The other two looked at him in alarm: had it suddenly all become too much?

'You've told us, Gilbert, that Vesalius had all sorts of enemies. So there was no way he was going to make it *that* easy. What better than a code to throw them off the scent?' They didn't look convinced. 'Look, it's mainly numbers and letters from the Latin and Greek alphabets. I've only just realized, but I've seen a group of similar symbols before.'

He took out Homs's notebook, and placed it on the table, open at the last page. There was a table containing symbols.

'We were wrong, these clearly are something! I'd bet anything that if we transpose what's here in this notebook with the symbols in the manuscript, it will be some sort of message.'

'Plus it would explain why Homs was so intent on getting the notebook back!' enthused the journalist.

'Let's see if you're right,' said Pau, resolve in her voice.

With renewed impetus, they split the job between them, each taking a third of the pages of symbols they'd copied out and checking them against the table in the notebook. They became so immersed in the task, Fleixa even forgot about his drink. What started out as a pile of incomprehensible signs, after an hour or so of feverish effort, gradually became clear: by the end, they had four pages of writing in Latin. Daniel translated out loud as the others listened expectantly.

The document you hold in your hands is Book Eight, con-
taining a store of knowledge of unsurpassed importance. I,
Andreas Vesalius, say to you who have come this far: it is
a huge responsibility you have in your hands . . .

They could barely contain themselves.

'It doesn't tell us where to find the *Liber Octavus*,' exclaimed Pau, 'it *is* the *Liber Octavus!*'

'Go on,' said Fleixa – which Daniel did.

I've dedicated my life to fighting illness and its final
consequence, which is death. Medicine is the highest sci-
ence, and my goal, that which has conferred meaning on
my days, has always been to add to its progress. In what
follows I shall refer to 'the process', which is something that
years of study have led to: a procedure with steps that must
be followed to the letter. None of the steps must be skipped,
meaning that you will need great humility if you are to
make it to the goal, which is supreme understanding.

First you must gather a certain amount of steel and glass

of the highest quality, prepared by a master craftsman: a
large receptacle must be made by the joining together of
these two materials.

Vesalius went on to set out, in the utmost detail, complex instructions and the materials required for the building of a device of some kind.

> *Truly, this is the sum of all that I know, the most perfect*
> *of the most perfect of all creations, the dwelling place for the*
> *immortal soul, an abode referred to by the ancients – not*
> *without reason – as 'microcosmos'.*

So ended the text. The trio sat in dumbfounded silence.

'Vesalius is describing how to build . . . a machine!' said Daniel finally.

'A machine capable of channelling an energy source as strong as a lightning bolt,' added Pau. 'Do you see? He's putting forward a system for manipulating electricity, almost a hundred years before it was even given that name. It's so far ahead of its time.'

'Wonderful, amazing – but what use is any of it?' said Fleixa. To this the others admitted they had no answer.

'Is this really all we have?' thundered the journalist. 'Maybe we haven't found everything!'

Daniel shook his head; he'd been through the notes twice, there wasn't anything else.

'Let's come at it from another angle. What could have made Homs so hell-bent on getting his hands on it?'

'That's obvious. He wanted the *Liber Octavus*.'

'It can't be that,' said Daniel. 'Homs already knew what was in here, and I think he even knew what Vesalius's machine could be used for. He hints at it elsewhere in his notes.'

'And so?'

'Homs has been trying to get both the notebook and the manuscript back. He's been trying to stop them from falling into our hands, but I just can't think why.'

'Fine,' said Pau. 'Let's suppose you're right and Homs is putting this machine into practice. How would he gather the energy that's needed?'

'He must have access to some lightning rods.'

'Well, there are any number of those in the city, but it would mean he'd need to wait for an electrical storm any time he wanted to use it.'

'No!' said Daniel, thumping the table. 'He doesn't need a storm: he's had all the energy he could possibly need, for weeks now!'

'As in?'

'The power station for the World Fair!'

'But Vesalius says the machine needs an *immense* amount of energy to function.'

'I've visited the station, and when I was there I saw generators capable of powering the whole of the Fair, as well as the squares and streets in the adjacent parts of the city.'

'So maybe it would be enough.'

'More than enough! And, when I was being shown around by the owner, Bertomeu Adell, at one point one of his employees came and told him about some incidents – no one knew what was causing them – that were undermining the stability of the whole system. It's possible that was Homs's work, tapping the electricity for himself . . .'

Daniel suddenly fell silent, his face bright.

'I've got it!' he said. 'This is the real reason Homs wanted to stop us from finding the manuscript! If we did, we'd be able to work out where he's hiding.'

'You've lost me, Amat.'

'He needs somewhere to dispose of his victims. What the *Liber Octavus* is telling us is that this place must be near to the power station, so he can have access to the electricity he needs. Do you see? My father had come to the same conclusion, and that explains why the last sighting of him was going down into the sewers. Homs is hiding somewhere beneath the grounds of the World Fair!'

LIES AND BETRAYALS

Nine days before the start of the World Fair

FORTY-NINE

No one dared actually touch the body. A group of fishermen, returning at dawn from a night trawl, had stumbled across it. One of the younger ones wondered whether it might be a washed up mermaid. She was covered in seashells and pebbles that marked marine shapes on her skin. Seaweed was strewn about her closed eyes and her mouth curved upwards in a smile. She looked as though she had simply fallen asleep on the marshy sand of the Barceloneta.

A few curious folk had come out of their houses and were milling around whispering – in the absurd worry that the killer might overhear. They all asked what they could have done to anger the Black Hound, to make it strike again.

A crunching on the pebbles and the neighing of some horses announced the arrival of two carriages up on the esplanade. The rotund figure of Inspector Sánchez emerged from the first, his considerable bulk causing the vehicle to tilt as he got down. He examined the grey sky and the incoming sea clouds, scowling at the likely rain. He had a hangover, his head hurt, and he did not much feel like examining some beggar's corpse.

A man got down after him, slight and with very pale skin, wearing a coat that hung off him. He carried a small briefcase in his left hand. Adjusting his spectacles, glancing indifferently around, he stood and waited for Sánchez's instructions.

Half a dozen Guardia Civil alighted from the other vehicle, an uncovered wagon, and set about clearing the area. The people were moved off amongst pushes, threats and hard looks.

With his assistant beside him, Sánchez trudged over to the corpse. As he pulled away the fishermen's blanket, a hush fell. The feet and hands were black as coal, a number of digits missing from each. The right breast was missing and the flesh at the edges of the wound looked singed. One of the men blanched and stumbled away, vomiting up his breakfast in the shallows.

Sánchez looked pensive as he took in the sight. He prodded one of the legs with his toe; it was bloated and stiff. The man with the briefcase knelt down next to the body and prepared to take out his implements.

'Take it easy, sawbones. Even the sergeant there can tell you she's dead.'

A few of the men chuckled nervously. The morning was cold and spirits were low. The doctor shrugged and withdrew to fill out the death certificate, while two of the men came forward to cover the body and place it on a stretcher.

Sánchez heard Sergeant Azcona come up behind him. He was young and ambitious, always willing to go the extra mile – too willing, in Sánchez's opinion. One of a new batch of police that had been brought in – the view was that Barcelona was in need of some good men on the force. Not a view shared by Sánchez. With a sigh, he turned to listen.

'I recognize her. Her name's Dolors. She worked the Raval.'

'Wonderful, Sergeant, that saves us having to identify her.'

'I found this,' said Azcona, handing over something small and gold. 'It was clasped inside one of her hands.'

'What is it?' said Sánchez, raising an eyebrow.

'It's a bit bent, but I think it's a tie clip. And look, its got someone's initials: *D.A.*'

'Great,' said Sánchez, pocketing the object. 'I'll look into it.'

The younger man nodded respectfully.

'So the usual M.O. with the body?'

'No, in fact. Take her directly to the Nord. I don't want any more bodies like this, any found in this state, to go to the morgue.'

Azcona looked shocked; it was a clear departure from procedure. Unidentified bodies were always kept at the morgue for three days before being buried in a mass grave.

'As you say, Señor, but—'

'But what, Sergeant?'

'A family member might come to claim the body.'

A know-it-all – a real know-it-all. Just what he needed.

'Who the fuck is going to claim a whore?' said Sánchez. 'For Christ's sake, just do as I say. And Azcona—'

'Yes?'

'Don't go blabbing this around.'

Fleixa was sitting on the beach – a few metres further up, with his back against one of the beach huts. Nervous spasms had taken over his body, and he was manically writing in his notebook, turning the pages and writing, knowing that if he stopped, his heart would stop as well.

His hand was bleeding. The pages became crumpled or even ripped, he was pressing so hard, but he little cared; he'd just turn to the next page and write his words there – and continue gasping for air.

Dead. Dolors was dead.

He repeated it over and over, as if the repetition might somehow stop it from being true.

He wanted to believe they were wrong, that it was another woman who had washed up on the beach, but when he received Vidal's message, he knew it could only be her.

If he hadn't have left the way he did – if he hadn't acted like a frustrated schoolboy . . .

Tearing out another page, he let the wind bear it away.

Suddenly a stab of pain in his gut forced him to double over. Something inside him shook, contorting his stomach and moving up into his chest. It was growing inside him, seemed to be about to rip him in two. He wanted to cry out, but couldn't. Writing was all he could manage. He carried on unspooling letters from his pencil until the pain took over his burning hand. He lifted the hand up – it shook so hard it wavered in the air. He tried to carry on writing. Blood soaked the already illegible pages, which were falling apart – much as he felt himself to be. Then, the pencil snapped in his hand. Fleixa let the notebook drop onto the sand and wept.

FIFTY

Daniel made his way along the earthen path, one which the recent downpour had turned into a muddy lake, the occasional dry island to hop between. Up above Collserola a few blue patches could be discerned in the ash-grey sky.

He came to a wrought-iron gate and rang the bell on one of the ivy-covered posts. The residence of the Marquis of Llupià i Alfarràs looked more like an Arabic castle than an aristocratic home: a hexagon with stout, crenelated walls and a tower. The Moorish windows and two enormous palm trees added to the illusion of having been transported to somewhere in the Rif mountains.

He'd spent the morning going over the *Liber Octavus* with Gilbert – Fleixa had failed to show. But their efforts had produced no tangible results; they were no closer to understanding what the remarkable Vesalius machine was intended to do. He'd been about to call a halt, so they could go and eat, when a message came for him: the Marquis had requested his presence, that very afternoon. It had given no indication of why he was wanted, but remained sufficiently intriguing for him to accept.

He heard footsteps, and then a manservant opened the gate. Daniel held out his card, but the man, without so much as looking at it, beckoned him in. He was expected.

They made their way into the house and through numerous rooms decorated in an oriental style, before finally arriving in a spacious salon. At the centre of the room, comfortably ensconced on a divan, sat an elderly gentleman. He appraised the visitor with some interest.

'Please come in, Señor Amat.' He indicated the armchair nearest to him. 'You'll excuse me if I don't get up: this blessed chaise keeps me prisoner for many an hour after I have lunched.'

Daniel crossed over and sat down. The Marquis was a tall man, and even with the blankets on his lap retained a distinguished air. He wore a dressing gown and, though haggard of face, there remained something regal about his large, prominent nose. Bushy eyebrows, light, sparkling blue eyes, and pince-nez resting on his nose completed the picture.

'Good, good.' His voice resounded as though from the depths of a cave. 'A pleasure to meet you, Señor Amat. My name is Juan Antonio Desvalls, owner of this estate and of the bombastic title of Marquis, thanks to having been born into a very old family. An outmoded detail, considering the middle-class deluge we've seen in Barcelona in recent decades. They're the new aristocracy now.' He paused to cough into a handkerchief. 'Would you like a drink?'

Daniel shook his head. Desvalls swirled a goldish liquid around in a glass.

'Bourbon's the only thing I can stomach at this hour. A vice that I allow myself, in spite of my daughter's constant vigilance.'

'I see.'

'No, no, I don't believe you do. But you will. Soon enough, you will. You're still young.'

'I beg your pardon, Señor. In your message there was mention of a personal matter. I cannot guess what that may be, though, seeing as we've only just been acquainted.'

'You're quite right, though I shouldn't be the one to enlighten you on this particular matter.'

'I'm afraid I—'

'Pass me my cane, would you, let's go outside.'

Daniel got up and brought Desvalls his ivory walking stick, before helping the older man to his feet. At the top of the gardens was an open area with uneven ground, and from this they passed through an iron gate flanked by two lion statues, into a delicate boxwood garden and along a path lined by expansive flowerbeds.

'What do you make of it?'

'Beautiful.'

The Marquis leaned on Daniel as they went, looking straight ahead and speaking in a firm voice. 'My great-grandfather initiated the construction of the estate almost a hundred years ago – Joan Antoni Desvalls i d'Ardena, sixth Marquis of Llupià. He used an Italian for the buildings, a man named Bagutti, and a Frenchman for the gardens, Debalet I think it was, something like that – never much liked Frogs, myself. And it's been added to and extended in the time since then, the flowerbeds, the irrigation, these small squares. Dozens and dozens of trees we've put in, expanded the overall surface area, even installed a waterfall.'

Daniel continued to support the old man as they walked on, with little idea of where the conversation was headed.

'We've had kings and princes here at the Desvalls estate. Fernanda and her sisters are dead set on having their masques here, open air theatre and the like. We'll end up giving the place away, mark my words.'

They came out onto a terrace with a viewing platform. To either side was a pair of shrines, with a statue in the centre.

'Ariadne and Theseus,' said the Marquis, pointing with his stick. 'Pretty story, you know it?'

'What I can remember from school. Ariadne helped Theseus find his way through the labyrinth. He killed the Minotaur, and the pair ran off together.'

'Oh, more or less, yes. Though Ariadne's always struck me as something of a scatterbrain, if I'm honest. Perhaps that's why I like her.'

His laughter brought on coughs and, once the fit had passed, he shuffled forward and rested against the platform balustrade.

An intricate labyrinth stretched out on the level below, formed of sculpted hedges. Daniel admired the maze of green with all its twists and turns, inviting unsuspecting souls to enter in. The weak afternoon light seemed to deepen the darkness of its paths, which branched off in all directions, with no apparent destination. In the centre, Daniel glimpsed what he thought was a statue covered in creepers.

'Our famed labyrinth,' said the Marquis. 'A kilometre, give or take, of cypresses, kept at a height of four metres throughout. You would have trouble imagining all the scenes that have taken place here.'

'This is all very interesting, Señor Desvalls, really it is. But I don't believe you've brought me here to show me the landscaping.'

Desvalls paused and looked at Daniel for a moment. Up above, clouds were moving in and covering the sky again.

'If you wouldn't mind following me, Señor Amat,' he said, hobbling ahead and leading the way down some steps. As they advanced, the vegetation began closing in on either side. The air became increasingly freighted with electricity and the odour of jasmine.

'There's just one last thing I'd like to say. The secrets of these gardens lie not in their beauty, nor in the exotic plants, nor the wonderful position they enjoy. The key to this place is its harmony. And that harmony is a delicate balance. Any new element, any kind of interference whatsoever, will cause it to wither and fade. Think on that.'

They came to a clearing presided over by an elegant statue of Eros. A pair of figures could be seen in the shadows on the far side of it. Irene, with a pretty young girl at her side, appeared beside the plinth. The pair shook hands lightly, and the girl came over to accompany the Marquis away, leaving Daniel and Irene alone together.

'Shall we sit?'

Daniel, not yet recovered from the surprise, let Irene lead him over to a stone bench. She seemed to want to keep a certain distance; in a dark dress and fitted overcoat, a veil obscured her face. Daniel spoke first.

'I didn't think I'd be seeing you again.'

'And that was how it should have been, but I had to warn you, and I could think of no other way to do it.'

'Warn me about what?'

'You're in danger.'

'How do you know that?'

'I overheard my husband in conversation a few days ago, with Inspector Sánchez. He often comes to the house – has done for a long time. They talked about you and your friend, the journalist. Bertomeu was apoplectic. He told the Inspector to take measures – whatever he had to do, he said, anything in his power.'

'I see . . .'

'No,' she said, shaking her head. 'I don't believe you're seeing this correctly at all.'

'But why is he so determined to stop us?'

'There's a lot of money at play. A scandal would be very harmful to him.'

'Much like what he told me when he and I talked, but for some reason I don't think that's everything. Perhaps your husband's worried what conclusions people might come to concerning the death of my father, and the deaths of all these poor girls.'

'Bertomeu is incredibly well connected, and he also happens to be capable of anything. Do you hear me? Just by being here I'm putting myself in danger.'

'So this is why we meet so far from Barcelona. You're afraid.'

'Of course I'm afraid!'

'How can you love a man like that?'

'Easy for you to say!' she exploded. 'You left, remember? You abandoned me. After that, he was the only one who would have me.'

Daniel was about to speak, but she stopped him.

'None of that matters now,' she said quietly. 'What matters is that you leave Barcelona and do not come back. It isn't just

380

Bertomeu – what if this murderer finds you, what if you end up like your father?'

Daniel shook his head.

'I can't, Irene. Not this time. I fled once, and it cost me my life, everything. The nightmares have never stopped. Not long ago, I thought I'd got my life back, but it was all a lie. I can't go away again, do you understand?'

She looked at him through the veil and, after a moment of hesitation, removed a leather-bound folder from her handbag and handed it to him.

'I was worried you'd say this. These are some documents I found in Bertomeu's office. They're to do with the sanatorium. They shouldn't be in his possession, and he's gone to great efforts to hide that he has them. Maybe they can help you.'

For a moment, as Daniel accepted the folder, Irene's gloved hands were in his.

'There's still time,' she said. 'You can still leave all of this behind.'

Daniel gently moved her hand side, and took out the pieces of paper.

It was a few loose sheets containing a medical report. The language was familiar to him from the many times his father had tried, in vain, to interest him in medicine. This one described the autopsy of the patient befriended by Homs in the sanatorium, with a detailed description of the wounds that had led to his death. Though inflicted with less precision, they were altogether of a piece with the dead girl at the morgue. It only underlined his certainty that Homs must be mad: who in their right mind could commit such acts on another human being?

He went on reading about the state of the body. The forensic doctor had been exhaustive – there was even a list of the infirmities suffered by the man during his lifetime. Daniel couldn't think why Adell would have wanted this information. There was nothing particularly noteworthy about it?

He'd nearly given up when one of the later paragraphs caught his eye. He would have skimmed past it if, in that moment, he hadn't remembered something Doctor Giné had said. He reread the passage slowly and carefully: 'the subject [it read] presented an advanced hepatocellular carcinoma.'

He felt the hairs on his arms stand on end.

'Can you make use of it?'

Though stunned, Daniel nodded.

'I have to go,' he heard Irene say.

They both stood up. Their bodies were very close as they faced one another. The leaves on the ground turned circles as a light wind picked up. A thunderclap boomed in the heavens, and the first drops of a storm began to fall. Standing motionless, neither seemed to notice.

'Why did you have to come back?' whispered Irene.

Daniel didn't know how to answer. He brought his hand forward, thinking to push back her veil. He felt a sudden urge to kiss her. She tried to avoid his hand, but it was too late; the black muslin fell clear away, and what Daniel saw stupefied him.

An enormous, puffy bruise extended up from Irene's left cheek and across her eye, which was all but shut. He ran his trembling fingers over the injury, until a blush appeared on the unbruised part of her face, and she turned away. Tears sprang to her eyes as she replaced the veil. Daniel, for his part, wanted to explode, but then she took his hands in hers.

'There's nothing to be done.'

'Leave him. Let me take care of you.'

A dejected smile spread on her face. She caressed his cheek for a moment.

'No. You don't understand.'

'Wait,' he said – but the words were left floating in the air as Irene ran away through the thickening rain.

FIFTY-ONE

The Adell mansion looked like a cake lit from within, all the windows aglow from the hundreds of blazing candelabras. In the front courtyard, in between the sumptuous carriages, coach drivers and butlers stood around in their cloaks and capes, sharing cigarettes and, with luck, a little hot punch purloined from the kitchens. The sounds of the revelry drifted down to where they stood.

Though not as frequent as in the past, and though most such affairs were held at the Liceo, Adell would put on a masked ball once a year at his home, always going to some lengths to bring together the great and the good of the city.

Amongst the ladies this year, the fashionable thing was to be seen in village-style dresses, Hindustani outfits, or the attire of a Hungarian princess. As for the gentlemen, the somewhat less imaginative Neapolitan gentlemen, Sevillian apprentices and Venetian senators were much in evidence. The orchestra, over sixty-strong and surrounded on all sides by enormous Antwerp mirrors, played the first movements of a polka, much to the delight of the younger ladies in attendance.

'Bertomeu, my dear, you can't deny me this time.'

The industrialist, dressed as the Doge of Venice, was in the middle of a conversation and, turning, looked annoyed at the interruption. But when his eyes fell upon the voluptuous Alpine peasant girl, and her eager face, he couldn't help but smile.

'My dear Julia, you know I don't dance. Please, go and amuse yourself.'

'Spoilsport!'

She pouted for a moment, though that quickly gave way to a mischievous smile, followed by a curtsey. Her neckline was somewhat more plunging than was decorous. Adell felt a pang of pleasure as he remembered that the two of them would be enjoying their own private dance in a matter of hours. The young lady, pleased at the effect she'd had, turned and moved off into the sea of masks around the dance floor.

Adell returned to the conversation, enjoying the envious looks of his interlocutors. A couple of them cast furtive glances in Julia's direction as the dancers came around, the music swelling and growing faster. A menacing gesture from Adell was sufficient to regain their attention.

'Splendid girl, your companion, splendid.'

'Quite lovely, Señor.'

'Oh, I hadn't noticed,' said Adell, concealing his smile behind his brandy.

'Your wife must feel truly indisposed to miss such an event.'

At this, everyone in the circle fell silent. Throats were cleared. Adell, taking the Havana from his mouth, appraised the young man who had made the unfortunate comment. He didn't even know his name.

'My wife, Señor, does not deal well with crowds. Which is why my beloved niece is here with me this evening, keeping me company.'

The younger man, realizing his imprudence, turned a deep shade of red. It seemed that would be the end of it, but Adell was enjoying his discomfort and, after a pause, added with a grin, 'I imagine you'll agree when I say that my wife's health is not your concern – or, perchance, are you her doctor?'

'Ah, yes, Señor – I mean, no.'

'You are her doctor, or you disagree with me?'

'No, I mean—'

'It's all right, I see. Now that you've had your say, Señor, I believe you've expended your welcome here this evening.' Adell nodded to a nearby butler. 'I'm sure you have other pressing engagements, and so good night.'

Adell turned his back on the younger man as the butler escorted him out. As if nothing had happened, the group resumed the conversation – the topic of which was the ongoing turmoil in Cuba. Cotton and cloth were up, very bad news for all. Adell opined that the natives needed to be taught a lesson, a view everyone else hastened to agree with.

Just then a commotion began over at the entranceway. Adell thought the young man must be kicking up a fuss, but as he left the group and approached, he found that wasn't the case. His last guest had finally arrived.

'Señor Amat! Thanks for your punctuality, I hadn't expected to see you so soon.'

'I'm sure you hadn't,' snorted Daniel.

Two butlers, dressed in the livery of Louis XVI chamberlains,

386

were holding Daniel back, as he struggled to shake them off. Adell's coach driver hovered nearby, looking ready to step in.

'Señor Adell,' said one of the men, 'he isn't on the list, but wouldn't hear a word of no.'

'Ah? How strange for you not to be invited.'

Daniel threw off the men and walked straight up to Adell. Daniel looked in a very poor state, with both his hat and overcoat gone and his clothes and hair soaking from the rain. Shaking with rage, he shouted into the host's face. 'Scoundrel! How dare you lay a hand on her?'

The orchestra stopped playing, dropping the salon into an unexpected silence.

'I don't know what you're referring to.'

'No? As well as a coward, then, you are content to be a hypocrite?'

'You would insult me in my own home?' But Adell's anger was feigned: he was enjoying this. 'This is unheard of.'

'Won't you introduce me, Bertomeu?'

Julia had come over – drawn, along with a number of other guests, by the argument. She unabashedly looked the recent arrival up and down.

'This is Daniel Amat, my dear. He lost his father not long ago, and he returned to the city for the funeral, though he isn't going to be staying long.'

'Sounds like he needs some sympathy,' she said, and the smile she gave was not at all to Adell's liking. Unlinking arms, he sent her back the way she'd come.

'Off with you, go and dance or something.'

She was about to protest, but seeing Adell's angry look,

387

decided against it. With a disdainful look she turned and went in search of some champagne.

'Bring your floozies into your own house?' spat Daniel.

Adell looked amused. More and more people were gathering: all the witnesses he could hope for. This was going precisely as he had hoped. And there were even a couple of reporters, so their encounter couldn't fail to make it into the society pages.

'Mind telling me why you've come, Amat?'

'I want answers.'

'Answers? Ha!'

'Why have you been trying to stop me from looking into my father's death? And what have you got to do with the spate of murders?'

Murmurs went around.

'I believe you're referring to the murders of all these poor girls, of which there's been so much talk in the papers? You wouldn't, by any chance, be saying that I am the Black Hound, would you?' He burst out laughing, and after a moment others joined in. 'You must be unhinged, Señor.'

'There is a link between you, the power station, and these murders. Sooner or later justice will be done.'

'Actually, I rather think that you are the one who ought to be doing the explaining.' Adell saw, much to his delight, that he had wrong-footed his adversary. 'Why don't you start by explaining to us the events of seven years ago? Hmm? How it was that your brother died, *and* your fiancée? It's something people here are very anxious to know about. I mean, a man flees after an incident such as that, and . . .' He threw his arms in the air theatrically, looking around.

Daniel became aware of just how many people had gathered now, all the expectant and inquisitive faces. When he spoke, he could hear how unconvincing he sounded.

'It was . . . an accident.'

'An accident?' Adell chuckled. 'How convenient. To me it seems the most extraordinary coincidence that these murders should coincide with, well, *your* return to the city. Murders you seem to wish to implicate me in? I, who do everything I can and strive in all humility to see this city progress and improve.'

A chorus of assenting murmurs followed his words.

'Tell us, why don't you, what the real reason is for your return, after so many years away? Sure the doggy demon isn't, in fact, *you?*'

'You know it isn't.' Daniel had balled his hands into fists. 'Someone who's prone to fits of violence, however, someone with a history of losing control – to the point he nearly killed one of his own servants – *that* is the kind of person who might easily turn murderer.'

Adell blanched, but managed to keep his smile in place. He now stepped closer to Daniel again, and spoke softly so that no one would hear. 'I told you not to see her again. You showed me just how much my wife is in need of a firm hand. And you can be sure she isn't going to forget it this time.'

'Son of a—'

Daniel unleashed the punch – as Adell had thought he would. Even so, the blow to his chin was harder than he'd expected, and knocked him to the ground. Horrified cries went up, and a number of butlers leapt upon Daniel. Inspector Sánchez's face appeared in the crowd. He was wearing a Scottish kilt, and his outfit, particularly with the large amounts of hair oil he wore, gave him a far from martial air.

'Señor Adell,' he said. 'Has this man just assaulted you?'

'What do you think, cretin?' said the industrialist, who was still on the floor. 'Do your job!'

Sánchez flushed and gestured to two of his men. 'Señor Amat, you are under arrest.'

Before Daniel could start to protest, Adell's coach driver stepped forward and jabbed him in the kidney with a cudgel. Daniel dropped to his knees, gasping. A second blow, to the base of his neck, sent the room spinning. He barely felt it as he toppled to the floor.

Julia, returning, stifled a cry and clung to Adell as he got to his feet. This time he didn't push her clear.

'Put that away,' Sánchez said to the coach driver, trying to assert his authority. 'Your help is not required.'

With a shrug of the shoulders, the strapping driver stepped aside as Sánchez's men came forward to put handcuffs on Daniel. As they hauled him to his feet, Adell stepped in and put a hand on his shoulder, whispering into his ear.

'Did you know I also bought your family house?' he said, before pausing. 'Think on this when you are behind bars: everything that was yours is now mine, and there's nothing you can do to change it.'

FIFTY-TWO

'Please, Señor Gilbert, have a seat.'

The dean's voice resounded as sombrely and with as much force as on the hospital wards. Pau sat in one of the two free chairs. Seated across from her was the rest of the University Council, all five of them looking very guarded.

The office was a circular room with the same arched windows, set between pillars, as the rest of the building. Pau admired the collection of antique surgical instruments on display and the real skeleton – from the days when study materials still came from cemetery graves. She was startled to see, up on the wall, a reproduction of one of the illustrations from *De Humani Corporis Fabrica*. Bringing her attention back to the men facing her, she hugged the bag containing the manuscript closely to her.

As yet Pau did not know why she'd been asked in. After bidding Amat farewell, she'd been about to return to the Raval to hole up again in Dolors's rooms, but had decided first to stop by the hospital to ask after the young girl. She wanted to see for herself that her recovery from the tuberculosis was complete.

And as she came through the entryway, an orderly told her she was being looked for.

Finding the whole Council gathered, and seeing that Professor Gavet was among their number, her first thought was that her excuses for her recent absence must have gone down badly.

'Señor Suñé, I can explain.'

The dean raised a hand for quiet.

'Thank you for coming, Señor Gilbert.' He paused to take a breath. Whatever the reason, something was clearly making him very uncomfortable. 'You are a model student. Everyone here present holds you in high esteem, for all that you have on occasion shown impulsiveness and a tendency to take unnecessary risks on your own account. Everyone knows you went too far in your conduct with regards to the consumptive girl, and you were lucky that your approach was effective. You acted without guidance, and put the health of the whole hospital in jeopardy.'

Pau nodded. Had they changed their minds and decided now to punish her for that?

'Fine,' said Suñé. 'That, however, isn't why we've asked you here. 'We've just been informed of a conspiracy against your person, the object of which is to damage your reputation, and as a consequence the reputation of the university. Do you know what it is I speak of?'

There was no need to hide her surprise. 'No, Señor. I haven't the first idea.'

'Of course, that's understandable. I myself am unsure of where to begin. It's rather an embarrassing matter.'

'Implausible, is what it is,' said Professor Segura, straightening his jacket. 'This sort of calumny cannot be allowed to stand, far less for it to call the honour of this faculty into question.'

'The scandal would be enormous,' added another of the professors, a man named Llompart.

'Truly.'

'Gentlemen,' interrupted Suñé. 'So that we may all put our minds at ease, and so that Señor Gilbert may do the same, let us come to the point.'

'Quite right, Professor,' said the dean. 'Call him in, please.'

Llompart went and opened the door, and in marched Fenollosa. His lips were pursed so hard they'd gone white. Without so much as glancing at Pau, he nodded at the faculty members and sat in the only remaining seat, alongside Pau.

Pau tried to give an appearance of calm, though she was far from it. Everyone in the room seemed on edge – aside from Gavet. The professor, sprawling back in his chair, seemed to find something about the situation amusing. He looked smilingly from Pau to Fenollosa, and back again.

'This morning,' said Suñé, 'Señor Fenollosa here came to my study in a state of real perturbation. The young man has shown great brotherliness. Acting out of a double concern for others – for you, Gilbert, and for this great institution – he came to inform me of certain rumours that have been going around. About you.' The dean again took a deep breath before continuing. 'This slander, these aspersions, would have it that you are, in reality . . . a woman.'

The dean cleared his throat uncomfortably, and a number of the others shifted in their seats. Pau could feel her heart begin to pound, and the blood rushing to her cheeks. Suñé went on, seemingly unaware of her state.

'It goes without saying that this is all utterly absurd, but there's no way we can ignore the potential repercussions of such talk – for your own person, Gilbert, or for the university.'

Pau stole a look at Fenollosa. The look of concern on his face was very convincing.

'And where are these ... rumours coming from?' she said, trying to stop her voice from wavering.

'Señor Fenollosa?'

'Ah. Well, I was on my way back to my rooms a few days ago when, by chance, looking down at the street from a window, I observed my colleague Señor Gilbert having an altercation with a beggar out by the hospital gates. I went to try and assist, but arrived too late. Then, some days later, I saw the same individual hanging around in a nearby street. Thinking he might have it in mind to attack Gilbert once more, I went up to him to warn him away – but as I began giving him a piece of my mind, he begged that I listen to what he had to say. He told me that he was an old acquaintance of Gilbert's – he'd been a servant for a time at his family home. Still, I said, that gave him no right to importune his old employer. At this he began to laugh, saying that Señor Gilbert had never been his employer, that, in fact, Señor Gilbert was a woman, and that he had taken it upon himself to make this common knowledge. I called him a rogue for seeking to sully my colleague's good name. I thought to take him to the nearest Guardia barracks, but he managed to get away from me, and ran off.'

'Well, Señor Gilbert, what do you say?'

'It's true, I do know the man. He was a servant at my family home in the past. He was dismissed when we found out he had violated a young woman. He accosted me the other day asking for money.'

'That undesirable seemed to know all about you, Gilbert,' said Fenollosa, looking at her for the first time. 'And I can tell you, he's deadset on muddying your name.'

Fenollosa had set this up very shrewdly. If Pau managed to convince them that she was a man, he'd be congratulated for having stepped in to save a fellow student's good name. And if not, Fenollosa would have uncovered an act of fraudulence, saving the university from dishonour and ensuring Pau's expulsion to boot.

'Your colleague is in the right,' said the dean. 'This lamentable episode needs clearing up, and promptly. Ridiculous though the question may be, Gilbert, would you please give us your word that you are indeed . . .' He coughed. 'That you are not a woman?'

'My word?'

'Yes, and we can consider the matter closed.'

A number of the professors nodded their agreement: all wanted this over and done as quickly as possible. Pau breathed a sigh of relief: she'd be coming out of this far better than she'd expected. She was about to answer when Fenollosa leaped from his seat.

'That won't cover it.'

The dean looked surprised.

'Sit down and explain what you mean.'

'The rumour, that there is a woman pretending to be a man inside the university walls, has already spread to the local shops and taverns. Other students are also talking about it, and they are quite unsettled by the idea. The jokes will start, within the week, and think of how much that will be to our discredit. The sick will have second thoughts about even coming to us for treatment. To nip these rumours in the bud, it is my view that a more . . . a more *active* solution is required.'

The dean didn't seem convinced but, glancing around, saw the rest of the Council, to a man, weighing Fenollosa's words.

'He's right,' said a pensive Segura. 'We can't allow doubts to linger.'

'It would be f-for the best,' said Gavet, an amused look still in his eye.

The dean cast a reproachful glance at Fenollosa, sighing.

'Any suggestions, Gilbert?'

Pau fell silent. She'd been furiously trying to think of a way out, and still hadn't come up with one. Perhaps if she could put the matter off for a while, until after the exams, at least that would win her time.

It was Fenollosa who spoke first. 'I have an idea, Señor.'

'Go on, then, but be brief. We've wasted enough time over this nonsense already.'

'We need to give the impression that the university is not concerned by this kind of slander,' he said. 'And for that, we need to tread carefully. You should organize a lecture and open it to the public, an Anatomy lecture. Then Señor Gilbert would simply need to offer himself as a volunteer for a check up, and by baring his chest put an end to all this. Students, staff, and every person present, would see the proof for themselves.'

'I can't say I like the idea,' said Suñé, 'but I can think of no alternative.'

396

'Could we wait until exams are over?' squeaked Pau.

'Swifter action surely needs to be taken,' said Fenollosa, smiling. 'The damage to the university's reputation in the interim would be irreparable.'

'You're right,' said the dean. 'The sooner the better, and we can all return to our rightful work. We'll hold this lecture within the next three days, and let that be an end to it.'

A yawning chasm seemed to have opened beneath Pau's feet. She had always feared being discovered, and though she'd said to herself any number of times that it might happen, it made her no more prepared now that it was. She stood up and, with tears in her eyes, jutted out her chin. The five men across from her looked back in surprise. She no longer affected the deep voice as she said, 'That won't be necessary.'

'What are you saying?'

'Gentlemen, the rumours are true.'

'If this is a joke, Gilbert, it's in poor taste, very poor taste indeed.'

'It isn't, Señor. I am a woman.'

The dean and the rest of the Council looked horrified. An uncomfortable silence spread across the room, only to be broken when Professor Martorell stood up in a fit of rage.

'But . . . It's unheard of!'

'I can't believe it,' said Segura, examining Pau for any feminine aspects.

Suñé simply gawped, while Professor Llompart gripped the arms of his chair as though he might fall from it.

'Women cannot be doctors, far less surgeons,' he exclaimed, his voice quavering with indignation. 'It's, it's . . . inconceivable.

Dear God! Your character is not fit, your mind is clearly limited. Your place is in the home, with the family. What on earth were you thinking?'

'How could you have? The sheer cheek of it.'

'The brazenness!'

'That's enough, g-gentlemen,' said Gavet. 'C-calm yourselves.'

'Gavet's right,' said Suñé finally. Pau thought she saw a glimmer of admiration in the dean's face, but it was quickly eclipsed. 'We must try to be calm. A most unexpected turn of events. This changes everything. You falsified documents, you tricked this institution and its staff, and overall you have taken advantage of our good faith. All of this is extremely serious.'

'Yes, Señor,' said Pau, her voice firm.

'Anything to say in your defence?'

'I'm sorry if you feel yourselves to have been mocked in any way. It has never been my intention to damage the university's name or my colleagues. But you cannot expect me to be sorry. There was no other way for me. Whatever you may think, a woman is just as capable of being a good doctor as any man.'

To this nobody responded, though the looks on their faces spoke volumes. The dean appeared as though he'd aged ten years.

'I hereby suspend you from all academic activities, with immediate effect,' he said. 'And you are not to leave your lodgings until further notice. In the meantime, we will seek to arrive at the happiest end to this we can. Professor Gavet will accompany you.'

Pau turned to leave. Fenollosa was beaming. She decided not

to give him the satisfaction, and didn't even look at him as she came past.

'One moment, Gilbert,' said the dean. 'One last question. I have always meant to ask: many years ago I met a Doctor Francesc Gilbert. You look very like him. You wouldn't happen to be . . .'

'Yes, Señor,' she said, somehow managing to prevent her voice from cracking. 'He was my father.'

'Ah,' he said thoughtfully. 'An excellent doctor, Gilbert, quite excellent. As you could have been. A pity that God made you a woman.'

'The pity, Señor, is that God made you all men.'

Gavet held the door for her as she walked out.

They made their way along the corridors with the rapping of Gavet's cane a rhythmical accompaniment, bringing to mind the drums on a gallows walk. Pau felt nothing, it was as though she had inhaled ether: she floated forwards as the walls around her distended and warped.

She was surprised to find that, in spite of all that had happened, her mind turned to the Vesalius manuscript and the revelations of the previous day. Somewhere in the city a murderer was patiently awaiting his next victim. If they didn't find a way of stopping him, another girl would soon be dead. She had considered bringing the Council in on their findings, but now they'd learned of her deceit, they'd never believe her.

Gavet's voice brought her from her reflections.

'I-I want you to know,' he said, 'that you've won my admiration.'

'That's kind, Professor.'

'There's no question, my dear, that you have shown quite extraordinary bravery. You're like our very own Agnodice.'

Pau nodded – she knew the story. In 300 BC, an Athenian woman had pretended to be a man in order to study and then practice medicine. She saved hundreds of people's lives before being discovered and condemned to death. However, her patients came to her rescue, threatening to throw themselves onto the pyre with her should it be lit. The difference being that Pau had no one to come to her rescue. No one would be saving her. She was alone in the world. Quite alone.

FIFTY-THREE

The room, which had low ceilings and grey walls, made it near impossible to breath. The furniture was minimal: a desk and three old chairs, a pair of filing cabinets and a coat stand on which hung a single jacket and an umbrella. The only light came from a lantern on the desk at half-flame; there were no windows.

Daniel was sitting in the centre of the space. They'd left his overcoat on and the heat was suffocating. What was more, his wrists had been badly scraped by the handcuffs. On the other side of the desk sat Inspector Sánchez. The policeman was unhurriedly looking over some papers as he chewed on some salted peas. Two guards were standing behind Daniel.

The fit of rage that had carried him to the party had now waned, to be replaced by a feeling of pent-up powerlessness. How foolish he'd been to fall for his old friend's provocations.

'Señor Inspector,' he said, 'I know I was wrong to go to Señor Adell's home uninvited. I accept that. However, I can see no reason to be arrested and treated like a common criminal.'

Sánchez put the papers to one side and fixed his small eyes on Daniel.

'Señor Amat, I didn't expect this of you.'

He spat out the pea shell, which bounced off the side of the waste basket and onto the floor. Annoyed, he lifted his heavy frame out of the chair and came around to Daniel's side of the desk.

'Really, I'm surprised. Killing all these girls – no easy task! Tell me, what drove you to it? Some form of madness you're prey to?'

'What's this?'

One of the guards stepped forward. The blow to Daniel's side nearly knocked him from the chair. Astonished, he steadied himself, as the pain in his ribs gave way to an excruciating prickling beneath the skin.

'I'll ask the questions,' said Sánchez, unperturbed. 'You only need to worry about the answers.'

'You can't—'

Sánchez clucked, before answering coldly, 'I can do whatever I please.'

'No—'

The second blow came as unexpectedly as the first, and this time Daniel was shunted off the chair and onto his knees. The sounds in the room became distorted, as on an old gramophone. He noticed a crimson stain in the cracks between the floor tiles, and it was then that he understood what this room was for, and the reason for its lack of windows. He was hauled up by the two guards and placed back on the chair. A shiver ran through him in spite of the heat. He heard Sánchez's booming voice as his ears continued to ring.

'Don't trouble yourself, Amat, I know who you are.'

'What are you talking about?'

'We've broken through your subterfuge. We know everything. But there's still time for you to save yourself a certain amount of unpleasantness – if you confess.'

'Confess?'

'Damn it all, Amat! To think, you even managed to fit in another quick kill on your way to the Adell home!'

The Inspector was thrilled by Daniel's bewilderment.

'Don't deny it. Just like the others, this latest one, chopped to bits and burned like some dog. Though this time she was an acquaintance, eh? You couldn't resist, when you found out she shared a bed with your friend the journalist, isn't that right? You hated the man so much you wouldn't need more than ten minutes to slay him with your bare hands, yes?'

Daniel looked back in utter astonishment. Dolors was dead? Dear God . . . How had it happened? Could it be an awful coincidence, or had the assassin found out where Pau was staying? He felt suddenly worried for Pau. Though he knew it would sound suspicious, he asked, 'And no other bodies have appeared?'

Sánchez squinted warily.

'You tell me. Should one have?'

'No . . . I don't know!'

'What do you mean, you don't know? It is you and you alone who have been the architect of all these deaths.'

Daniel fell silent. In part it was the truth. He was culpable: if he had given up trying to find out about his father's death, Dolors would not be dead, and the mysterious killer would not be after Pau. And if he hadn't come back to Barcelona, nor would Irene be in such dire straits. He fell back in the chair and put his head in his hands.

'While you waste time with me,' he groaned, 'the real killer is out there. He could strike again at any moment.'

'Amat, your comedy's over. It's beyond all doubt.'

Sánchez leaned back against the table looking pleased. He had the tie clip in his hand.

'Recognize this? It has your initials on it.'

Daniel nodded. 'Where did you find it?'

'The last woman to be murdered had it clasped in her hand. Seems she put up enough of a fight to tear it off as you did away with her.'

'It isn't true! I haven't seen it since my luggage was stolen when I arrived in the city.'

'Of course! Naturally! And now you bring it up, I must say how surprised everyone was at your sudden appearance in the city. I mean, all that time away, it was rather unexpected for you to come back. Tell me something: how was it that you learned about the passing of your father?'

'I told you before, a telegram came.'

'Ah, yes. You said that the Señora Adell wrote to you. The only thing is, we've looked into that one, and it's nothing but a lie. She neither knew where you were, nor did she ever get in touch with you.'

'A telegram came, I swear!'

'Then I don't suppose you'd mind showing me the telegram.'

Daniel shook his head. 'That disappeared too, when my room at college was ransacked.'

404

'So convenient! I cannot deny your cunning in all this, but sooner or later you're sure to trip yourself up.'

Sánchez began circling Daniel, launching into the version of events agreed by he and Adell.

'Firstly, you have been resident in Barcelona for several months now, rather than several days as you would have us all believe. I'm certain that we could inquire in a few hostels in La Lonja, or say down in La Barceloneta, and a man fitting your description would have registered at one of them – under a false name, naturally.' He clasped his hands behind his back before going on. 'And thus you maintained your anonymity in the city as you carried out your criminal acts, but then your father learned of your presence, and your involvement in the murders. So he had to go. Which was a bother, wasn't it? Unlike the girls, your father was a well-known individual, no way he wasn't going to be missed. But fortune smiled on you, and your father's death went down as an unfortunate accident. Then you could breathe easy – for a time – until you found out about a certain journalist who knew of your father's research, and who you thought would sooner or later put your operation in jeopardy. So then came your prodigal son moment, popping up after all those years abroad, attending your father's funeral, doing your turn as the grief-stricken successor. The alibi was in place: everyone thought you'd only just arrived. Very cunning, really very cunning, but there's one problem: you needed to invent the infamous telegram as a way of proving you'd been notified. A loose end.'

'You only have to ask at Magdalen College, they'll confirm that I was in England all that time.'

405

'Of course,' said Sánchez, waving a fly away. 'We've already been in touch. And I'm quite sure their answer will confirm your guilt. Now if I might go on with my exposition?' He leaned in close to Daniel. 'The problem comes after the burial: you've got no reason to stay on in Barcelona after that, have you? But once again, Lady Luck has a hand in things, in the shape of a certain Bernat Fleixa. The two of you meet, he fills you in on the work your father had been doing, and asks for your help in solving the crimes, which leads you to the next step of your ingenious plan. Joining forces with the journalist, you come to us with the idea that your father had found the murderer, a certain Doctor Homs, a man of unsound mind who had fled the New Bethlem Sanatorium and ended up including your father in his manic killing spree. A quite ingenious lie.

'You set yourself up as you father's avenger – even identifying yourself to us and insisting on your commitment in hunting down the killer. And so the alibi is complete: you can stay on in the city and continue with your sick, cold-blooded murders.'

'Are you quite mad? Why on earth would I want to go around killing young girls? None of this makes the slightest bit of sense.'

'For the same reason you fled to England seven years ago, having murdered your fiancée and your brother, and having burned down your own home to cover your tracks. Your father's influence meant you got away with that one, though you did find it necessary to leave the country. Word is that London has also lately been prey to a series of murders, crimes altogether similar to the ones that have been taking place here. It would be little surprise to me to learn that you've also been applying yourself over there – perhaps the British authorities were close to finding you, and you saw it necessary to flee. I've been in touch with Scotland Yard about the matter.'

Daniel blanched. 'None of what you're saying will stand up. There's nothing to any of it.'

'Well,' said Sánchez, taking a piece of paper from the desk. 'Actually it's all written down here. This is your confession. Just put your name to it, and all this will be over.'

'You *are* out of your mind! I'll never sign it.'

The two guards, at a nod from Sánchez, took out their truncheons and began beating Daniel all over his body. The first blows knocked the wind from him and he fell to the floor again, where they set about him. One of his ribs was cracked, and in his left elbow he felt something snap. He was on the point of passing out when they lifted him up and got him into the chair again.

'This is all really rather disagreeable, Amat.' Sánchez's tone became one of compassion. 'If you would simply sign here, I will personally see you declared insane, and you'll avoid execution, possibly be sent to New Bethlem with others of your kind. You know the place.'

'I didn't . . . kill them. This is all . . . a mistake.'

'Impressive, Amat! You know you're done for, and yet still you try to make us believe your fantasies.'

At a signal, the guards dragged Daniel over to the table. Putting down quill and confession paper, Sánchez fished in his pocket for something, finally coming up with the cigar cutter. The guards stretched out Daniel's handcuffed hands – but then one looked up, shaking his head.

'He's passed out.'

FIFTY-FOUR

After leaving the dean's office with Gavet, the reality of Pau's situation had come crashing down upon her. She'd avoided falling apart in front of the Council and Fenollosa, but now, alone in her quarters, she began to see how far the implications stretched. The tears she'd been holding back for so long – she could resist them no more.

It was over. Her medical career, just like that. She was going to be expelled in short order, that was a formality. She'd be lucky if the situation didn't become worse still. The university could go back to Edinburgh with her false documents, and the consequences would be extremely serious.

Minutes passed and, as she grew calmer, she tried to put her thoughts in order. Being confined was torture, but she shouldn't let despair get the better of her. No point in feeling sorry for herself. She needed to occupy herself, turn her mind to other things.

Feeling resolved, she went over to the desk where her bag was. She took out the Vesalius manuscript and the notes she'd made in the meeting with Amat and Fleixa, laying them both out carefully before her.

Turning the yellowed pages, she felt as though in the company of an old acquaintance. The shining constellations they'd found had now faded, and the illustrations looked out at her with their usual sinister aspect. She ran through her jottings and came to the part about the need for a huge energy source of some kind. What was the process intended to achieve? How was it tied up with the spate of killings? Once more she couldn't help but feel that something was missing from the *Liber Octavus*, something that would answer these very questions.

Letting out a sigh, she went on reading.

It was only by chance that the secret book had fallen into their hands. Vesalius's evasions had been quite brilliant – for three hundred years his enemies had failed to uncover the secrets hidden in each of the illustrations.

Wait though – *not each and every illustration.*

Pau tried to contain herself, turning the pages as swiftly as the delicate vellum would allow. The emotion got the better of her, and she missed the page, flicking back again until she found it.

In the image a skeleton, seen side on and leaning an elbow on a stone plinth, was resting its cheek on its hand: a pensive posture. She knew the engraving well – it was one of the most celebrated in the whole *Fabrica*. This was the only one in which they hadn't found any hidden symbols. A coincidence, or was there something to it?

She tried to see if there were any other differences between this and the other illustrations. It was the only one, she realized after a few minutes, that bore an inscription.

HVMANI COR-   PORIS OSSIVM CAE
TERIS QVAS SV-   *STINENT PARTIBVS*
LIBERORVM, SVÁQVE   *SEDE POSITORVM EX*
latere delineatio.

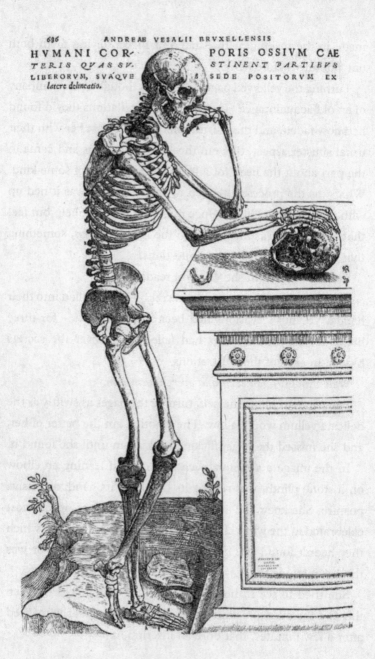

At the base of the plinth, Vesalius had included a few words in Latin. The lettering was tiny. As her excitement grew, she rummaged around in her desk drawers, her hand finally alighting on a magnifying glass, which she placed over the text.

Vivitur ingenio, caetera mortis erunt.

Pau was overcome. *Man's ingenuity is his only way to eternal life,* she thought, remembering Amat's translation. The same phrase repeated so obsessively in Homs's secret laboratory! The same one Amat had used to point his son towards Homs's notebook! Now this couldn't be chance – it must mean something. But what?

The idea of this image seemed to be that the skeleton was meditating on resurrection: man's great works, like his soul, are eternal. But could there be another, hidden meaning, something to do with the secret of the manuscript?

Her eye came to rest on the page number in the bottom corner. Page 696. She remembered Fleixa pointing out the mistake in the pagination – and, checking the previous and following pages, found that it was this page to which he'd been referring. It was in the wrong order.

Not that it could be counted as especially unusual. In earlier times, errata in printing and typesetting were commonplace – yet this was the *only* page where such a slip had occurred. Vesalius had shown himself to be most adroit when it came to hiding his tracks. And above all meticulous. It just couldn't be chance.

Following the thread of her own thoughts, she went in search of the real page 696. She flicked through and came to the last page – 695. There was that idea, dashed. Another dead end.

She leaned back in the chair and shut the manuscript, resolving to give up the ridiculous quest – when she had a thought. It *was* absurd . . . but she had to check.

She turned the book over and began feeling the binding, testing for anything anomalous. She examined the small gap between the cover and the dust jacket, and ran her fingers over the flyleaf. Her hand stopped on something – there, the texture was different.

The dust jacket seemed disproportionately thick at one point – thicker than the cover itself. Pau sat up tall, her heart pounding. She checked the front and back – and, yes, the back jacket did seem thicker at that point. No one would ever notice unless they were intentionally looking for it.

She took out a letter opener and had just brought the tip of the blade between the vellum flyleaf and the leather of the binding, when doubts suddenly overcame her. What was she thinking? This manuscript was priceless, and she was about to damage it because of some momentary hunch? It was madness. If the page number was a mere printing error, and if she'd simply let her imagination get the better of her, she'd have destroyed this great treasure for nothing.

Biting her lip and shutting her eyes, she plunged the blade in, as far as the hilt. She ran it up, then side to side between the flyleaf and cover, before reaching in with her fingers.

Nothing.

A shiver coursed through her. She began to think she'd made a terrible mistake. She fished around in the gap again, almost tearing the vellum. Nothing. Pushing her fingers in as far as they would go – desperation, and she knew it – suddenly she found something. Holding her breath, slowly, trying her hardest not to tear the page, she managed to trap whatever it was and slide it out.

Trembling with nerves, she considered the piece of parchment between her fingers. The wax seal, bearing the coat of arms of the University of Padua, gleamed as though it had just that very moment been stamped, and not centuries before. Pau couldn't stop herself. She broke the seal and, with utmost care, unfolded the parchment and lay it on the desk.

And was presented with the most extraordinary image.

In the middle, Vesalius stood pointing at the open chest of a corpse laid out on a table to his left. Some kind of ropes or cables emerged from the head, the chest, and the thighs and extremities, marked with circles and symbols; the ropes ran together and were collected in a large capsule to one side of the anatomist. Other lines, seemingly ropes as well, emerged from the contraption and rose up to the ceiling, where a series of scrolls and carved angels had been depicted. Here it was, she thought! The mysterious machine that the *Liber Octavus* had described.

Several containers on stone pedestals were positioned around the man and corpse – for incense, most likely, she thought. Two figures floated by the head of the corpse: a skeleton wrapped in a cloak and bearing a scythe, and a young girl in a toga stroking the corpse's forehead. For beauty and sheer detail it was far superior to any of the other illustrations in the manuscript. She ran her fingers reverentially over the parchment. And in that moment she realized that the last person to lay eyes on it – there could be no doubt – must have been Vesalius himself.

She found a fragment of text on the reverse: a passage in Latin entitled 'Vitalis Punctis'. She set about translating it, writing in her notebook. Her Latin was no match for Amat's, but she worked systematically, and saw the sense of the passage begin to take shape. She stopped after half an hour and looked over her work.

She was astonished by what she found.

It had to be a mistake. She reread the text, and cast her eye over the image once more – and suddenly it made sense.

Before her lay the fragment that completed the *Liber Octavus*.

Hurriedly she began gathering her notes, folding up the parchment and the manuscript. She could barely control the trembling of her hands. She had to get this to Amat and Fleixa immediately, it couldn't wait. The ban on leaving her rooms now couldn't have mattered less. Placing everything in her bag, she got to her feet. They were going to expel her whatever happened anyway.

Slinging the bag over her shoulder, she sensed something move behind her in the room. Then there was a sharp pain, and she cried out. Spinning on her heel, she just had time to make out a shadowy blur as it leaped at her. She tried to reach for the letter opener, but a sudden wave of exhaustion took hold of her, and her legs gave way. Her assailant caught her before she hit the ground. She tried to cry out for help, but all that came from her throat was a gurgle. Her eyes shot open in surprise as she recognized the face of her attacker – before immediately passing out.

FIFTY-FIVE

Stable hands paraded the horses as an anxious crowd looked on. Betting slips in hand, they did their best to surmise which beast would be fastest, which would last the course. Those that had already placed their bets looked on with self-satisfied smiles and fingered the stubs.

A young man in a striped suit and straw hat, up on a podium, put a metal cone to his mouth and called out the names of the animals, the stables they hailed from, and the riders' names. At the windows they were attempting to close all bets.

The horses were taken to the starting cages, where they stamped and hoofed the earth as the riders gripped the reins. An expectant hush fell. The stands were a quarter full. Then the starting gun was fired, the gates flew open, and the horses burst onto the track, followed by the roar of the crowd at the Can Tunis hippodrome.

The empty glass fell onto the table, to disapproving comments. Fleixa glared back at the other people in the bar with sunken eyes; the protests immediately died down. Utterly indifferent, the journalist poured himself a new glass – all the way to the top. He downed it, sloshing brandy over his hands and onto the floor, and slammed the glass down among the torn-up slips and stubs littering the table. His clothes were covered in sweat, drink stains and foodscraps, and his checked jacket hung crumpled over the back of the seat along with his boater. Swaying in his chair, with his bloody, bandaged hand he raised the glass once more.

A young waiter came over and took a deep breath, before addressing Fleixa.

'I'm sorry, Señor, but people aren't happy.'

'Don't give me that!' he slurred, filling the glass again.

The boy turned back to his colleagues at the bar to see who would help eject Fleixa, but then felt a hand on his forearm.

'Don't worry, I'll take care of this.'

The waiter withdrew, clearly relieved. Fleixa looked up, blinking as he tried to focus. They had the lights *far* too bright in here.

'Well, hello!' he cried. 'Have a drink.'

Inspector Sánchez gave him a disdainful look before glancing around at the other customers. Fortunately, they were concentrating on the race.

'You're drunk.'

'Very. Yes indeed. Joining me?'

'I hardly have time for that.' Sánchez pulled up a chair and sat down, crossing his legs impatiently. 'I received your message. What have you got?'

The journalist, as if he hadn't heard, pushed a full glass of brandy Sánchez's way. Sánchez, grimacing, simply moved the glass to one side.

416

'I've got information,' blurted Fleixa, turning anxious. 'Lots of information. Worth your while. Just want to be sure you'll keep your word.'

'That remains to be seen.'

Sitting up, Fleixa peered at him over his smudged spectacles.

'I know who it really is, the Black Hound. And I know where he's hiding out.'

Sánchez shifted in his chair and looked around to check if anyone was listening.

'The drink's rotted your brains. We've already got the man: it's Daniel Amat.'

'You arrested Amat?'

'He's currently a guest at Amalia Prison. He'll confess soon enough. Now give me something I can actually use, or you'll be joining your friend.'

'Amat's no friend of mine, no, Señor. He can rot in the Amalia for all I care. There are certain things he needs to make up for, but he isn't the killer everyone's looking for and you know it.'

Fleixa lifted the bottle to fill his glass once more, but it slipped from his hand and rolled across the table. Sánchez waved at the waiter to bring another.

'Tell me everything. And I mean everything.'

Fleixa proceeded to fill him in on all that had passed since he'd met Daniel at the Montjuïch Cemetery, emptying and refilling his glass as he went: the discovery of the notebook; the visit to New Bethlem and the start of their suspicions about Homs; and the conclusions they'd come to when they studied the Vesalius manuscript. Though Sánchez took a few notes, to him it seemed little more than the ravings of a sot. When he started on the part

417

about the *Liber Octavus*, Sánchez stopped him. 'Do you take me for a fool?' Putting away the notebook, he began to get out of his chair.

'No!' said Fleixa, his eyes bulging as he grabbed Sánchez by the arm. 'The manuscript's fucking real! I've held it in my own two hands. And the secret inside it, that's real too.'

'Get off,' said Sánchez, shaking himself clear.

Fleixa wiped his mouth on his sleeve and cast around for a drink. Sánchez pushed his own, undrunk glass in Fleixa's direction.

'Finish the story, then. What's this secret you're so het up about?'

'There are instructions, instructions for how to build some mysterious machine, one that requires a huge energy source.'

Fleixa's slurred speech was becoming harder to understand. Sánchez leaned closer, in spite of the smell.

'We don't know what the thing's for, this gizmo. But it has led us to the murderer's hiding place . . .'

Sánchez nodded brusquely for him to go on. Fleixa explained how Homs was using the sewers to move around the city unseen, and how that meant he was also able to tap the power station.

'That seems to be the reason for the power cuts,' he said in summary. 'It could lead to an explosion, an enormous one, so big it would send half the World Fair sky-high.'

'The opening ceremony's so soon now,' Sánchez said to himself. 'The power station will be at full capacity for that.' Sitting up, he tugged on Fleixa's lapel. 'You said you knew where he was hiding. Out with it.'

'There's an abandoned chamber down there, somewhere

under the grounds of the Fair. He's hiding there. In La Barceloneta, if you go and find Vidal, he's got a boy, Guillem is his
name – he knows the sewers like the back of his hand. He could
guide you to it. And I've done this map.'

He brought out a crumpled, blotchy sheet of paper. Sánchez
took it warily, glanced at the picture, and put it in his jacket
pocket.

'That all?'

Fleixa nodded.

'Right.'

'Not so fast, Sánchez! You have to help me.'

The Inspector looked at him with naked contempt.

'Help you?'

'I've done what you asked of me.' Fleixa's eyes filled with
tears.

'Perhaps in our last meeting I didn't make your situation
completely clear. You're still in my debt, until I check your story.
If you've lied, if you've skipped any details, if you've wasted my
time, I'll make you wish you hadn't. I think you can probably
still do a little scribbling with one or two fingers less.'

He forced an expression similar to a smile and dropped a few
coins onto the table.

'Don't spend it all on drink.'

FIFTY-SIX

'My God, Sánchez, do we always have to meet in such unseemly locations?' Llopis knocked dirt from his trousers with his straw hat as he looked around in disapproval.

Sánchez, accustomed to the reporter's complaints, didn't bother to answer. They were meeting the day after he'd seen Fleixa at the races, and he'd chosen this depot as the rendezvous point. There was a table, and on it stood a large tallow candle, the flame bright enough for them to see each other's faces.

Before Llopis could go on with his objections, a deafening round of applause broke out above their heads. The reporter thought the ceiling boards were about to come crashing down, but the noise came to an abrupt end as a cornet blast announced the next round of the bullfight above. Sand came showering onto their heads, again sending Llopis into protest.

'Amazing,' said Sánchez, spitting out one of his pea shells. 'We must be right beneath the pen. Quite the line-up today: The Lizard, Fat Face, and Valentín Martín, taking on six of La Conde de la Patilla's best.'

'To be honest, I couldn't care less about bullfighting.'

'Honest? You? Don't make me laugh.'

Sighing, Llopis decided to bite his tongue. They'd been meeting for almost half a year now, half a year in which he'd put up with Sánchez's constant banter – but still, there were limits to everything. Sánchez had supplied him with very good information – robberies, murders, a good amount of scandal among the well-to-do. No one could match Llopis's pen, but every man needed his sources. And his stock had risen these past months, he was looked upon now as one of Barcelona's up-and-coming men. Even his colleagues were baffled by the quality of his information – Sánchez only came to him. He felt he was probably outgrowing the *Correo* – he hoped *La Vanguardia* might offer him a position, or maybe even one of the nationals. The retainer was not inconsiderable, and Sánchez also insisted on some kind of eulogy in each report, but the agreement was still to Llopis's benefit. But none of that made the meetings themselves any more agreeable.

The Inspector, misreading Llopis's look of disgust, tried to mollify him.

'It's a safe spot. Who's going to guess we're here, just beneath the very spot where all those eyes are watching? Nice touch, in a way – don't you think?'

Llopis didn't answer, but dragged a chair over, trying to find a place where the sand wouldn't continue to cover him. The cheering and clapping continued to ring out above them. It was the turn of a new toreador. The show was heating up in the bullring.

'Come on, let's get to it,' said Sánchez. 'I want to catch the next round.'

'It's you who asked to meet,' said Llopis. 'Why the hurry, anyway?'

Sánchez seemed to agree with him for once. He quickly summed up everything Fleixa had told him at the hippodrome.

'Seems you made good use of the information I gave you about his debts. Fleixa's a drinker, he'd probably turn in his own friends at a pinch, but I don't think he's a liar exactly. He was a good reporter in his day.'

'The thing is, I've already got a man in the cells for those crimes, and the Mayor himself has sent me his congratulations.'

'And if another body turns up? Rius isn't going to be your biggest fan if that happens.'

'That *would* complicate matters,' Sánchez conceded. 'But I still need to keep Amat locked up.'

Llopis thought for a moment. Sánchez must have some reason for wanting to keep Amat off the streets. Maybe Sánchez had been paid to do so – anyway, what did it matter? Instinct told him that the murderer presented a tremendous opportunity – he quickly came up with a plan that would benefit them both. But first he had to convince Sánchez.

'Inspector Sánchez, I don't see why there should be any issue with keeping that man under lock and key. Why should it matter if he killed one or a dozen people? You can pin the most recent murder on him, that prostitute, say it was down to some kind of feud with Fleixa – maybe you could say he copied the killer in an attempt to disguise his act.'

'That's actually not bad.'

'Well, with that solved, there is a way we could use Fleixa's information, and both come out of it pretty well.'

'Pretty well how?'

Llopis couldn't fail to notice Sánchez's clumsy attempt to conceal his interest.

'You already suggested it yourself, my good friend. A most brilliant idea, I ought to add.'

'I did?'

'You catching the murderer yourself.'

'Have you lost your mind?'

'You, accompanied by a group of your best men, will go and detain him, on the day of the Fair's opening ceremony. With what Fleixa's given you, you won't have any trouble locating him.'

'But that would mean going down into the sewers. Easier just to send a detachment, problem solved. Me, go down there? Ha! All that ink must have gone to your head.'

Llopis managed to hold back an insult as Sánchez guffawed at his own joke.

'Inspector. Don't you think your talents are wasted in your current post? Do you really not want to see them recognized at the level they deserve? You ought to carry out this arrest in person – one: your decisiveness, your cool head, will ensure that it comes off, avoiding a disaster with significant implications – and, two: throw into the bargain the fact you'll have saved the lives of the Queen Regent and the King. You know what that would mean?'

Sánchez's face lit up.

'And,' said Llopis, 'if you agree, at the same time I'll organize a large gathering of people, so that the capture of the murderer, and your role in the arrest, will become the main event. I can already see it: the whole city calling you a hero. A promotion, perhaps some even greater reward, who knows?'

'It all sounds very good, but what are you going to want in return?'

'The exclusive will be enough for me – as usual. I'll be the only journalist who gets to interview the killer when you put him behind bars. Are we agreed?'

The Inspector tongued his gums as he considered his answer. He found the offending scrap of pea shell, brought it to his lips, and spat it between Llopis's feet – much to Llopis's horror. Sánchez looked pleased.

'Llopis, I believe we have a deal.'

INTO THE INFERNO

Four days before the start of the World Fair

FIFTY-SEVEN

Francisco Casavella crossed the courtyard with short steps, as though pacing out the ground he covered. Known amongst the workers as hard but fair, none had a bad word to say about him, and more than one among them owed him their livelihoods. He didn't drink, wasn't much of a talker, and was rarely given to nerves. And yet that morning he was muttering to himself as he went, casting anxiously around to check that everything was ready. He kept glancing up at the clock at the far end of the bay, and from there to the building's entranceway, where a young boy was stationed, ready to call out as soon as the owner came into sight.

Adell was beaming. After the tensions of recent weeks, it seemed everything was going to turn out as it should. He was in his coach on the way to the World Fair site, and sat rereading the note that had arrived from Inspector Sánchez first thing. A stop had been put to the investigations, once and for all. After Amat's arrest at the party, he'd been named as the prime suspect for the murders, precisely as Adell had hoped.

Implicating his old friend had been brilliant, an inspired idea. With a little luck he'd be found guilty, but even if that didn't come to pass Amat would still be out of the way for a few weeks, behind bars. Amalia wasn't the safest of places to pass the time, and any kind of misfortune might befall him during his stay.

He was also delighted at the thought of Irene's reaction when she heard the news. Her old lover, a killer. He'd worked out about her getting her hands on the autopsy report, but that didn't matter now. Nobody, absolutely nobody, would meddle in the affairs of Bertomeu Adell and get away with it. Perhaps, finally, the obstinate bitch would understand.

The vehicle pulled up outside the power station. Elies Rogent was standing at the entrance with a group of men, all in morning coats and top hats. The town council's Monitoring Committee. Amat's arrest had also placated the Mayor, who had agreed to give the inspection the go-ahead.

Adell got down from the coach and cast a triumphant look over the building. The work had been completed on time; the steam system and the generators had been installed and were in perfect working order. Several days had passed since any malfunctions, and that meant several days since any power cuts. The World Fair, and the streets adjacent to the site, would have all the electricity they needed.

He noticed a testy look on the architect's face, and frowned. Approaching, he thought through the steps that had led to this juncture. He had to congratulate himself on how well it had all come off; modesty, after all, was the stuff of commoners. No one, least of all that fop Rogent, had the first inkling of the capital he'd pocketed from the project simply by using cheap materials.

It wasn't as if the building needed to last long. After all the Hotel Internacional itself, the work of the celebrated Domènech, was due to be knocked down soon after the end of the World Fair. That had cost three times as much to build, and no one had batted an eyelid.

The unfortunate thing had been the way that capital had evaporated in a couple of bad investments – pure bad luck. He who dares, wins! True, his creditors were breathing down his neck, but his mind was at ease. All he needed was a little time. He planned to use the success of the power station to win contracts for a further three. They wouldn't refuse him. Investors would be queuing up for a share, and all the money problems would evaporate, just like that. All of which would pale in comparison with his other project if, as he expected, it came off. He'd chosen the day of the inauguration to unveil his genius to the world. Then the true plaudits would begin – nothing would be the same again. He was beginning to wonder whether a position as a Deputy might not, in fact, be aiming too low.

Yes, it was going to be a great day.

'Gentlemen.'

His greeting was returned by all. Elies Rogent stepped forward, though without proffering his hand. An insult not lost on Adell.

'Good day, Señor Rogent.'

'We've been standing here waiting for ten minutes.'

'And I'm quite sure that the tour today will more than make up for it. Now, if you'd like to follow me.'

The group turned to go inside.

'Lucky turn of events,' said Rogent. 'Them catching the killer.'

'We can only be thankful for the diligence of the police.'

'The Mayor was on the point of rescinding your contract, but luckily for you the feared scandal was averted.'

'The matter has been dealt with, more than dealt with.'

'Let's hope so. A week on Sunday and the great and the good will be here for the opening – everyone's confirmed. You have to get through that yet.'

'I'm sure they'll be more than happy,' said Adell, biting his tongue. 'Now, if you'll allow me.'

He pushed open the main door. Casavella was there to receive them, cap off and eyes lowered. Adell was pleased at that: in this world, people needed to know their place, that was all.

'I trust that everything is in order.'

The plant manager gave a faint nod.

'Well? Is it or isn't it?'

'Yes, Señor Adell, yes,' said Casavella nervously, before standing aside and allowing the group to pass, with Adell at its head. They advanced through the great archway entrance and were met in the brightly lit vestibule by the plant workers standing in a row.

The group made its way through the installations, with Adell as the guide, with contributions from Casavella on the more technical points. They led them to the viewing balcony, where murmurs of astonishment went up, and then down to the immense bays with the steam engines and the generators. Adell gave a running commentary, including a number of grandilo-quent pronouncements on the astonishing output of the plant.

When he came to the construction of the building, one of the inspectors made a comment praising the wrought-iron metalwork, and Adell couldn't help but smile. Elies Rogent had suggested the use of riveted iron to absorb the shocks produced by the pounding of the steam engines, but Adell, spying an altogether avoidable cost, had opted for the less robust wrought-iron. Not the only corner he'd so cleverly cut. In the early stages of the building work they'd discovered some halls beneath the ground that had formed part of the old citadel and, though there hadn't been time to give them full inspections, Adell could see the opportunity they presented. He'd simply ordered the old installations to be reused, with slight modifications, for the foundations: more money in his pocket.

Not that the inspectors knew anything about that. Their initial circumspection gradually gave way to praise and acclaim. By the looks of things, even Rogent seemed impressed. Just then, a discreet cough from Casavella drew Adell's attention.

'What? Come on, out with it.'

Casavella looked down at his boots and then over at the inspectors, who were admiring one of the generator pods. He seemed to hesitate. Adell thought this was simply one more of the man's usual infuriating silences, and let out an exasperated sigh.

'The problem of the overloads hasn't been solved,' he said finally.

'What do you mean?'

'Everything's working for now, but—'

'So no problem.'

'Far be it from me to contradict you, Señor, but I'm afraid there is. The generators are functioning, but not by any of our doing. Before we could get to the root of the problem, the charge in the transformers went down, the gauges on the engines returned to normal, all on their own account. We still don't actually know what was causing the overloads. It could happen again at any second, and no one can say what the knock-on effects might be.'

Adell glanced at Rogent out of the corner of his eye – the architect was coming over. He forced a smile, and at the same time pulled Casavella to one side.

'I don't want to hear another word about this. Understand? Everything must run like clockwork, that's what I expect of you. If it doesn't, I'll hold you responsible.'

'But, Señor—'

'Casavella, think of your family. If you want to avoid them ending up begging in the streets, do as I say, and let that be an end to it. Now, out of my sight.'

Adell turned back towards his guests, who continued to sing the praises of the works. Straightening his jacket, he assumed a cordial expression and went over to join them.

'I hope the tour has been to your liking, gentlemen.'

This was met with a chorus of enthusiastic agreement.

'And now, you must be tired. I've taken the liberty of preparing some refreshments. This way, please.'

One hour later, free, finally, of the inspectors, Adell breathed a sigh of relief. They had left amidst hearty congratulations, and even the meddling Rogent had promised to pass on his favourable impressions to the Mayor. A nervous smile crossed Adell's face. He turned and hurried back in the direction of his office. During the tour the only thing he'd thought about was the moment he'd be on his own again. As he arrived at the office and pushed on the door, Casavella suddenly materialized beside him.

'Dear God,' Adell said, 'you gave me a fright. What is it now?'

'Apologies, Señor Adell. I hope I'm not bothering you. I came to tell you that everything's ready. I've personally checked the steam system and the generators. They seem in perfect working order. And I've sent the men home until morning, as you asked. If you wanted someone on site during the night, I myself wouldn't mind—'

'No, no,' said Adell impatiently. 'Everyone out, like I said.'

'As you wish, Señor. You're staying here?'

'That's none of your business, Casavella. Now off you go . . . Oh! And give me your keys, I'll close up myself.'

Though clearly concerned, Casavella obeyed without a word. Adell waited as he left the premises, and only when he heard the main door shut did he close the office door as well. He hastened over to his desk and, taking a key from a chain around his neck, opened one of the drawers. He reached inside and flicked a small switch; behind him there came a thud, and a section of the wall slid back. A copper lamp illuminated a service lift, inside which Adell went and stood, before lowering a lever. With a hiss, the section of wall slid back into place. All in the power station was silent once more, save for the ongoing whirr of the generators.

FIFTY-EIGHT

The eight people in the circle regarded one another in silence. All lanterns had been extinguished and velvet curtains kept out the afternoon light. A black sheet covered the table, on which there stood a water jug, a glass and, in the centre, a lit candle. Otherwise the narrow room was in darkness and thick with cigarette smoke. The five men and three women held hands. Their faces were masks of contained emotion.

Llopis took a moment to observe the others. To his right sat Countess Berenguer, the meeting's hostess. Her thick make-up could not hide her excitement, clearly there could be nothing more exhilarating than this in all the world to her. Beyond her was Francisco Aguirre, the Secretary of the Barcelona Chamber of Commerce. Something about his dark suit, his stiff bearing and his wan face made Llopis shiver. To Aguirre's left sat a fidgeting Alfredo Comins, a textile tycoon, a regular at these meetings and an enthusiastic proponent of the theories of Volapüka. Llopis didn't know any of the others.

'Marina, show yourself.'

Madame Palatino was a medium of great renown. After appearing in the best theatres in Vienna, London and Paris throughout the previous twelve months, she'd been invited to take part in Barcelona's International Spiritualism Conference. A number of her followers had decided to make the most of her stay, convincing her to hold a few private sessions such as today's.

The table was circular but everyone's attention was now firmly on the medium. The candlelight played on her stony features. And though she barely moved her lips, her voice could be heard loud and clear.

'Marina,' she said again. 'I feel your presence. Come forth, have no fear.'

The atmosphere grew heavy around the group and the candle flickered for a moment as though someone were softly blowing across it. Stifled exclamations went up. Llopis looked around, trying his best to disguise his scepticism.

Then, suddenly, the table began to tremble. One of the ladies shrieked. People's eyes grew wide in alarm, the more experienced in the group looked pleased, though even they could not help but betray a certain amount of trepidation.

'Marina!' she commanded. 'Come, be with us now!'

Llopis's eye was drawn to the older gentleman next to her, who had generous white sideburns and a sallow face. Before the start of the session, he'd stood silently in a corner of the room, accompanied by the smooth-faced young man who now sat beside him. Now, his expression had quite altered, and he gazed in yearning at the medium who, eyes closed, intoned a sort of prayer in Italian.

Abruptly, the table ceased its trembling, and the door opened and immediately slammed shut again. The room seemed to become several degrees colder. The medium spoke once more, but this time not in her own voice. Everyone shuddered to hear the childish timbre she articulated.

'Grampa,' the voice said, 'are you there?'

'Yes!' cried the old gentleman. 'I'm here, yes!'

An assistant came over to prevent him from leaping to his feet and thereby breaking the circle.

'H-how are you, sweet child?'

'I am well, Grampa. Well.'

The whole group, including Llopis, were completely captivated. The medium's eyes were still closed and her back was straight as a rod. The old man began asking more questions.

'Where . . . What is it like, where you are? Oh, my sweet little one . . .'

'It's lovely here. There's lots of light, always lots of light.'

The voice grew quieter, as if it might fade away at any moment. The man tried to say something else, but could only sob.

'Don't cry, Grampa. It's all right. I'm happy now.'

His face had completely drained of colour. He dabbed at his eyes and stammered something that Llopis could not make out.

Suddenly the medium arched her back and began to shake violently. Everyone held their breath. Shortly the convulsions subsided, as swiftly as they'd begun, and she gradually opened her eyes once more. She looked around, blinking as if just waking from a deep sleep, apparently unaware of where she was. An assistant handed her a glass of water, and she thirstily gulped it down. Then, her eyes narrowed, she spoke in a voice so hoarse she might have had a mouth full of earth.

'I'm sorry. She's gone.'

The curtains were drawn back. The weak afternoon light broke into the room, and lanterns were lit. Sighs went around as people ceased holding their breath, and they took their hands back and began to converse in whispers, deeply stirred by the experience.

Meanwhile the older gentleman, with his face in his hands, continued to sob. The younger man tried to console him, though he himself seemed somewhat embarrassed. An assistant brought over a cordial and the older gentlemen quickly drank it down before gathering his coat and hat, standing up from his chair, and leaving the room.

Llopis was impressed. He hadn't managed to work out how they'd made the table vibrate like that, nor where the ghostly sounds had come from, but he imagined neither could be particularly difficult tricks to pull off. But the change in the woman's voice had been so real, and really quite hair-raising. For a moment he'd almost been convinced it was the child speaking. A good sign, he thought.

The group moved through into a small and charming salon, one room along. Coffee, tea and servings of pasta had been prepared, along with some stiff drinks to steady people's nerves. A fire burned in the hearth, making for an atmosphere altogether different to that of a few minutes before.

They spread out across the room and the conversation, already animated to begin with, intensified. Llopis approached the medium while she was speaking to a couple of the guests.

'Signora Palatino?'

Turning to face the journalist, she looked as though a fly had landed in her soup. She looked him up and down, her indifference giving way to a courteous nod.

'Yes?'

'Good afternoon, Señora. My name is Felipe Llopis.'

'I don't believe I've had the pleasure.'

She spoke with a slight Piedmontese accent. Llopis was now able to get a proper look at her. Eusapia Palatino was thirty-five years old, though she could have been over fifty. Thin as a wire and dressed entirely in black, her work in the occult seemed to have taken its toll. Her face was covered in lines, her eyes were a startling green, and her nose, in contrast to the rest of her lean, ill-proportioned features, looked clearly southern European. Her hand lightly gripped the silver handle of a wooden malacca cane with a metal tip.

'We've spoken before, I'm a reporter from the *Barcelona Correo*.'

'Ah, I remember. This was your first time. How did you find it?'

'Most . . . suggestive.'

'I'm pleased for you.'

Breaking away, she turned back to the people she'd been speaking to. Undaunted, Llopis went on.

'If you don't mind, Señora, I'd like a moment of your time.' Then, in a lower voice, he added, 'Alone, if possible.'

'Everyone you see here,' she said, gesturing across the room, 'is a trusted friend. You may speak openly.'

The journalist did not appreciate that.

438

'It's to do with some deaths,' he said.

'Deaths, you say?'

Llopis felt the attention in the room turn towards them. There was no turning back now.

'I don't know if you've heard, but in recent weeks the bodies of a number of young ladies have been appearing across the city, the victims of a series of cruel murders. It's been in all the papers, and I myself have covered the story. In fact, perhaps it's not very modest of me to say, but it was I who broke the story.'

'I've heard about it,' said a gentleman with a bushy moustache. 'Prostitutes, aren't they saying?'

'It isn't safe to walk the streets any more,' someone else said.

'It's the authorities, I tell you: they ought to spend less of their time putting on exhibitions and more worrying about the city.'

'Yes, well, of course . . .' Llopis tried to wrest back the conversation. 'What I wanted to say, you see—'

'Señor reporter,' said Madame Palatino abruptly. 'Would you describe yourself as a materialist or, rather, would you say you believe in the existence of the soul?'

Nobody spoke as Llopis, taken aback by the question, struggled to answer. The conversation wasn't going as he'd envisaged, but he had little option but to follow these maniacs' lead.

'It's my understanding that God duly provides us all with a soul.'

'And, from there, do you believe in the fact it outlives the body, that it goes on after death?'

'Well . . . I suppose so, yes.'

'That's our entry point. Spiritualism is catching on, as it must. The goodness in life belongs to those who believe.'

439

This statement was met with a chorus of assent. Llopis managed a thin smile.

'You have seen it for yourself,' she continued. 'The gentleman was suffering unspeakably following the untimely death of his granddaughter. He came to us for succour, we put the two in contact. Now, knowing the child is well in the great beyond, it is a great relief for him. Of this there can be no doubt.'

In fact, it was just this idea that Llopis doubted.

'You, Señor, seem unconvinced,' said Comins. The businessman, seemingly affronted, moved his eyebrows energetically as he spoke.

'Forgive him,' said Madame Palatino. 'Our dear Alfredo is a most impassioned believer.'

'I take that as a great compliment, Señora. You already know my view. This doctrine of ours should to be taught in schools across the land, and that just for starters—'

Madame Palatino touched his forearm delicately.

'Comins, *amore*, would you be so kind as to bring me some sherry?'

He, delighted at the attention, hurried over to the drinks stand. Madame Palatino turned back to Llopis.

'So,' she said. 'What is it you want from Madame Palatino?'

'As I was saying, there have been these murders, and no one's been able to find the culprit.' Llopis quickly summed up the details of the cases, exaggerating certain aspects sufficiently to draw, as he'd hoped, astonishment, horror and indignation from the room. 'There are those that would lay the blame at the feet of a certain Black Hound – an old curse, a malediction. I'd like to know what you think of that.'

Madame Palatino paused before answering. 'The source of these terrible murders clearly cannot be human. Only a spirit could be responsible for the things you have described to us today. These actions are a cry of anguish, a call for help, a soul clearly in search of peace.'

A murmur went around the salon.

'And that is precisely why I have come, Señora. I am in agreement with your view, entirely in agreement, you see, and I was wondering if there's anything that might be done.'

'Done in what regard?'

'Do you believe it would be feasible to contact the spirit in question?'

'Without a doubt, *possible*. Disembodied souls are around us all the time, Señor reporter, every second of every day.'

Llopis felt a chill. The woman was so convinced, it was a kind of fanaticism. Her listless aspect, allied with her affected manners, made him feel most uncomfortable. He took a deep breath and focussed on why he'd come. Now to come to the point.

'I was wondering whether it might be possible to organize a meeting, such as the one we have today enjoyed, and to call on this very spirit. As a way of helping it back to its . . . proper path?'

The woman nodded. 'I don't see why not. We hold it here, perhaps.'

'That would be wonderful! Though of course—'

'Go on,' said their host, the Countess.

Llopis looked at her as though reluctant to say anything further. 'Forgive me for speaking plainly, but in my view, if we were to call on such a spirit it would need something more than a private meeting such as this. An event of such considerable importance ought to be made available to all of Barcelona.'

'Such a session would not be so straightforward,' said Madame Palatino.

'But the whole city lives in fear of these crimes. People need to know that their mothers and daughters are safe to walk the streets, they need to know this malign spirit has been dealt with.'

'*Possibile, possibile*, but—'

'I should mention that I have an excellent relationship with the owner of the Lírico, and it would be quite straightforward should we wish to hold it there. I could make all the necessary arrangements.'

A brief silence ensued, one soon interrupted by the Secretary of the Chamber of Commerce. 'It's a wonderful opportunity to expound our school! It could be our only chance to tell the world about the great good spiritualism can do.'

Everyone agreed. Llopis, trying to hide his satisfaction, encouraged the idea, nodding and smiling at everyone. Madame Palatino raised a hand, and the room fell silent. A few seconds passed before she spoke again.

'Spiritualism is a serious discipline, not a variety show.'

'But of course, Madame. You have my word that the whole thing will be carried out with the utmost delicacy.'

The medium's green eyes came to rest on the journalist.

'The theatre will make money from this.'

'And your fees will come out of them, on top of any costs you might require, of course.'

'Let me think about it.' With the help of one of her assistants,

442

she got up from her chair. 'Now, ladies and gentlemen, if you will excuse me, I am tired. Today's meeting was so taxing.'

With that the group got up from their chairs while Madame Palatino, leaning on her assistant, withdrew.

Llopis left the house a little while later. Coming around the corner, he breathed a sigh. He thought for a moment he wasn't going to pull it off, but luck had been on his side, along with the fact that the enigmatic Madame was as fond of money and fame as any other mortal. Hook, line and sinker. What did it matter if to him it was all some fantastical charade? The people wanted to hear that the crimes were the work of occult forces, and he didn't mind giving them what they wanted. His readers had already shown themselves delighted at the idea of a murderous spirit, and the theatrical event would be its culmination. To make it coincide with Sánchez's sewer raid, that was if the fool didn't make a mess of it, had been a stroke of genius.

FIFTY-NINE

Inspector Sánchez gave a pensive nod. Before him he had a detailed map of the city's sewer system, alongside Fleixa's smudged and blotchy effort. An 'X' in the centre of Barceloneta marked the point where, that night, he would enter the sewers. The tunnels that ran beneath the old Parque de la Ciudadela had also been highlighted, up to the point where they came together in the abandoned reservoir also ringed by the journalist.

He puffed out his cheeks. The map showed only the principal channels. The older chambers and ducts, some of which could be as old as the Roman occupation of the city, weren't there. As many as four layers deep beneath street level, and reaching right down into the depths of the earth, the network of tunnels spread out like a spider web, hundreds of kilometres long. In that maze he'd struggled to decide which was the best route to the hideout of this Homs character. They were going to need a guide, little as he liked to admit it.

He'd kept the preparations quiet. He didn't see any point in forewarning either the Mayor's or the Governor's Office. If they found out about the possible threat to the opening ceremony, they were quite capable of calling the whole thing off, and there would go his chance of emerging as saviour and town hero. He could kiss goodbye to that promotion.

Just then, the door to his office opened and Sergeant Azcona walked in.

'Señor, I wanted a word.'

There you go. Hadn't even bothered to knock. How the hell he'd let them saddle him with Azcona was beyond him. As soon as he could be rid of the young idiot he would be.

'Sergeant!' he said peevishly. 'What is it? I'm extremely busy.'

'I've heard you're putting together an operation to apprehend a killer of some renown.'

Sánchez grimaced. The barracks were worse than the fruit and vegetable market for secrets. After his promotion he'd put an end to this sort of thing.

'I wasn't aware,' he said, 'that I was under any obligation to keep you abreast of my decisions.'

'Of course not, Señor. But I know the area from my previous posting, I think I could be of use to you.'

'Very good, Sergeant. So then what, given your vast experience, is your advice?'

'The sewers in the Barceloneta are hundreds of years old. It's a labyrinth, Señor, an enormous and very dangerous labyrinth. I had a few scrapes down there – criminals in the area use the sewers all the time.'

'Fascinating.'

Azcona, mistaking his superior's enthusiasm, went on. 'It's very easy to lose one's bearings. There are dozens of different

445

chambers with submerged shafts and culverts that could swallow a group of men, just like that. The flow of water is incredibly strong in places, and the air, or rather the gas, in some of the chambers is impossible to breathe. We once had to send a search party for a couple of men who took a wrong turn; they nearly didn't make it.'

'Really,' said Sánchez.

Azcona shifted uncomfortably on his feet.

'What, cat got your tongue now? Please, how else can you enlighten me?'

'At all costs you must avoid the community that inhabits the lower levels.'

'You mean the so-called Pickers?' said Sánchez, arching an eyebrow. 'Do me a favour, Azcona! I didn't have you down as quite so gullible.'

'I can assure you they're real, Señor, and there are a great many of them. They're organized, they abide by their own rules, have their own leaders. It's like a bloody city unto itself.'

'Language, Sergeant!'

'Yes, Señor, I'm sorry. But it's the truth. I once had a run-in with some Pickers. We were pursuing a pickpocket, we'd chased him from the Estación de Francia, and he tried to throw us off by heading down into the sewers, but we followed right after. I went ahead of my men and, once we were down quite a way, I became disoriented. I thought I'd found the man, but then I heard a terrible cry. Instinctively I blew out my lantern. Then, a second later, I saw a group come along the parallel chamber bearing the pickpocket in their arms – he was dead. They moved along in total silence, like they were the shadows of the sewer

446

itself. I don't mind admitting I've never been as frightened in all my days, but I was lucky and managed to escape a different way. I learned an important lesson that day: down there, they rule, not us.'

'What a load of utter . . . I'm not going to make my decisions based on some group of reprobates. If we come across them, which I sincerely doubt, we'll apprehend them, and that will be that.'

'Forgive my insistence, but honestly, mark my words. During my time there, a number of disappearances—'

'Yes, yes, I know this one. These Pickers kidnap anyone foolish enough to go roaming around in the sewers, kill them and then use the fat from their bodies in exchange for goods in the market. Fairy tales to frighten children, Sergeant! You're more grown-up than that.'

'But Señor—'

'Let's move on to more serious matters. You'll be wondering how I'm planning to involve you. I've thought up a crucial role for you.' Sánchez observed, amused, the way the young officer stood tall in anticipation. 'You'll stay here.'

'Pardon? I don't understand. Here?'

Sánchez almost broke out in a smile at Azcona's dismay.

'That's right. I need someone to man the place while we go and catch that killer. It's up to you.'

'But—'

'There's nothing more to say, off you go. I've got a lot of work to get through.'

Azcona, bewildered, saluted and turned to leave. At the door he turned back again.

'Señor—'

'You really can't take a hint, can you?'

'Yes, Señor, I only wanted to suggest you take a couple of dogs with you.'

'Dogs? And what do you imagine we'd do with them?'

'They're very useful for following a scent, and they can sniff out a Picker. They'd give you advance warning.'

'Sergeant, be sure to shut the door on your way out.'

Alone once more, Sánchez sat down again, rummaging in his drawers until he found one of the paper wraps. He grinned, took one of the dried peas and threw it in the air, catching it in his mouth. This was going to be a doddle.

SIXTY

'Señora, you . . . you can't be here.'

Oriol Pascual, Deputy Governor of the Municipal Correctional Facility, or, as it was more commonly referred to, Amalia Prison, rubbed his eyes for the third time, trying to make sense of what he was seeing. Usually at lights out he'd be in bed enjoying the bottle of brandy he kept stashed in his office, and, perhaps, the company of a female inmate (in exchange for an extra crust of bread). But instead here he was, still sitting in his uncomfortable office chair, feeling dog-tired. Adjusting his tie and trying, for the life of him, to comprehend what this woman was doing in front of him at such an ungodly hour.

No lady of good standing had ever set foot in the prison before. Nor was it hoped that any ever would. But now this. He personally had never had dealings with such a lady before, he had to admit it. It wasn't often he found himself rubbing shoulders with gentry, and even if he did he doubted he'd find among all their number someone such as her.

'Señor Colonel—'

'No, no, Señora. *Deputy Governor*. Just an officer. You can call me Pascual.' He sat up tall in his chair, pleased at having been mistaken for a superior, and a man of military bearing.

'Forgive my blunder, Señor Pascual, I'm just so upset.'

Irene let out a sob, before covering her mouth with a handkerchief from her maid. The girl cast an embarrassed glance at Pascual, before averting her gaze. He had better find out what this was all about before he really woke up – and dashed any chance of sleep.

'Let's see now, Señora. You say a terrible injustice has been done. Would you mind explaining in a little more detail?'

'There's an innocent man in this prison.'

Pascual gave an uncomprehending look.

'You see,' she said, stifling another sob, 'Señor Amat fought in Cuba a number of years ago, where he was wounded in action. After recovering from his injuries he was transferred to Barcelona. But the pain he continued to suffer meant he had to avail himself of certain substances, and these fogged his mind, robbed him of all reason. I blame the opium mainly – those dens he has to visit, awful places! Very occasionally he has become involved in brawls, though never anything very serious. We had word yesterday that he'd been detained, accused of public affray. I was horrified at the news and, in spite of the hour, thought I should present myself in order to clarify the matter, which is doubtless an awful misunderstanding. Señor Amat must be freed as soon as possible.'

Pascual leaned back in his chair, eyeing the woman suspiciously. It was Inspector Sánchez's case. And it wouldn't be the first time that a woman had tried to save her lover when the husband brought charges – for that they'd always come up with the most incredible stories. The strange thing here, though, was that they'd never usually come in person, but just send a servant with a heavy purse, and that would be that. This was different – there was something more to it.

'You know he stands accused of murder?'

Irene, eyes wide, covered her mouth, before quickly regaining her composure; her stupor gave way to a cold expression.

'That's ridiculous. Señor Amat is simply incapable of such things. He's unwell, not dangerous. Clearly it's another mistake. Amat is an old, and very dear, friend of the family, I can answer for him.'

'Friend of the family? Really?'

'I understand your confusion, I do. It's really a rather awkward situation, and I am sorry to be such a pest. It seems quite reasonable that you should be compensated. Perhaps the fine needs a little topping up.'

A small purse slid across the table, coins tinkling inside. But rather than reach out and take it, Pascual studied the woman more closely. He took in the waist, ran his eyes up the corseted midriff to her heaving bosom. The lanternlight picked up a sheen on her ebony skin, and a faint blush in her cheeks. He moved the purse nonchalantly to one side and leaned forward.

'Really,' he said, yawning, 'this seems quite a singular affair. Yes? Perhaps we'll need to talk to Inspector Sánchez. What do you think about that?'

Irene's face dropped.

'I thought so.' Pascual gave a small smile. 'Though perhaps there's a way we might avoid troubling the Inspector, as well as ensuring your "poor man" gets out tonight.'

A look of renewed hope crossed Irene's face.

'I mean, the conditions in the cells really are quite awful. Tuberculosis, dysentery, it's all rife, not to mention how thuggish these prisoners can be with one another. I want to help your friend, I really do . . . Perhaps,' he said, reaching out a hand to touch her, 'we can come to some agreement?'

Irene, stifling her instinct to recoil, shut her eyes, and when she opened them addressed her maid. 'Encarnita, you go out to the coach.'

Even Pascual was taken aback. Her gentle tone, the sobbing demeanour, had gone. Not the prude her performance had so far suggested.

'But, Señora—' protested the maid.

'Out to the carriage, I said. Leave us.'

Encarnita crossed the office with her head low. She stopped at the door and cast a look at her mistress, as if hoping for a change of heart. Irene ignored her, and the young girl closed the door gently after her.

'Good, good,' said Pascual, coming around Irene's chair and standing behind her. 'Now it's just us, we can talk more freely.'

A shudder went through Irene as she felt his fingers on the nape of her neck. He leaned in closer, she felt his beard against her skin. The smell of him turned her stomach. She shut her eyes and tried to stay calm.

'You have to promise,' she said in a small voice, 'that Señor Amat will be freed.'

'You have my word,' said Pascual, excitement entering his voice. 'Oh, I've never been with a woman such as yourself . . .'

Tittering, he reached around and began kneading her breasts

like lumps of dough. His breathing became heavier as he began to tongue her ear.

That was as much as Irene could bear, and she made to stand up and move away, but Pascual didn't feel like stopping now. He clasped her around the waist and lifted her, with ease, over to the table. Irene gasped as her body struck the top. She tried to twist around to face him, but the man grabbed her arm and bent it up behind her back, before forcing her, face down, onto the table. He slurred a few lascivious words; she felt his saliva on her skin. With his free hand he undid his belt. Irene realized there was nothing she could do, and wished she had some way of making herself pass out. Pascual cursed as he struggled with the buckle, before finally dropping his trousers. He was about to hitch up her petticoat when a loud bang behind them resonated through the room.

'What on earth?'

Another blow shook the door, and the sickly figure of Fleixa appeared in the doorway, struggling with a pair of guards. Encarnita, looking terrified, stood on the far side of the men.

'Let me go! Let me go, I say!' The journalist barked the order with such authority that the men obeyed. He straightened his checked jacket and placed his crumpled straw hat back on his head. He looked furious.

'What's going on here?'

The Deputy Governor, moving away from Irene, fumbled with his trousers.

'Who are you?'

'What, you don't know who I am?' bellowed Fleixa as he came into the office. 'I, my good man, am Bernat Fleixa, renowned reporter and head of the current affairs desk at the *Correo* itself.'

'What are you doing in my office?'

'I have just spent the most wonderful evening with the Señor Governor and his wife, and on my way home was importuned by this young lady, and in quite a state she was too. Her mistress is being ravaged by some degenerate, she says to me. Looks like I arrived in the nick of time.'

'It isn't how it looks,' protested Pascual.

Fleixa took in the man, shirt undone, trousers around his ankles, with an arch of the eyebrow, and gave a sardonic nod in the direction of the guards.

'How did he get in?' shouted Pascual, while the two men shifted on their feet in the doorway. 'Get him *out* of here!'

'I wouldn't do that if I were you, Señor. You'd be making quite the mistake. You evidently don't know who you're dealing with.' He moved purposefully over to Irene, whose cheeks were gradually regaining their colour. 'Are you all right, Señora Adell?'

Hearing her surname, Pascual jumped.

'You can rest assured, Señora,' said Fleixa, ignoring Pascual's growing alarm, 'all of Barcelona will know of the events here tonight.'

'What's that?' stuttered Pascual, glancing at his men, who remained in the doorway, eagerly watching the drama unfold.

'Oh yes, in tomorrow's first edition, I'll explain to my reader-ship – which, by the way, includes most of the city – about the dire conditions of this place, about all the many kinds of corrup-tion it is a haven for, not omitting to describe the treatment of decent members of society should they set foot inside the door.

454

Two front page columns, minimum. The repercussions will go right to the top.'

'You can't do that.'

'I'm afraid that's where you're wrong.'

Irene cast a grateful look in the direction of the journalist and moved delicately closer to Encarnita, who'd hurried to be by her side.

'At least,' she said to Pascual, 'do as you promised.'

Pascual glanced from Irene to Fleixa, and back again, before addressing his men. 'Everything's under control. Out, and shut the door.'

The men hesitated, but seeing their superior's look, obeyed. With them gone, Pascual turned to Irene with a look of annoyance.

'What is it you want from me?'

'Free Señor Amat immediately.' Then, looking at the journalist, she added, 'In exchange, the events of this evening will stay in this room.'

'Very well,' said Fleixa, inclining his head. 'If that's what you wish, I won't write a word.'

'What guarantee do I have that this . . . *incident* won't get out?'

'Isn't the word of a lady enough?' retorted Fleixa.

'Yes, all right, yes.'

Why, the Deputy Governor asked himself, why hadn't he just stayed in bed?

SIXTY-ONE

Llopis rested his legs on the desk, lolling back in the chair. A good week's work. Following Madame Palatino's note two days earlier agreeing to put on a public session, Barcelona had been flooded with wall posters advertising the event in the Lírico, which was due to take place that night.

The *Correo* had gone to press with a special edition focussing on the spiritualist event, and the response had been overwhelming. He himself had written a long piece in praise of Madame Palatino, talking up her enigmatic personality and the spectacular nature of her conferences with the spirit world. As though this were the answer to all the city's prayers, the tickets had sold out in a matter of hours, and the requests for more kept flooding into the offices of the *Correo*. He was almost sorry not to have been able to convince the Lírico managers to let more people in – they were obviously at capacity. The anticipation levels couldn't have been higher.

In his subsequent articles he'd returned to the murders, fuelling the nervousness and the morbid interest that were by now

456

palpable on the streets. As he'd expected, his reports had been a success. It was simply a matter of echoing people's fears; thereafter he'd demanded, quite vehemently, a spiritual resolution for the murders, at the same time as haranguing the authorities for their failure to act. His words had been sparks to a mound of dry leaves, and all of Barcelona was caught in the glow. Many other newspapers had ended up taking the same line. A number of opposing voices had been raised, like that of Reverend Monsignor Català, but that only further stoked the fire by drawing still more people into the debate.

From the most select gentlemen's clubs down to the most disreputable taverns, the talk was of nothing but the murderous Black Hound, a diabolical spirit made flesh. The details of the state of the corpses – partly Sánchez's information, partly his own imagination – had had just the impact he'd hoped. The horrific tales enthralled readers.

People started reporting fresh sightings, followed by many more. They spoke of attacks by an enormous mastiff, eyes like embers, a fire emanating from its snout. In Barceloneta, and in the barrios of Las Atarazanas, El Born and Raval, groups of men had gone around killing any dogs they came across in the night. They city was in the grip of a new madness.

And Llopis couldn't have been happier. Tonight would be the culmination. Madame Palatino's session would go down in the history of the city, and he'd be famous, not to mention a good deal better off.

He just hoped Sánchez could manage his part. The announcement of the madman's arrest ought to coincide with the close of Madame Palatino's show. Then Llopis could draw links between the two in the paper. According to what Sánchez had told him, Homs was just some poor devil, with neither family nor any friends to speak of, recently escaped from New Bethlem. Once he was behind bars, Llopis would be allowed to interview him. He imagined the piece he'd write on the man: how a dastardly spirit had corrupted his soul and turned him into a merciless killer. The greatest interview of his life.

A dozen Guardia Civil waited in a group. Muttering to one another, they covered their nerves with deep puffs on their cigarettes and stamps of the feet. From the shadows, Inspector Sánchez watched in silence. The whole company was dressed in thick wool coats, gloves and gumboots. Armed with pistols and flintlock rifles, each man carried a triple quota of bullets. Distributed across a number of haversacks there were seven oil lamps and four lanterns, ten metres of hopsack rope, and enough water to last two days. Nobody could say they hadn't come prepared.

Off to one side of the company, three bloodhounds strained against their leashes, eager to begin the hunt. They moaned and growled, and no one would go close save their handler, an old, taciturn officer who only had words for his dogs. The beasts' muscular legs, and their sharp fangs – which they bared at the slightest provocation – were a sight to behold. Their sense of smell would be of great help in trapping the killer. They were trained hunters of men.

Everyone looked up in the direction of some faint footsteps approaching. At last, thought Sánchez.

A street urchin appeared at the far end of the street, overseen by two men. Sánchez frowned. Coming over and stopping in front of him, the larger of the two men removed his cap, revealing a bald pate streaked with dirt.

'Here he is, Inspector. Wasn't the easiest to find.'

Guillem looked amused.

'And we made sure it's definitely him,' said the man, spitting on the ground. 'Little man knows those tunnels like the inside of his own underpants.'

'That's good news,' said Sánchez, turning to Guillem. 'Show us around down there and there'll be payment for you.'

'Give me ten pesetas and I'll take you wherever you want,' said the boy. 'But I'll be damned if this is a good time to go down in the sewers.'

'Do a good job, you'll get your money. Got it?'

Guillem shrugged. Sánchez called out to one of the younger guards.

'You. Your task is to keep your eyes on this one at all times. If he tries anything, if he so much as thinks about running off, break his arm.' Then he called to the rest of the men, 'All right, we've wasted enough time, let's go.'

A pair of guards prised open the manhole cover with a pole and deposited it to one side. There were iron rungs set in the sewer wall; one by one the men climbed in and descended. The yellow glare of the lanterns was engulfed in the darkness below. The main challenge was the dogs, which had to be lowered in improvised harnesses, a job which required the assistance of several men while the handler tried his best to soothe the beasts.

The spot they came down into resembled a large cistern. Water leaked through the walls and a fetid stream ran over their feet.

The cold, damp air slicked their faces and hands, but the most striking thing was the silence, so dense it seemed palpable.

'Bring me some light.'

Guillem was ushered to Sánchez, as one of the men opened out the map on top of a haversack.

'Seen one of these before?'

The boy nodded.

'All right, now you tell me our best route if we want to get to this point here.'

Sánchez indicated the old reservoir, and Guillem took a moment to study the lines that represented the underground network.

'There's nothing there you know,' he said. 'Just more tunnels.'

'I didn't ask for your opinion, boy. Just tell me how we get there.'

'Whatever you say. You're in charge.' Leaning close to the map, he ran a finger along one of the lines. 'You go through this gallery, it ends up at Las Ramblas. Walk that way for a bit and you come to a place where there are five different channels. Dangerous going along there. Once you're past that, drop down to the second level. Could be a lot of water at that point. The tunnels get much tighter there, not nearly as high and nowhere near as wide. And they start forking off every five yards, more than a serpent's tongue, mostly leading under the citadel. That's where you want to get to.'

'Fine, doesn't sound so hard.'

'Maybe, maybe not.'

Whispers went around among the men nearby. Sánchez straightened up and addressed the company.

'Well? What are you waiting for? Get the bags and get moving.'

They were soon underway, the handler and the hounds going first, Guillem and the man guarding him next, and then the rest of the group. At the end of the cistern three tunnels presented themselves, and at the boy's signal they entered the middle one.

They moved forward in silence, accompanied by the occasional yelp from one of the dogs. The tunnel floor became progressively steeper, and they began to hear the echo of small splashing sounds all around. Guillem said it was rats running off as they heard the men coming, and one of the men joked that they should trap one, a big one, and cook it with some rice. Nobody laughed.

Gradually, as the tunnel continued to dip, the thin strip of water spread into a torrent, forcing the company to proceed along a thin overhang to one side. Sánchez could see how difficult it would be to rescue anyone if they were to slip into the noxious waters. He was careful to situate himself between the wall of the tunnel and one of his men, and just as careful to make sure no one could tell he was doing so.

Guillem led them deeper into the sewers. Each of the watery cavities they entered was worse than the last; the smell got into their clothes, and a constant stream of freezing air blew through them; where it came from, no one could tell. After what seemed an eternity they came in earshot of a huge rushing body of water somewhere up ahead.

The tunnel they were now in emerged into a chamber of some considerable size. Down below, occupying almost the entire space, there was a channel the size of a public square, into which four separate chutes emptied water. Spray hung on the air. They had arrived at the culvert.

Guillem pointed the way. To the right was a narrow wooden gangway that ran over the top of the twenty-metre culvert. The wooden planks were extremely slippery, rotten in places, and the only handhold was a rope, also slick with moisture, hanging from a series of wall rings.

Again the dogs were sent ahead. They resisted to begin with, but their handler managed to goad them forward and they advanced cautiously, and finally made it across. The men came along afterwards in single file.

Sánchez did not like the look of that half-broken gangway, but he'd be damned if he was going to show fear in front of his men. He proceeded, making sure not to look down at the churning waters a few metres below. Sodden by the time he was halfway across, cursing under his breath, he wiped the water from his face with his forearm.

And, with that brief distraction, he lost his footing and toppled onto a particularly weak and ancient crossbeam, to a loud crack. He tried to regain his balance but his weight made his momentum difficult to arrest. He flung out an arm and grabbed the rope, panic overtaking him as the mortar around the nearest ring came loose. The boards tilted and he fell, to cries from his men. He tried to catch hold of anything he could, the roar of the culvert growing louder. As he hit the eddying waters, he desperately flailed around. His fingers sought some kind of handhold, anything, but all they encountered was more water.

Everything around him seemed to slow down. His chest felt

462

crushed under a huge weight, and all air was knocked from his lungs, which began to burn. Little by little the pain gave way to a strangely peaceful sensation. The current carried his body down, darkness closing over him.

SIXTY-TWO

The man came and stood in front of the column. Its surface undulated with light from the carbon filament inside, which sent out coppery flecks. Coming close, he gazed once more at the cylindrical form of the column, and the perfect finish of the dome. He tested the four iron braces that kept it upright, and checked the variety of cables that hung down from the ceiling like so many spiders' legs. He could feel the vibration emanating from inside the column – the whole laboratory was buzzing with it. His fingers grazed the metal, which sent a tremor up his arm. Bringing his face close he was met by his distorted reflection in the burnished metal. A moan escaped his lips. Soon, so soon . . . But not yet. There was still a great deal to do.

He moved reluctantly away from the device and over to one of the walls. A little way from the capsule, set into the wall, was a console dotted with dozens of small, flickering lights. The cables ran from its base and up the wall, disappearing behind the column. With some expert flicks of the hands he manipulated a few needles and dials, bringing the temperature, the oxygen levels and the energy up by fractions. In answer, a soothing, bubbling noise began to emerge from the capsule.

Satisfied, he turned his attention to the bench bearing the new specimen. Although, in this case, he wasn't sure if the term applied. The young girl's breast rose and fell serenely. In contrast to the others, he'd covered this one's body with a sheet. She was different. Her eyelids continued to move due to the light movement beneath. He took the pulse at one of her bound wrists and nodded to himself, pleased. The morphine was working well.

Pau Gilbert had shown uncommon daring. Who would have imagined that such a brilliant student was a women disguised as a man? Her determination, the willingness to do whatever it took to reach her goals, was in his eyes rather impressive. She reminded him of himself, in a sense. They'd both been made to conceal their true identity. Misunderstood and rejected by the world, they'd also both been willing to do anything to achieve their dreams.

Her keen mind was still a surprise to him. She'd shown intelligence to equal that of any man. Perhaps with a little more time she, along with her colleagues, might have managed to track him down and detain him.

And how close he'd been to taking her in the library, though that would have been a shame seeing as he'd been of a mind, at the time, to deal with her as he had the old man. If that had happened, he wouldn't have the key, as he now did, to complete the process. The irony of it!

He ran his fingers across the cover of the manuscript. He held himself back from opening it and losing himself in the contents, much as he would have liked to. Next to the book he had the girl's notes and the parchment that had lain hidden for three hundred years. Vesalius's final illustration.

Everything was prepared. He'd spent the previous several hours working on the modifications contained in the *Liber Octavus* – now a group of cables, slightly different from the others that ran into the machine, hung from a rail over the dissecting table. He couldn't help but look on in admiration. The process had been devastatingly simple, which was precisely what made it a thing of such wonder.

Checking, again, that the sawdust covered the floor around the dissecting table, and that all the bottles of saline were in place on the metal stand, he hooked two blood bags into a transfuser bearing the Coll y Pujol brand name.

He opened a nearby trunk and extracted a black satin case, opening its lid with his gloved fingers. Reverently he removed a glass vial and held it up to the light. The liquid inside was green. A dose that had been hastily concocted – but luckily he was a dab hand by now.

He smiled. The first times he'd used the serum, with his early specimens, it had not gone well. He lost them before there was any time to intervene. A waste: a corpse was of no use to him. It had taken dozens of unsuccessful attempts. In fact, he'd perfected the formula to such a degree that he could now adapt it according to the constitution of the individual and the time of the operation. This had led to some unexpected results. The singular combination of cocaine with other opiates in the formula had provoked hyperalgesia in the subjects; rather than sending them to sleep, it made them more sensitive to pain. This made their reactions to his work all the more fascinating.

Putting the vial away, he placed the case to one side on a small metal worktable. Shutting his eyes, he isolated the pain in his maltreated bódy. He loved the feelings that preceded each intervention. He'd miss them when it was all over. It was an instant of such exquisiteness, entirely unique. The specimen intact. *As yet untransformed.* Bringing the scalpel to bear on the skin, a slight alteration to the fragile equilibrium. If he didn't work swiftly and in perfect synchrony, the anatomical harmony would be lost irrevocably. His skill was the one thing separating his achievement – his art – from a bit of bungled surgery. An artist – that was precisely what he was.

SIXTY-THREE

Daniel moved his arm gingerly, trying to ease the pain provoked by each jolt of the carriage. His hair was clumped with dried blood and his lips were puffy and cracked. He looked down at his clothes in disgust – he looked like he'd crawled out of a sewer. Pushing away the proffered glass, he took a long swig directly from the brandy bottle itself.

'Thanks,' he croaked.

'Your friend Fleixa was most persuasive,' said Irene. 'He came to the house and insisted on seeing me, wouldn't take no for an answer. He told me about your arrest, and that you needed help. I did warn you – Bertomeu is capable of anything. This,' she said, holding out an elegant leather wallet, 'has a ticket for the express train to Montpellier, your passport, and the small amount of money I've managed to get together. Whatever's at the college you'll have to leave behind. I'll get it to you later, somehow.'

'You're very generous, it's far more than I deserve. And you've risked a great deal in helping me. But I can't leave.'

'Your life is in danger! What more proof do you need?'

The carriage came to halt under the Arco de Triunfo, the entry point to the World Fair. It was the eve of the opening ceremony, and silence reigned across the grounds. The carriage door opened and Fleixa's face appeared.

'Get in,' said Irene. 'And tell Encarnita to as well, it's so cold out there.'

'She's wrapped herself up in a cloak,' said Fleixa as he climbed in. 'She says she'd rather stay outside and keep watch.'

'Fleixa,' said Daniel. 'I don't know how I can ever thank you.'

'It isn't me you owe your freedom to, I was just the driver!'

'And I'm so sorry for your loss,' said Daniel, his face darkening.

Fleixa's laughing expression gave way, and he nodded solemnly.

'How are you?'

The journalist didn't answer straightaway, but pushed back the window curtain and looked off down the street.

'Much better now.'

'You know they'll be after you when word of my escape gets out?'

'Don't worry yourself. My guess is that Inspector Sánchez has more pressing concerns.'

There wasn't much light inside the carriage but Daniel was sure he'd seen a smile spread on Fleixa's face.

'I'll explain,' he said, anticipating the question. 'Not just now though. Señorita Gilbert is missing.'

'How?'

'As far as I can tell, one of her fellow students worked out the disguise and reported her. She was confined to her rooms but then when they went to take her dinner, she was gone. The rooms had also been ransacked. No one seems to have any idea what's going on – but we know, don't we? It must be Homs, he's got her.'

'It wasn't Homs.'

'What do you mean?'

Daniel turned to Irene. 'Where's your husband right now?'

'Bertomeu? Why?'

Daniel took her hands in his, squeezing them and looking directly into her eyes.

'It's just important we know, extremely important. Where do you think he might be?'

'I don't know what to say to you. It's been a number of days since I've seen him.'

'And is it like him to just disappear?'

'These past months, since he's been working on the power station, he's often gone off for two or three days without a word. I imagine he works late and sleeps in his office.'

Daniel nodded pensively, the others watching him expectantly.

'You remember the papers you brought me? They had the results of the autopsy that was carried out on the person befriended by Homs in the sanatorium, the one Homs was presumed to have murdered before he fled. The man wasn't survived by any family, so his body was sent to Santa Creu for student exercises. Your husband somehow managed to get his hands on the report, to stop the truth getting out.'

'Really?'

Daniel paused, taking another drink from the bottle. Looking

470

from Irene to Fleixa, he went on. 'The dead man was suffering from cancer of the liver.'

'Dear God!' exclaimed Fleixa.

Irene simply looked confused.

'It means the man killed in the sanatorium was Homs.'

All three were silent for a moment as they took in the revelation.

'But in that case, who was the other man?'

'A man in your husband's employ.'

Irene covered her mouth, stifling a cry. 'That isn't possible!'

'When Adell was in the sanatorium he struck up a friendship with Homs. He learned of Homs's work, he found out about his discoveries. He had a sense of their value and tried to buy them from Homs, but was refused. When Adell came out, he needed someone to keep an eye on Homs, and when this man took up with Homs they struck a deal, with money perhaps changing hands. After a few days the man sent word that Homs was about to be released. My guess is that Adell himself went back to the sanatorium to try, one last time, to get Homs to share his secret, but when he still didn't get the answer he wanted, lost his temper – he has a history – and killed him.'

'So the wounds on the cadaver . . .'

'Adell is well versed in aspects of surgery. He might have been expelled from his course, but until then he'd been a brilliant student. To throw people off the scent he disfigured Homs's face and dressed him in the clothes of his friend, hoping everyone would assume Homs was the killer.'

Fleixa and Irene looked unconvinced.

'I'm not so sure—' Fleixa began to say.

'Irene,' said Daniel, 'this coach belongs to Bertomeu, does it not?'

'Well, yes. But I'm not sure I see what—'

'Even in the dark,' he said, 'I managed to notice that a new lamp has been fitted, and there are scratches down the side; they've been badly filled, and the silver edging on the door, that's damaged too. They aren't that obvious, but then I was looking for them. This is the carriage we pursued along Las Ramblas!'

'God, you're right!' exclaimed Fleixa.

'Why would he do such things?' asked Irene, trying to stop her hands from trembling.

'Adell wanted to find the secret of Vesalius,' explained Daniel, 'and Homs wouldn't give it to him. For that he has carried out the most horrible experiments on all these girls, to the point of robbing them of their lives. For that same reason he was trying to find the manuscript in the library, but mistakenly seized the wrong manuscript from Gilbert. We've been chasing the shadow of a dead man. Adell is the real killer.'

He thumped the seat. Adell had Gilbert – who was to say he hadn't already done away with her? And he had the original manuscript. 'We have to rescue Gilbert and apprehend Adell.'

'I'm with you,' said Fleixa. 'But how? We know he's underground somewhere near the power station, but not exactly where – and even less, how to gain access.'

'The way down can't be in the power station itself, it would be too much of a risk to transfer his victims through somewhere as busy as the site of the Fair . . .' Daniel fell quiet. For the past few hours he'd been running through the encounter with Adell just before the arrest. He had the feeling he was missing something.

What could it be? What had Adell said that was so important? Then it came to him. 'Fleixa, quick, get us to my home.'

'You mean your rooms at college?'

'No, I mean my family mansion. And dear Lord, we have to hurry.'

With a nod the journalist jumped out of the cab and got up into the driver's seat. The carriage set off and was soon flying along the Paseo de la Industria, deserted at that hour. They came past the Cuidadela Park and turned into La Ribera. Threading their way through the backstreet, after a few minutes they arrived in front of the old mansion.

Daniel opened the door to get down, but stopped himself, turning to Irene. 'How will you get back?'

'Don't worry, Encarnita was raised by a coachman, she knows how to drive the carriage as well as any man.'

'I—'

Irene touched her gloved finger to his lips. 'Be careful,' she whispered.

They gazed at one another. Daniel wanted to say something further, but Fleixa interrupted.

'Sorry to hurry you, Amat, but the nightwatchman's bound to be about at this hour. And I'm freezing out here.'

Irene nodded – a brief gesture, all but impossible to see in the darkness of the cab. Without another word, Daniel got down from the carriage and followed Fleixa. They made their way out and along the street, in the direction of the house, which stood dark against the cloud-covered sky.

SIXTY-FOUR

Half opening the stage curtain, Llopis stole a look out into the concert hall. He glimpsed Evaristo Arnús out in the foyer receiving the city's elite. The owner of the Lírico was carrying out his role with aplomb, welcoming his patrons with endless gracious smiles. They would get down from their carriages on Calle Mallorca, the gentlemen in their finest suits and the ladies resplendent in dresses and jewels, and make their way into the theatre.

The tiers were full of the splendour of great occasions. A sumptuous chandelier illuminated the space. The upper stalls and the three tiers above bubbled with conversation and with people arriving. A full house was guaranteed. No one wanted to miss this.

The hottest ticket of the year. Ticket prices had shot up, with the general admission of one peseta doubling on the resale, and tickets for the best boxes going for as much as fifteen. The ticket vendors, with a little over two thousand tickets released, had sold out in an hour and a half; there had been demand for another thousand at least. A mounted guard had been posted on the street outside in case of disturbances. The whole of the staff from the town council were said to be in attendance, even the governor and his wife were coming.

Llopis could feel the expectation in the air. He caught sight of two gentlemen having a heated discussion, and was delighted to see that one had a copy of the *Correo* in his hand. Doubtless they were talking about his latest column.

At around this time Sánchez had to be down in the sewers, about to apprehend Homs. He hoped to God the man didn't ruin it all at the last.

He was struggling to keep his hands dry – nerves always brought them out in a sweat, he couldn't help it. Reaching into his pocket for a handkerchief, he felt the touch of another hand.

Madame Palatino was standing right beside him. How had she come up so quietly? She almost reminded him of those spirits she was so convinced she could see.

'Madame!'

She gave a few languid blinks and then tilted her head in greeting.

'I startle you, Señor Llopis?'

He thought he glimpsed an amused look, though it vanished immediately behind the grey pall of her countenance.

'No, Señora, of course not. I suppose I'm a little anxious, is all. Are you not?'

She didn't seem to hear him. Llopis, unsettled, changed the subject. 'Everything to your liking?'

In answer, she turned and looked behind them. Some theatre hands were placing chairs at a series of tables that had been arranged to form a semicircle across the stage, a black satin cloth draped over them. A young boy was lining up candles as another placed a tray with glasses and a jug of water in the centre. In accordance with Madame Palatino's wishes, the stage was otherwise entirely bare.

'Only the spirits know what destiny holds in store for us.'

'Well, quite,' he said.

The woman peered through the crack in the curtains.

'All of Barcelona is here!' said Llopis.

Madame Palatino showed no emotion, but, turning to him again, she looked sombre.

'There is something I ought to warn you about.'

'Pardon?'

'I sense a negative aura about the place. An energy I have never before encountered.'

Llopis couldn't help but shudder. What did she mean by that? Was she getting cold feet? He hadn't even considered the possibility of her calling it off at the last moment. Cancelling the event now would be a disaster, he'd never hear the end of it. Perhaps she thought she could get more money?

'You're unhappy with our agreement?'

'No, it is not that.'

Then Llopis saw something in her eyes that he recognized: fear. He breathed a sigh. So she was flesh and blood. He sought to reassure her. 'It's nerves, Señora. It'll pass once we're underway. Truly, everyone is here. Tonight will go down in the annals of the city, and you are the title role.'

She turned to look out at the concert hall once more. 'That is what worries me, Señor Llopis. That is what worries me.'

★

A short while later, and not without certain complications, the public occupied their seats. The conversations quietened to whispers. A sea of faces turned towards the stage. Then, as the lights were dimmed, silence fell.

Up went the stage curtain and Madame Palatino, all in black, appeared at the front of the stage, lights projecting upwards onto her. The shadows they cast gave her lean features a still more cadaverous aspect. A woman in the crowd let out an exclamation, quickly to be hushed by those around her. A shiver went through the public. Llopis had convinced the theatre operator to turn the heating down to give the place a glacial ambience, but he now realized how unnecessary that had been. The woman's presence alone was sufficient to chill the concert hall.

A gentleman came forward, one Llopis recognized from the private sessions.

'Good evening, ladies and gentlemen, and welcome. We've come together tonight in this magnificent theatre to take part in an event quite beyond the usual fare, a most memorable occasion. Whatever happens this evening, the whole world will hear of it. You are fortunate enough to be present, the first and only time in this city.'

The smile on Llopis's face grew broader. People would be talking about this for a great many days to come.

SIXTY-FIVE

The young officer had disappeared from before his eyes as though he'd never existed. The eyes of the group remained glued to the torrent of water, which crashed steadily down.

Sánchez, wet through and gasping for air, had survived. By a whisker. When he fell he'd caught hold of one of his men, and together the pair had been dragged into a niche as the water continued to buffet them. There hadn't been space for them both, and he'd only just managed to cling on – at the expense of the lower-ranking officer, who'd been swallowed by the culvert. Sánchez's men had thrown down a rope and he'd somehow escaped with his life.

He heard the men muttering nervously amongst themselves; they were glancing around in terror, whispering like old women. He had to impose some order, he realized, otherwise the whole operation would slip through his fingers.

'Bad luck,' he said, moving to the middle of the group. 'We've had an awful bit of bad luck. Your colleague saved my life, giving his own in the act. We'll remember him in our prayers, always. For now we need to carry on.'

'Inspector, Josep had the backup lanterns and the map.'

'We ought to go back,' whispered one of the men, transfixed by the pounding water below.

Sánchez strode over to the man and shoved him up against the wall. 'What are you saying?' he cried, making sure that everyone could hear. 'You're going to let his sacrifice be for nothing? Come on, get your things. Right?'

A murmur of agreement went up.

Sánchez cast around for the boy, whom he finally saw huddling over by the entrance to the tunnel, away from the group.

'You! Get over here!'

Sniffing, Guillem came closer.

'You lived down here for a time, am I right? Think you can find the way?'

'Maybe . . .' he said in a small voice.

'Maybe's no good,' hissed Sánchez, and he slapped him on the neck. 'You have to, boy. Understood?'

He watched, pleased, as the boy's frightened expression gave way. His face hardened. For a moment Sánchez thought he saw a glimmer of resentment, but the boy quickly looked down, seeming to come around.

'Yes, Señor. I'll do it. I can do it, yes.'

'Well, then. Let's get on with it.'

Guillem picked up his bag and paused uncertainly, before turning and moving off. The group, rousing itself, followed after him. Sánchez rummaged around in his pocket, but it was empty

– his dried peas had been lost. Bad to worse, he thought, bad to worse.

The light from the lanterns lit them up as in a street procession. They moved along in silence; no one felt much like speaking. After a few minutes the watercourse widened and the passage they were coming along grew still narrower, forcing them to shift to single file. This stretch of the sewerage network bore the effluvium from the Concepción, Audiencia and Born barrios, added to along the way by the waste of dozens of factories. The stench became so bad they had to cover their mouths and noses.

'Is there far to go?' Sánchez asked Guillem, putting a hand on his shoulder.

The boy, who for his part seemed unaffected by the smell, pointed up ahead. 'One more chamber after this, Señor Inspector.'

He'd said exactly the same half an hour earlier. Sánchez was beginning to think the idiot child was lost. Maybe it hadn't been the best idea to place so much trust in him. But then, after a couple of minutes, the passageway widened, opening out into a semi-circular space that broke into two tunnels.

They'd arrived at the fork.

Next to the wall was an abandoned handcart, left on its side with a number of tools and sandbags tipped out across the floor – the sand inside had solidified – almost completely barring one of the doors.

'Looks like a barrier to stop people coming in,' said one of the officers.

480

'It's to stop them coming out,' said Guillem.

'Coming out?' said the man. 'Who?'

'That's enough chat,' said Sánchez, cutting them off. 'Clear this lot out of the way.'

The men formed a line and passed the bags back along it. The moist air had left an intricate tracery of rust across the door, but it still seemed solid. A heavy iron bar sat across it, which needed two officers to lift it away. They went to open the door, but it had fused with the lintel and sides. Improvising crowbars from a number of the rifles, finally they forced it wide enough for a man to pass through. The flames in the lanterns shook at a blast of air, rancid like the breath of an old man. They came through to the top of a spiral staircase.

'Load your weapons and be on your guard!' said Sánchez. 'It won't do us any harm to be ready. And just three lanterns from here on.'

They descended, the handler with his dogs at the front, Guillem, Sánchez and the others in the rear. Feeling the boy trembling, Sánchez chose to put it down to the cold. At the next level down, they came to a tunnel that split off into five further tunnels. They were now in one of the network's oldest stretches. The tunnels here had been excavated from the stone itself and the floor was like clay. Guillem made directly for the third opening from the left, the roof of which was much lower; most of the men had to stoop. The tunnel opened out every few metres into cross-connecting passageways, wide enough for a man to pass through and leading into the adjacent tunnels.

After several minutes the dogs began to moan, and then refused to advance, turning circles around a spot on the ground.

The handler yanked on their leads, reprimanding them, but still the animals whined and clawed the ground.

'Shut them up!' cried one of the guards. 'They'll drive us crazy.'

Suddenly a screech was heard, followed by the sound of curses. The dogs, free from their leashes, fled forward into the darkness, baying furiously. The old handler was in a heap on the floor; a couple of the officers stepped forward to help him up.

'Can't you keep your mutts under control?'

'Of course I can, but not if one of them bites me. They've been beside themselves since the moment we set foot down here.'

Then, the barks suddenly ceased, and silence fell – a resounding silence. The men looked at each other uncertainly.

'What on earth—'

'Forward,' said Sánchez, hefting his pistol.

The men advanced along the underground passage, rifles out in front. In puddles along the way they saw that the water had turned red. Once more the passageway narrowed so that the men were more tightly bunched together; they gripped their weapons. At a point where the passageway rose slightly and bore to the right they found one of the dogs, lying in the middle of the tunnel. Badly wounded, with a large gash across its back, it was still breathing. Sánchez and two of his men moved forward – and saw another of the hounds a little way ahead, lying on a large rock with its neck clearly broken. And not much further on they came to the third, whose head had almost been separated from the body. The walls were splattered with blood.

'Who could have done this?'

'No matter,' said the handler. 'Whoever it was, they're dead, I swear it.'

One of the older officers came forward to speak to Sánchez. His voice trembled, though he tried to hide it.

'It's them, Señor Inspector. They're watching us.'

'What are you on about? Who?'

'The Pickers.'

Sánchez sighed – just what he needed, old wives's tales again.

'We have light and we have weapons. I'm not going to turn back on account of a ragbag bunch of beggars.'

'But this is their domain, Inspector. We ought to get out while we still can.'

Sánchez pointed his pistol at the man's head and cocked the hammer. The man stumbled back away, scraping his shoulder against the wall.

'Not even God gets out of this now,' said Sánchez. 'Do I make myself clear?'

The man nodded hurriedly.

'Say it.'

'Not even God, Señor.'

'Quite right.' Sánchez lowered the gun. 'Wait, where's the boy?'

They cast around, but Guillem had disappeared. Sánchez managed to prevent himself from crying out curses. Damned boy. But he could remember the map, and he knew they weren't far from the abandoned reservoir. No way he was turning back now, not after what they'd been through to get here.

'Forget him. Onwards, I say, just be on your guard. Whoever did this can't be far off.'

The group began forward again, looking apprehensively at the shadows flickering around them. Sánchez glanced at the guard next to him, whose expression suggested that he, too, had heard the sounds in the adjacent tunnels. He was about to call out for all of the lanterns to be fully lit when he caught sight of some silhouettes up ahead. As Sánchez's men came closer, the figures fled, with the handler and three of the men close behind. Sánchez cursed – they'd taken two of the lanterns with them, leaving them with just one alight. But before he could bemoan their departure, three shots rang out, followed by a cry. Then, once more, silence.

'Quick, the reserve lanterns!'

The order came too late. Like ghosts passing through the solid walls, suddenly a group of figures surged forward from the adjacent tunnels, surrounding them. Dressed in rags, they gave off a pestilential smell. These were no ghosts, as Sánchez could see only too well: men, and some women, all very much flesh and blood – about thirty of them. Most were missing teeth and displayed hands bent and curved due to some illness or malnutrition. They bore dirks and rudimentary little lanterns that cast hardly any light. Many were dressed in cowls, and some had faces covered in pustules and scars. The most terrifying thing, though, were their unblinking, milky eyes.

'I'm an officer of the law,' said Sánchez, as firmly as he could. 'Stand down, or we'll take you in.'

None of them answered.

'Do you hear?'

For a moment he thought they might comply. Then a man stepped forward; Sánchez barely saw the motion of his arm. The

484

officer next to him let out a cry and fell to his knees staring down at his hand – all but severed. The lantern he'd been holding rolled away along the floor, guttered, and went out.

And then the attack began.

In the gloom, the air filled with the sounds of blows, wails, muffled cries. One of Sánchez's men managed to get a shot away. Shouts went up. Sánchez groped frantically in search of the nearest wall. Then, suddenly, pain burst out in his leg. One of those tramps had stuck a blade in him. Backing away, he thrust the pistol into the dark and pulled the trigger. This had turned bad – nothing for it now but to run. He'd surely die if he stayed. Stumbling backwards, he crashed into one of his men, who recognized him.

'Inspector, what are your orders?'

Sánchez merely shoved the surprised officer to the ground. Straight away, three shadows were on the man, wrestling him down. He heard metal puncturing flesh, men crying out. Sánchez ran.

Passing through the stretch of tunnel containing the dogs, he made his way into the part he thought led to the staircase. Feeling he'd put enough distance between himself and their assailants, he took a reserve lantern from his haversack. His leg hurt, but there was no time to examine it. He could hear the ongoing fight behind him. Several shots rang out in quick succession, then a few more, this time further apart, before quiet descended once more. He hoped, in the uproar, that his escape had gone unnoticed.

After long minutes of searching, he found the stairs. He hobbled up, completely out of breath by the time he reached the top. As he was about to stop for a rest, he thought he heard footsteps behind him. He squeezed through the door and into the next chamber.

He needed to bar the door. He leaned and pushed with all his weight – the corroded hinges protested, began to give way, and inch by inch the door drew shut.

It was almost there when a man appeared on the other side – an officer. He'd been separated from the group, had lost his coat, his shirt was torn at chest-height and he was holding his forehead, which bled profusely.

'Señor Inspector, open the door!'

But Sánchez, to the younger man's astonishment, continued to push. Just then the first of his pursuers reached the top of the stairs. The officer howled like a cornered animal. The Pickers fanned out around him, taking their time. The officer, trying to push the door open, appealed to Sánchez.

'Open it! For the love of God—'

The door inched shut, cutting off the officer's appeals. The iron bar was too heavy for Sánchez to lift alone, and he grabbed an abandoned shovel and rammed it between the rings. Muffled cries issued from the far side.

He moved on with a feeling of great relief. He couldn't tell how long the door would hold them, but long enough, with any luck. His leg throbbed. Bringing the lantern close, he saw that his whole trouser leg was soaked in blood. He made a tourniquet of his neckerchief.

Now was a time for a clear head: the three initial galleries opened out in front of him. Which one was it? Before he could decide, he heard the echo of a cracking sound, followed by a metallic creaking. They'd broken through. Without another thought he bolted forward into the middle passage, his tiny lantern light as his only guide.

'...eeeeng, 'they'd gotten through.' When another
.... its hold forward and the middle portion, like tiny
.... as it settled in place.'

SIXTY-SIX

'Oh, good. You're awake.'

Pau heard her captor's voice like a distant echo. She tried to bring her hands up but couldn't; leather straps kept them in place. A shiver ran through her unclothed body, over which a sheet had been draped. She couldn't feel her back, it had gone numb from the cold hard surface on which she lay.

'My apologies for the tethers, they're just to keep you from hurting yourself as the serum takes effect. I'll untie you later, I promise.'

Her captor wore a white shirt, a bow tie and a leather medical apron over the top. He showed an unsettling stillness as he contemplated her through his glasses.

'How can it be? You?' Pau tried to stay calm. She'd thought that the last thing she'd seen before losing consciousness had been a hallucination. But no.

'You seem surprised.'

'I never imagined . . . Why?'

'Don't worry yourself. Everything will become clear, all in

due course. A few surprises still await us tonight. And in the meantime there's still much work to do.'

The man moved out of her field of vision. He reappeared a moment later carrying a basin of water and some objects wrapped in a cloth. Coming over to the bench, he sat down beside her. He pulled his gloves tighter. And, dipping a piece of fabric in the basin, he began dabbing it on Pau's scalp.

'Wh-what are you doing?' stammered Pau.

'The process requires a few preliminaries, as you surely know only too well. This won't take long.'

He continued with his task until satisfied, finally putting the fabric back in the basin and then pressing his fingers down on the girl's temple. His other hand held a barber's razor. As the blade came towards her face, Pau flinched, before feeling a sharp pain. She let out a scream. A trickle of blood ran down onto her cheek.

'Better keep still. It doesn't mater to me if your face is kept intact, so bear that in mind. I'll complete my work, whether you struggle or not.'

In spite of the fear she felt, Pau obeyed. With a sob she saw clumps of her hair falling to the ground. The man worked quickly and efficiently; it was over in a matter of minutes.

'What a lot of trouble I had finding you. So ingenious, shacking up with a prostitute! Was that your idea, or your friend Amat's?'

'What did you do with Dolors?' said Pau, choking.

'A most valiant woman. She really didn't want to give you up.'

Pau shut her eyes to try to hold back the tears. 'They'll get you, sooner or later.'

'You'll permit me to disagree. You and your friends were close, but not that close.'

489

Putting away the barber implements, he came and sat next to her again. 'I really can't tell you how pleased I am to have you here, dear. You're the only one who can truly appreciate my work. Remotely intelligent conversation has, with my previous specimens, been quite out of the question – for obvious reasons. But with you, Gilbert, that's far from being the case.'

Pau didn't say anything.

'You, more than anyone, will be able to appreciate the finer points of the process. As you know, Vesalius was a far greater man than any other medical person has even dreamed of being. How brilliant of you to unravel the *Liber Octavus's* secret, you made my job far easier; I really ought to thank you. And now, a once in a lifetime opportunity, do you see? You're going to get to experience it for yourself. I almost envy you.'

Pau was having trouble controlling her feelings, the horror that threatened to overwhelm her. Amat and Fleixa didn't know she'd been abducted, and even if they did they'd never find her; she didn't even know where she'd wound up.

'Stop, please! This is insanity, all of it!'

The man turned his head round slowly, and looked at her silently for a moment.

'I'm sorry to hear you say that.' He sounded genuinely sad. 'I thought you would understand.'

Turning away, he took the vial containing the serum from the black satin case on the side table. 'A tiny amount leads to total immobility in the patient, but leaves their thinking faculties untouched. The heart rate and blood pressure also stay the same. Unlike the morphine I used on you in your rooms, this formula has no analgesic effects, which means the body also produces

490

large amounts of adrenalin, which makes for better results. Quite the stroke of luck. The procedure is rather lengthy. You have to wait a number of hours for it to spread throughout the whole system, but all in all it's very effective.'

He proceeded to suspend the vial from one of the metal hangers, unscrewing the lid and attaching a rubber pipe.

'You're going to feel a prick now, my apologies again.' He expertly introduced the needle into a vein on her inner elbow. 'There we are, now we just have to wait.'

Just then, the copper lamps flickered and the lights dimmed, leaving the space half in darkness. The man cursed, leaving Pau and going over to the wall console. He adjusted a few dials, muttering to himself in concentration.

Pau took a moment to think. She had to find a way to escape. If the serum entered her body, she'd be paralyzed, and that would certainly be the end of her. Her only chance was if she could stop the liquid entering her veins, and try to run when the opportunity arose.

With one eye on her captor, she reached up for the rubber tubing, bending her hand back and stretching the strap to its limit. She could just graze it with her fingers. She took a breath – the man was still busy at the console. This was her chance. Squeezing her eyes shut and gritting her teeth, she stretched her arm out once more, this time in the direction of the metal hanger from which the glass ampoule hung. She managed to reach it, hooking a finger around the frame and yanking it towards her. Now the tube was closer. The straps cut into her forearm, but she withstood the pain, twisting her hand back again towards the tubing. Just as she was about to give up, she felt her fingers brush the tube, and managed to trap it and pull it closer. She bit her lip, managing to hold back a cry of delight. She'd done it. But the tubing got caught up in the leg of the side table, and escaped her fingers. It was out of reach again. Just then, the lights came back on.

'You'll have to forgive me,' said the man, smiling as he came closer again. 'Something's come up – I have to go to the theatre. Please don't worry, I won't be very long, and we can pick up on our interesting conversation again. If you wish, cry out whenever you like, no one will be able to hear you down here.'

With that, he went over to the far end of the cavern. He pressed some controls, and there was the sound of pulleys. The doors of a service lift parted, and the man got in, shutting the doors behind him.

Pau, unable to hold back the tears any longer, began to sob.

SIXTY-SEVEN

Daniel and Fleixa crept along the side of the Amat mansion wall. In the dark the place was even more sombre than during Daniel's previous visit. His throat knotted at the memory. In one way or another everything began, and ended, here.

'How's your arm?' Fleixa asked.

'It's nothing, I can carry on.'

Fleixa could see how stiffly his companion was moving, but didn't insist.

'What are we doing here?'

'I've been a fool.'

'What do you mean by that?'

'Adell made me believe he'd bought the house to spite me, but not at all – do you follow?'

The journalist nodded, though he wasn't sure if he did.

'I got the wrong end of the stick. That wasn't why Adell wanted the house.'

'But why else—' Fleixa stopped before finishing the sentence. He did see.

493

'Perfectly situated, isn't it?' continued Daniel. 'Just between La Barceloneta and the Parque de la Ciudadela. The rumours about a curse mean no one's going to come anywhere near – convenient, don't you think? I'd never have thought of it if Adell hadn't mentioned the purchase. It's the perfect spot.'

'Not so near the power plant though—'

'Not so far away, either – just a couple of streets.'

The journalist nodded. He reached into his jacket and pulled out two pistols, proffering one. Daniel gave an inquisitive look.

'I thought we'd need guns to get you out of Amalia,' shrugged Fleixa.

Daniel hesitated, but finally took the weapon. He'd never fired a gun – but the weight of it in his hand made him feel safer. Taking a deep breath, he turned and made his way towards the entrance.

The gate chain was on the floor when they arrived. They exchanged looks.

'Let's try not to make any noise,' said Daniel.

Once they were into the gardens they lit the lamp they'd brought from the coach. Daniel led the way. They came along the flagstone path, with the old linden and the collapsed summerhouse watching over them. When they came to the steps leading to the entranceway, they both felt a sensation as though the old mansion had been expecting them.

Entering the building, they made their way through the deserted rooms, their footsteps echoing off into distant reaches. Daniel could feel the journalist's nervous breathing close behind. They reached the kitchen far more quickly than the last time he'd been there. He held up the lantern: before them stood the charred remains of the door leading down to the cellars.

'This is the entrance to my father's laboratory. He must be there.'

Cautiously, cocking the guns, they entered and began down the steps. Daniel was filled with misgivings as he recalled the strange sounds he'd heard on the previous occasion, and all that followed his stumble.

This time, however, they reached the foot of the stairs without any mishaps. The lantern light revealed a sizeable space in which the fire had evidently been more severe than anywhere else, since the blaze had begun here; the lab chemicals had made an inferno of the room, leaving only a few charred remains. There was one long table that hadn't been entirely consumed, and the frame of a chaise longue. Broken glass crunched underfoot. What remained of some wooden shelves, and the precious library, had subsided against a wall.

'A long time since anyone's been here,' said Fleixa, who was taken aback by the sound of his own echoing voice.

'Let's look, maybe something will turn up.'

They ranged around for a few minutes in the semi-darkness. Daniel was beginning to lose hope, when he heard Fleixa's voice. 'Over here, Amat.'

He was holding the lantern over a small pallet bed in one corner – it looked unaffected by the fire. Dark yellow stains covered the wooden boards, and they both supressed tremors as they guessed what they were from. Leaning closer, Daniel lifted away some shackles that were attached to a hitching ring on the headboard.

'Maybe I wasn't completely wrong!' he said.

Fleixa nodded, though he wasn't as enthused as his colleague. 'Seems like it, though this place isn't what I'd imagined.'

Daniel didn't answer. He'd come to the same conclusion. Adell's experiments called for certain macabre prerequisites – a laboratory and utensils, light, running water. And there was none of that. They checked the room with utmost care, but aside from some bandages lying near a lamp that looked in working order, found nothing further.

Daniel kicked the remains of a chair.

'Damn it all! No! There's hardly any time—' The words died on his lips.

Then Fleixa voiced what they were both thinking. 'We guessed wrong, and now Gilbert's got no chance.'

SIXTY-EIGHT

The dimmed lights did little to obscure the expectancy inside the theatre. The occasional nervous cough went up, or somebody clearing their throat, and then someone would hiss at the offender to be quiet. All eyes were riveted on the same point on the stage.

Beneath the table, Llopis kept drying his perspiring hands on a handkerchief, little good that it did. To his relief, the candle flames meant he couldn't see the faces of the people in the crowd. Until now he'd thought it would be a wonderful idea to take part in the act – he'd have been directly involved in the thing he was planning to write about, and what an article that would make for. Sánchez would have made the arrest by now, and would be waiting at the barracks for the event to end. He eyed the medium's water jug thirstily, once more wiping his palms and asking himself if he wouldn't have been better to stay in the wings.

Beside him, Madame Palatino was sitting with a straight back staring straight ahead; erect as the stem of a plant. Her jaw trembled very slightly, suggesting to Llopis that she wasn't as calm as she appeared. Sensing the journalist's eyes on her, she turned brusquely, regarded him for a moment, before turning her gaze out into the room again. After that Llopis kept his eyes firmly ahead.

The candlelight played on the black satin of the tablecloth, and cast a yellowish hue on the people's faces. There were a dozen more sitting at the table, men and women, all looking guarded.

The compère continued with the introduction. 'Ladies and gentlemen, the terrible events of these past weeks have afflicted us, one and all. Poor innocent girls, murdered in the most abominable ways. Such vile acts can clearly only be the work of a troubled soul. A spectre that was barred from passing through into the great beyond, and that has become evil incarnate. Tonight, with your help, we are going to free this distressed soul, and put an end, once and for all, to its terrible actions.'

A murmur went around the stalls. Madame Palatino wetted her lips on the water glass, and went on looking out with half-closed eyes. She seemed not to be listening to the compère, who went on.

' . . . truly exceptional. We have the privilege of welcoming here tonight one of the world's most brilliant minds. Her pre-eminence has been acknowledged across Europe, in its most glittering cities, in London, Vienna and Paris! And as evidence of her generosity, which knows no bounds, she has offered to help us in this time of great need.'

Applause went around, which the medium acknowledged with a slight nod. The compère cleared his throat.

'Madame Palatino would now like for you to all join hands.

Silence is then required, and, ladies and gentlemen, absolute seriousness among you all.'

There were murmurs as the audience members joined hands with their neighbours. One or two titters broke out, and some whispers, hushed immediately by other members of the public.

Llopis joined hands with Madame Palatino on one side – hers was rough and bony to the touch – and a portly gentleman on the other – who grimaced at Llopis's sweaty palm. He shrugged an apology.

Madame Palatino dropped her head and brought it up again with eyes closed. She took a deep breath in and exhaled, and then once again. Everyone looked on expectantly. She allowed a few seconds to elapse before speaking, in her usual deep, calm tones.

'Spirit, I call on you.'

Though she appeared not to exert herself at all, her voice reached every corner of the auditorium.

In the silence that followed, Llopis unknowingly held his breath – as did almost every other person there. When next Madame Palatino spoke, it was like the prelude to a storm, building louder and louder.

'We hear you. Come, come to us, have no fear.'

The candles flickered and the temperature all across the space suddenly dropped. People shifted nervously in their seats. And then the table on the stage began to float up above the ground – to the amazement of all present.

'It nears . . . I can feel it . . . It approaches . . .'

Llopis felt a lump in his throat – it was so *real*. Then, without warning, Madame Palatino's chair was thrown violently back

499

as her spine arched – Llopis almost lost hold of her hand. She made a guttural sound, and adopted a hunched posture, her eyes still squinted but now with an added malevolence to her features. And when she spoke, in resounding tones, it was with the voice of a man.

'I have been called, and here I am.'

'Tell us who you are!' someone called out.

'I have many names, but you may address me as Belial. Prince of treachery, Sodom's own demon. The Antichrist!'

Cries went up, and two women in different places in the audience fainted, causing a commotion around each of them. Theatre hands came to remove them. Llopis was furious: this wasn't what they'd agreed at all.

'Cease your evil deeds!' cried one young man. 'Murderer!'

A chorus of protests went up, deaf to added calls for silence. Then a hoarse cackle issued from the medium's mouth, and again the auditorium fell quiet. The men who had got to their feet now stood motionless.

'Fools. You're nothing. There's nothing you can do to stop me. I, Belial, have come to tell you: great suffering awaits you, calamity untold. The Black Hound has been raised, and only blood can sate it, and it will be sated. A dark time awaits, oh terrible—'

Suddenly the voice stopped, and Madame Palatino's eyes shot open. She looked startled. She struggled to her feet, only to stumble back, sending the chair clattering to the ground. She wavered, grabbing onto the table to keep her up – suspended from thin wires in the rigging, it swung in the air. The audience looked on, rapt. Then the woman tottered to one side, taking the

500

tablecloth with her. Unintelligible noises issued from her throat, and then a pinkish froth appeared on her lips. With Llopis's help, she regained her balance for a moment, but then, grimacing, let out a shriek and collapsed.

An uncertain silence settled. Two men came forward and, identifying themselves as doctors, approached Madame Palatino to check her pulse. Their faces reflected the astonishment of every person present.

'She's dead.'

SIXTY-NINE

Sánchez had been going around in circles in these repugnant sewers for hours, losing his way and having to backtrack on at least three occasions. This time, though, he was sure he was on the right track. A little further and he'd be at the stairwell they'd descended to begin with, all those hours ago.

The lantern began to gutter. He struck the sewer wall, which clanged emptily. It didn't matter. He hadn't heard his pursuers behind him for quite some time now. He'd given the scum the slip. He laughed to himself – a sound returned, with interest, by the echoing tunnels.

He was sick of this darkness, sick of his soaking clothes, sick of the smell that clung to his skin. To top it off, the wound in his leg was burning horribly; he had to shuffle along like some kind of cripple. Dear God, he said to himself, don't let it become infected. The moment he got out he'd go straight to the baths at Casa Emilia, spend a whole day there. Then he'd put together a new expedition, with more men and many more guns. They'd come down here barrels blazing, exterminate those Pickers like the rats they were.

A waterfall came into sight – one he was sure he recognized. What a relief – not long now. He had a terrible yearning to see the sky again. He'd survived, and that was all that mattered. He was a survivor; damn it, a hero.

He heard a heavy booming sound in the air overhead. Stopping, he thrust the lantern up into the darkness, but could see nothing there. After a few seconds it came again, stronger now and resonating around the walls for longer. This time he understood: a thunderclap.

As if in answer, the sound of drains emptying resounded along the chamber he was in. Sanchéz looked down at his feet. He was ankle-deep; what moments earlier had been a centimetre or two of water had transformed into a stream.

He remembered someone saying the sewers would flood when it rained, and trembled at the thought – his joy at having got away vanished. He was going to have to hurry now. He tried to get going again, but his bad leg wouldn't budge. The scrap of cloth he'd tied around the cut had fallen off, and the leg of the trouser on that side was entirely steeped in blood.

Literally having to lift his bad leg forward, bracing around the thigh with both hands, he got underway again. Within a few steps he was panting and, with the water up to his knees, it was becoming harder to make headway. Gritting his teeth, he forced himself on. Salvation was so close, he couldn't stop now.

Then one of his feet came into contact with something soft, and he slipped, letting go of the lantern. He tried to fish it out, but then his leg gave way and he fell. Twisting around to keep his head above the water, he let the current take him. Looking up, he realized that fate was smiling on him once more: he was being carried in the direction of a down-hanging metal ladder. He could see it a few metres ahead, caught in the streetlight from the manhole at the top.

Before he knew it he came beneath the ladder and threw out an arm, grabbing hold of the bottom rung. Cursing, he heaved himself up and got hold of a higher rung. His body was firmly against the ladder, but the water continued to rise – it was up to his chest already. He managed to lift the top half of his body clear of the water, his leg still smarting, and his considerable bulk not making things much easier. Puffing out his cheeks and calling on unknown reserves, he hauled himself still higher, until his feet were also above the surface. Exhausted, he glanced up to see that only a few rungs remained. It was all he could do to stop himself from shouting with jubilation. He climbed. Then another thunderclap came – it seemed as though the tunnel would implode.

For all he knew the sewer might indeed be collapsing. He gripped the ladder with both hands and peered away into the darkness. A gust of warm, moist air began to blow, whipping his hair then growing more intense, taking his breath away.

He looked up again. Above his head, a perfect circle could be seen, and the light of the city above. He even thought he heard the wheels of a carriage, voices. Then came a deafening roar.

The wave hit him, tearing him clear of the ladder. His body fell into the furious torrent and was dragged away like a rag doll.

Sánchez came to with a start. It took him a moment to get his bearings: he was lying on his back in some sort of tiny space. A chink of light entered from somewhere, so the darkness wasn't total. He recognized it as one of the many ventilation shafts that lined the sewers just beneath ground level. Then it all came back: the spate had dragged him along and, after battering him against the walls of the sewer, probably knocking him out, it had deposited him here on its way out to sea. He'd been extremely fortunate.

He heard, down in the depths, the waters crashing along, continuing their vertiginous descent through the tunnel below. His body felt as though a streetcar had driven over it. When he moved his right arm, cramp seized him at the elbow – though it didn't appear broken. There was a warm, throbbing lump on his forehead; maybe that was why everything was spinning.

But he was alive. And the way out couldn't be far off. Once the torrents receded, he'd come out of his little sanctuary and be away from this watery hell. He could wait.

Reaching down into his jacket pocket, he was surprised to find a number of candles and a lighter – how had they not fallen out? He thought he heard a small animal scurrying nearby. He hurried – whatever it might be, it wouldn't like the light.

The flint was soaked, but after several turns did strike. More luck. But then the feeling that he wasn't alone in the small space grew stronger – holding the small flame out in front of him, he gasped.

Two enormous rats were hunched over his wounded leg. The light sent them scuttling away into the shadows before he had time to kick them off. Blood was oozing out over the part of his thigh where the trouser was still intact. The rats had gnawed down to the bone, which was visible, lit white by the flame.

He vomited immediately, and had to prop himself up on his elbows to avoid passing out. The flame trembled in his hand. How had the pain not woken him up?

Running his hand down each of his legs he found, to his dismay, that he could feel nothing. He couldn't move either of them. He broke out in a sweat. This, this really was not good.

Over to his right, he heard agitated scrabbling. The rats, he'd forgotten the damned rats. He held the candle up and, as the light fell on one corner, nearly dropped it. He saw, barely a few metres from his body, a seething, innumerable mass of rodents, a profusion of grey fur. The light sent them into ferment; they piled away from it, over to one side of the shaft, eyeing the intruder all the while. A number sniffed the air, while others scratched at the floor and bared their teeth. There was a nest they were protecting. The light kept them from attacking – for now, at least.

Sánchez gulped. He'd lost a good deal of blood, and he was losing strength, that was clear. It wouldn't be long before he'd surely pass out – he shuddered to imagine what they'd make of him once he was unconscious.

Avoiding looking at his ruined leg, he moved the candle around to try and find some way out, provoking further squeaking and scuttling. After a moment – which felt like an awful lot longer – he found what he was looking for.

An opening, half a metre above his head – not dissimilar to a chimney flue. Just wide enough for an adult to squeeze through. Usually such ducts led to the surface. The candlelight fell on the bottom rung of a ladder, and his hopes revived.

He dragged himself to sitting, being sure to place the candle between himself and the increasingly unsettled rats. The stone

506

floor scraped his back – the least of his concerns. He manoeuvred himself so that he was directly beneath the flue. The rats began to approach and he waved the candle from side to side.

'Get away! Away!'

And, as though they knew he'd soon be out of reach, they swarmed forward, retreating only when the circle of light touched them directly. They hissed, a high, keening sound – like a knife against a whetstone.

His energy was fading. He had to move, now. Keeping the candle aloft, he managed to insert his upper body into the flue, which was tighter than he'd expected. He heaved himself up, hand over hand on the dilapidated rungs, with his back and arms wedged against the slippery brick sides. A square of light from outside could be seen at the top. The flue ascended on a slight angle – he knew he'd never have made any headway had it been vertical.

He drove himself up, his temples pounding, his breathing ragged. His legs were a dead weight, almost impossible to lift. The smoke from the candle was getting in his eyes, which had begun to stream. He stopped for a few seconds to rest. He was a little more than halfway up the flue. It had grown narrower still, but he was going to make it. He could hear the rats below, their screeches of frustration.

He took a deep breath and pushed on a little further. His arms trembled violently with the effort, though he didn't have far to go now. The small shaft that connected to the manhole cover was almost within touching distance. The night air tasted glorious – he pushed on. Then cried out in pain and surprise – the final rung had shorn, and, protruding from the wall like an iron paling, part of it stuck out – he'd gashed his hand on it. He dropped the candle, which went bouncing back down the flue into the darkness, and lost his grip on the ladder too, slipping and sliding down himself now – try as he might to arrest the fall, it was no use. He fell in a heap onto the floor of the shaft. Without the candlelight, the darkness gathered close to him like a shroud.

Silence ensued – though only briefly. A chorus of fevered screeches went up all around him. His cries were drowned out by the sound of hundreds of tiny paws. A lean year: they were hungry.

SEVENTY

Pau exhaled, trying to rid herself of tension. The straps over her wrists had dug in so deep as to draw blood, but after a number of attempts she'd finally managed to get hold of the tube again.

She pinched it and doubled it back on itself, stopping the flow of serum; then she began rubbing it back and forth against the edge of the table, with short sharp movements, until she saw that her hand had began to puff up with the solution. Her escape plan was straightforward: when her captor came to untie her, she'd simply try and grab one of the scalpels on the table, see if she could inflict some sort of wound, and while he was recovering make off in the service lift. She dearly hoped that the serum hadn't fully entered her system yet. Now all that was left to do was to wait.

After a while – forever, it seemed to her – Pau thought she heard his footsteps. A spasm of worry flipped her stomach. What if he came and checked whether the serum had taken effect before untying her? Or saw the damaged tube? It would all be over.

'I hope you were comfortable in my absence. A very worth-while evening. No exaggeration, one of the best spectacles I've ever witnessed. Such a shame you couldn't be there.'

He followed his words with a burst of hesitant laughter. Pau was about to make some sign of agreement when she remembered she needed to feign immobility. Donning the leather apron once more, without another word, the man began his preparations again.

Pau eyed the ampoule on the stand, and saw that it was practically empty. Letting go of the tube, it swung away from her and out of sight. Her arms felt slightly rigid – she put it down to the nerves. She wouldn't get another chance. She could do it – she *had* to do it if she wanted to get out of this alive. She tried to focus on that thought alone.

Meanwhile her captor yanked on a cord that hung down from the ceiling, releasing a bundle of cables that unspooled over Pau's head with a rasping sound. At the end of each cable was some sort of bracket, and a needle finer than any she'd seen in her life. The overall impression was of the tips of an enormous spider's legs. Paralyzed by the fear, for a moment she forgot her plan to escape.

'As you know, my dear, the key to the process is in creating the right connection between the body's vital points. It's a very delicate process – each of the perforations must be in its precise place, not a millimetre either way.'

He came over and undid the straps on her legs. 'Priceless, this serum. Allows me to work with such a minimum of fuss.'

He reached out and brought one of the cables nearer, clamping the bracket over her ankle and then, with utmost care, inserting the needle into her instep. Pau felt the metal slide into her flesh. It was all she could do not to flinch – move her leg, and the game would be up.

Having inserted the second needle into her other foot, her captor moved along the side of the table and made to unstrap her arm – but suddenly stopped. Taking Pau's hand in his, he exclaimed. 'Well, well! Someone's been a bad girl.'

At that, Pau felt all her hope drain away. She gathered herself – she'd try, even though still partially tied down. The man lifted her wrist up, turning it over and inspecting the lacerations.

'You really shouldn't struggle, Gilbert.' His tone was one of reproach. 'Your efforts have all been in vain.'

Pau averted a sigh of relief.

He finished unstrapping her and inserted the remaining needles into the backs of her hands, one into each of her breasts near the clavicle, and one into each thigh. Then he laid a strap, part leather, part metal, over her forehead and secured it on either side. Nodding, satisfied, he went over to a chest and took out a leather briefcase. Onto a metal tray he deposited – ceremoniously and in a neat row – a set of scalpels, and some saws and forceps, before rolling up his sleeves and plunging his hands into the basin, scrubbing vigorously to get them clean.

Now, this was it. His back was turned, he'd taken his eyes off her. She took a breath and readied to get up. And she tried – tried to leap to her feet – but her body didn't respond. She couldn't even raise herself to sitting – her arms didn't seem to belong to her. She tried again with her legs, but couldn't move them, not a single centimetre. Her heart began to pound, so hard she could hear it, and a wave of panic washed over her. She couldn't move.

Her captor came back over, a gauze in one hand and a smile on his lips.

'You'll have to forgive such rude and basic methods, it's the only way to stop you from screaming. No one can hear you, as I said, but my hearing is rather, oh, sensitive. I could have cut out your tongue, like with some of the others, but time really has flown.'

He placed the gauze over the mouth of the unresisting Pau and brought the metal tray over. His hand hovered over a lancet, then a bone cutter, and finally, with a satisfied sigh, he opted for a small scalpel. Pulling down the sheet, Pau's breast was exposed, shining with sweat.

'Ready, dear? I'll talk you through it as I go. I *know* you'll find it interesting. Your last anatomy lesson, I suppose!'

Carefully he placed one hand on her sternum, squinting. 'I'll be needing some of your organs – later on.' He nodded towards the glass receptacles up on the shelves. 'My collection needs constant updating.'

The moment the blade touched her skin a thin runnel of blood sprung forth. Pau felt as though a thousand tiny needles had been inserted between her ribs. She wanted to scream, she tried to, but the gauze dropped down to the back of her throat and she let out nothing but a weak cry, a whimper. Tears welled in her eyes and dropped onto the marble. The pain subsided as he removed the blade once more. Her captor gave her a commiserating look.

'Now, you'll really want to keep still for this next bit.'

SEVENTY-ONE

Daniel looked apprehensively at the stains on the pallet bed. He'd made the most terrible mistake. With each minute they spent there, Gilbert's demise grew more likely. That was if it hadn't already come to pass.

He looked around, trying to calm himself, think clearly.

'So it doesn't seem Adell used this place to carry out his gruesome experiments,' he said. 'But doubtless he used the house as a bolt-hole. What if he hid his victims here until any fuss around their disappearance had died down, before transferring them to another location?'

'Another location?' asked Fleixa. 'Where? And, sorry, but transfer the girls, how?'

'I don't know. But there must be some kind of clue here, something that will help us find him.'

He looked around the space once more, but it was just the same as before: full of shadows and blackened furniture. He punched the wall in exasperation – the pain in his knuckles was no consolation. But then his gaze came to rest on a wardrobe. Its charred doors blended in almost entirely with the walls behind. He'd noticed it before, but only now saw that something didn't fit.

'Bring the lantern over here, Fleixa.'

A circle of light fell on the wardrobe.

'Why hasn't it been destroyed like everything else?' said Daniel.

'What do you mean?'

'Look at it. The doors are virtually intact.' He pulled on the bolt, but it didn't budge. 'Locked. That's strange, don't you think?'

'What I think is that we need to hurry.'

Ignoring the journalist, Daniel raised the pistol and pulled the trigger. The report resounded around the room, and the acrid gunpowder hung on the air.

'Have you lost your mind?'

Where the bolt had been there was now a gaping hole. Daniel, without replying, slowly pulled the doors open.

It was empty inside.

Kneeling down, Daniel began rummaging around inside the wardrobe, his hands quickly turning black from the soot. Fleixa sighed. To him this all seemed an enormous waste of time. They had to get out of there, head straight for the power station.

'Bring the light here.'

'What are you looking for? Don't you see there's nothing in there?'

Daniel looked up, a hopeful expression on his face. His hand was pointing to some marks on the wooden base, where some heavy object seemed to have been dragged along.

'Look here, look at the . . .' He stopped, peering closely at the lantern. 'Did you see that? No, keep it still.'

They both focussed on the lantern the journalist was holding. At first nothing happened, but just when Fleixa was about to lose patience the flame tilted, twice – as though prodded by an invisible finger.

'An airstream!'

Daniel grabbed the lantern and moved it from side to side. Again the flame slanted when he held the lantern in a certain place. Placing it down on the floor, he began feeling around at the back of the wardrobe, until his fingers encountered a thin fissure in the wood, running from top to bottom. Rapping his knuckles on the spot, it gave a hollow sound.

'Quick, find something to prise it open.'

They found a poker next to the remains of the fireplace. Slipping it between the opening, they both threw their weight against it; the wood creaked and then gave way with a loud crack. And before them, bathed in a yellowish glow, was the entrance to a narrow tunnel.

Daniel, without any hesitation, headed in – followed by a cursing Fleixa. The tunnel had been excavated from the bedrock and they had to stoop as they went. Every fifteen paces, a bronze lamp hung down.

'Electricity, down here!' exclaimed Fleixa.

The way grew narrower still until eventually they arrived at the top of a spiral staircase, and as they made their way down the steps the air grew moist. They came out at an unlocked door, on the other side of which there stood a small pontoon, little more than a few planks jutting out over a dark, underground stream, and with a small rowboat floating beside it.

'Must be part of the city sewers.'

'Seems that way from the smell,' said Fleixa. 'Well, now what?'

'Where the lamps go,' he said, pointing down at the series of lights hanging above the water, 'we go.'

Fleixa followed Daniel into the boat, grumbling. 'I hate water.'

Daniel took up the oars and, with the assistance of the current, they made their way beneath the lamps, which stretched into the distance like a string of fireflies. In the base of the boat Daniel noticed the same stains he'd seen on the pallet bed, and shivered to think of all the terrified girls who had made this same journey – terrified, and with no idea as to their fate. He rowed harder.

After a number of minutes the tunnel curved to the left, and, as they entered a larger chamber, the quiet plashing of the water-course gave way to a deafening roar. Fleixa pointed to some steps that had been hewn into the wall to their right, above a barely visible metalwork jetty. They'd certainly have missed it without the lantern light.

Daniel rowed them over, they fastened the boat to a wooden post and climbed the steps. Reaching the top, they looked at each other in surprise. The door ahead was ajar.

'I don't like this, Amat. It's just too easy.'

'What can we do? That madman has Gilbert, we don't have any choice. You wait here if you like.'

'Well I'm hardly going to do that.'

Holding the pistols out in front, they advanced and went in. The sound of the water, along with its suffocating smell, died away. The flooring, which was original to the old station, could barely be seen for all the shelves – shelves lined with glass vials. There was a constant buzzing in the air.

'What's that sound?' asked Fleixa.

'It's the generators in the power station. We're right beneath it. Fleixa, we've found Adell's secret laboratory!'

They cocked their pistols and ventured forward into the labyrinth of shelves. Fleixa observed the range of containers, of all different shapes and sizes; there were hundreds, perhaps thousands. He asked himself what they might be for. They soon came to a tall glass vat with an iron base and sides, reinforced by bronze rivets – tall as a man and, in circumference, wider than four people with arms outstretched. The lantern light picked out golden flecks inside, and it gave off a pungent odour.

'What could such a large container be for?'

'Doesn't the smell tell you anything? It has to be some kind of antiseptic. Formaldehyde, perhaps, or phenol. Something like that.

Fleixa rapped his knuckles against the side and peered in.

'Careful. If I'm right, that kind of liquid is highly flammable – anything can spark it,' said Daniel.

'Wait, did you see that?' said Fleixa.

'What?'

They peered in, and were both dumbstruck at the sight. Like an apparition, a floating figure emerged: a naked man, suspended in the dark liquid. His blue, lifeless eyes stared back at them – a look of incredulity. His hands were up in front of him in a final gesture of desperation. He'd surely have screamed, if he still could. Thin threads of blood floated out of his mouth, along with the occasional tiny bubble. Bertomeu Adell wouldn't be giving orders any longer.

Then the lights went out.

*

Holding the pistol out in front, Daniel groped the air with his other hand. The outage could be anything. The generators above had fallen silent – a silence that only made the darkness more unsettling. He wished to God they hadn't left the lantern behind in the rowboat. Taking a breath, he took a step forward. He heard glass knocking against glass somewhere in the dark.

'Where are you, Fleixa?' he hissed.

'Over here. I knocked into a shelf.'

The voice came from over to Daniel's right, further away than he'd expected. He wondered if his own voice sounded as terrified as Fleixa's.

'You stay there,' he said, 'I'm coming over.'

Carefully he advanced in what he thought was the right direction. Suddenly he felt someone push him in the back, and fell to the floor. Then he heard some kind of thud, and someone moaning. Something heavy and metallic struck the floor, and after a brief rattle all was silent again.

'Fleixa?'

No answer. Before he could decide what to do, he felt warm breath on his ear, and a sharp edge was being pressed against his throat.

'Don't move.'

There was a click, and the generators started up again. The carbon filaments in the bulbs above glowed red for a moment, and suddenly the space was brightly lit once more. Dazzled, Daniel caught a glimpse of Fleixa, who was slumped at the foot of one of the shelving units. The journalist was grimacing and fingering the back of his head.

'Up,' said the voice.

Daniel stole a glance at the hooded figure with the scalpel at his throat. 'You!'

'Now, Señor Fleixa, pick up your gun, and that of your colleague, if you don't mind,' ordered Doctor Gavet – all hint of a stutter gone. 'Pick them up by the barrels, and place them down – slowly – on this table here. Your friend will pay for it if you try anything unwise.'

Glancing at Daniel, Fleixa did as he was told, placing the pistols on the table Gavet had indicated. The doctor picked one of the weapons up, pointed it at the journalist's chest, and pulled the trigger.

'What—'

Daniel flinched at the gunshot, which was immediately followed by another. Fleixa toppled over with a groan, blood pooling quickly around him on the floor. Doctor Gavet calmly placed the gun back down on the table.

'Madman!' cried Daniel.

He rushed at him, but Gavet stepped deftly to one side and, with a smooth, precise motion, struck Daniel at the base of his neck with the gun. His vision bloomed with lights for a brief moment, and everything went dark.

RESURRECTION

The start of the World Fair

SEVENTY-TWO

The pain in his head told him he was still alive. He'd been tied to a chair, and could barely feel his arms or his legs. His jacket was off and his shirtsleeves had been rolled up. To one side, on a metal stand, hung a glass ampoule containing a greenish liquid.

He felt a burst of anguish as he remembered what had happened before he blacked out. He couldn't believe that Fleixa was dead. He'd grown fond of the man, and now, that was it, his lifeless body lay somewhere in that underground cavern.

Looking around, he found that Gavet had dragged him through into another room. Over to the right, to his astonishment, he saw the very machine detailed in the *Liber Octavus*. A golden pole in the middle reached up almost as far as the ceiling. Cables sprung from it at different points, running away at various angles across the room, while one, thicker than the rest, rose directly out of the top of the pole and ran through ceiling rivets to a point directly above the marble table on which Pau was laying.

The girl lay motionless. As though she'd been pinned down by some insect, thin metal filaments emerged from different points across her body. Even her shaved head had a leather strap to keep it down, with lots of tiny wires attached, and each one of these connected up, via silver rods, to the main cable above her. Might she still be alive? Then an affected cough interrupted Daniel's thoughts.

Over on a divan, half hidden in the darkness, Gavet was watching him and dandling his cane. He grinned – it was as though they were taking coffee together, and Daniel had just said something amusing.

'Finally,' he said. 'It's after midday already. I started to think I was going to have to wake you myself.'

'Let me go.'

'Oh, I think not. You're fine as you are for now.'

'Murderer!'

'You mean your colleague? Bernat Fleixa had really become quite the nuisance, I can tell you. Believe me, I'm glad he's gone.' He looked over at Pau. 'Your excellent young friend there, on the other hand, is in perfect health. Your arrival, for all that I expected you to come, interrupted us. Now, with all these unfortunate loose ends tied up, we can start again where we left off.'

'Have you lost your mind? What are you planning here?'

The doctor shook his head, though more to himself, it seemed, than as an answer to the question.

'You never understood a thing, Daniel.'

The man Daniel had been thinking of as Doctor Gavet stood up – without use of the cane. The limp was gone, and he no longer stooped as before. Making his way over to a table where a lantern stood, and with his gaze fixed on Daniel, he removed his glasses. Then, to Daniel's astonishment, he lifted his chin and tore away his beard, which came away like the sloughed skin of an animal. Piece by piece the rest followed: the moustache, the eyebrows, the hair on his head. He rubbed his face with a damp towel, removing the adhesive and the make-up. In the end it was a far younger individual standing there smiling at Daniel.

Daniel gaped. He couldn't think – surely his own mind had gone. He'd seen him die. Wept for him, borne the guilt of his loss all these years. Like in one of his nightmares, he heard himself murmuring his name.

'Alec.'

'Dear brother, you have no idea of the trouble it takes to keep up such a disguise.' His scarred face looked all the more mangled as he let out a hearty laugh.

'You're . . . alive?'

'Well,' said Alec, spreading his arms theatrically, 'it looks like it!'

'I saw the fire take you, I saw you die. It can't be possible. How—' He couldn't find the words.

His younger brother raised his hands appeasingly, and sat back down, crossing his legs.

'Doubtless you'll have one or two questions. I'll try to answer them, in the time we have.' He sighed. 'Time, Daniel, time really is the most fickle judge. So. It's a long story. A story that began one night, seven years ago.' His hand twitched on the arm of the divan. 'Do you remember Ángela?'

'Of course. I've never forgotten her.' The words tasted very bitter in his mouth.

'Then you'll have been asking yourself, all these years, what she was doing at the house that night.' He waited for Daniel to nod before going on. 'Simple: after your engagement was confirmed, I sent her a note, in your name, asking her to stop by.'

'You? But why?'

'When she arrived I took her down to Father's laboratory. She was excited; she thought you'd be there to meet her. The way she was so gleeful – it was annoying, but I put up with it – thinking of what would happen when she understood.'

'Understood what?'

'Oh, I told her about how you'd never loved her, how you preferred her half sister.'

Daniel was profoundly confused.

'Thought that was a secret, did you?' Alec continued. 'Ever the fool! Think I didn't notice the glances the pair of you shared? The little caresses when you thought no one was looking? Think I didn't know about your furtive meetings? Well I did, dear brother, just as I knew that you didn't really want Ángela. And I'd have done anything for her.' He grimaced. 'I told her everything about your relationship, including your plans to run away together. And after that I confessed my feelings for her, and asked for her hand. Know what she said?'

Daniel just shook his head.

'Nothing! She just laughed. I told her not to, I told her *quiet*, but she ignored me. She laughed, I felt so foolish. A red mist came down, I couldn't help it . . . By the time I knew what was happening, I was on top of her, my hands over her mouth . . .'

Alec, seemingly unaware of the tears rolling down his face, and of Daniel's horrified expression, continued his tale, whispering hoarsely now.

'She was unconscious – still breathing – but I couldn't help her, not just then. In my fury, I'd torn the laboratory down, a rug had caught fire – I'd knocked over a lantern. The flames were around us in an instant, there was no way out. Then I saw you, you were coming down the stairs. I cried out for you to help us, I begged you to help me get Ángela out, but then you were gone. You ran off, you left us there to perish.'

'That's not what happened!' said Daniel.

He could hardly put his memories of the night in order. After being separated from Irene, he'd drunk so much he'd almost collapsed. He did remember, though, having tried to reach them, before a flaming bannister had fallen on top of him. And that was the last thing he remembered. He woke hours later in a hospital bed, his father telling him that his brother and fiancée were dead.

'I passed out,' Alec continued. 'I later learned that some of the servants came and dragged me out. Too late for poor Ángela though. I begged for God to let me die along with her, but He refused, He forced me to live.' He took a deep breath. 'Once I'd recovered somewhat, Father decided we should go to Vienna. There was an eminent doctor there, a man named Eduard Zeis, who'd had some success with reconstructive surgery. Can you believe it? Nowadays very little surprises me.'

Daniel didn't answer. Why wouldn't his father have told him? Why did he let him go off to England? But then the answer came to him: because his father thought that he'd been the one to start the fire.

'I had more operations than I can remember. Gradually I regained the use of my arms and legs. And if the state of my face surprises you, you should see the rest of my body. Zeis used grafts from dead bodies, he put me back together as best he could.

527

He turned me into a presentable monster, and in return I'd be in pain for the rest of my days. Fair exchange, considering my sins, wouldn't you say?'

The laugh that followed sent a chill through Daniel's blood.

'It took me a long time to recover. For all the sedatives they gave me, there were times when I believed I would split in two. A number of the grafts had to be replaced, because I ripped them off with my own hands. I had to be tied down. Night after night, Ángela would come and visit me, sitting next to me, telling me she loved me, stroking my wounds.' He batted away some tears. 'I was moved from hospital to hospital – Vienna, Munich, Prague – a squadron of new doctors in each place. Two nightmare years. One morning I was stupid enough to confess to Father what I'd done. I begged him to take me back to Barcelona, which he agreed to immediately. I didn't know at that point what he had in mind for me.' Alec sucked in air sharply through his nostrils, making a rasping noise like broken bellows. 'Upon our return, Father took me straight to New Bethlem. Didn't want his loony son to go around ruining the family name, so off I went – he admitted me under a different name, as one of his own patients. He told people I'd had an accident, which was the reason for all the bandages. Even the director, a close friend of his, never found out. I'd be able to use that later on to my advantage, but at the time I simply loathed Father for leaving me there. I still didn't know then what destiny had in store for me.

'As you saw for yourself – yes, I knew of your visit there too – there wasn't a great deal to recommend that place. I put up with it as best I could, and then, at the beginning of my third year, a new patient was admitted: Doctor Homs. Thanks to my

528

medical studies, we became friendly, we'd chat about this and that, and then one afternoon he told me about his efforts to save his wife, including mention of the *Liber Octavus*. It was so extraordinary – my ears pricked up straight away.'

Suddenly enthused, Alec now sat bolt upright.

'Homs, however, didn't share my elation. Daniel, the man had the kind of knowledge to make the Lord God jealous, only he was too stupid to realize. He thought he'd been wrong to go down that path, and he refused to reveal the fundamentals of what he'd uncovered. He was worried about what would happen if it got into the wrong hands. Nature's laws are not to be toyed with, was his view. Fool.'

Alec lay back on the divan and grunted.

'We built a little laboratory together, over the course of a few months – something to amuse ourselves. During that time we didn't speak of it again – until that arrogant pig showed up.'

'Adell!'

'Exactly. Which reminds me . . .'

He got up from the divan and left the room, leaving Daniel on his own. When he returned, he was dragging the industrialist's corpse behind him – a yellow sludge in its wake. Alec seemed able to lift the deadweight with ease.

'I knew it was him the moment he was admitted, but he didn't recognize me. I wasn't surprised to see him there, he'd always been of unsound mind – did you know he was expelled from university for striking a nurse? Apparently she was overly informal with him. Lost an eye, poor girl. Adell told me all about it – he thought he was in the right!

'Insane he might have been, but he wasn't stupid, and he saw the value of Homs's discovery straightaway. My only choice was to make him think I was on his side, and that we might share the spoils – that wasn't difficult: Adell thought everyone was born to serve him. He was allowed out after two months – family contacts.'

'It was him who helped you escape?'

'Very *good*, Daniel. We agreed that I'd try and talk to Homs, and Adell would find some way to get me out. But then Homs's release was announced, which threw things up in the air. There wasn't any time. The night before he was due to leave, I tried to make him share what he knew with me again. I'd made a rudimentary scalpel for our experiments . . .' The patches of Alec's face that could still move wrinkled up in a grimace. 'I used it all night long on him. A very obstinate man, unfortunately: he died without letting on at all.

'I realized that when they found the body, that would mean my true identity coming out. But I was lucky. Homs and I, though far apart in age, had similar complexions – only our hair was different. But mine was always shaved, so I shaved his, cut his face so no one would recognize him. I left my bandages – soaked in a bit of blood – next to his body. Then, with the help of Adell's driver, I escaped.'

He brought Adell's body over to the middle of the room and lay it next to a metal hatch in the floor.

'Adell wasn't happy when he learned of Homs's death, but I managed to convince him that, if he provided me with the means, I'd be able to solve Vesalius's secret myself. I persuaded him to buy our family home as well – he of course didn't know it was *my* family. And he liked the idea. Then, another stroke of luck:

the workers discovered the cellars of the old military hospital beneath the power station – the perfect spot for the laboratory in which you find yourself. We knew from Homs that we needed a large power supply, and here we have the biggest generator in the whole country! But the mansion was still useful for hiding the girls, and we came up with the idea of joining the two buildings via an old section of the sewers.'

Alec opened the hatch. The sound of rushing water filled the space, making his words hard to hear. 'Adell provided me with the materials I needed for the machine, and the equipment for my experiments. He even loaned me his horse and carriage, as well as keeping me informed about your investigations. I must admit, I found your pathetic attempts exciting, in a way. You only had me worried at one point, when you showed up at the house – I was there, down in the cellar with one of the girls. Hearing you coming down, I just managed to gag her. Luckily you didn't get all the way down, otherwise I'd have been obliged to kill you there and then!'

He shimmied the corpse over to the edge. 'You had your uses, but all your demands, and oh, those airs you constantly put on, did become quite tiresome.'

Placing his foot on Adell's chest, he pushed, and the body rolled over and fell into the sewers. Alec closed the hatch again, and the roar of the water became a muffled murmur once more.

SEVENTY-THREE

A huge crowd had gathered at the entrance to the World Fair. People were intent on catching a glimpse of the royal retinue as it passed beneath the Arco de Triunfo, and a cry went up each time they thought they recognized a city grandee, or some foreign ruler. A festive spirit reigned in Barcelona.

'Enjoying the show?'

'Mellado, my friend! Wonderful to see you here. Good trip?'

Ferrán Gadea, director of the satirical weekly magazine *L'Esquella de la Torratxa*, shook hands with the man who had just appeared next to him, Francisco Mellado, his opposite number at the *El Imparcial* newspaper.

'You know how it is, Gadea,' he answered with a laugh. 'The express train from Madrid is usually quite pleasant, but since we had all these big shot politicians aboard this time, the train simply carried on through all the usual stops. We were here in no time at all!'

'I'm sure it must have been an entertaining trip, with all those personalities. And lots of *piquant* quotes for you, no doubt.'

'Well, yes, the eyes of the country are on the Fair. A great moment for Barcelona.'

'Couldn't agree more, my friend.'

'I've heard there have been sabotage threats.'

'Oh, there are all kind of rumours going around. Anarchists, syndicalists . . . It's all nonsense. But in any case, all security measures have been taken, all eventualities mapped out. The whole of Catalonia's taking part in the celebrations. Nothing can go wrong.'

'I hope God is listening to you. Look,' he said, pointing, 'there's the Mayor at the head of the retinue. We ought to hurry, we don't want to miss this.'

'I'm right behind you.'

Mayor Rius i Taulet, dressed in tails and a top hat, was in a carriage alongside his First Deputy, Eduardo Romero, and the President of the municipality of Paris, who wore a tricolour sash; Paris would be hosting the World Fair the following year. The conversation between the trio was extremely animated.

After them came the members of the organizing committee, accompanied by the ambassadors and chief executives of the countries and companies taking part, including representatives of the overseas colonies of Cuba and the Philippines.

A detachment of trappers stood in full regalia at the entrance to the Palace of Fine Arts. The orchestra struck up a lively song, to a flapping of wings from the birds resting in the nearby trees, and a line of Guardia Civil formed a barricade to keep the public from entering the Hall of Ceremonies.

Gadea and Mellado made their way into the Palace vestibule,

slotting in behind a large group of luminaries awaiting the arrival of the Queen. Different coteries had formed, and numerous spirited discussions were being held.

Don Práxedes Sagasta, President of the Government, was holding forth to a group of dignitaries, while the Marquis of Miravelles and the Marquis of Castor Serna listened on, nodding and trying to stifle yawns. Over by the windows stood the Bishop of Barcelona, Vice Admiral De la Pezuela and the Marquis of Sierra Bullones, each expressing hopes for the good weather to hold, so as not to spoil the arrival of their Highnesses. The marquis asked the bishop to intercede on their behalf to help with that, drawing polite laughter from those gathered around them.

The pair of journalists had moved over to one side and, pads in hand, each took constant hurried notes.

'You could hardly ask for a greater gathering of leading lights in a single place,' said Gadea. 'It's the year's major event, no doubt about it.'

'They're expecting huge number of visitors, aren't they?'

'Five or six million, they're estimating.'

'Really, *that* many?'

'So I hear. Look! The foreign royals are arriving.'

The orchestra began the Royal March, to announce the arrival of representatives from the European houses. The Duke of Genoa, himself once a candidate for the throne of Spain, entered the vestibule alongside Prince George and the Duke of Edinburgh, all in full regalia.

The cavalry bugles began to sound, followed by the guard band and the halberdiers with their whistles and drums. After a slight delay the royal carriages themselves appeared, the opulent d'Aumont style of carriage, with a full cavalry escort.

They passed through a tunnel formed of two rows of halberdiers and entered the Hall itself, followed by a rush of ladies whose impatience to see the Queen had brought them out to wait on foot beyond the guards, rather than keeping their appointed place.

Casavella could hear the excited crowds through the power station windows. He, however, was not in a mood for celebrating.

One of the machinists stood next to him making notes on a record sheet, frowning continually as Casavella himself took in the dials and barometers before them, comparing the current state of affairs against previous readings. He'd already checked each of the pressure gauges innumerable times, as well as the valves regulating the temperature and pressure of the colossal steam engines. Everything seemed in order, but the decision had been taken to carry out scrupulous readings of the entire system at two-hour intervals. The machines had a 4,000-horsepower capacity, though at that particular moment the output stood beneath 3,000 h.p. Over by the coal trolleys a group of workers took a break from feeding the engines. The late afternoon light was fading, but the streetlamps around the Fair were yet to be lit, leaving the demand for energy still relatively low.

Casavella made his way over to the centre of the bay, where the generators stood. The combined hum of the six dynamos meant speaking at the top of one's voice here. Together they had an output of three kilowatts, more than enough to light half of

Barcelona. He noted with satisfaction the efficient work of his men. But then his face dropped.

In spite of his long years of experience, he'd never become accustomed to the continual bee-like drone. The sound had a menace to it, as though instead of electricity the generators contained some beast straining to escape its steel and ceramic cage and devour them. It was all he could do to stifle the shudder produced by that image. Dismayed, he hoped the young man taking the notes hadn't picked up on his show of fear; the sudden, inexplicable surges and drops in pressure these past months had affected not only the machines, but also his state of mind. They still hadn't identified the cause of the fluctuations, which meant they'd have a hard time solving the problem should it arise again. Señor Adell had refused to upgrade the cooling system because of the cost involved; he'd even refused the idea of installing two new machines. There was a chance it could happen again at any moment, and that the generators or the steam engines themselves would be unable to withstand the pressure. The demand for energy they were expecting in the coming minutes would require the power station to shift to full capacity. The potential for an accident was higher than ever. Though he wasn't entirely sure what the consequences might be, he knew that any kind of chain reaction would blow up the whole of the World Fair, and every single person in the grounds.

For the past few days everything had been functioning as normal. But still he felt unsure. He'd never been a superstitious man, but he couldn't shake the ill feeling that kept on touching his heart, time and again.

At a shout from the machinist, Casavella jumped: his nerves

were well and truly shredded. He tried to calm himself and focus on the sheet the man was handing to him. The owner might have decided to show a complete lack of interest, but he for one would not leave his post.

SEVENTY-FOUR

Drying his hands on a towel, Alec set about organizing his equipment. 'Once I was out of the sanatorium,' he said, 'my aim was to get hold of the original Vesalius manuscript. Homs once told me, quite by the by, that the *Liber Octavus* was to be found inside the same manuscript, and that the manuscript itself was safe inside the university library. But since he died without going into detail, I had to come up with some chicanery if I was going to avoid people noticing my search.' A hint of a smile crossed his face, all but lost amongst the scars. 'You'll remember how much I loved theatre, all my dress-up shows for everyone. So it won't come as any surprise how easy I found it to pass myself off as Doctor Gavet, a self-important little man whom no one had ever taken very seriously. Thanks once more to Adell's contacts, I was taken on as a lecturer and as a doctor at the hospital, it was all quite straightforward.'

'Why did you kill our father?'

'He helped Homs when his wife fell ill, so he knew about the manuscript and its secret, though not its precise whereabouts.

538

When he examined the girl's corpse he noticed the similarities to the work of his old colleague, but also its differences. He became suspicious, and over time his doubts about my death began to grow. Until, one day, he just came too close to uncovering the truth.' Alec clicked his tongue. 'His death was unavoidable, but at least it meant you came back to Barcelona.'

'The telegram! You sent it.'

'Naturally. Father often came and saw me at New Bethlem, and on one occasion Homs, who was suspicious about all the interest I showed, passed the notebook with the codes in it to him. I guessed he'd sent it to you, so I had to bring you back.'

'To me? Why?' Daniel stopped himself. 'So it was you who had my luggage stolen, you who came and ransacked my room after failing to find the notebook?'

'Yes, Daniel. You were always his favourite. Father secretly admired your obstinacy, the fact you refused to become a doctor. Even I admired you for that. He kept an eye on you while you were at Oxford, he was very proud of your success there.'

Daniel shook his head. 'Why, Alec? Why would you do all this?'

'I thought you'd have worked it out by now.'

Moving over to the console, he pulled back a drape to reveal a chrome lever. A light tremble entered his hand as he reached for it. And as he brought it down there came a suction noise, followed by grinding, swishing sounds as chains and tackle blocks unwound. With a loud snap, the metal sheet at the base of the golden column parted, the two halves moving back to disclose a glass capsule beneath. Inside, submerged in a yellowish liquid, floated the naked body of a woman.

One of Vesalius's prints immediately came to Daniel's mind. Her flesh had been cobbled together: large stitches lined the joins between the torso, limbs, and the other parts his brother had added. The arms and legs, and part of the torso itself, had doubtless originally belonged to other individuals. Flaps of flesh hung from her face, becoming tangled in her hair. Cables held her in place, adding to the impression of an old marionette. Daniel almost vomited when he recognized the face.

'I dug her up as soon as I had the chance,' explained Alec. 'Unfortunately time had not been kind to her beautiful body.'

'You were using the girls to *remake* Ángela.' Daniel couldn't hide his horror.

'I'm not the monster you think me to be, brother. I didn't have a choice. The girls I took, I chose for their similarities with Ángela. I could recall, exactly, every strand of her hair, the smoothness of her arms, those lithe fingers of hers, and her eyes, oh her precious eyes . . . ' He sighed. 'It was no easy task finding all those girls, but the result, as I think you'll agree, couldn't have been better.'

'And the awful wounds you inflicted on them? Why did you feel the need to torture them?'

'I built the Vesalius machine in accordance with what I gleaned from Homs, but unfortunately that didn't do it. I spent days and weeks trying to arrive at the final process. I needed to do some tests, you see, that was all. *Thus has science progressed,*' he exclaimed. 'Isn't that what father used to say? Then again,' he laughed, 'it was also rather convenient that the wounds should be confused with bite marks, the work of some diabolical animal.'

Daniel shut his eyes to stifle the horror of it all. He tasted bile in his throat.

'Ángela's gone, nothing you can do will change that.'

'You still don't understand, do you? Vesalius's studies pre-empted thousands of years of human evolution. That was why the Inquisition went after him. He was like a new Prometheus! He stole the gift of life from the Gods themselves!'

'You mean . . . You intend to bring Ángela back to life?'

Alec seemed to delight in his brother's bafflement. He went over to Pau and began caressing her motionless torso. 'Your young friend found the final piece in the puzzle, revealing the concluding element. I spent such a long time looking . . .' He sighed deeply. 'The human organism possesses a series of connection points that capture external energy and join it to the nervous system, the endocrine glands and the organs. The *Liber Octavus* image details it very clearly. Vesalius found a way of connecting them and, using electricity as a catalyst, transferring the vital essence of one body to another.' His eyes glistened with excitement. 'Yes! Ángela will live!'

'I beg of you, stop this madness. It's useless, and you're going to create a disaster. Your machine has been causing outages at the power station, and the knock-on from that could easily be an explosion – an enormous one. Not just you and me, but thousands of people will lose their lives.'

Alec looked disappointed. 'I was hoping for better from you. I thought you of all people would understand. That's why I wanted you to be here.' He looked at his watch. 'Anyway, no time now. All the lights at the World Fair were turned on three minutes ago. The power station is at full capacity. Now's the time.'

'I beg of you, don't do it.'

Alec turned his back, focussing on the console again – Daniel ceased to exist for him. Having checked the gauges, he flicked a long row of switches, the lights next to each blinking on. He lowered a number of levers and pressed a series of buttons in a precise order. There was an alteration to the hum of the generators above; a sharp, whining tone was emitted, cutting through all other sounds in the space. The lamps shone brilliantly for a moment and everything began to vibrate. The cables twisted and writhed as the energy began to course through them, and down in the capsule the liquid began to simmer, streams of bubbles obscuring Ángela's corpse.

'It's the twentieth of May! Exactly seven years since the fire,' shouted Alec over the noise. 'An incredible coincidence, don't you think? Destiny, some might say.'

Without awaiting a response, he adjusted more dials, and the tremors grew stronger. Two specimen vials danced off a shelf and shattered on the floor. The machine began to give off large gouts of steam, a thick mist spilling out and blanketing the floor.

The noise grew so loud that Daniel thought his eardrums would burst. He pulled on his straps. During the conversation he'd been struggling with the knots and, in spite of the constant pain in his injured arm, had managed to free one of his hands. He set about trying to free the other.

The tone of the thunderous reverberations deepened slightly, while the cables above Pau shook and began to emit a bluish glow. The girl's body shook and, as the cables drew taught, was lifted clear of the marble top. The whites of her eyes showed. The gag muffled her cries.

A flash of light exploded from the capsule, and the body

inside began to convulse. The air was suddenly full of the smell of chemicals, making it all but impossible to breathe. Louder and more piercing grew the clamour, and the lights dimmed. The corpse began to convulse less, gradually ceasing to move.

And then Ángela opened her eyes.

She looked around uncertainly, as if waking from a deep sleep. She turned her head stiffly, like an automaton at a fair, and her eyes met Alec's. Then, with an ungainly lunge, she reached out and pressed her gaunt hand against the glass.

Alec leaped down next to the capsule and embraced the surface. Tears fell from his eyes as he murmured words tinged with love and madness.

SEVENTY-FIVE

The Palace of Fine Arts was sumptuously decked out, with flags on the walls and yellow and white pennants hanging down. The throne they'd brought in for the ceremony was quite unostentatious: a white backrest adorned with a fleur-des-lis and lined with a red plush trim. The canopy had been embroidered with the royal coat of arms, and to either side stood rows of wickerwork chairs for the officials.

The atmosphere was solemn; people knew this to be a historic moment. The floor of the hall and the balconies alike were thronged with guests. At the back journalists from across the country, and from the principal European capitals, contended for a good vantage point. Gadea and Mellado, exchanging greetings with their colleagues, arrived and took up positions.

'Have you noticed the lights, Gadea?'

'What about them?'

'Look. They're failing.'

He pointed to a chandelier above them: the bulbs were

flickering and then, for a brief instant, they went out, before returning once again to their full brightness.

'And those two over there,' he said, 'I saw them do exactly the same a minute ago.'

Gadea saw that his colleague was right: something was indeed happening with the lights. But everyone in room was too intent on the arrival of the King and Queen to have noticed.

'I'm sure it's nothing.'

'But if there were to be a power cut, with all these grandees, and the royal family inside, it would be a most compromising situation.'

'Let's not get carried away, Gadea. Doubtless it's a momentary drop in voltage, nothing more.'

'You're probably right.'

Just then the orchestra, situated on the platform in front of the throne, began playing a march, and the royal entrance began.

'Long live the King! Long live the Queen!'

The two journalists joined in the cheering.

A square of halberdiers came out with the son of the royal couple at their centre, in the arms of a wet nurse; the boy was dressed in the modest attire of the upper classes. Next came the Princess of Asturias and María Teresa, the Infanta, both in white, and after them the Queen, wearing a dark dress with a gold and silk trim. She wore little jewellery and greeted the spectators with warm smiles.

His Highness the King was shown to an armchair, at the foot of which the Princess and the Infanta – now with the boy in her arms – settled on an assortment of large pillows. The Queen left the pre-eminent position to her son and took up a place on the left, to

545

be joined by the Princess of Edinburgh and the Duke of Geneva, while to the King's right sat the Duke of Edinburgh, Prince George and the Prince of Bavaria. Leading palace officials formed the next row back, with government ministers and members of the Fair Commission to the right, and ambassadors, squadron commanders and high-ranking officers from the Spanish Navy to the left. Preferential positions were also given to the deputation from the Catalan Courts, representatives of all the Catalan provinces, and committee members from the invited municipalities.

As the murmurs and scrapings of chairs died down, Mayor Ruis i Taulet stood and began his speech.

'Señora, a thousand times may the peace be blessed!' The ebullient Mayor spoke with an assured voice. 'Thanks to the influence of this precious gift of heaven, we see in the current day a flourishing in the sciences, a fine moment in the arts, growth in agriculture, developments in industry, and profits in business: nations walking steadily forward along the path of progress, the pride of the century in which we live, and a force, too, for fraternity among all peoples. And now, in all modesty, Barcelona looks to be a leading light in the universal manifestations of the activity and progress of the human race.'

The speech was met with cheers and applause, at which point the head of the Fair Commission, Don Manuel Girona, stood up somewhat laboriously from his chair and came over to the lectern. Mellado leaned close to his friend.

'Not bad, the Mayor. Brief and to the point. Pro-peace.'

'Yes, very positive. Don't suppose that many of the people here will have swallowed it.'

*

546

Casavella dabbed at his brow; he was dripping with sweat. He neither felt the heat surrounding him nor registered the frightened cries of his men or the strident whistling of steam engine valves. The pressure gauges before him occupied his full attention.

It had happened again. The pressure in the generators had shot up not once, not twice, but three times, in quick succession – and it continued to rise. He'd ordered the safety valves to be opened to allow steam to escape, as well as adjustments to the transformer to bring down the overall energy input. But in spite of his efforts the claxons continued to go off. If things continued the way they were heading, not only would the World Fair be plunged into darkness, but so would every street in the city that had electric light.

Though not keen on provoking his employer, he saw no other option. He wished the man were there in person. He'd sent one of the lads with a message, over half an hour ago now, but no reply had come.

Suddenly some new claxons began to sound.

'Not again!' bellowed Casavella. 'Turn it off.'

A youth came running over. Stripped from the waist up, he was bathed in sweat and seemed terrified.

'Señor Casavella—'

'Easy,' he said. 'Take a breath, and tell me what it is.'

'It's the steam engines, Señor, the pressure. Two of them are about to blow and another is going to fail any minute.'

'I said no more coals to the furnaces.'

'We haven't, Señor.'

'And still . . . You've opened the steam valves?'

'It's been tried, but they won't open. They're blocked!'

'They can't be. All right, come on.'

Casavella hurriedly crossed the storage tank room, bypassing the ponderous pulley lift and taking the stairs two at a time. The boy tried to keep up.

Entering the bay with the steam engines, he found a number of wild-eyed men attempting to open a spigot with a large iron key. Seeing Casavella, they stopped.

'Can't get them open, Señor,' said one man. 'None of them.'

'Nothing to be done,' said another. 'Pressure's too high.'

Casavella approached the enormous boiler and, though the heat made his eyes stream, thrust his head close to the spigot. It looked in a bad state. The coat of paint that was there to hide the rust had peeled away with the first wave of heat, and the metal was completely corroded. The tap itself seemed to have fused shut. The steam was sending the boiler pressure sky-high. Adell had bought second-hand parts to save a few pesetas – and now they were all doomed.

Casavella cursed, turned and retraced his steps. He took a moment. Even cutting the input wouldn't do much now, he realized with a groan. A disaster. His men watched him nervously, awaiting instructions. He felt thankful for their loyalty – they trusted him, but he was damned if he could see the best course of action. This was a nightmare.

'Everyone out. And tell everyone downstairs as well, evacuate.'

The men didn't need to be told twice, and ran off towards the stairs. The boy, however, did not move.

'Didn't you hear? This place is about to go sky-high! Get out now!'

'What about you?'

'I don't know, boy, I honestly don't know.'

SEVENTY-SIX

Alec was sobbing and laughing at once. Arms splayed against the glass, he spoke Ángela's name over and over. Daniel, paralyzed, watched on – he couldn't believe what he was seeing.

The Vesalius machine had taken on a silverish brilliance, too bright to look at directly. The cables seemed close to snapping under the huge surge of electricity running through them. Pau's body was giving off a blue glow – growing duller as the moments passed, Daniel noticed. Whatever she was undergoing, it would be the death of her. And he wasn't going to get over there in time to free her.

Then the lights on the console began to flash frenetically. A series of cracking sounds was followed by a prolonged, high-pitched noise, like the rusty hinge on an enormous door. Pau's straps shook for a moment and then went slack, and the girl collapsed back down. The halo that had encircled her disappeared.

Alec, until this moment unaware of anything that was happening in the room, spun around in alarm. Before he could react, the generators screeched – Daniel's hairs stood on end – and fell silent. Most of the lightbulbs blew immediately – a series of loud pops – and the ground stopped shaking. A dim half-darkness settled in the space, along with a curious silence.

Ángela's outstretched arm wavered for a moment, her palm against the glass, before falling back beside her body. The life in her sunken eyes went out. Her body lost all tension and began to float once more, inert inside the capsule.

'No!' cried Alec, dashing over to the console. He feverishly began checking and altering switches and dials, but to no effect. All the gauges showed the same thing: the system had gone down.

'It can't be!' he spluttered. 'How? Why, why, why . . .'

As if in answer, he heard a groan from the far side of the cavern. Fleixa, lying propped up on his elbows, threw up a hand. Behind him lay a trail of blood where he'd dragged himself into the space. In his other hand he held a bundle of cables he'd evidently torn from the circuit.

'Imbecile,' howled Alec, grabbing a scalpel, 'you've no idea what you've done! You're supposed to be dead – this time you will be.'

'I don't think so.'

It was Pau. Free from her binds, wrapped in the sheet, she was pointing one of the revolvers at Alec.

Daniel could see her blinking as though struggling to focus, and her raised arm trembling. It was taking great effort to stay on her feet, but she valiantly concealed her precarious state, bracing herself against the marble top.

'What a surprise, you're up,' said Alec, his voice serene. 'I doubt, though, that you'll manage to fire by the time I make it over there.'

Straightening her arm, she cocked the hammer.

'You may put that to the test.'

Studying her carefully for a moment, Alec smiled and took a step closer.

The echo of the gunshot resounded off the walls. Alec was still standing – stock-still. The bullet had grazed his shoulder. He looked up at Pau, with renewed interest it seemed, and still just as calm.

'Fine,' he smiled, 'you can pull a trigger, but there's slightly more to it than just that.' A grim look replaced the smile. 'I know a murderer when I see one, and a murderer you are most certainly not.'

He took another step forward – he was just a few paces away now. Pau hesitated.

'You're right,' she said, lowering the gun.

Alec looked triumphant.

'But,' she said, 'I have no objections to shooting at a dead person.'

She turned, raised the gun again and fired it at the capsule. Alec's cries were drowned out by the ensuing detonation.

The capsule exploded in a shower of tiny glass fragments. The alcohol solution came pouring out and the cables attached to Ángela couldn't bear her weight, leaving her body to collapse to the floor in a mound of bones and torn flesh. The metal filaments hanging from what remained of the machine, Daniel noticed, had begun to writhe like a nest of lice; they were still conducting the current, and within seconds sparks

552

began to fly from their frayed ends. By the time he'd figured it out, it was too late.

The cavern lit up as though in broad daylight. Pau and Alec disappeared. Momentarily blind, Daniel felt the explosion lift his body up off the floor and, along with the chair he was still tied to, throw him several metres back. Huge flames immediately sprang up and began to devour everything in their path.

Pau got unsteadily to her feet. The marble table had shielded her from the enormous explosion and, except for the dull ache in the shoulder she'd fallen onto, and how faint she felt, she was unharmed. But she'd lost the revolver. She tried to locate Daniel but the chaos in the laboratory made it difficult. The far side of the space, where she'd last seen Fleixa, was clearer, and she decided to try and reach it.

It wasn't long before she found the journalist. He was on the floor, half-lying, half-sitting against a wall. Miraculously, he seemed unscathed by the explosion, though his shirt was soaked with blood. She thought she'd reached him too late but, putting her fingers to his neck, was relieved to feel the pulse still beating – weakly, but still beating. A moan from Fleixa confirmed that he was alive.

Pau passed her arm around Fleixa's back, thankful he was so thin. Fortunately, not a great deal of the serum had entered her system. Its effects had begun to tail off while the brothers were arguing, and little by little she'd been regaining full movement of all her limbs.

Coming to, Fleixa looked at her with slitted eyes.

'Gilbert? What happened?'

'Come on, help me. I can't manage you on my own. We need to get over there.'

She indicated the service lift at the end of the laboratory. The fire hadn't yet reached that section, though the shelves nearby had started to go up.

'And Daniel?'

'I lost sight of him in the explosion. The fire's spreading, it would be suicide to stay. We need to get out and try and find help.'

'You're better off leaving me, dear.'

'What are you saying?'

'I'll hold you back. You'll never get out if you try to carry me. Go. There's still time.'

'Of course, and have you accuse me of abandoning you. No chance.'

A bloody smile spread on Fleixa's face.

'You're going to have me thinking you've gone soft on me.'

'Don't you believe it. I'm only taking you because I don't have a choice. Now come on, you idiot, move.'

Ignoring the journalist's look of surprise, Pau grabbed his jacket under the armpit and, puffing out her cheeks, heaved.

When Daniel awoke the flames were about him. For a moment he recognized the scene: it was the same nightmare he'd been having, night after night, for the last seven years. The heat was so intense that it felt as though his skin would fall away if he moved. To one side of him lay the remnants of the chair he'd been tied to. His muscles had stiffened after being tied up for so long, he could barely move the wounded arm, and the scars

554

on his raw neck seemed like open wounds. As if all this weren't enough, he felt stupefied by fear – the voice that screamed, over and over, for him to flee.

Shutting his eyes, he took a deep breath and got up, meaning to locate his brother in the blaze. He didn't intend to leave Alec. Not this time.

He staggered forward into the wall of smoke, struggling to distinguish the objects that reared up before him. It wasn't long before sucking air into his constricted lungs became a torment. This was useless, he thought – at which moment he spied his brother. Lying in the broken remains of the machine, Alec was cradling Ángela's body in his arms; it was covered with sores and gave off a putrid smell, but Alec didn't seem to notice. He smiled and stroked his lover's hair, unaware of the clumps that came away in his hands.

Daniel grabbed him by the arm. 'Alec, we have to get out of here.'

His brother looked up at him.

'Daniel, what a surprise!' he said, a note of genuine happiness in his voice. 'Ángela and I were just this very moment talking about you. You've always been a good judge of these things. What do you think, white or red?'

'What are you talking about?'

Snickering, Alec whispered in Ángela's ear – in the ear of a ragged corpse – before turning back, his look a mix of forbearing and amusement. 'The flowers, Daniel, the flowers for the wedding. Should we have daisies, or should we have roses?'

'There isn't gong to be any wedding, brother. Ángela's *dead*. You have to leave her now, leave her and come with me.'

Alec seemed confused, before giving a dry laugh. Daniel was about to insist further when a string of explosions went off at the far end of the cavern. The vials and containers fed the fire, and as the flames reached the human specimens the smell of burning flesh grew more intense.

'Alec! Please!'

With the little strength that remained in him, he managed to separate Alec from the corpse, which subsided onto the wet floor tiles with a small splash.

Daniel cast around for a way out. Alec, in his arms, seemed suddenly to lack all energy. The path to the service lift was no longer clear; part of the roof had caved in, and huge piles of rubble blocked the way.

'Alec, is there some other exit?'

Alec seemed not to understand – though, a moment later, he shook his head. Then, suddenly, as if remembering something, he pointed to his right. When Daniel looked, all he saw was a huge wall of fire.

'I won't let you take her from me again.'

A blow between Daniel's shoulder blades brought him to his knees. Behind him, Alec held a stool aloft. Rage distorted his scarred features, and the reflection of the spreading fire danced in his eyes. Daniel rolled away to one side, avoiding another swing of the stool. The shards covering the floor punctured his back and he stifled a cry, tried to stand. Alec rushed at him again and, instinctively, Daniel threw up his wounded arm to protect himself. The blow sent a wave of pain into his body, and his vision turned blurry. Badly injured as he was, he made a poor combatant. He needed somehow to get the upper hand – before

Alec came again, Daniel himself leapt forward, taking his brother at chest height and knocking the stool to the floor. The pair crashed into a shelving unit, knocking down vials, laboratory instruments, and books, and a satchel whose contents scattered across the floor. The impact left them both winded.

Alec recovered first, a twisted smile on his face as he got to his feet. He was brandishing a scalpel. Daniel moved aside just in time to avoid the thrust of the blade. He tried to back away but, having to negotiate some flaming curtains, stumbled into the divan. Before he could regain his balance, he felt a sharp pain in his chest. Blood began gushing out over his shirt.

A mighty rumbling drowned out the ongoing din. The pair looked up. Above their heads, the part of the ceiling from which the cables hung seemed for a moment to judder, before earth, metal and stone came showering down.

Daniel threw himself to one side, and was fortunate to find himself beneath the dissecting table. He tried to regain his breath. The slightest movement had become torture, his whole body screamed in pain; though the wounds were mostly superficial, he'd lost a great deal of blood. He tried to ward off the dizziness with some deep breaths. Casting about, he wondered whether his brother had survived the caving-in of the roof.

He didn't see him coming. His brother punched him in the jaw, throwing him back against the marble block. Alec, covered in dust and blood, dropped on top of him and threw a flurry of punches – it was all Daniel could do to try and shield himself. The blows rained down – the cavern, glowing orange from the flames, began to turn blurry in his vision.

Alec, straddling Daniel's torso now, began to strangle him.

557

Try as Daniel might to prise away the fingers, all he left were scratches. He felt himself begin to pass out, unconsciousness gripping mind and body. His vision shrank as though he were entering a tunnel.

Suddenly he wasn't being strangled. He sucked air into his lungs – a wave of heat scorched his throat, sending him into a series of racking coughs. Confused – he was still alive – he tried to get up.

His brother was standing with his back to him. His attitude seemed to be one of surprise, as if he'd just woken to find the fire blazing.

'Alec,' Daniel croaked. 'We have to get out.'

'Oh, it's too late now.'

Daniel looked where Alec was looking: the flames had engulfed the whole cavern now, reaching as high as the ceiling in places, and licking at the enormous, alcohol-filled vat in which Adell had been kept.

Daniel lay his head on the floor, feeling thankful for the fog that had begun to cloud his thoughts. Perhaps this was what destiny had always had in store for him. Fire it was that had sent his brother mad, that had led to innumerable deaths and untold pain for so much time, fire that had failed to kill him seven years before. Now it would have its man. He felt a certain relief: at last, it was over. He closed his eyes and dedicated his final thoughts to Irene.

He barely felt it as Alec came and shook him. Since Daniel didn't respond, his brother lifted him under his armpits and dragged him, passing straight through the flames, dropping him to the floor again after several metres. It was pointless, thought

Daniel numbly; he didn't know why Alec still kept on. If the fire didn't finish them, another explosion surely would.

Then he heard a metallic scraping nearby, and a cool gust of air. Again his brother's burly arms took hold of him. As his eyes opened he was confronted with the sight of a drop, and then the rushing torrent of the sewers. Glancing back up at his brother, in whose eyes the enormous flames continued to roll and leap, it seemed that all hint of madness had departed. Daniel tried to speak, but Alec just shook his head and smiled.

And pushed Daniel over the edge.

As he fell, Daniel flailed about for a moment, only a moment, before crashing into the water. Above him there came another explosion, and flames spurted briefly from the circular gap. It was the last thing he saw before the waters engulfed him, sweeping his body away into the darkness.

SEVENTY-SEVEN

The lights blinked off and on and the ground itself seemed to shake for a moment, sending up cries and protestation from the audience. Then, with no warning, everything returned to normal.

'Dear God, Gadea, what was that? Not an attack?'

His colleague, glancing around ashen-faced, couldn't summon an answer. He knew as little as Mellado.

Guests began to exchange confused looks, and gradually the murmurs grew so loud that Mayor Ruis stood once more and returned to the podium. He swept the room with his gaze.

'Ladies and gentlemen, please stay calm.' His steady tone immediately hushed the murmurs. 'It would seem the fireworks planned for later in the day have started a little before time.'

Sighs went around, along with some nervous titters.

'Following this minor interruption, I suggest we continue with the order of events.'

Ruis took his chair once more, and a respectful silence resumed. The room was heavy with anticipation as His Excellency Práxedes

Mateo Sagasta came forward: it was the role of the Cabinet President to make the announcement officially inaugurating the Fair.

'Her Majesty, the Queen Regent, in the name of her august son, King Alfonso XIII, has ordered me to say –' he paused, smiling – 'the Barcelona World Fair, in this, the year 1888, is now underway.'

Clamorous applause broke out, along with cheers for Catalonia, for the King and Queen, and for the Countess of Barcelona. Maestro Blasco, the orchestra conductor, swept the musicians into life, and the opening notes of *Hymn to the World Fair* filled the Hall of Ceremonies. A hundred white doves with pink collars were released from beside the Raw Materials Pavilion.

The Queen Regent rose and led the way offstage, followed by the Princes, the other officials, and then the rest of the guests. They went through into the Palace of Fine Arts, accompanied by further clapping and cheering. They were met outside by a jubilant crowd. So began, as planned, the royal tour of the pavilions.

The director of *El Imparcial* turned to his colleague.

'Well, Gadea. That's that then, I suppose.'

The journalist finished taking some notes and looked up, a euphoric tear in his eye.

'Yes, Mellado my friend. We're lucky; we've seen a bit of history. Today will be remembered by generations to come. There's no turning back for the city now. Barcelona will never be the same again.'

'Such high hopes for the Fair?'

'Not the Fair, my friend, but the people of Barcelona.'

*

561

Casavella was sitting on the floor beside a pillar, staring around in disbelief. He patted his filthy clothes, checked his pulse: incredible that he was still alive. Thick white plumes rose, filtering out through the shattered windowpanes. By some miracle the power station still stood.

Legs trembling, leaning on the wall, he lifted himself to his feet. A layer of ash fell from his shoulders. He took some tobacco out, rolled a trembling cigarette – dropping more tobacco than he managed to get inside the paper. Licking and rolling it, he patted his pockets, then stopped, laughing: he had nothing to light it with.

With the unlit cigarette dangling from his lips, he decided to check on the damage. The blaring of the klaxons had ceased, leaving behind a strange silence, broken only by the sound of a familiar hum.

To his astonishment the generators, though covered in ash, were still going – as if nothing had happened. Their never-ending buzz seemed, for once, rather lovely.

Then he heard something from the nearby passage – the one that led to Adell's office. He thought the building might still come toppling down at any moment, but decided to investigate.

It was thick with steam but as he advanced something else began to fill the air: a sour, pestilential odour. He gulped, casting back to the last time he'd encountered such a smell. Years ago, he remembered coming past the cemetery of Poble Nou in his father's carriage. That's what the dead smell like, his father had said, when the bodies are burned. It was the smell of death.

Rumours had gone around among the workers since the day work had commenced: the station was being built on the foundations of the old citadel hospital, a place that had seen a great many deaths. Some of the men claimed to have heard voices, cries and moans, while they'd been working.

He shivered in spite of the heat, trying to tell himself it was all in his mind. Taking a deep breath, he entered the foul haze, and soon came to Adell's office. It seemed to be more badly affected than anywhere else in the building; the roof had collapsed and the windows had been blown out. Though thick with ash and smoke, Casavella didn't see fire. Then he started – he heard a person cough. He froze. Some planks fell to the floor and, after a moment, two dark figures emerged from billowing smoke. He crossed himself, took a step back, and watched, dumbstruck, as a young lady, half-naked, appeared with a blood-spattered man leaning against her.

Casavella opened his mouth and the unlit cigarette dropped to the floor.

SEVENTY-EIGHT

The sunset over the port promised a calm night ahead. Dozens of boats had docked for the Fair – the great success of which was being celebrated all across the city – and every single berth was taken.

Beyond the freighters, the passenger steam ships and the packet boats, three small fishing boats were moving to and fro. The men aboard cast large nets, dragged them in, and cast again.

On the jetty, a young boy paced back and forth, peering out nervously across the water. Suddenly he stopped and, after a few moments' hesitation, his excitement redoubled.

'There!' he cried. 'Over there!'

Guillem's shouts alerted the others. A number of men hurried over and looked in the direction he was pointing. The fading light made it difficult to see.

One of the boats approached the spot, the men holding out lanterns and scanning the water. Eventually one of them pointed to a bulk floating in the water a little way ahead, next to an old tugboat at anchor. They used poles to manoeuvre the body to the side, before heaving it up and in.

Guillem kept hopping excitedly from foot to foot, until he felt the prod of a walking stick in his back.

'Settle down, lad. They won't come any quicker with you thrashing about like a lizard.'

Vidal, chin lifted, looked vacantly out over the water, as if his sense of smell itself might read the sea air. Sitting in a chair with several of his men around him, the blind patriarch turned the cane about between his fingers. 'Down there,' he said to the boy, 'you did well.'

Guillem, surprised at the praise, stood a little taller. He did his best to keep still then, still like one of those streetlamps along the paseos.

As they waited for the boat to pull in, Vidal cast his mind back over the agreement with the journalist – the request had at first come as a surprise: to ensure the police lost their way down in the sewers. Fleixa would make sure the police got as far as entering the sewers, they would do the rest. He'd spoken of a grudge, some deep-seated resentment. Vidal didn't ask for explanations, he needed none – he was only too pleased to help on such a job. The result being, no sign of Inspector Sánchez in the city, or of his men, for several days. Their disappearances remained unexplained.

The boat reached the jetty, was fastened, and the body lifted out. The man's clothes had large holes in them, and the upper part of his shirt was covered in bloodstains. One of his shoes was missing, and his arm stuck out at an unpleasant angle. He smelt of the sewers.

565

Guillem made to approach, but the old man's stick prevented him.

'Easy. If he's going to live, he'll live.'

The boy gave him a hateful look, but did as he was told.

They laid the body out flat. At a nod from Vidal, they lifted the head up and an old woman stepped forward, a pot of blue crystals in her hand. Wafting it beneath the man's nose, nothing happened; the men shook their heads. The woman withdrew, but Vidal ordered her to try once more.

This time, everyone staring in silence, the man's eyelids fluttered. Then his whole body shook, and the hands holding him lost their grip. His back arched and he began gasping for air, followed by a coughing fit. With a moan, he began to vomit over the side of the jetty.

'Everyone back. Give him room to breathe.'

They waited for him to recover. The woman brought him a gourd of watery wine, which he gulped down. When he'd finished, the man looked around wild-eyed.

Vidal got up from his chair and approached, followed by a beaming Guillem. The dwarf hid his smile.

'About time, Señor Amat. We've been waiting for you.'

FORGIVENESS

Two weeks later

SEVENTY-NINE

The buildings in that barrio were so close together that the narrow earthen streets were little more than tunnels. Fleixa looked at the way the beams bowed with the weight of the accumulated rot. The walls hadn't been painted since the buildings had gone up, and the flaking, peeling layers called to mind the warts on an old woman's face. The single streetlamp barely cast enough light to read the sign above the hostel door, which hung loosely.

The journalist stepped inside; the interior was just as uninviting. On the landing you were met with a mound of rubbish that must have dated from the days of the First Republic. At the top of three uneven steps, where the stairwell to the building proper began, there stood a reception counter that was falling to pieces; the bell seemed long inoperative. Visitors were not expected.

He thought he'd been in some foul-smelling places in his time, but this was unbearable. With a cloth over nose and mouth, glancing back along the street in case he'd been followed, he started up the four flights at a hobble – the wound in his shoulder had yet to heal. He avoided putting weight through the rickety bannister in case it should come away in his hand, and the groaning boards announced his presence, though nobody came out.

Arriving at the top floor, he made his way along a corridor to a begrimed door. Knocking, he stood and waited. He heard nothing inside. He knocked again, this time more forcefully.

The door inched open – it was on a chain. A pair of bloodshot eyes looked out from between the crack.

'Señor Malavell? Are you Albert Malavell, and did you once work at the Gilbert household?'

'Possibly . . .' said the man suspiciously.

'I'm here because we have a friend in common, someone I'm worried about.'

'What should I care?'

The door began to shut, but Fleixa quickly thrust his foot in.

'I can make it worth your while.'

'There's money in it?' The man couldn't hide the anxiety in his voice. He half-opened the door again.

Fleixa stepped to one side, and La Negra came out from a recess in the hallway. At a nod, the old circus strongman at her side kicked down the door. The chain snapped, splinters of doorframe flew. Malavell fell down, dropping the bottle he'd been holding, which spilt its contents across the floor.

La Negra stepped over Malavell, followed by her bodyguard.

'You . . . you can't do this!' he stammered.

La Negra smiled, before replying in her feline tones. 'Oh, my dear, but we can.'

Fleixa turned and headed back along the landing, rolling a cigarette as he went.

Pau's lip was bleeding – she'd been chewing on it without realizing.

She'd been waiting by the door for almost an hour. She kept adjusting her dress and corset, unable to get comfortable. How were you supposed to breath in all this? After the time she'd spent in shirts and trousers, it made her feel like some kind of bonbon. She longed for the roomier outfits to which she'd become accustomed.

She lifted a hand to her heart – the needle pricks had healed, but the thin scar across her breast would be a constant reminder of that subterranean nightmare. Her hair had grown a little – she still wore a hat to hide it. Happily, the transfer of her life force to the body of Alec Amat's dead lover had not been completed; by yanking out the cables, Fleixa had interrupted the flow of electricity, thereby saving her life. She'd suffered the occasional dizzy spell, but otherwise was in good health.

She sighed. Her hands were sweating inside the fetching brown velvet gloves. Señora Adell had been kind to lend her the clothes, but the attire of a man would still have been far preferable.

The faculty was very busy that morning: it was Finals day. In different circumstances, she'd be sitting those exams herself, doing her best to answer the questions set for prospective surgeons. But instead, here she was, her former peers eyeing her as they passed. She tried to ignore them, turning her thoughts to the real worry: why she'd been asked to come. Recent events meant there hadn't been time for her expulsion to be made official.

She took a deep breath, saying to herself perhaps it would all be quite straightforward, a few signatures, done in a matter of minutes.

The sound of the door interrupted her reverie. It swung open, and out stepped Fenollosa. He looked ashen, as though having received some terrible news. Seeing Pau, he seemed about to speak, only to decide against it. Pau held his gaze, until finally Fenollosa dropped his head and walked away along the corridor without a backward glance. She found, to her surprise, that his sudden appearance awoke no ill feelings; she did not hate him. After all that had happened, she felt a kind of liberation: there was no space in her for any rancour. Then someone was saying her name, and again she started. With a deep breath, smoothing down her dress, she entered the Anatomy lecture theatre.

On this occasion, the tiers of seats were all empty. Only the armchairs of the board of professors were occupied; five grave-faced men watched as she made her way to the centre of the room. Her presence seemed to discomfort them – all, that is, except Doctor Segura, who gave her a sympathetic nod.

'Señorita Gilbert,' said the dean, his voice echoing up and around the empty space. 'Take a seat, please.'

Pau did so, and tried to make herself comfortable, but the dress was so inhibiting. She shifted awkwardly in the chair until one of the men cleared his throat, and she looked up again.

'Firstly, I would like to request your strictest confidence. The matters we're about to discuss must stay in this lecture theatre. Agreed?'

Pau nodded, though at what she wasn't sure.

'Good. Three days ago we received a message bearing the

royal seal. In it the Queen's secretary told us of the crucial role you've played in certain recent events, though, out of discretion, he was unable to go into detail.' He paused. 'It seems that you and your friends helped divert a most egregious disaster, saving the lives of many people, including, no less, that of Her Majesty and the heir to the throne.'

Pau gave an uncertain nod. She didn't know what to say. The dean looked up from the piece of paper before him, removing his glasses.

'And I'm right to think you probably won't be able to enlighten us on the matter?'

'Yes, Señor, I'm afraid that's right.'

'Fine.' He put his glasses back on. 'The Queen has requested that we make an exception of you. She has communicated her desire for you to take the Surgeon's exam. If we were to allow you, she would consider it a personal favour. Your consent is all that's now required.'

Pau tried to conceal her amazement.

'Furthermore,' continued Suñé, 'Her Majesty would wish to make a donation to the University coffers, in the hope of supporting the wisdom, bravery and daring of which you . . . are such a fine example.'

An awkward silence ensued; none of the other men seemed to want to say anything.

'Well, we've met, we've discussed the matter, and though the request is far from orthodox . . .' He cleared his throat. 'We've decided to go along with it.'

Pau had to clasp her hands together to keep them from trembling.

'So then, do you, or do you not, wish to take the exam? You can say no, we'll understand.'

'Oh, no, Señor. I'd be more than happy to. When would it be, though?'

'This very moment.'

'Right now?'

'All the tests you took while masquerading as a student here, you passed with flying colours. It's our view that you ought to be given a practical examination with no delay.'

The dean turned and gestured behind him: two orderlies entered bearing a stretcher. Depositing it on the dissection table, they drew the cloth away to reveal a corpse underneath, as a third man sprinkled sawdust on the ground. The familiar smell of decomposition cut through the smoke from the freshly lit incense.

'There's no shame,' said one of the professors, 'if you don't feel up to it.'

'It would be quite understandable,' said another.

'Gentlemen,' said Segura, 'I believe we ought to let the Señorita make up her own mind.' Then, with a wink: 'She usually does.'

'But of course,' said the first professor. 'Only to make it clear, there would be nothing wrong with refusing. At the end of the day, you are still a woman. You don't have to go through this if you do not wish to.'

Pau clenched her jaw. They all had reservations – all except for Segura, and perhaps the dean. None of them thought she was up to it. She reflected for a moment. Here was the final proof: even if she passed the final exam, in their eyes she'd still be more woman than doctor.

She stood up with a sigh. Hands still clasped, she scanned the men, taking them in one by one. Then, without a word, she turned and made her way towards the door. A satisfied murmur went up behind her. When she reached the exit, she proceeded to remove her gloves, along with her hat, which she placed on one of the pews. Taking the surgical gown from the assistant, she smiled – for the first time in a good many days.

'Whenever you want. I'm ready.'

Pau and Fleixa walked in silence along one of the jetties at the port, seagulls calling and circling overhead. After each wave the boats would strain at their anchors, anxious to get back out to sea. As the sun set, numerous fishing boats were coming ashore, unloading the day's catches.

The journalist's torso was still swathed in bandages, and he walked stiffly – though, unusually for him, he hadn't been complaining. Pau carried a small suitcase; Fleixa had offered to take it for her but she'd refused.

'I haven't said "well done" yet.'

Pau nodded, her eyes sparkling.

The exam had lasted three long hours. The questions they'd asked had exceeded the level of knowledge usually required, including reference to a number of cases generally reserved for very experienced doctors. But it hadn't mattered: she'd passed. She was now a certified surgeon.

'So, you're leaving?' said Fleixa.

She felt moved by the note of concern in his voice. She realized it was going to be painful for her as well.

'It's a great opportunity.'

'Morocco is a complicated place.'

'I've been made a medical officer. Given the state of affairs in the country, it won't matter to them whether it's a man or a woman patching up their wounds.'

Fleixa nodded gravely. They continued along the jetty.

'Was the evening at the Lírico Alec's work as well?' asked Pau.

'It seems like it. Amat's brother saw a chance to spread the idea of the Black Hound, to create more of a smokescreen. He made a deal with the medium to predict the coming of a demon, that way to stir up more panic. Poor woman didn't know that Alec had his own plans. He went to the theatre disguised at Doctor Gavet, and managed to drop some cyanide into her water before the event began. Then, when she collapsed onstage, everyone was stunned – they thought the demon spirit had really come.'

'My God, what a to-do.'

'I know.'

'And what's become of the journalist you were up against at the paper?'

'Llopis? The whole affair hit him quite hard, but he'll get over it. I'm sure he'll be writing articles again soon enough.'

Pau gave him a concerned look. 'I do hope, Señor Fleixa, that you aren't still unemployed.'

'Well, not exactly. The *Correo* offered me my old job back.'

'This is great news!'

'And I turned them down.' His eyes lit up as he remembered Sanchís's face. 'I received a better offer: you have before you the new head of current affairs at *La Vanguardia*. They set up the desk this year, they're doing interesting work. And,' he said with a wink, 'the salary isn't bad.'

'I'm so pleased for you.'

The journalist preened his moustache. The thought of Dolors came to mind, bringing a tear to his eye. How he wished she was still around to share in his good fortune. He missed her, and like a badly healed wound the memory still pained him – he thought it probably always would.

They came eventually to the embarkation point. A couple of sailors walked by, looking admiringly at the young lady.

'And what about Daniel,' she said, her tone changing. 'Have you seen him again?'

'I haven't. By the time I left hospital, he'd already recovered from his injuries.'

'His own brother – who would have thought it?'

'I know,' said the journalist. 'And all those years he spent, thinking the fire had been him, carrying the guilt around like that.'

Pau remembered the letter she was carrying in her luggage – Daniel had written some kind words of goodbye. He'd signed off in a way that moved her: 'Wherever life may take you, never stop fighting for your dreams.' The fabulous Vesalius manuscript came to her mind; it had apparently burned in the fire at Amat's laboratory. How incredibly valuable it had been, she thought; and the process discovered by that doyen of anatomists was an incredible medical advance. Though it might change the world, what a danger it represented in the wrong hands. Perhaps it was better off lost.

Fleixa sighed, bringing her from her reverie. 'I have to thank you,' he said. 'You saved my life.'

'Your watch did a pretty good job too.'

577

'Yes!' He took it from his pocket. There was a large dent in the metal where it had caught Amat's second bullet. 'But it was still you who got me out of that inferno.'

In answer, Pau took him by his good arm and drew him close. Fleixa walked a little taller as they took the final steps to the steamer gangway – the steamer that would take the young lady far from Barcelona.

A detachment of soldiers waited to board as the sailors finished loading the cargo. Orders from officers melded in the air with the voices and bustle of the crew. The sea air was impregnated with smells of leather, steel and animals. A bell rang out, and gouts of smoke began to rise from the ship's chimneys.

'Oh, I forgot,' said the journalist, fishing in his pocket. 'This is for you.'

He held out a brown envelope. Pau put down her suitcase and took it. Inside was a wad of money.

'I don't understand.'

'I paid a visit to a friend of yours, took along a couple of people I know. We had a lovely chat, one that helped him see reason, anyway: he decided to return the money he extorted from you. He also said to say sorry – he seemed quite sincere. He won't be bothering you again, of that I'm fairly sure.'

Pau then did something that came as a surprise to them both: she threw her arms around Fleixa and kissed him on the cheek. Fleixa felt his face flush. For the first time in his life, he was speechless.

'Thank you so much, Bernat. I'll miss you.'

'As shall I, my dear. As shall I.'

*

Daniel adjusted the sling. The stitches on his arm bothered him, and it still hurt his ribs to breathe. The doctor had advised rest, but he couldn't have left Barcelona without coming to the cemetery.

It had been only a few weeks since his father's burial, and yet to Daniel it seemed so much longer. He stood before the grave and read the epitaph on the headstone – one he himself had requested: 'Don Alfred Amat i Roures, eminent doctor, dedicated father.' And beneath that, the family motto: '*Vivitur ingenio, caetera mortis erunt.*'

A mound of earth to the right indicated his brother's final resting place. Though it hurt to do so, he leaned down and introduced his fingers into the broken soil, still wet from the previous day's rain. It was the closest he'd ever be to his brother again.

The Vesalius manuscript, the original, was in there too, buried with Alec's remains. No one would ever find out whether the brilliant anatomist's machine would truly work or not. During his stay in hospital, he'd spoken to a number of doctors who told him that a strong electric shock could have the most incredible effects on a dead body. Lifting the legs, moving the arms, even causing the eyelids to open – but to bring it back to life, that was beyond all possibility. And yet . . .

He heaved an enormous sigh; what a relief to know that none of it mattered any longer. He sifted the soil with his fingers. While in hospital he'd also gone through the moments leading up to the explosion in the laboratory, over and over again. Alec had saved his life. Daniel liked to think that, in those final moments, his madness had ceased to torment him, and that he would have died at peace.

Getting to his feet, he took his train tickets from his pocket. He'd be boarding the service to Paris in two hours, where he'd transfer to the Express to Calais. He'd reserved compartments to himself all the way, wishing to be alone. He had much to think about.

After a final look at the graves, he gathered his bags and readied to leave. The wind picked up, rustling in the trees, and he caught a faint hint of a smell: jasmine.

Irene was dressed in black: widow's black. On this occasion, it was she who approached him; she moved slowly, the gravel crunching beneath her feet. Stopping at Daniel's side, she looked at the two mounds.

'You're leaving?'

'Today.'

It was quiet in the cemetery; they could hear the leaves in the trees.

'What will you do now?' asked Daniel.

'I still don't know. Bertomeu was ruined. Your journalist friend wrote an article two days ago in *La Vanguardia*, going public about the fraud with the investors' money. The family's standing, any position it might once have held, has gone now – forever. Death saved him from prison. Perhaps I'll stay on in Barcelona, perhaps I'll return to Cuba. It's a long time since I've been back.'

Daniel simply nodded; a sudden sensation of loss left him unable to speak.

'You'll be pleased to know my father and I have seen each other again,' continued Irene. 'It'll take time, but we'll get there.'

She moved closer; the warmth of her body felt like a comfort. 'It's time you forgave yourself,' she whispered.

Daniel let out a sigh. It was no simple thing, after such a long time thinking of himself as guilty.

'Here.' She was holding out a sealed document. 'I've arranged things with my lawyers – before Bertomeu's creditors come knocking. It's the deed to the mansion. It's yours.'

She reached up and caressed his cheek, before laying a resolute hand on the scars on his neck. They were close enough now that strands of their hair began to intermingle. Daniel ran his fingertips over the corner of her mouth, tilted his head, and lost himself in the fullness of her lips. As he shut his eyes, all the pain disappeared, as if it had never been there in the first place. They separated – she was smiling. Lowering her gaze, she turned and went back along the path, leaving that fragrance of jasmine floating in her wake.

Arriving back at the carriage, Irene's breath was ragged. She stopped and took a few moments before opening the door and climbing in. A silhouette moved about in the diffuse light inside. The girl, her skin brown and her hair black, could barely contain her nerves. Her large grey eyes searched her mother's face expectantly.

'What are we doing here, Mama? Who's that man?'

Irene didn't answer. She stroked the girl's hair, moved a strand off her forehead. Seven years old, she felt an immense curiosity for the world – just as Irene herself remembered having at that age. She pursed her lips, showing her impatience – which made her mother smile.

'He's a friend,' she said eventually.

'Oh . . .'

'Make room, go on.'

Irene settled back into the leather seat, and with a jerk of the horses the carriage got underway.

'Will we see him again?' asked the girl, leaning out of the small window.

The sound of the wheels on the path drowned out her mother's reply.

The girl watched the man, who was standing in front of the mounds of earth, suitcase in hand. Barcelona rose behind him in the distance. As they approached the first corner, the wind picked up, clearing, for a brief moment, the smog of sea mist and the factory fumes. For the first time in days the blue of the sky could be seen, and the sun, setting over the peaks of Collserola, shone gold across the rooftops. The carriage had almost exited the cemetery grounds, and the girl watched as the man, looking out over the city, put down the suitcase and took papers of some kind from his jacket. After a moment's pause, he scattered them in the wind. In spite of the distance, the girl caught his smile in the late afternoon light as he watched them flutter down in the direction of the sea.